so
all

progresses. With various parallel story strands deepening the mystery before they all come together in a flurry of unwelcome truths, this makes for an altogether excellent thriller'
– *Crime Time*

'This debut novel is intelligent and arresting. And grim'
– *Morning Star*

'This debut novel upholds the recent tradition of dark Nordic noir. A girl goes missing on her way home from the party in the forested village of Gullspång. Enter a Stockholm detective with a secret of her own' – *i Newspaper*

'A brilliant, dense crime novel' – *Dagens Nyheter*

'The next big Swedish crime sensation' – *Dagbladet*

'A wonderful debut' – *Dziennik Zachodni*

Lina Bengtsdotter grew up in Gullspång, Sweden. She is a teacher in Swedish and Psychology and has published a number of short stories in various newspapers and magazines in Sweden and the Nordic countries. She has lived in the UK and in Italy and today resides outside of Stockholm with her three children.

Agnes Broomé is a literary translator and Preceptor in Scandinavian at Harvard University. With a PhD in Translation Studies, her translations include August Prize winner *The Expedition* by Bea Uusma.

FOR THE DEAD

LINA BENGTSDOTTER

Translated from the Swedish by
AGNES BROOMÉ

ORION

First published in Great Britain in 2020 by Orion Fiction,
an imprint of The Orion Publishing Group Ltd.,
Carmelite House, 50 Victoria Embankment
London EC4Y 0DZ

An Hachette UK company

1 3 5 7 9 10 8 6 4 2

A CIP catalogue record for this book
is available from the British Library.

ISBN (Paperback) 978 1 4091 7938 2

Typeset by Deltatype Ltd, Birkenhead, Merseyside

Printed in Great Britain by Clays Ltd, Elcograf S.p.A.

www.orionbooks.co.uk

For my sisters,
the ones who walk beside me
and the ones who went before

It is a strange thing to be an unlovable child.
You're unhappy but also free.

Johanne Lykke Holm, *Natten som föregick denna dag*

Prologue

A group of boys stood huddled behind the chapel. I approached from the lake; they didn't notice me until I was much too close. In the faint light from the church, their faces looked weirdly spectral against their black tailcoats. It was the odious little gang with the royal names, Erik, Gustav, Oscar, Magnus and him, Henrik Stiernberg, my sister's conceited boyfriend.

Henrik was the first to spot me. I must have scared him because he looked terrified when he asked me what the fuck I wanted. I stared at his face for a second, then burst out laughing.

'What are you laughing at?' he said. 'What the fuck's wrong with you?'

I didn't reply, because I had no idea why I was laughing or what was wrong with me.

'Go back to the ball, weirdo,' Erik said. 'Aren't you supposed to be inside, dancing?'

'My escort's missing,' I said.

The moment I said it, my mood shifted; I suddenly felt on the verge of tears. Paul had been gone forever and the autumn ball was pointless without him. He'd promised me both the first and the last dance and the orchestra in the gym was

I

gearing up to play the closing song. Maybe they already had. I don't know why it made me so sad, because I definitely wasn't the kind of girl who cared who I danced with, or if I even got to dance at all, but this was Paul.

'Check his room,' Erik said. 'He probably got too hammered and conked out.'

I told them he wasn't in his room.

'Well, he's not here,' Henrik said, 'so move along.'

I stayed where I was because I couldn't think of anywhere else to look. I'd already checked the lake and the Weeping Willow and there was no one at Pine Point. This bench next to the family graves behind the chapel had been my last hope.

'What's the matter with you?' Henrik said when I suddenly staggered to one side.

'I'm ... dizzy,' I said and reached out to lean against a headstone. I misjudged the distance and fell. Sprawled on the ground, I spotted the rose, the one that was the same shade of yellow as my dress and which Paul had been wearing in the breast pocket of his tailcoat.

'Paul must've been here,' I said, holding the rose up for the boys to see.

'What are you on about?' Henrik said. 'We haven't seen your little boyfriend.'

It was around that point our stories began to diverge.

I

Charlie tried to make herself comfortable in the tilted-back chair. Eva, the psychologist, was sitting diagonally to her left.

Eva had just gone over the guidelines for their conversations. It was important to start and stop sessions on time, important to be honest if something didn't feel good, important that Charlie knew everything she said in that room would stay in that room.

Eva's tone was friendly, but her eyes revealed she could be stern if the need arose. Charlie had looked her up and knew she was a member of the Swedish Psychologists' Association and had fifteen years of professional experience. That had been Charlie's first counter-demand when Challe ordered her to see a therapist, that it had to be someone with a proper education, not some smug git with an eight-week diploma in personal development. She didn't want to waste her time on someone who spouted banalities or talked too much about their own life. Most importantly, though, she wanted to avoid doing it at all, which was why she had postponed this meeting for as long as she could. She'd tried to show Challe she was doing fine, that she was completely capable of taking care of herself and doing her job, but after the events of the summer, she didn't exactly enjoy her boss's full confidence.

LINA BENGTSDOTTER

Either way, there she was, in a strangely constructed chair in Eva's office. Outside, the leaves of an enormous oak tree glistened gold and orange and rain trickled down the window-pane in tiny rivulets.

'Tell me why you're here, Charline,' Eva said.

'You can call me Charlie.'

'What brings you here, Charlie?'

'My boss. It was an ultimatum. He feels I need help.'

'I see.' Eva gave Charlie a probing look; Charlie figured she was making a mental note: *Possible lack of self-awareness.* 'Do you agree with him?'

'About needing help?'

'Yes.'

'I guess so, but I might not have come if it weren't for the fact that I want to keep my job.'

'Can you tell me a bit about yourself, in general terms. I know what you do for a living but that's about it.'

'What more do you need to know?' Charlie said.

Eva smiled and said a person is more than just their job. Maybe Charlie could just give a brief description of herself.

'Sure,' Charlie said. 'I like to ...' She paused. What did she like? Reading, drinking, being alone. She couldn't think of anything that didn't sound depressing off the top of her head. 'I like to read.'

When she realised Eva was waiting for more, she had an urge to add she loved working out as well, but what was the point of lying about something like that?

'Have you been to therapy before?' Eva said after a while.

'Yes, a handful of sessions as an adult and a longer period of counselling as a teenager. My mother died when I was fourteen.'

4

'That's a difficult age to lose a parent.'

Charlie nodded.

'And your father?'

'Unknown.'

'I see.'

'What was your relationship with your mother like?'

'It was ...' Charlie didn't know what to say. Complicated? 'My mother was unique.'

'In what way?'

'I suppose she wasn't like other mothers. I guess you might say I'm fighting hard not to become her.'

'That's natural, though, don't you think?' Eva said. 'Wanting to avoid repeating your parents' mistakes? But if your aim is to avoid being your mother, you're still using her as your reference point. You may not be able to step out of her shadow until you start acting without reference to her.'

'Sure.'

'We can come back to that. Right now, I want you to talk a bit about why your boss gave you an ultimatum. Why he is requiring you to see a therapist.'

Charlie suddenly heard Betty's voice in her head. That thing she used to say when she was having a down period: *I feel like the undertow's pulling me down. If I lie still and think about it, I'll sink. It's best not to think, not to talk. It only makes things worse.*

'I imagine it's because of my drinking,' Charlie says. 'Sometimes I drink a bit too much. And the reason I'm here now is that until recently, I was able to keep it under control, drinking only when I was off-duty and never even the day before work, at least not in any significant quantities, but these days I find myself having a few drinks even if I'm working the next day, so I guess there must have been alcohol on my breath. Challe, my boss, has an incredible sense of smell.'

'Maybe you're lucky he does,' Eva said. 'I mean, because it induced you to seek professional help while there's still time.'

'How can you be so sure there's still time?' Charlie demanded.

'You're aware of and open about your problem. That's a pretty good place to start.'

'I've been aware of it for a long time, but that hasn't meant I've been able to do anything about it, so I don't know if that's true.'

'I thought you just told me you've been able to keep it under control?'

'There have been times when I lost control,' Charlie said.

'But now you're here.'

'Yes, now I'm here.'

A few minutes of trivial small talk followed. Then silence fell. Charlie studied the paintings behind Eva. Framed pictures that looked like ... Rorschach tests, Charlie suddenly realised. She tried to see patterns in the blots as a way to gauge her mental health, but was interrupted by Eva, who wanted to know more about her job.

Charlie told her about what she did as a detective working for the National Operations Department, about how she and her colleagues were dispatched to assist local law enforcement with particularly difficult cases across the country.

'And what does the rest of your life look like?' Eva asked.

'Single, no children,' Charlie replied.

'And if we go back to your drinking,' Eva said, without commenting on her lack of partner. 'How long has it been a problem?'

'I'm not sure. I suppose it depends on who you ask.'

'I'm asking you.'

'Ever since I had my first drink I've really liked alcohol, and I've always had more of it than the people around me. The one-glass-only mentality is incomprehensible to me. But I wouldn't call myself an alcoholic just because I drink more than other people. I suppose sometimes I drink a lot, but there are calmer periods, too.'

'And the uptick that led to this meeting, when did it start?'

'I honestly don't remember exactly, but I went back to Gullspång, the town I grew up in, a few months ago. It's a small town in Västergötland,' she added when Eva looked nonplussed. 'I lived there until my mum died. That's when I moved to Stockholm.'

'Did you have family here?'

'No, I ended up in foster care.'

'What was that like?'

Charlie didn't know how to respond. What was there really to say about her life in the small terraced house in Huddinge? She pictured the garden, the raked gravel path, the flowerbeds where everything grew in neat rows and the tiny apple tree that never bore fruit. She thought about her first meeting with her foster parents Bengt and Lena and their daughter, Lisen, how the three of them had stiffly welcomed her into their clinically clean house. On the surface, her new family was exactly what she'd used to wish for whenever Betty went off the rails: calm, orderly people with regular sleep schedules, sit-down family meals and a mother who packed gym bags and cooked traditional food and didn't have mental breakdowns. Lena never once curled up on the sofa for days, desperate to shut out any trace of sound and light. She never threw parties and invited people she didn't know. Charlie thought about her room in the terraced house, the laundered sheets, the smell of soap and roses. *I want you to feel at home*, Lena had told her that first night. *I really hope you will feel at home here, Charline, and that you and Lisen will be like sisters.*

But Charlie had never felt at home in the house in Huddinge and she and Lisen had never become anything like sisters.

Eva cleared her throat.

'It was functional,' Charlie said, 'my foster family. Everything was neat and orderly and I was able to focus on school.'

'That's good,' Eva said, 'but back to when this period started. You went to Gullspång at the start of the summer. How come?'

'It was for work; a young girl had disappeared, Annabelle Roos, you might have read about it in the papers.'

'Yes, I remember.'

'We went down there to help the local police and as it turns out, being back was pretty rough, much worse than I'd thought it'd be.'

'In what way?'

'It stirred up a lot of memories and I was ...'

Charlie saw Annabelle's thin body being pulled out of the black waters of the Gullspång River, saw Betty's boyfriend, Mattias, disappear into the same black depths two decades earlier, saw two little girls with a crying toddler between them, even further back in time, long before she was born.

'You were what?' Eva said, leaning forward in her chair.

'I suppose you might say I got personally involved in the case, to some degree. And I made a mistake down there and was suspended and that obviously affected me as well. When I returned to Stockholm, I thought everything would go back to normal, but it didn't. It got worse.'

'What got worse?'

'My anxiety, the futility of it all, my sleeping problems. I have a hard time falling asleep and once I do, I have bad dreams.'

'Describe them.'

'My dreams?'

'Yes.'

'They started when I got back from Gullspång, but then they were slowly going away, until I started working on this case that's getting to me more than I'd like to admit.'

Eva asked what kind of case it was and Charlie told her about the two young women from Estonia, the ones who had been found murdered and dumped in a wooded area in the suburbs. One of them had a three-year-old daughter, a hollow-eyed, hungry girl who had been locked alone in a flat for at least two days. The daughter still hadn't said a word, even though it had been two weeks since they found her.

Eva said she wasn't surprised Charlie felt affected by it, that an abandoned child would make most people feel the same way. But the little girl was okay, wasn't she?

'She's alive,' Charlie said. 'But that's about it. Last night, I dreamt she was my child, that I was her mother. I wanted to run home and rescue her, but I couldn't, because I was dead. And then, in my next dream, I was the child and, well, you get it.'

'Are you on any kind of medication?' Eva asked without commenting on her dreams.

'Sertraline,' Charlie said, 'one hundred milligrams.' She didn't mention that she sometimes complemented the sertraline with oxazepam or sleeping pills or both.

'Nothing else?' Eva said.

Charlie shook her head.

'Are you aware nightmares are a common side effect of sertraline?'

Charlie nodded. She knew that, but since she'd been on sertraline for years, she felt it was unlikely to be related.

Eva folded her hands around her knee.

'This mistake you mentioned,' she continued, 'I would like to talk some more about that.'

Charlie thought about that night at the pub for a minute. The liquorice shots, the wine, the beer, Johan. Her decision to dig up everything she could about him after she got back to Stockholm had been foolish. If you wanted to move on, you had to put a lid on things and leave them well enough alone, she knew that, but instead, she'd left no rock unturned. It had started with her wanting to find out where he lived, to check if he was married, if everything he'd said about being Betty's boyfriend's son was really true. It seemed to be.

'Charlie?' Eva was looking at her.

'I'm sorry, what were you saying?'

'I asked you to tell me about that mistake you mentioned.'

'Right. I actually don't remember all of what happened, but in a nutshell, I had too much to drink and took a journalist back to my room. The next day, privileged information was printed in the papers. I wasn't the leak, though everyone obviously thought I was. And, well, it was a problem, to put it mildly.'

Eva said nothing for a minute, as if waiting for Charlie to continue. Then she asked: 'Do you think you would've spent the night with this man if you'd been sober?'

'God, no!'

'Why not?'

Charlie didn't quite know how to answer that, so she told it like it was, that she couldn't really remember the last time she'd gone to bed with a man sober. And was there something wrong with that?

'What do you think?' Eva retorted.

'I obviously think that particular instance was ill-advised, but in other contexts, I mean, when I'm not working? Do you think one-night stands are wrong?'

'Is what I think important to you?'

Charlie said it wasn't, but that was a lie, because if there was one thing she despised, it was judgemental people.

'Either way, it's not for me to say,' Eva said. 'But I will tell you that using sex to feel better might not be entirely constructive.'

'It's better than alcohol, though, right?'

'As far as I understand, you use both.'

Charlie sighed and looked out the window, watching a blackbird fly past.

'I'm not saying it's wrong to have sex with strangers. I'm just saying you should think about why you do. What you hope to achieve by it.'

'Isn't it enough that it makes me feel better? Does there have to be a deeper purpose? Why can't people just do what makes them feel good?'

'I suppose they can. But maybe what makes you feel good in the moment isn't what makes you feel good in the long run.'

Charlie nodded. Sad, but true.

'I mean, a drug addict feels good getting high,' Eva continued, 'but that doesn't mean ...'

'Yeah, I get it.'

Charlie was starting to regret demanding a trained

psychologist. It would have been easier to see a happy-go-lucky life coach who'd tell her about new kinds of yoga and meditation. If she was serious about wanting help, she was going to have to dig deep and she didn't know if she was up for it. She was so tired.

'Going back to your mother,' Eva said. 'What was she like?'

'She was ... different.'

Charlie glanced at her watch. Not that it mattered how much time was left, she wouldn't be able to describe Betty if she had a lifetime. Betty had been so full of contradictions and contrasts, of darkness and light, drive and apathy. Back when Charlie studied psychology, she'd tried to find a diagnosis that fit her, but none of them had felt spot on. It was as though all descriptors were too narrow to encompass Betty Lager.

2

Half an hour until the morning meeting. Plenty of time to get there from Eva's office.

The rain had stopped and the air was crisp. Autumn was Charlie's favourite season. *The season of decay*, Betty used to call it. Betty, who would grow anxious before they'd even made it to midsummer, as soon as the cherry blossoms fell. But to Charlie, autumn was a time of rebirth, a promise of routines, order. She loved the smell of rosehip and new books; they reminded her of school starting again after the endless, unpredictable summer holiday. But this autumn had been different. It was as though she was just pretending to care about the world around her, pretending to work, pretending to participate in conversations, pretending to live, while, paradoxically, everything also seemed portentous and frightening somehow. The other day, she had seriously considered hanging a blanket over her bedroom window to block out the light seeping in through the gaps in the blind. The thought alone had scared her. She mustn't become like Betty. Never like Betty.

Charlie pulled out her phone to check if Susanne had called back. She hadn't. When Charlie was going back to Stockholm, after the Gullspång case was wrapped up, they'd promised to keep in touch and meet up again soon. In the weeks that followed, Susanne had called almost every night when she took her dog out. They'd talked about her marriage, which was rockier than ever, and all the things that hadn't turned out the way they'd thought they would. But a while ago, Susanne had stopped taking Charlie's calls, sending only brief texts saying she was fine, just a bit overwhelmed, when Charlie asked if something had happened.

Charlie listened to the phone ring and hung up the moment the call went to voicemail, thinking that perhaps she ought to respect the fact that Susanne wanted to be left alone.

Kristina, the receptionist, was back from her vacation abroad; even though she'd talked about little else for weeks before she went, Charlie couldn't remember where she'd been. But apparently she was back, standing by the coffee machine in the kitchen by the conference room, telling everyone what a wonderful time she'd had, the balmy air, the warm sea, the pool. Going had been a matter of survival, she said, because the Swedish summer had been miserable, aside from that one heatwave in June, but she'd been stuck at work then. And after that ... summer had never really got going properly.

Charlie tried to recall the summer. She hadn't given the weather so much as a passing thought. The few days she'd been off work after coming back from Gullspång, she'd spent large parts of asleep.

Kristina said she was already dreaming about next summer.

'I'm not,' Charlie replied and took a cinnamon bun from the plate on the table.

'Are you serious?'

'Yes. I don't like summer or being off work or holidays or

anything like that. I don't even like to travel,' she added. Then she wished she hadn't, because she knew all too well discussing her idiosyncrasies with Kristina was a waste of time. When was she going to learn to keep her mouth shut? How many times had she got stuck in interminable arguments about the most insignificant details simply because she was annoyed about something or even just bored. Safe topics of conversation with Kristina included recipes, weather and property prices. Things that were concrete, simple and normal.

'That's actually kind of sad,' Kristina said, 'not liking summer.'

'What's sad about it? Given as how there are three other seasons, living only for summer seems even sadder. And if overcast days make you upset, well, then how often do you really get to be happy; since greatest possible happiness seems to be your goal?

Kristina stared at her blankly.

'Jesus,' she said after a pause. 'I hardly think me being unhappy about the weather and the season is cause for you to get so angry.

'I'm not angry, I just didn't appreciate you calling me sad.'

'I never called you sad.'

Hugo entered the room. Kristina lit up.

'Looks like you've had some sun,' he said.

He smiled at Kristina and gave Charlie a curt nod.

Kristina forgot about Charlie and once more launched into a paean about the heat, the surroundings, the daytrips. Then she suddenly stopped herself and congratulated Hugo, saying a little bird had told her.

'Thanks,' Hugo said. 'I'm really chuffed about it.'

He glanced at Charlie.

'Did you hear, Charlie?' Kristina said. 'Did you hear some-one's going to be a daddy soon?'

'No, but I'm hearing it now.' Charlie turned to Hugo and put on as big a smile as she could muster. 'That's exciting. I'm so pleased for you.'

'Thanks,' Hugo replied and flushed.

At least he has the decency to be embarrassed, Charlie thought to herself. That's something, at least.

'So how's Anna doing?' Kristina went on, oblivious to the tension in the room.

'She's actually been rather poorly,' Hugo replied. 'But I think she's turned a corner now, thankfully.'

'Aren't you staying for the meeting?' Kristina said when Charlie got up and moved towards the door.

'Yes, but it doesn't start for another three minutes.'

Charlie went to the bathroom and ran ice cold water over her wrists. It was something Betty had taught her. *When your blood boils and your head's burning, ice cold water's what you need. Hold your wrists like this, no, don't pull them out, soon, you won't feel a thing, you'll be numb. Keep them there, sweetheart. Endure. There, feel that? Can you feel it all just going away?*

Charlie closed her eyes, tried to make it all go away, tried to think of nothing at all, just a white room, white floor, white ceiling, white, windowless walls. But Hugo's wife's face kept popping up, her hands on her belly, Hugo's protective arm around her shoulders, his joy at the unborn child.

Charlie had last slept with Hugo less than a month ago. He'd turned up in her regular bar, standing there with a stupid grin on his face, pretending his presence there was sheer coincidence. When he wanted to have a drink with her, she'd told him no, that they were done with each other, but he'd

insisted. Surely, they could have one little drink and talk about
what had been. Charlie had eventually agreed, but only to the
drink, she'd told him, not the trip down memory lane; she
had no desire to reminisce about their affair. She already knew
everything she needed to: that Hugo was a lying coward who
thought far too highly of himself. She knew, but her heart
seemed not to care. Charlie was often told she was a rational
person, but as far as Hugo was concerned, her intellect was no
match for her lust; all she'd wanted to do while they sat there
with their Long Island Ice Teas was to take him home and
have sex with him all night long. Which was why, after the
third drink, she'd done just that.

*Just be happy he's not yours, Charline. What good is a dishonest
man to you? Why moon after a man with no conscience?*

Charlie opened her eyes. She didn't want Hugo. She'd
thought she wanted him because she'd convinced herself he
was someone he wasn't, that there was depth to him. But he
was just ...

He's just an ordinary man, sweetheart. Don't waste your time.

Someone tried the bathroom door.

'Sorry,' she heard Anders' voice say. 'I didn't realise it was
occupied.'

Charlie turned off the taps. Dabbed her wet fingers under
her eyes, wiped her hands with toilet paper and opened the
door.

'Are you okay?' Anders asked.

'Sure, just have a bit of a cold.'

'Want to go for a drink after work? We haven't been out
together in ages.'

'Eight months,' Charlie said.

'Has it really been that long?' Anders frowned as though

he didn't believe her. 'I suppose that's right, actually. Because I didn't go out at all the last month before Sam was born and since then I've … I haven't been out once since.'

'Maria's not going to let you out of her sight,' Charlie said with a smile.

'I actually have a mind of my own.'

'Alright then, great. We'll go for a drink after work.'

'I just have to call Maria to doublecheck,' Anders said.

'Fine,' Charlie said. 'We'll see how it works out.'

3

When the morning meeting was over, Challe asked Charlie for a quick word in his office. She followed him in and closed the door behind her.

'I've reviewed everyone's overtime and annual leave,' Challe said, sitting down behind his desk.

'And?' Charlie said.

'And I wasn't surprised to find that you've taken less leave than anyone else.'

'Okay.'

'Are you ever going to use your leave?'

'I took two weeks in July.'

'You took a week and a half,' Challe corrected her, 'and not even one week the summer before that.'

'Sure, but I'm in the middle of an important investigation right now.'

'All investigations are important,' Challe replied. 'There's always work to do.'

Charlie knew where the conversation was going; soon, he would point out that no one was served by her becoming personally involved in her case. He'd seen the pattern, he'd told her the last time the subject came up; he'd noticed that cases involving vulnerable young women tended to make her overly invested, which in turn meant she risked running herself into the ground and no one, not the victims, not their loved ones and not she herself, was helped by that.

Charlie recalled the pictures of the women's naked bodies; the eyes of the three-year-old found alive in the flat. How was she supposed not to become emotionally involved?

'I'm not saying you have to take time off this minute, Charlie. I just think you, like everyone else, need periods of recuperation from time to time.'

Charlie said that was true, but that recuperation might mean different things to different people.

Challe agreed, but it was nevertheless his job to put his foot down when he felt his staff needed rest. Because no one is indispensable. The cemeteries of the world were proof of that.

Charlie didn't smile at the stupid saying. Instead she asked if their conversation had anything to do with what had happened the previous summer.

'It has to do with a lot of things,' Challe said. 'The events down in Gullspång, your partying and the fact that you look exhausted. I've seen too many ambitious people burn out in this line of work and I can't afford to lose you.'

'You won't,' Charlie said, refraining from adding: *Didn't you just say no one's indispensable? You can't have it both ways.*

'You don't know that; you can't just decide you won't hit the wall. You of all people should know that.'

'I do know that, but I would have by now if I was going to. And I've started seeing a therapist. I've done everything you've asked me to.'

'Which is good,' Challe said, 'but I still think you should take a few consecutive weeks off. Maybe after you wrap up your current investigation. I'm not going to force you,' he went on when he saw the look on Charlie's face, 'but consider it.'

'Sure. I'll consider it.'

Charlie left Challe's office feeling slightly suffocated. She liked Challe a lot more when he played the demanding boss than when he veered towards the fatherly.

And if he was so attuned to what was good for her, he should realise a long vacation would be disastrous at this point. What would she fill her days with? Books? And then what? Chances were, she'd go out for a pint and then another and when she got back to work, she'd be in greater need of recuperation than ever.

When Charlie got back to her office, she resumed the time-consuming task of getting in touch with people who had moved in the two Estonian women's circle. It was a jumble of nicknames, pay-as-you-go phones and dead ends. It made Charlie stressed that they weren't making any progress in the case. They'd had no match for the DNA on the women's bodies and the few leads they'd had hadn't yielded any results.

After a few hours, she needed a break. To take her mind off the case, she googled *Johan Ro*. It had been a while since she last checked up on him. An article she hadn't read before appeared in her search results. *What happened to Francesca Mild?* Charlie clicked to read the rest of the article. *On the night of the 7th October 1989, sixteen-year-old boarding school student Francesca Mild disappeared from her family's farm, Gudhammar, outside Gullspång.*

Charlie paused, then reread the sentence. *Gullspång.* And the year, 1989. Why hadn't she heard a word about this when they were looking for Annabelle? She shook her head, kept reading. The parents had been away at a dinner party that night, leaving Francesca and her older sister home alone. The sister had gone to bed early; Francesca had not been missed until the next morning.

It has been twenty-seven years since Francesca Mild went missing, but we still don't know what happened to her. Numerous theories have been posited. Her passport was gone, so her disappearance was at first assumed to be voluntary.

Charlie scrolled down, reading about suspicions of suicide, the dragging of the lake and interviews with classmates, friends and relatives. All fruitless. There was a picture of the Mild family standing on the wide stone front steps of the family manor. A man and a woman behind two teenage daughters who looked about the same age. All smiling stiffly except one of the daughters, who was looking into the camera with eyes that were both dejected and defiant. Francesca Mild.

Further down there was another picture. It was from Adamsberg Boarding School, students in dark blue uniforms, the boys in trousers and the girls in pleated skirts. And there, a younger version of Francesca Mild. She was the only girl in the front row, her arms crossed.

What had happened to her?

Charlie's eyes lingered on Johan's name under the article. Should she call him? But no, what was the point?

Francesca

The light hurt my eyes when I walked out the hospital doors. Having spent over a week in bed, I felt strangely fragile. It was as though the world had changed, turned into something different. I don't know if it was the colours, the sounds, the air, but something was different. I grabbed Dad's arm, closed my eyes and let him lead me to the car.

'Why are your eyes closed, Francesca?' Mum asked.

'It's the light,' I said. 'All this light hurts.'

Dad removed my hand from his arm, but I kept my eyes closed, groping my way. When I squinted, I saw Mum shoot Dad a look and shake her head. If there was one thing she had no time for, it was me acting like a lunatic.

'Where are we going?' I said after squeezing into the back seat of Dad's sportscar. With my legs, you would've thought she might have let me ride shotgun, but I don't think a circumstance existed that would ever persuade Mum to sit in the back.

Dad said we were going to Gudhammar. He'd postponed all meetings in Switzerland for a while. That was when I finally realised how seriously they were taking this. Dad had never cancelled a meeting before. A meeting was a meeting, an appointment an appointment, an agreement an agreement. And Gudhammar, where we only spent high holidays and vacations.

'And then what?' I said. 'What are we going to do at Gudhammar?'

'We're going to talk about how we can help you,' Dad said. 'We need time to talk things through before we decide what to do about everything.'

'Why am I not going back to Adamsberg?'

'I think you know why,' Dad said.

I said I didn't; if anyone should be forced to leave that place it ought to be Henrik Stiernberg and his friends.

'Let's not talk about Henrik Stiernberg,' Dad said. 'We're done talking about him.'

I thought to myself that I would never ever be done with Henrik Stiernberg, not done talking about him and not done thinking about how he should be punished. Because even if it was true what they'd said, the royals, that they hadn't even seen Paul on the night of the ball, they were all to blame for his death. Ever since Paul came to Adamsberg, they'd bullied him about his clothes, the way he gesticulated when he talked, his dialect. They'd mocked him for his constant reading, his philosophical digressions in class, his interest in the human brain and body, in life and death. They had refused to laugh at his jokes, even though he was the wittiest out of all of us. And it wasn't just psychological stuff either; they'd often walked into him in the hallways, shoving him aside as though he were invisible.

I'm like a swan, he used to say when I asked how he kept from punching them, *it's water off my back*. Once, I corrected him and said it was supposed to be water off a duck's back, not a swan's. Paul laughed and replied that it was the same thing with swans, the cold never penetrated to their skin either. I said I didn't know much about the repulsion mechanisms of different fowl, but that there might be a reason people usually said duck instead of swan. Because ducks were dumb.

Paul said he wasn't dumb, he just didn't care. He didn't care what a bunch of bellends thought of him.

Had I believed him when he said that? I remember thinking it might be the best approach, after all, to just let the bullying roll off you, but later I realised it hadn't worked, that the cold must have penetrated through all the layers of Paul, straight to his heart. And while all this was going on, my own sister went and got together with Henrik Stiernberg, the biggest bully of them all. She hadn't even dumped him after what happened to Paul. When I asked her why, she just offered her condolences as though we hardly knew each other: *My deepest condolences on your friend's death, Francesca.* And then she said she believed Henrik, that she loved him, that it could never be another person's fault that someone took their own life.

I thought about my sister for a while, about when she visited me in the hospital. The first time, she cried as though I were dead and the second time, when she realised I was going to live, she cried about me spreading terrible lies about her boyfriend. I'd done similar things before, she said and brought up that thing I'd accused Erik Vendt's older brother of. I was too weak to argue.

'And Cécile?' I said when Dad turned out onto the motorway. 'What's going to happen to Cécile?'

Dad met my eyes in the rear-view mirror and said nothing was going to happen to Cécile.

'I can't believe you're going to let her stay there.'

'You're focusing on the wrong things, Francesca,' Mum said. 'The only thing you need to think about is getting well.'

I said I was fine, that the sick thing was that they were letting their daughter stay at a school that ...

'This is not the time to talk about that,' Dad said. 'Let's talk about something else.'

I had no desire to talk about anything else. I was fed up with Dad deciding what subjects we could and couldn't talk about, so I closed my eyes, pretended to fall asleep and let the relief at them pulling at least me out of school wash over me.

But first we still had to go by Adamsberg to pick up some clothes for me.

'Come with us,' Mum said after we parked the car. 'You can at least come along and say bye to Cécile.'

I shook my head because I didn't want to say bye to Cécile, and I didn't want to risk running into Henrik Stiernberg or anyone from his gang. If I did, I might cause a scene. It was one of my many shortcomings, that I wasn't always able to control my impulses.

After Mum and Dad left, I climbed into the front passenger seat and looked up at Adamsberg's imposing, white main building. There was something unwelcoming and cold about the whole place. It struck me that it was incredible I had endured it as long as I had. For five years I had said grace before every meal and sung stupid songs about the grandness of the school. I had worn the ill-fitting blazer with the big-beaked eagle on the chest, tried to toe the line and be a good classmate and all that stuff, but the truth was I had hated it from the moment I got there.

The dormitories were scattered around the school building: The Major, Pine Point, The North and Högsäter, the building that had been my home since I first started. *Esse non videri*, read the inscription above the entrance to my dormitory. *Being without being seen*, Dad had explained the first time we walked through the school gates. He said it as though the words were beautiful and not unsettling in the slightest.

I was only eleven when I moved into Högsäter, the youngest person at Adamsberg. Cécile and I were both starting sixth grade, but we were not going to be in the same class or live together. To give us a fresh start. It was time for us girls to have a fresh start, Mum felt. When Dad carried my bags up to the small building on the hill that first day, I was barely able to hold back my tears. I didn't want to spend nights with people I didn't know; couldn't I at least live in the same dormitory as Cécile? But Dad just patted me on the head and said I would have the time of my life. He knew I would, because he had.

But I wasn't like Dad, not like Mum and not like Cécile. I was a stranger in the world, a stranger in my own family.

Describe them, Paul had urged me once when I was complaining about how I didn't belong. *Describe your family.*

I gave him the short version, that my sister was a hypocrite, my dad a liar and my mum ... my mum was nothing but a paper doll, flapping in the breeze.

Dad must have felt it was a failure to have his own daughter expelled from the school he called the *springboard of his career*. Rikard Mild had certainly made the most of his time at Sweden's poshest boarding school. His face was on the wall outside the dining hall together with all the other students who'd graduated with top grades in all subjects.

Dad looked silly in that old photograph. His neatly parted

hair was combed flat across his forehead and his teeth were crooked.

I don't know how he managed to bag Mum, Cécile said once when we were studying his picture together. *How he bagged Stockholm's prettiest girl, with that face.*

I asked her how she knew Mum had been Stockholm's prettiest girl and Cécile replied that Dad had told her.

I countered that Dad was a very unreliable source when it came to Mum. According to him, she was a perfect person, but he was wrong about that; anyone who'd spent more than five minutes with Mum would know she had her fair share of flaws. Dad, usually so perspicacious, was completely blind to them.

Cécile said she supposed that was what love was all about, seeing the good in another person. When she married, it would be to a man who saw the good in her.

I replied that if I ever married, it would be to a man who could make me laugh and who didn't sleep around. Because what good was him telling me I was best person ever if he cheated on me?

Cécile said I shouldn't talk about things I didn't understand.

So I reminded her about Mum and Dad's nocturnal fights on the subject, about how we'd stood behind doors and heard Mum cry about what Dad claimed were malicious lies. But I'd seen enough of Dad's wandering eye to know Mum's accusations were not without foundation.

Mum and Dad were taking a long time. I grew restless and got out of the car. I dug a pack of cigarettes with one cigarette left in it out of my bag. I stood there, defiant, in plain sight, in broad daylight, smoking. I was almost hoping one of the seniors or a teacher would see me. It would feel so good to be immune to their threats. I had been expelled; I was alone. There was nothing to fear; nothing could get worse. I stepped onto the gravel path that led through the school gates to have a closer look at the gold letters on the iron plate that held them closed and read the Latin words (at Adamsberg, Latin was still a world language): *Non est ad astra mollis e terries via.* I had forgotten what they meant, but remembered I had thought it sounded ominous when I was told, once upon a time.

There was no sign of Mum and Dad. They'd probably got caught up in a servile conversation with some teacher or the other. Without really knowing why, I walked over to the chapel. God's house was always open, so I stepped inside. I slowly walked up the aisle to the pew where Paul and I had always sat during services. I took a seat and looked up at Jesus on his cross. How many times had I sat here while my mind was elsewhere? I traced the letters Paul had carved into the bookrack: *God is d.* That's as far as he'd made it before Miss Asp had stopped him and made sure he was given a warning. I searched my pockets for something sharp. At the hospital, they'd confiscated anything potentially harmful, but when I was discharged, they'd at least given me my keys back. I pulled them out and finished what Paul had started. *God is dead.*

Then I went back to the car.

Twenty minutes later, Mum and Dad returned with a suitcase.

'Cécile says hi,' Mum said after asking me to move to the back seat.

I asked why Cécile hadn't come to the car to say hi in person. Mum said it was because she was studying for the national English exam.

I told her the national exams took place in spring.

Mum sighed and said she must have misunderstood then. Either way, it didn't matter since I refused to speak to my sister anyway. It wasn't particularly pleasant to talk to someone who pretended they couldn't see you.

I wanted to tell her I would talk to Cécile again when she believed me, when she believed her own sister over her idiot of a boyfriend, but there was no point. Mum and Dad always believed Cécile's version of events. With me, it was as though they assumed I was lying until they had proof otherwise. They made no secret of it and justified it by pointing out that I had brought it on myself by lying all the time. But my lying could, arguably, be said to be caused by me never feeling like they believed me. It was, as Dad himself liked to say, hard to know which came first, the chicken or the egg.

'I found this in your desk drawer,' Mum said, handing me an envelope.

I took it and saw my name written in Paul's beautiful hand. It made me confused. Had he left a suicide note after all?

'Is it from *him*?' Mum asked.

I nodded.

'Well, don't you want to open it?'

'Later,' I replied.

4

It had just gone five when there was a knock on Charlie's door. It was Anders, wondering if she was almost done. It took her a moment to recall their plans for an after-work drink.

'You're allowed?' Charlie asked before she could stop herself.

She hadn't thought it would actually happen. Truth be told, she would have preferred to stay at work, to sit in her office while night fell, to keep looking for a way forward in her investigation. But she knew new angles and ideas often came to her when she allowed herself to take a break and think about other things.

'I can make my own decisions, you know,' Anders replied; Charlie resisted the impulse to say that from where she was standing, it didn't really seem like it.

'Your part of town or mine?' she asked instead.

Anders pretended not to understand her, but his face lit up when she suggested Riche.

Riche was already loud, despite it not even being six yet. Anders quickly managed to make eye contact with a waiter and they were shown to a small table near the back.

'Because you're hungry, right?' Anders said.

Charlie nodded.

'What do you want?'

'Just pick for me,' Charlie said. 'I'm so hungry I can't choose.'

Anders looked up at a waiter who promptly came hurrying over. Anders ordered two beef fillet carpaccios and two glasses of a red wine Charlie didn't catch the name of. Then he stopped himself and asked if she maybe preferred another wine. She shook her head and said she trusted his judgement. The ins and outs of wine didn't interest her. Had it been so long since they'd been out together that Anders had forgotten she couldn't tell one wine from another anyway? Besides, she preferred beer over wine, but she didn't have it in her to tell Anders that right now.

Anders' phone dinged. He picked it up and smiled.

'What?' Charlie asked.

'It's Sam,' Anders replied. He turned the phone so she could see and played a short video of his son sitting on a blanket on the floor with a trickle of saliva running down his tiny chin. 'He's sitting up unaided.'

'That's early,' Charlie said, though she had no idea if that was true. She knew nothing about child development.

'I think he's pretty average,' Anders said, 'but to us, it's still a miracle.'

He pressed play again. Charlie tried to compensate for her utter lack of interest by taking the phone from him and paying extra close attention.

'He's sweet,' she said when she handed back the phone.

'My god, I'm starving,' Anders said. 'I think it's the sleep deprivation, I never have time for proper meals, it's all snacks these days.'

'Same here,' Charlie said. 'Sleep deprivation turns me into a relentless grazer.'

'You're sleep deprived?'

'Yes.'

'What's keeping you up?'

'I don't know. Thoughts, swirling around.'

'What thoughts?'

'Well, we're working on a horrific case, for instance.'

'So it's just about work?'

Why had she steered the conversation in this direction? She'd known Anders was bound to start asking questions. He'd always been interested in who she was and how she was feeling, but since the Gullspång case, he'd been asking more about her background and health than ever. She didn't know if it was out of concern or curiosity, or maybe both.

'It's just regular insomnia,' she said. 'You know, that vicious circle. I think about how I have to go to sleep and that keeps me awake and ... well, you see what I mean.'

'I get it,' Anders said. 'Maybe that's why you're a bit low. Because of the insomnia, I mean.'

'I'm fine.'

'You're not fine, Lager. You haven't been fine since we got back from Gullspång and not before that either, come to think of it. Actually, I'm wondering if you've ever been completely fine.'

Charlie could feel her hackles rising. Anders was without a doubt her favourite colleague to spend time with. Even though their lives and backgrounds were completely different, they clicked. They rarely agreed on anything, bickered often and laughed together even more. But now, something between them had changed. She hadn't forgotten how he'd sold her out to Challe after her misstep in Gullspång. Maybe she would have done the same in his shoes, but it still chafed at her.

'I'm seeing a therapist,' she said tersely. 'I'm trying to sort things out.'

'What happened?' Anders asked. He stopped fiddling with his cutlery and fixed her intently. 'What really happened in Gullspång?'

'What happened?' Charlie met his eyes. 'A seventeen-year-old girl disappeared and was found dead by the dam gates. Her name was Annabelle Roos. I thought you were there?'

'A lot of other things happened, too,' Anders retorted. 'Don't you think I know that? You really weren't yourself.'

Their food arrived. When the waiter put it down in front of her, Charlie suddenly realised just how hungry she really was. She took a bite of the meat, the rocket and the pine nuts. It was delicious.

'Anyway, it's good to be out together again,' she said, 'good to see you feeling better.'

'I'm not feeling better,' Anders said.

'How come?'

Anders put oil, salt flakes and pepper on his food.

'It's Maria. I think we're going through our first real crisis.'

Charlie put her cutlery down.

'What do you mean by crisis?'

To her mind, Anders and Maria's relationship was pretty much a permanent crisis.

'We're bickering and arguing about every little thing,' Anders said. 'And a few days ago, she told me she was unsure about her feelings for me. I mean, it was in the heat of the moment, obviously, but still. I can't stop thinking about it. "Is this it?" she said. "Is this the rest of our lives?" Like it was hell or something.'

'Maybe you need a break from each other,' Charlie suggested, 'room to breathe, to think things over and ...'

'I don't want that. I really don't want us to be apart.'

'I understand,' Charlie said, though she didn't. She'd only met Maria a handful of times; they had disliked each other on sight. And things hadn't exactly improved when Maria found out that Charlie had been having an affair with Hugo. Apparently, she knew Hugo's wife. After their affair came to light, she'd banned Anders from working alone with Charlie, and not even that had provoked objection from Anders. Instead, he'd lied to her about them working together. It was incredible, when you thought about it, that anyone could be with a person like Maria.

'She's unhappy,' Anders went on. 'She's not happy.'

'Are you?'

'Sure, I suppose so, though obviously I'm not jumping for joy every minute of the day, but ... It's just that I don't see divorce as an option.'

'Why not?'

'Because in my world, I mean the world Maria and I come from, it's ... well, it's just a big enormous failure, simply put.'

Where I come from, failing is not standing up for yourself, Charlie retorted inwardly. Being born and bred on the sunny side of the street seemed to have its drawbacks.

'But maybe you're right,' Anders said. 'About needing time apart. I'm just afraid the end result will be a permanent separation. And being alone ... it frightens me.'

'What's so scary about being alone?' Charlie said.

'The real question is why it doesn't scare you.'

'I never said it doesn't. It's just that the idea of there being this one person you belong with, the notion that you can become immune to loneliness through promises, rings, children, that scares me even more.'

'But does it make you happy?' Anders asked.

Charlie thought he must be asking ironically.

'What do you mean by happy?' she retorted.

'Just happy,' Anders replied.

'I think happiness means different things to different people.'

'And to you?'

'I don't know,' Charlie said. 'If by happiness, you mean that bubbly, tingling, intoxicated feeling, then I don't think it's a state you sustain for very long. To me, it's more about not having anxiety. I think I appreciate that feeling more than most. Being anxiety-free is happiness to me.'

'That sounds terrible.'

'What's so terrible about it?'

'That happiness is nothing more than being anxiety-free. Makes you sound like a pretty unhappy person.'

And you sound like a person who has never experienced anxiety, Charlie thought to herself.

They ordered a bottle of the wine they'd had a glass each of. Anders' phone rang. Maria, of course. He muted it.

'She knows I'm out,' he said, 'but I can't keep telling lies about not being out with you. I'm just going to text her to make sure Sam's alright.'

Do whatever you want, Charlie thought.

'Don't look to your right,' Anders said, 'but there's a guy at the bar staring at you.'

Charlie immediately turned right and the guy at the bar met her eyes. She recognised him instantly. Johan Ro. No, she thought. Not now.

Gaps in Time

So you've seen dead people? I ask Paul when he tells me his father is an undertaker. We've only known each other for about a week but I could tell from the first day he was different.

Of course I have, Paul replies. I've probably seen more than a hundred. My brother and I help out during breaks.

Sounds like an exciting job, I say.

I reckon most people find it creepy. People want to live as though death doesn't exist. They prefer not to think about it.

I think about death every day, I tell him. Ever since I could think abstract thoughts.

But then, you seem different from most people, Paul says with a smile.

I ask him to tell me more about what he does at work. Is he allowed to ... touch the dead people?

Paul nods. He prepares them for their coffins, combs their hair, puts on the clothes the loved ones have picked out and places their hands neatly.

Would you prepare me? I ask.

What do you mean?

I mean, like a dead person.

Why?

I don't know, it would be … exciting.

Sure, Paul says, I could, but I would feel weird about it.

What are they like?

Who?

The bodies. What do they look like? What do they feel like?

Well, they definitely don't look like they're sleeping, I can tell you that, Paul replies. They're stiff, cold, have cadaver spots and look dead, simply put. But the most distinctive thing about them is the smell.

I ask him to describe it, but Paul shakes his head and says he can't. It's kind of an … ineffable smell. If you've ever encountered it, you'll never forget it. Sometimes, during warm summer days, he thinks he can smell it everywhere in their house.

And the maggots, I say, where do they come from? I don't understand how they can just appear out of nowhere.

They don't appear out of nowhere, Paul says and smiles. Dead people attract flies that lay eggs that become maggots.

I always thought they appeared out of nowhere.

But nothing comes from nothing.

5

Charlie took a big gulp of wine.

'Who is he?' Anders asked.

'You don't recognise him?' Charlie said. 'Could you please stop staring.'

'He looks familiar,' Anders said, 'but I'm terrible with faces, am I supposed to know him?'

'Johan Ro,' Charlie said, 'the journalist from last summer.'

Anders brightened.

'Right, I remember now.'

Charlie couldn't help feeling bothered at how happy he sounded. Had he forgotten the aftermath of this particular acquaintance?

'He's the guy who got me suspended.'

'Well, if we're being honest, you sort of got yourself suspended, didn't you?' Anders said. 'Because I'm assuming he didn't force himself on you and then pump you for classified information.'

Charlie had forgotten how brash alcohol made Anders.

'I never gave him any information about the case,' she said.

'And yet it was in the paper the next day,' Anders retorted. 'Aren't you the one who's always saying you don't believe in coincidence?'

'Of course I believe in coincidence,' Charlie replied.

'Why are you so angry? I thought you were over that now.'

'Anders,' Charlie said, leaning in closer. 'I never told him anything about the case.'

'So where did he get his information?' Anders kept smiling as though their conversation was amusing. 'Maybe we should ask him,' he went on and got to his feet.

'Cut it the fuck out,' Charlie said. 'Sit down.'

'Relax. I'm going to the bathroom. But maybe you should go over there and say hi.'

'Why would I?'

'Why not? He clearly wants to talk to you. Right now, he's staring at your profile in the mirror behind the bar.'

Don't come over here, Charlie thought when Anders left. Stay over there and leave things well enough alone. But Johan was already on his way.

'Hi,' he said. 'I thought it was you.'

'Hi.' Charlie tried to look pleasantly surprised. 'Good to see you. How are things?'

'Not bad,' Johan said with a smile. 'And you?'

Charlie realised she'd managed to block out the way his smile affected her.

'Great,' she said.

'I've been trying to call you.'

'You have?' Charlie said and cringed at how fake she sounded.

At first, she'd been happy and planned to call him back, but then she'd decided not to. It had been pure self-preservation, because the last thing she needed in the days after Gullspång was to talk to a person who reminded her of what had happened there, a person who knew so much about her family history. Johan, Mattias's long-lost son.

'Yeah, I called a few times and even left a message, but I took the hint when you never called me back.'

'I've had a lot on, I ...'

'No worries,' Johan cut in. 'I get it.'

And something in his eyes said he meant what he said, that he really did get it. Charlie remembered what Betty had said about his father, Mattias: *He's the only person who knows everything about me and still likes me.*

Was it possible Johan was as patient with lost souls as his father? And then, a moment later, she thought that she really couldn't take that for granted. Johan might know her secrets, but he didn't know her. They didn't know each other and maybe that was for the best.

'Do you want to join us?' Charlie asked. Why had she said that? But it was too late now.

Anders came back from the bathrooms and greeted Johan enthusiastically. Charlie realised he was pretty drunk.

'I bumped into an old friend from school,' Anders said. 'She wanted to buy me a drink at the bar, would it be okay if I ...'

'Sure,' Charlie said. 'I'm leaving soon anyway.'

Anders disappeared, leaving her and Johan alone.

'Want some wine?' she said.

Johan nodded; she topped up Anders' glass and handed it to him. They gazed out at the room in silence for a while. The music thudding out of the speakers was loud, unrhythmical and discordant. Charlie spotted Anders and his friend at the bar. They were talking with heads close together. Maybe to hear each other over the music, Charlie mused, because Anders really wasn't the type to encourage close physical contact with women he wasn't married to. Or was he? If there was one thing life had taught her, it was that you could never truly know another person, that the ones you thought were the most predictable and straightforward could do things that were completely contrary to their nature. She liked to think she was the master of her feelings for the most part, but nothing could be more wrong. Like now, for instance, now she was sitting here with a man common sense told her she should say a quick, polite farewell to, but instead, she raised her glass to him and said it was good to see him, that she'd thought about him from time to time since the summer.

'You have?' Johan said, breaking into another smile.

'Why wouldn't I have? It's not every day you discover a long-lost brother.'

'I would prefer if you didn't think of me as a brother.'

'How come?'

Charlie felt warmth spread through her chest when Johan said it wasn't exactly sibling love they'd felt for each other last summer.

'Then what was it?' Charlie said, putting her wineglass down. Given how unguarded she tended to be, she should probably slow down her drinking.

'You tell me,' Johan retorted.

'Lust?' Charlie reached for her glass again. 'Temporary insanity? The offspring of two lunatics seeking comfort from each other?'

'Or maybe just two unrelated grown-ups and instant attraction?' Johan replied.

'That definitely has a better ring to it.'

Charlie sipped her wine. Thought about that article again, the teenage girl she couldn't stop thinking about.

'I read an article you wrote, by the way,' she said. 'The one about Francesca Mild. Do you know anything else, other than what you wrote?'

'No, most of it's in the article. It was hard to get people to talk about Francesca Mild. It was almost like they were afraid of something. Why?'

Charlie shrugged.

'I think it's weird no one in Gullspång mentioned her. I mean, when we were looking for Annabelle. That would be natural, right, bringing up that another girl disappeared before?'

'I suppose so. But it was a long time ago, maybe people forgot.'

'People in small places don't forget, believe me.'

Charlie recalled the pictures of Francesca, a boarding-school student standing in front of her school with her arms crossed and a rebellious look on her face.

They drank the last of the wine. Anders was still at the bar with his friend.

'Want to go?' Charlie said.

'Where to?'

'My place.'

Repetitions, Charlie thought as they went to pick up their coats and left Riche. Is life just an endless series of repetitions?

6

Johan looked around the living room. Charlie followed his gaze to the books piled high on the floor and windowsills. This was one of the reasons she preferred to go to other people's houses rather than her own. She didn't like being scrutinised, for people to look at her home and judge her.

'Why don't you have any bookshelves?' Johan asked.

'Because the walls are concrete,' Charlie replied. 'Everything I put up falls down.'

'I guess you need plugs?'

'Maybe, but I hate having to deal with things like that.'

'It feels like you just moved in.'

'I didn't. I'm just not into buying lots of crap or doing DIY.' Charlie went into the kitchen. 'Come on.'

Johan pointed to Lillith's old food bowls.

'You have a cat?' he asked.

'Had,' Charlie replied. 'I brought an inbred wild one with me from Lyckebo last summer.'

'What happened to it?'

'She died.'

'Traffic?'

'No, I didn't let her go outside; I was worried she wouldn't be able to navigate an urban environment. She got sick.'

Charlie thought about how the cat had seemed to thrive for the first few weeks. She had dewormed her, her fur had grown soft and the contours of her ribs had disappeared, but then she'd suddenly refused to eat. Charlie had tossed out the dry food and bought expensive packets of the poshest cat food instead. When that didn't work, she'd taken her to a vet who quickly established that it was serious; the cat was dying. Charlie had started to cry, had blamed herself. She'd yanked the poor animal from its natural environment. It was all her fault. The vet said that wasn't the case, absolutely not, but if she really wanted to do something nice for the cat, she should put it to sleep.

Charlie had asked him to try to save her. She didn't care about the cost, or the impossible odds. *Save her*, she'd said, too desperate to care how she sounded, *do everything you can*. But the vet had said it would only prolong her suffering; in the end, Charlie had given in and let him stick a needle in Lillith. She'd sat there holding the warm little body on her lap. Just before Lillith closed her eyes for the last time, she'd looked up at Charlie with sad eyes as if to say: *Thank you. Thank you for trying.*

She looked at Johan.

'What would you like to drink?' she said.

'Maybe tea?'

'Black, white, red or herbs I dried myself?'

'You're joking, right?'

'Yes.'

'Me too. When I said I wanted tea. So, what do you have? Whisky?'

'All gone. But I have beer.'

Johan laughed when she opened her fridge.

'I'm sorry,' he said when she gave him a querying look. 'It's just not what I would expect from a woman's fridge. I forgot that you're rather ... unpredictable.'

Charlie smiled at the joke from last summer. She handed Johan a bottle and grabbed one for herself. They went back to the living room and sat down.

'Francesca Mild,' Charlie said. 'How did you decide to write about her?'

'I had the idea when I got back from Gullspång last summer,' Johan said. 'I figured it would give me peace of mind to visit the place my dad disappeared, see Lyckebo, talk to you about him, but I just ended up wanting to know more. I couldn't stop thinking about it.'

'Welcome to my world.'

'And what about you; why do you find it so interesting?'

'The place,' Charlie said. 'And ...'

'What?'

'Maybe the Annabelle case, that another girl her age disappeared from Gullspång.'

'But it's almost thirty years ago,' Johan said.

'Still.'

Charlie took a big swig of her beer and thought to herself that there must be another reason she couldn't stop thinking about Francesca Mild. She could neither formulate any clear thoughts nor put into words what it might be.

'Anyway, I stumbled across the Francesca case and started digging,' Johan explained. 'It wasn't easy because there was practically nothing about it online. That made me curious. And the harder it was to get information out of people, the more important it seemed. When I contacted the boarding school she attended to get information about her classmates, they were uncooperative, to say the least. Maybe that has more to do with wanting to protect the school's reputation, but it's still curious.'

Charlie nodded. The simple movement made her dizzy. She tried to fix her eyes on a pile of books by the opposite wall, but everything blended together. She was unfocused.

'And when I managed to get hold of some people who had been to school there around that time, none of them wanted to talk.'

'Are you surprised?' Charlie said. 'Haven't you read about the culture of silence those places foster?'

'Sure. But it's so long ago. I didn't think people would still be so prickly about it.'

'They've been trained to be for generations.'

'How come you know so much about boarding-school students?' Johan smiled.

'Adamsberg isn't that far from Gullspång. Sometimes they'd come into town, the students and … laugh.'

Charlie remembered the Adamsberg gangs with their expensive clothes, their requests for various goods in the shop, their rolling eyes when their wishes couldn't be fulfilled.

'Laughed?' Johan said. 'At what?'

'I never asked. At all the things we didn't have, perhaps, or all the things we did have. They called us …'

'What did they call you?'

'I can't recall. I honestly don't remember, but it was incredibly fucking condescending.'

'Pretty brave of them,' Johan remarked.

'To go into town in big groups and laugh at kids who hadn't been lucky enough to be born with their kind of privilege?'

'I wouldn't have dared to laugh at you.'

'The question is really whether you would have wanted to?' Charlie said. 'Besides, I wasn't very tough back then.'

'I reckon you were.'

Charlie opened her mouth to tell him he was wrong, but just then, Johan leaned in and kissed her.

'Wait,' she mumbled.

'I'm sorry.' Johan pulled back. 'I thought you wanted to.'

'I do,' she said. She leaned towards him. 'I just wanted to ...'

'What?' Johan asked.

'Nothing,' she said and kissed him.

Johan started putting his clothes back on the moment they finished. Charlie felt a bit dazed by what had just happened between them. They'd clung to each other as though their physical union was their only means of survival. And now he was leaving.

'I have to get up early tomorrow,' Johan said.

'Sure,' Charlie replied.

What's with me? she wondered. I hate sleeping with other people. I should be happy he's sparing me the inconvenience of kicking him out. And yet, she felt disappointed when Johan bent down and kissed her on the lips.

'I didn't come home with you just for this,' he said.

'Then why did you?' Charlie asked. She grabbed the blanket from the sofa and pulled it over her naked body.

'Because I wanted to talk to you.'

Charlie let out a laugh.

'I mean it.'

'I'm sorry, it just sounded a bit rehearsed. I like talking to you too.'

*

Charlie fell asleep and dreamed of Betty. Betty's hands in her hair, plaits so tight they hurt. Betty putting on red lipstick, bending down to press her cheek against Charlie's. *Do we look fancy? Are we good enough now?*

And then, a tree-lined road, Betty's pale face in the moonlight, hazy mist around their legs. Are they in heaven or on Earth?

Where are we going, Mummy?

To a friend's.

What friend?

No reply.

Charlie was woken up by her phone buzzing on the coffee table.

Susanne, the screen informed her.

'Susanne?' Charlie said and cleared her throat when her drowsy voice cracked. 'How are things?'

'Things are fucked.'

'What happened?'

'Two things,' Susanne replied. 'Isak moved out and mum started drinking again.'

'Oh my god,' Charlie said.

'I know it's an uncivilised hour, but I'm falling apart,' Susanne whispered. 'I'm completely falling apart, Charlie.'

'You're going to hold it together.'

'I'm not so sure.'

'Do you want me to come down?'

There was a brief pause.

'Could you?'

'The moment I close the case I'm working on.'

*

After they hung up, Charlie was unable to go back to sleep. She spent a long time staring at the ceiling, thinking about Susanne, the parties they'd suffered through together out in Lyckebo, the laughing, the screaming, the drunken rows, the parents who turned into children. *The two of us are the only adults here, Charlie.*

Then she remembered her dream: Betty, the moonlight, the trees lining the road on both sides. It all felt strangely familiar. It took her brain a few more minutes to piece it all together. She got up, fetched her laptop from the kitchen, opened the article about the missing Francesca and studied the picture of the family's manor. Gudhammar.

Debris from the day before, Charlie thought to herself. According to what she remembered of the various theories on dream interpretations, dreams were nothing but the brain cobbling together sensory information from the day before to make a complete picture. She didn't believe dreams were a secret door to a person's psyche, that they contained messages or expressed subconscious thoughts and fears. She'd seen that picture, had thought about Betty and then the two had been merged in her dream.

She put her laptop away and resumed her attempts to fall asleep. She couldn't. Eventually, she got up and wandered about her flat aimlessly. I'll just walk around for a bit, she told herself. I don't need benzo to sleep and besides, I've been drinking and ... that was as far as she got before she found herself in the bathroom with two diazepam in her hand. Just tonight, she thought, then I have to be done with this.

In her dream, Betty returns. She's sitting by her make-up table in Lyckebo. Her bedroom window is open and the sheer white lace curtain is billowing in the summer breeze. *Come, sweetheart. Come help me button up my dress.* Betty holds her hair up and Charlie walks across the floor. Then she stops, because Betty's back is hollow like an old tree trunk.

What's the matter? Betty tilts her head to one side and looks at her with sad eyes in the mirror. *What's wrong now?*

Francesca

Gudhammar. Mum always said the place gave her cabin fever, but I didn't mind that it was so isolated. I loved that you could look as far as you liked in any direction and see nothing but fields, woods and water. I even loved the tiny high street in the nearby town. Mum and Cécile always complained about the things that weren't available there. They found it incomprehensible that anyone would choose to live in such a godforsaken place. Neither one of them had much time for the locals. Cécile would giggle at them. On account of their social clumsiness, she said; because they said hello to us even though they didn't know us. That, coupled with their ugly dialect, made her unable to suppress her laughter. Personally, I thought their dialect sounded warm and I liked that people I didn't know said hi to me. I would chat with old ladies in the narrow aisles of the supermarket and buy lottery tickets from the peculiar man who sat outside its entrance.

Dad didn't like me talking to strangers. A manor like Gudhammar and old money like ours attracted crackpots, he claimed.

Dad turned down the tree-lined road leading to the house. When we passed the gatehouse, I almost expected to see old

Vilhelm sitting there with his kerosene lamp in the window. It had been almost three years since Vilhelm died; even though he'd been old and sick, his passing had come as a shock to me. Vilhelm had always been there and I'd spent countless hours playing cards with him in the gatehouse kitchen. I had loved listening to his stories about what the farm had been like in the olden days, when my grandparents were alive and still kept animals. And even though I'd never experienced that time, I felt like I missed it. Vilhelm's son Ivan had worked for us, too, when his dad got too old to keep up with his duties, but he'd quit now. I was happy about that, because Ivan was nothing like his dad. There was something unpleasantly bitter about his face and his presence always made me uneasy.

'The rhododendron's still there,' Mum said, pointing to the flowerbed outside the north wing. 'I told Adam to remove it.'

'And I told him to leave it be,' Dad said.

'Why?' Mum asked.

'Because I wanted it there.'

They started bickering about the rhododendron. Dad thought the flowers were beautiful, but Mum disagreed. She didn't enjoy the colour and besides, they only lasted a week.

I sighed loudly and thought to myself that I, for better or worse, would never become the kind of person who cares about bushes.

'What's that?' I said, pointing, when Dad pulled up next to the front steps.

'Lions,' Mum replied. 'Isn't that obvious?'

'What I meant was what are they doing on the front steps?'

'They're welcoming us.'

Mum told me she'd bought them at an auction in

Switzerland, that they weighed over two hundred pounds each, that she'd had to hire a specialist firm to ship them here. Lions didn't seem like particularly welcoming animals to me, but Mum tended to lose her temper when people criticised her purchases, so I just walked up to one of the lions, put my hand in his open maw and said I could tell the material was expensive.

'Adam!' Mum called out to a shadow in the garden. 'I'm glad you're here.'

I looked over at Adam, the man Dad simply called the 'gardening boy', and quietly agreed with Mum. Adam was the kind of person who eased tension. He was pleasant to have around. Cécile liked him, too; she'd admitted as much one evening when we'd seen him in his bathing suit on the jetty. But she wasn't interested. He was too simple, didn't have enough depth. I laughed out loud when she said that, because all the boys Cécile had liked had one fundamental thing in common: they all had the depth of a murky puddle of water. At least Adam wasn't conceited, and he made me laugh occasionally. That was more than could be said for most.

'Hi, Francesca,' Adam said and smiled.

'Howdy,' I replied, wondering how much he knew about recent events.

Mum and Dad never talked to staff about private matters, but he could probably tell something was wrong since we'd come in the middle of term, and I still had a cannula stuck in the back of my hand.

'I have a fire going for you inside.' Adam nodded towards the house.

'Thank you,' Mum said.

'Did you use up all the kindling?' Dad asked.

Adam shook his head. He hadn't used any kindling at all.

'I need to talk to you later, Adam,' Mum said, 'about the rhododendron. Tomorrow, perhaps?'

The first thing that greeted any visitor to Gudhammar was a framed wall hanging my great grandmother had embroidered: curlicue letters surrounded by blue butterflies and lilies-of-the-valley.

Good thoughts
Good words
Spread joy on this Earth.

Reading it always made me feel like a bad person. My usual thoughts returned. *I'm a stranger. I'm a stranger in this family.*

I went to the bathroom and pulled out Paul's letter. If it was a suicide note, I'd expected a beautiful farewell or perhaps an attempt to explain or at least an apology for leaving me alone in a place that was utterly unendurable without him. But mostly, I wanted to know why he hadn't taken me with him. But there was nothing like that in the short text:

Two explorers were captured by cannibals and put in a cauldron of boiling water. All of a sudden, one of the explorers burst out laughing.

'What's so funny?' said the other explorer. 'Is being boiled alive amusing to you?'

'Yes,' replied the first explorer, 'because I peed in the soup.'

Mum and Dad were in the parlour. My stomach felt empty so I shuffled out into the kitchen. Tacked to the noticeboard next to the fridge was a piece of paper with the numbers of all the people who helped out at Gudhammar. There must have been fifty names, some of them crossed out and replaced with new ones. Why did we need all this help, even when we were here? Why couldn't we clean gutters, defrost the freezer and oil the garden furniture like regular people? If I was ever accused of being out of touch, these were the kinds of things I'd blame. Before I went up to my room, I tore down the paper, crumpled it up and threw it in the bin.

The room on the north side of the house had been mine since Cécile and I moved out of the big nursery next to Mum and Dad's bedroom. We had both wanted the room with the southern exposure, so to make it fair, we'd pulled straws out of Dad's hand. It goes without saying Cécile drew the longer one. When I demanded a do-over because it hadn't been done right, Dad laughed and said I was the world's sorest loser. Besides, it wasn't a big deal, he felt, since the rooms were practically identical. The only difference was the balcony.

I disagreed and said it was other things, too, the walk-in closet, the climbing roses on the outside wall, the light and the view of the water. I would have liked to sit on that balcony on balmy summer nights, watching the sun set over the lake. In the room on the north side, the view was obscured by an enormous oak tree. But Cécile had pulled the longest straw. She'd been luckier than me. It was fair.

I put my bags down and went into Cécile's room. I stood in the middle of the room and just stared into space for a good long while. Then I walked over to her perfectly made bed and groped around a little. I found one of her silky nightgowns under her pillow. I took off all my clothes, pulled it over my head and studied myself in the full-length mirror at the foot of the bed. With my pale skin and bandaged arms, I looked like a ghost. Then I walked over and sat down at the antique desk and stared at Cécile's cork board, which was covered with a billion photographs. Cécile at various ages with her arms around friends who were almost as pretty as her: Cécile in a yellow bikini on the jetty, Cécile with a big smile next to the Connemara pony she had one summer. And everywhere, those friends. I couldn't understand how Cécile could bear to have them around all the time, people she had to talk to, who couldn't just sit in silence, thinking, drawing, reading. A wave of grief washed over me when I realised I would never find a friend like Paul again. I was convinced no one else would ever be as right for me, no one would ever be as wise and funny and like me for me. I thought about the note he'd written. Paul had often left little missives for me to find. I would discover them under my pillow or in my maths book. Anything from ironic in-jokes to quotes from philosophers he was reading. If he had in fact killed himself, he would have left a note, I was pretty sure about that.

I studied one of the photos of Cécile more closely. It was from our ninth-grade spring ball. A pale pink two-piece dress, her arms around two classmates. At the edge of the picture I glimpsed a corner of the green fabric of my dress. Without thinking, I tore down the picture, ripped it in half and threw it in the bin under the desk before stomping off. Cécile would know I'd been in her room (it was as though she could smell me; she always knew, even when I hadn't touched a thing) and then she would notice the picture missing and then she would complain to Mum and then Mum would give me her usual lecture about the importance of respecting other people's privacy; when was I going to stop transgressing against social convention?

I went back to my room and started unpacking my neatly folded clothes. I managed to put three pieces of clothing in my closet before I deflated. Then I didn't know what to do. I felt tired but far too restless to lie down. It was as though something was missing inside me; it took me a while to figure out I needed to smoke. I was pleasantly surprised to find half a pack of Blend in my nightstand. I opened the window, sat down on the windowsill and lit a cigarette. Gudhammar had a unique smell. After a while, you grew immune to it, but right then, I could smell that undefinable blend of wood, soil and gravel.

Between the branches of the oak, I could just make out the outline of the jetty down by the lake. I was reminded of when Cécile and I were little and used to compete over who could stay under water longer. It didn't matter that I was vastly superior at holding my breath; Mum always said we were equally good.

I could stay under longer, Cécile said once after I teased her for giving up so easily. *I could stay under as long as you, if I didn't float up to the surface.*

I offered to help and pushed her head under water. It's not that I wanted to drown my sister, which was what Mum shouted at Dad when he came running down from the house. For god's sake, I just wanted to help her beat my record.

'Francesca,' Mum suddenly said (she'd always had an unpleasant ability to sneak up on people).

I dropped the cigarette.

'How many times do I have to tell you not to sit in the window like that?' she went on. 'Do you know how long the fall is?'

I looked down at my glowing cigarette and said I'd estimate about twenty feet.

'It's over thirty,' Mum corrected me.

'Did you want something?'

'Have you been smoking?'

I shook my head.

'This is what I'm talking about,' Mum said. She walked up to the window and mopped up some ashes with her finger. 'How are we supposed to trust you when you're always lying?'

'You've never trusted me anyway, so it makes no difference.'

'And why do you think that is?' Mum sat down on my bed, looking unhappy. 'Why do you think we don't trust you? You're like the boy who cried wolf.'

'What are you talking about?'

'You don't remember the story? You heard it quite a few times as a child, but it doesn't seem to have stuck. Maybe I should tell it again?'

'No, thanks,' I said, because I actually knew that ridiculous story by heart.

'There once was a young shepherd boy,' Mum began.

'Not now, Mum, I'm too tired. I actually don't feel well.'

'Don't you think I know that?' Mum said and abruptly got to her feet. 'Don't you think you've just put Dad and me through the worst thing that can happen to a parent?'

'The worst actually didn't happen.'

'But it would have, if it weren't for...' Mum's voice broke into a sob.

'It's not that I was planning to kill myself,' I said.

Mum said that if that was true, slicing my wrists open had been a strange thing to do. Not the kind of thing people who wanted to live usually did.

'But I don't want to die. There was just a lot of anxiety; I was sad about Paul. I suppose I wanted to dull the pain inside. It wasn't a suicide attempt.'

'I know,' Mum said and picked a withered leaf off a plant in the window. 'It was just a cry for help.'

'Was there anything else?' I asked.

'I was thinking about this business with your school. I understand that you're upset, Francesca, but ...'

And then, before I could tell her I was anything but upset about being pulled out of school, she launched into a long rant about how it was okay if I graduated a year later. I was a year ahead anyway, since I'd skipped a grade. And when this situation, when I felt a bit better, then ... well, then I could pick up my studies where I'd left off. I wasn't permanently expelled. The headmaster had explicitly said I was welcome back when I was doing better.

'Maybe,' I said. Was she ever going to leave?

'Francesca,' Mum said. 'Just because something sad happened in your life ...'

'My best friend's dead,' I said, cutting her off.

'Yes, that's exactly what I'm saying.'

'No, you're not. You're saying something sad happened.'

'Okay.' Mum bit her lip. 'But listen to me. You don't get infinite chances in life.'

'You don't say.'

'I'm serious, Francesca. You can't keep making bad decisions again and again and expect to be given more chances. I'm not telling you this to make you feel bad, that's the last thing I want, but as your mother, I have to tell you bluntly that if you throw away too many opportunities, some doors close.'

She looked at me mournfully.

'Answer me, Francesca.'

I didn't know what to say since I hadn't heard a question.

'When the lord closes a door, he's supposed to open a window,' I said.

Just then a gust of wind blew my window shut with a bang.

'I choose not to take that literally,' I said.

'Maybe you should.' Mum smiled.

'Are we done?' I asked.

'Cécile doesn't like you going in her room.'

'I haven't been in there.'

'Then how come you're wearing her nightgown?'

7

Charlie sensed something was wrong the moment she woke up. A quick glance at her watch made her leap out of bed. It was one in the afternoon. One! Had she forgotten to set an alarm? She picked up her phone and let out a series of curses when she saw all the missed calls from Challe. And a text from Anders: *Give us a shout unless you want a patrol to stop by. Challe thinks you're dead.*

She called Challe. He picked up straight away.

'I'm not dead,' she said.

'Pity,' Challe replied. 'That would have been the one acceptable excuse.'

'I'm so sorry.'

'Come in,' Challe said. 'We need to talk.'

No excuse Charlie could come up with in the taxi was plausible or good enough. And just admitting that she'd overslept obviously wasn't going to work. No functional person slept until one in the afternoon. She gave up trying to think of a credible lie that would hold up under Challe's scrutiny and instead turned her thoughts to her conversation with Susanne in the middle of the night. Susanne was one of the strongest people she knew. Or had been when they were young, at least. The Susanne she'd met last summer had been broken by life and circumstance and now the situation had gone from bad to worse. *I'm falling apart, Charlie, I'm completely falling apart.*

When Charlie got to the office, Challe was in a meeting, so she went to the kitchen.

Her head was pounding from hangover and benzo. She needed coffee.

Kristina was standing by the sink, holding forth on one of her favourite topics: that women need to stop talking behind each other's backs and be supportive instead. Hugo was sitting at the table, nodding his agreement.

'There you are!' Kristina exclaimed when she spotted Charlie. 'Challe has ...'

'I know,' Charlie cut her off. 'I know.'

She could feel Hugo's eyes on her back as she shuffled over to the coffee machine.

'I couldn't agree more,' Hugo said to Kristina. 'Women treat women worse than men. What?' he demanded when Charlie chuckled.

'I just don't understand what you mean,' Charlie replied. She carried her cup over to the table and sat down. 'Are there scientific studies that show that?'

'That show what?' Kristina said.

'That women treat women worse than men.'

'I thought everybody knew that,' Kristina said, rolling her eyes at Hugo.

Charlie wanted to say something about that not being a valid argument, but she knew it would be a waste of time. Kristina wasn't susceptible to things like facts and statistics. Her own unshakeable conviction was good enough for her.

'Say you're right,' Charlie said, 'that women talk more behind each other's backs than men do, then maybe the underlying reason for that is our social structures.'

'I don't know why you're so upset,' Hugo said. 'We're not exactly the only ones who think women treat women worse than men.'

'What kind of argument is that?' Charlie exclaimed. 'You can't just point to the fact that lots of other people are wrong, too.'

She wondered where the man she'd thought she knew had gone and reached the same sad conclusion as before: he'd never existed.

Kristina's ignorance didn't upset her as much. Kristina hadn't been out in the field and seen what men were capable of. She wasn't in the middle of an investigation in which two young women had been murdered and dumped in the woods like so much rubbish. She'd never interviewed devastated rape victims or looked after children whose fathers had killed their mothers right in front of them. She was just a person who lacked analytical ability, blind, even to the most obvious things.

'I hope we can agree on one thing, though,' Charlie said. 'That assault, rape and murder is worse than talking about someone behind their back.'

Kristina said that of course they agreed on that.

'Alright then,' Charlie said. 'Women don't murder, they don't rape, they don't hit. That's what men do to women.'

'That's not exactly what we meant,' Hugo said.

'Fine, then maybe I misunderstood. I thought you said women treated women worse than men.'

'It's impossible to discuss things like this with you,' Hugo said.

'Back at you,' Charlie retorted. 'And besides, I don't believe that stuff about women talking more shit than men. I've met enough men to know most of them are full of shit.'

She stood up, grabbed her coffee mug and left the kitchen.

'I'm free now,' Challe said as she walked past his office. 'You can come in, Charlie.'

Charlie sat down facing Challe. She'd sat in his office so many times, had good conversations, been given praise, been promoted and received a raise, and yet it was the unpleasant conversations she remembered best. The one about her drinking habits after the office party, about her unprofessional behaviour in the Annabelle case and the most recent one about her annual leave. She suddenly felt exhausted. She didn't have the energy to defend herself, to beg him to let her keep working, to assure him everything was fine. Because things weren't fine. And before Challe had a chance to speak, she told him she'd been thinking. Challe spread his hands and asked her to go on. What had she been thinking?

'My annual leave,' Charlie said. 'I think I need time off.'

'I thought you wanted to finish the investigation first?' Challe said.

'I know,' she replied. 'But I have a childhood friend who needs me. I was thinking I might go see her.'

'Where does she live?' Challe asked.

'Does it matter?'

'No, I was just curious.'

'In Gullspång. Is that a problem?'

'I don't know,' Challe said. 'I mean, you weren't exactly doing great when you came back from there last time.'

'Who said it had anything to do with the town?'

'No one. Anders just mentioned in passing that you grew up down there. I thought maybe ...'

'What did you think?'

'That maybe it would be unwise for you to go back again.'

'This isn't about whether it's wise or not,' Charlie said. 'This is about my friend who needs me.'

Challe stood up and walked over to the window. There was a long pause before he finally turned round.

'I understand. But what about your therapy? It's important that you follow through with the therapist now that you're finally going.'

'Absolutely,' Charlie said. 'I'm not quitting therapy. Just taking a break.'

'And when were you planning on leaving?'

'Today.'

'Today?' Challe scratched his head. 'Alright. Fine, consider yourself on leave.'

'Good.'

'And hey, Charlie,' Challe said to her back. 'Look after yourself.'

8

Ten minutes into the drive, Charlie called Susanne to say she was on her way. Melker, Susanne's oldest son, answered.

Charlie introduced herself and asked to speak to his mother.

'She's asleep,' Melker replied. 'We're only allowed to wake her if it's a matter of life or death. Do you want me to give her a message when she wakes up?'

'Tell her I'm on my way,' Charlie said. 'I'll be there in three hours.'

'She said you were coming, but not today.'

'I moved some things around. I'll be there today.'

'I'll tell her when she wakes up.'

After she hung up, Charlie tried to remember how old Susanne's children were. The twins were six and Nils a few years older, but how old was Melker? Eleven? Who looked after them while their mother was asleep? She concluded they were probably fine on their own. She'd been considerably younger than Melker when she started handling cooking, homework and bedtime without any involvement from Betty.

After about an hour, Charlie stopped at a Seven Eleven for petrol and a big latte. Night was already closing in. Charlie liked it. Darkness seemed to have the opposite effect on her than on other people, who seemed to yearn for the light.

When she turned back onto the motorway, the image of Francesca Mild's face popped into her head again. What had she seen? What lies had she uncovered? Why had she disappeared? And how was it possible that no one in Gullspång had mentioned her disappearance last summer? Was it because Francesca hadn't been a local girl? Because she was a child of the upper class who attended boarding school and only spent holidays in the area?

Several streetlights were broken, so Gullspång's high street was partly shrouded in darkness. Maybe the local youths still entertained themselves by kicking lampposts until they went out. She and Susanne had done that. They'd learnt how from older boys. A hard kick with the flat of the foot about three feet from the ground. It had taken a long time and a lot of failed attempts before she finally succeeded and the light flickered and went out.

The pub was lit, however; she could see people inside. She wondered what the mood was like in there now, if the regulars had already gathered and started drinking. A swaying sign by the side of the road next to the pub read HARVEST FESTIVAL and the coming weekend's dates. Waterfall Day and the Harvest Festival, Charlie mused. How long had those traditions existed? Betty had loved them, loved the beer tents pitched in the field between the pub and the river, loved that the bands playing were proper ones for once, able to keep a beat and stay in key. If there was one thing that made Betty happy, it was dancing to a proper band.

The memory of Betty in her dream again. Her hands in her hair, the plaits, the gravel, the moonlight.

Where are we going, Mummy?
To a friend's.
What friend?
No answer.

The road to Susanne's house was unlit and pitch black. Charlie passed the small cottage in which an old woman had lived with her adult son. They were relatives of hers, Susanne had admitted once, distant ones, but still. She wasn't thrilled about being related to crazy people. The son used to sell lottery tickets outside the supermarket, hollering and shouting so loudly he scared the out-of-towners. What's wrong with him? Charlie had asked Susanne's mum Lola once, but she'd just looked at her like she didn't understand the question. There was nothing wrong with him. He was just a bit nervous. When he wasn't selling lottery tickets, he liked to stand at the intersection holding an orange snow pole that he raised in greeting to the passing cars. It was because it soothed his nerves, Lola reckoned. One time, Charlie and Susanne, buzzed from the beer they'd drunk, had sneaked by his cottage, stolen his pole and discarded it in the woods some way away. Why? Charlie didn't know.

She was so deep in thought she almost missed the narrow road leading down to Susanne's house. She felt relieved when she saw the welcoming, bright windows of the large wooden house.

Charlie was just about to knock when the door was thrown open by one of the twins. His fleece trousers were too short in the leg and his stained top too long in the sleeves.

'Dad's moved out,' he said instead of hello.

'I heard,' Charlie said, trying to figure out if it was Tim or Tom standing before her.

'Mum's still sad, even though it was a lot of days ago,' he said and pushed the dachshund that was trying to escape back inside. 'Stay, Hibby.'

'Do you remember me?' Charlie said, extending her hand.

'Of course I do, you're Charlie, mum's bestie.'

'And you must be Tim, right?' Charlie guessed.

'Tom,' the boy corrected her.

'It's not easy to tell you apart,' Charlie said.

'I know,' said Tom.

'So, where's your mum?'

'She's in her room. I'm afraid to look if she's awake yet because she gets really mad.'

I see,' Charlie said, holding back a smile. 'Where are your brothers?'

'Nils and Melker are upstairs and Tim's in the living room.'

The house was a mess, Charlie noted. Shoes were scattered all over the hallway, the kitchen was cluttered with dirty dishes and smelled faintly of cat litter and old food.

Tim was sitting on the sofa, eating chocolate. He was watching a violent film and didn't seem to register Charlie's presence. His eyes were glued to the screen where a man with a knife was chasing a woman through a forest. Charlie said hi but got only a nod back. She grabbed the remote on the table and pushed the red button. Nothing happened. She looked around to see if there was another remote and deduced from Tim's smug look that he had it.

'Hi,' she said again.

'Hey,' Tim said and waved his hand about. 'You're blocking the TV; this is a really exciting part.'

'I don't think this a good film for you to be watching.'

'I've seen it a thousand times. Mum lets me.'

Charlie gave up and moved out of the way. She had more urgent things to care about right now than the boys' film choices.

'Don't wake Mum,' Tim said when she walked towards the stairs.

The bedroom was dark and Susanne was completely hidden underneath her duvet. It was like a scene from Charlie's own childhood. She was the tiptoeing child and Susanne was Betty, who had bailed on parenthood and the world.

'Don't,' Susanne whispered when Charlie turned on the overhead light. 'Let me sleep a bit longer.'

Charlie walked up to her nightstand and checked the backs of the many blister packs scattered across it: Largon, Oxazepam and Zoloft.

'Susanne,' she said, pulling the duvet down. 'Your boys are downstairs.'

'I know. And you don't have to say it,' Susanne replied. 'I already know I'm completely fucking useless. I can't do this.'

Charlie felt like ripping the duvet off the bed and telling her she had no choice, that she had to do it, but she couldn't, because she knew that it could have been her in that bed.

'I'm not judging you,' Charlie said. 'I'm here to help.'

Susanne sat up.

'Thank you, Charlie,' she said. 'I'm so happy you're here.'

Then she burst out crying.

Francesca

When Mum finally left my room, I went out into the upstairs hallway and called the Major. One of the younger girls answered. It took Cécile a while to come to the phone.

'Francesca?'

'Yes.'

'Are you at Gudhammar now?'

'Yes.'

There was a long silence.

'Did you want something?' Cécile said finally.

'How did the exam go?'

'What exam?'

'The national one. In English.'

Cécile didn't answer. I could hear talking and laughing in the background.

'Why did you lie?' I asked.

'I guess I just didn't want you to start yelling at me again.'

'Is it really so strange that I'm upset when my sister's dating a murderer?'

'I don't want to talk about it any more.'

'Cécile,' I said. 'I'm pretty sure they did something to Paul, that Henrik, Erik and ...'

'I don't know where you get that from,' Cécile said. 'He did it himself, Francesca. He was a wreck. Everyone except you seems to have grasped that.'

I hung up.

Mum had decided to sleep on the sofa bed in my room. I told her she really didn't have to, that after a week in the hospital with people coming and going at every hour, I really needed to be alone. But Mum insisted. Given the situation, she wasn't about to take unnecessary risks. She was going to sleep on the sofa bed and if that bothered me, I was free to pretend she wasn't there; she wasn't going to make a peep. I said she might be able to ignore people like that, but I didn't know how. Besides, my insomnia was always worse when I wasn't alone.

'How long have you had trouble sleeping?' Mum asked.

'Since my first night at Adamsberg,' I said. 'It started when I had to share a room with strangers.'

That wasn't true. My insomnia had started long before Adamsberg, but I didn't want to miss an opportunity to make Mum feel bad for sending me there.

'Your housemistress always brings it up during our parent-teacher conferences,' Mum said. 'She thinks lack of sleep is the root cause of your problems.'

'My housemistress is an idiot,' I said.

'In what way?' Mum asked, without commenting on my word choice.

'She's just an idiot.'

After Mum fell asleep, I peeked underneath the bandages on my arm. The cuts were actually really deep. The doctor who'd been in the room when I came to had told me I must have had a guardian angel: a few minutes longer and it would've been too late. I spent some time pondering what would have happened if the housemistress hadn't called for help, if she'd been on one of her long evening calls with her sister and not bothered with the lights-out routine; everything would have ended very differently. I thought about my funeral, about all the phonies at Adamsberg who would have attended it in their school blazers, the boys with slicked back hair and lowered heads and the girls with their waterproof mascara, fake crying, like at the memorial service for Paul. They would have shaken Mum and Dad's hands, bowed and curtsied and offered their condolences. They would have said I was such an amazing person, so happy and colourful (Adamsberg really was lousy with liars). Then the headmaster would have talked some rubbish about how I'd been a gifted girl with big dreams, how it was incomprehensible that such a young, vibrant person could be gone from one moment to the next.

That was more or less what had been said about Paul. The memorial service had taken place a week after Paul's death; at that point, I still hadn't had the capacity or wherewithal to work through my impressions from the night of the ball, but as time went by, my fuzzy memories grew clearer. When I was in the hospital, I tried to talk to the staff about it. 'His trouser legs,' I whispered to a poor nurse's assistant. She shrieked, because she probably thought I was asleep and of course it was frightening to have your arm grabbed by a psych case spouting nonsense in the middle of the night. His trouser legs were wet,' I called after her when she fled into the hallway. 'They were dripping!'

The next morning, I'd wanted to call Cécile, but they hadn't let me. I wasn't allowed to call anyone. The staff gave me no other reason for my phone ban than that I needed my rest. In my condition, it was important to take it easy and have as little contact with the outside world as possible.

I tried to explain it all to a young resident doctor: the rose, the water, their inexplicable agitation.

The doctor said he certainly didn't want to trivialise my experiences, but he still advised me to let things sink in properly. I had ingested a drug that could induce hallucinations and that, coupled with the significant quantity of alcohol I'd drunk, was enough to cause considerable memory loss. In other words: I could not trust my memories. My brain had been poisoned. It hadn't been working right at the time.

I'd thought he might be right, that it might be for the best to do what I was told, to rest and not get myself worked up. But I couldn't.

I turned over in my bed at Gudhammar. Mum was breathing far too loudly. Once I'd noticed, it was impossible to ignore. Why couldn't she just leave me alone? How was I supposed to get back to normal if I couldn't sleep?

When I closed my eyes, I suddenly remembered something Paul had told me before we parted ways to get ready for the ball:

I think I've found someone. I think I'm in love, Francesca.

With whom? I screamed inwardly. With whom? But there was nothing.

I sat up. Whom had Paul found? It had to be someone at the school, I figured, because back home he saw only his father, brother and grandmother. And he wasn't the type to head into the nearest town, looking for fun. I fetched an old yearbook and started flipping through it. Beautiful girls' faces in almost every class, but none of them could, as far as I was aware, keep up with Paul intellectually. But love's not only about being well-matched, I mused. Hadn't Paul said that once, in fact, that the strangest thing about love was that it was irrational, that it would not submit to reason.

9

It was seven o'clock, but given the mess in the kitchen and Susanne's mental state, Charlie was fairly certain it had been a while since anyone in the house had had a proper dinner.

'Are you hungry?' she asked he boys.

Melker and Nils had come down from their rooms and greeted her a bit awkwardly. Charlie wanted to tell them that they shouldn't feel embarrassed, that she was the last person on Earth they should feel ashamed in front of.

All four said they were hungry.

'How about pizza?' Charlie suggested.

Tim and Tom cheered and immediately started to make requests.

'Can we have Coke, too?' Tim wanted to know. 'Stop it,' he went on when Nils elbowed him.

'Pizza's plenty,' Nils said.

The twins and Nils wanted to go with her to the pizzeria. Melker said he'd stay home in case Susanne needed help with something.

'Is being a copper fun?' Tim said when they'd climbed into the car.

'Most of the time,' Charlie replied.

'Why not all the time?'

'No job's fun all the time,' Charlie said, 'and sometimes police officers have to deal with things that aren't very nice.'

'Have you ever killed anyone?' Nils asked.

Charlie hesitated while images flashed before her: Mattias's hands flailing in the water. The stillness after the ripples had subsided.

'Have you?' Tim said. 'Have you killed anyone, Charlie?'

'No.'

They turned in and parked in front of the big window of the Happy Salmon. Tim pointed to the charred lot on the other side of the street where the other pizzeria had once stood and said it burnded down.

'Burnt down,' Nils sighed. 'It has burnt down or it burnt down.'

'That's what I said. It burnded down.'

There were only two people in the pizzeria, each seated in front of a gambling machine. Charlie asked the boys to choose six drinks from the fridge while she went up to the counter to pay.

'Won't that be too expensive?' Nils asked anxiously. 'I can run over to the supermarket and buy a big bottle instead.'

'No,' Charlie said. 'We're far too hungry for that. But thanks for offering.'

The penny pinching, she thought to herself, the constant fear of not being able to make ends meet. She could still feel it sometimes, even though she earned a good salary. Maybe living on the breadline was something you could never fully get over.

'Well, well, well, Betty's daughter's back again,' one of the men by the gambling machines said.

Charlie realised it was Svenka. He was holding a bottle of lager.

'Hi,' she said. 'How's things?'

'Fantastic,' Svenka replied. 'It's good to be rid of all the journalists and out-of-towners who took over the town last summer. Because we're not in for some new crap now, are we? No new murders?'

'Murders?' Charlie said. 'Didn't you read what those out-of-town detectives concluded and what those journalists wrote? There was no evidence of murder.'

'That doesn't mean it didn't happen, though, does it?'

'Do you know something I don't?' Charlie said.

'No.'

'Then I don't understand why you ...'

'I suppose I don't trust you to do your job, simple as that,' Svenka grinned. 'I've had bad experiences with coppers.'

'I see,' Charlie said. 'Are you winning?' She nodded towards the gambling machine.

'Sure, but I always lose more than I win, though I guess that's the whole idea.'

Charlie studied Svenka. His sallow skin, his eyes, which looked blearier than last summer.

'Can I ask you something?' she said.

'I didn't drive here,' Svenka said and put his hands up. 'I haven't driven a foot since they took away my licence.'

'I believe you,' Charlie assured him. 'I'm not here in a professional capacity.'

'Then why are you here?'

'I'm here as a friend.'

'Fine, ask away.'

'Do you know anything about Gudhammar?'

'The farm?'

Charlie nodded and Svenka took a sip of his beer.

'It's a bloody shame.'

'What?'

'That people will let a beautiful old place like that fall into such disrepair. And no one can do anything about it since the owners refuse to do it up or sell it.'

'Who owns it?'

'The Mild family, but they haven't been back since their daughter took off.'

'Took off?'

'Well, that's what they said happened. It was a long time ago.'

'Why won't they sell the place?'

'No idea.' Svenka shrugged. 'I suppose they can afford not to. Maybe they'll come back one day and do it all up.'

'Did you know the family?'

'Know?' Svenka laughed. 'They didn't exactly stoop to socialising with us mere mortals.'

'And the daughter? The one who disappeared? Do you know anything about her?'

Svenka sipped his beer.

'She had a reputation of being less stuck up than the rest of the family; that's all I know. Maybe that's why she left.'

'Are you sure she left?'

'What do you mean?' Svenka said.

'I mean they never figured out what happened.'

'So that's why you're here?' Svenka grinned as though he'd stumbled onto a big secret.

'I just heard about it and was curious.'

'You are a curious one, aren't you,' Svenka observed. 'Just like your mother.'

He glanced towards the door.

'Well, well, well, look what the cat dragged in.'

It took Charlie a second to recognise Sara, Svenka's daughter. Her hair was a different colour and she wore a lot of eyeliner. It was a harder version of the girl Charlie had sat next to at the top of the diving tower last summer.

'Hi, Sara,' Charlie said.

'Hi.' Sara looked at her. 'What are you doing here? I mean ...' She smiled uncertainly.

'I'm visiting a friend,' Charlie said with a nod towards the boys lined up at the counter.

'What can I do for you, my heart?' Svenka asked.

Sara rolled her eyes and said he'd forgotten to leave the key out. Again.

'Bloody hell,' Svenka said. He patted his shirt-like jacket. 'Then where the fuck did I leave it? Don't you have your own?'

'You're using mine,' Sara replied wearily. 'You lost yours.'

'Right,' Svenka said. 'So you need to get in?'

'Never mind,' Sara said. 'I'll stay over at Jonas's.'

She turned around and left.

Call her back, Charlie wanted to say. Get a locksmith. Do something!

Their pizzas were done. Nils and the twins carried the boxes.

'He lied to you,' Nils said as they got in the car. 'That old man you were talking to, he lied.'

'About what?' Charlie said.

'He did drive here.' Nils pointed to a yellow Volvo 240 in the car park. 'That's his car.'

'Maybe someone gave him a ride,' Charlie said.

'I don't think so,' Nils replied. 'I don't believe that old man.'

Charlie looked at him in the rear-view mirror.

'Do you know him?' she asked.

'He said weird things to Mum in the supermarket once. I don't like him.'

When they returned with the pizzas, Susanne was up. She'd showered and met them in the hallway with a towel wrapped around her hair. Charlie told her what Nils had said about Svenka and Susanne rolled her eyes and said something about overdramatic kids.

'You hang out with him?'

'I guess I've bought booze from him on occasion.' Susanne lowered her voice. 'It's cheap, locally produced and creates jobs. What more can you ask for?'

'Maybe for it to be legal, if we're being pedantic,' Charlie said.

'Good thing we're not pedantic, then.'

'What are you talking about?' Nils asked.

'Nothing,' Susanne replied. 'Why don't you get out cutlery and glasses?'

Charlie had barely put the boxes down on the table before the boys had devoured most of the pizzas. But she was relieved to see Susanne was eating her fair share, too. She'd lost a lot of weight since the summer and in times of crisis it was important to get enough food and sleep. It sounded easy, but when you were barrelling towards rock bottom, nothing could be more difficult.

When they had finished, the twins wanted to play with Charlie. They had a race track in the living room and the cars all had names and personalities. Charlie couldn't help getting swept up in their imaginary world.

Susanne watched them without participating. After a while, she glanced at the clock on the kitchen wall and told Tim and Tom it was late, time for them to put on their pyjamas, brush their teeth and turn in.

'You're really good at playing,' Susanne said after the twins went upstairs.

'You think?'

'At least compared to me. I've never understood grown-ups who can play with children and not get bored. Whenever I'm pressed into playing, I'm the infant who just lies there and if we're playing hospital, I'm a dying patient who can't move.'

'I assume it's different when you're with them all the time,' Charlie observed. 'And the notion that parents should play with their children has to be fairly new, no?'

'Maybe,' Susanne said. 'I certainly can't remember Mum or Dad ever playing with me.'

Charlie thought about Betty. She hadn't exactly played with her, but during her sunnier periods, everything they'd done together had been a game: going to the bakery, night swimming, dancing. *You're the man and I'm the woman.*

'Sometimes I feel like I'm no better than my parents,' Susanne said.

'You do the best you can,' Charlie said.

'I suppose they did, too. But let's be honest: it wasn't good enough.'

'No, it wasn't.'

Susanne took a deep breath.

'I did something heinous the other day,' she said. 'I had a fight with Melker. He provoked me; I was exhausted and I ...

I pushed him up against the wall and yelled and cursed in his face.'

Charlie didn't know what to say. She remembered how scared she had been when Betty lost control. *Everything's goddamn bloody fucked.*

'Maybe you're making it a bigger deal than it was,' she said.

'I came this close to hitting him; I grabbed him so hard and ...'

'I don't know how many times Betty grabbed me too hard,' Charlie said. 'But it happened a lot.'

'But Betty wasn't like other people.'

'All I'm saying is I don't think you should be too hard on yourself right now.'

'Would you have said the same thing to a man who'd pushed his wife up against a wall?'

'No.'

'I pinned Melker to the wall and shouted at him an inch from his face. It's definitely assault. He was so scared and shocked he didn't even cry. And it doesn't matter how many times I apologise; I can't undo what I did. I can't change the way he sees me now.'

'But you can do everything you can to make sure it doesn't happen again,' Charlie said.

She reached for the kitchen roll on the table, tore off a sheet and handed it to Susanne. She wanted to say something about guilt being a good sign, maybe even a guarantee she would never do it again, but then she remembered all the remorseful wife beaters she'd encountered and realised her words would be meaningless.

Gaps in Time

I didn't know you play the guitar, I say.

I don't, really, Paul replies. I can't even read music.

We're in the chapel, at the very front, right underneath Jesus on his cross. Paul is sitting on the little ledge where brides and grooms can kneel and I'm facing him, my back against the baptismal font. Paul has found a guitar. His fingers move across the strings.

What does not being able to read music matter if you can play like Paul? It's a hauntingly beautiful melody I've never heard before. I close my eyes. Then Paul begins to sing. He sings the song 'Francesca' about a girl who's free.

Afterwards he says that's what my name means: Free.

Francesca means free.

IO

Minutes after Susanne came back down after saying goodnight to her children, her phone went off.

'Speaking of good mothers,' she said after glancing at the screen.

She got up and walked away with the phone pressed to her ear. After about a minute, she returned.

'I don't know why I bother to pick up,' she says. 'I suppose part of me hopes she'll be sober.'

She sighed.

'But who am I to criticise her? I want nothing more than to do the same thing. After what happened last summer ... I feel like I'm falling, like there's nothing to hold on to. Do you know that feeling?'

'All too well.'

'I'm not saying I would ...' Susanne shakes her head. 'I would never do that, Charlie, but sometimes I feel like I'm going to die from sheer exhaustion, like I want to lock myself in a soundproof room. It's never quiet around here, and even when the boys aren't fighting, just talking, I want to cover my ears, even when they want to tell me what they did in school that day, normal things. I often think to myself that it would feel so good to be ... dead.'

Charlie wished she had something uplifting to say about the value of life, but nothing came to mind. She'd often had the same thoughts.

'I wish Isak could look after the children sometimes, that he hadn't just dumped all of this on me; if I could just get some uninterrupted sleep and manage to finish a thought or two every once in a while ...'

'How long since he left?'

Susanne said she didn't know, that the days blended together, but that she thought it had been almost two months. He'd called a few times but hadn't wanted to see the children; he had a lot of things to sort out, he was busy with himself.

'And you're not?'

Susanne shrugged.

'Well, I'm here now,' Charlie said. 'Now you can sort things out, sleep, think about whatever you want.'

'It's not just this thing with Isak. It started long before he ... hold on.'

Susanne went into the kitchen and returned seconds later with a pack of Prince. Without asking Charlie if she wanted one, she handed her a cigarette and took one herself. They lit them with the long BBQ lighter.

'I should have left him a long time ago.' Susanne tapped her ash off into the fireplace. 'I wanted to divorce him years ago. I'm such a fucking idiot. Where's my self-respect? Who is this person I've become?'

She turned to Charlie as though she expected her to answer.

'You're not the first to ...' Charlie didn't know how to finish her sentence. The first one to believe in love and get screwed?

'I trusted him for so many years.' Susanne laughed. 'It was as if my brain was refusing to understand that he was lying

87

to me, even though it's obvious in hindsight. He had other women. I don't care if it happens all the time,' she said as though Charlie had made a comment. 'It's still hell when it happens to you. He should have left me instead. Why didn't he just leave me?'

Charlie thought about Hugo and his pregnant wife.

'Maybe because he wanted it all,' she said and almost added Betty's mantra about all men being pigs.

And what about me? she mused. I'm not exactly monogamous myself, but then, I've never promised anyone I'll be faithful.

'But what really gets me is Annabelle,' Susanne said. 'I can't stop thinking about her. I see her face. I see her dad in the shops, he's all shrunken and old. And I feel ... I feel so damn guilty.'

'Why?' Charlie asked. 'Why should you feel guilty?'

'Because of what I did,' Susanne replied. 'Because I yelled at her that day, because I was so blinded by my own jealousy that I took it out on the wrong person, because I didn't tell the police about her relationship with Isak. And I know it's pointless to beat myself up like this, but tell my brain that.'

'It'll pass,' Charlie said, then she corrected herself. 'It will get better at least, in time.'

She didn't know if that was true, but what else was she supposed to say?

'I know Isak didn't kill her,' Susanne said, 'but I can't help thinking she might be alive if he'd stayed away or if I'd talked to her instead of laying in to her. Now her dad walks around like a ghost and her mum's in the loony bin. Bloody hell.'

Susanne put her glass down and tossed her cigarette into the fire.

'I don't know about you, but I need something stronger.'

'I'll have whatever you're having,' Charlie replied.

She felt a flutter of anticipation in the pit of her stomach. I should say no, she thought. I should say we need to steer clear of alcohol, that we have to handle the crap life throws at us without anaesthesia. But I don't have it in me.

Susanne returned with two plastic cups.

'Everything else is in the dishwasher,' she said, handing one of the cups to Charlie.

'What is this?'

'A mix of what I had available. It might not taste great, but it's strong enough to warm your insides.' Susanne took a big swig from her glass and looked around the room. 'I might have to sell the house and leave all this. I assume Isak's going to be demanding his share any day now.'

'Surely he's in no position to make demands, with things the way they are?' Charlie said. 'He wouldn't be that stupid, would he?'

'I don't know him,' Susanne replied. 'I have no idea how stupid he is.'

'Where is he now?'

Susanne shrugged. The last time she'd spoken to him, he'd been in Stockholm, but she didn't know now. He might never come back.

'He will,' Charlie said.

'How do you know?'

'I don't. It's just what you say. But I hope he does, I mean, for the boys' sake.'

'I hope he comes before it's too late, before they start to hate him.'

'Children are ... very forgiving,' Charlie said.

'Not all children,' Susanne retorted.

They sat in silence for a while.

Charlie had forgiven Betty for all the times she'd made a fool of herself at parties, for the days she'd spent in bed, barely answering when spoken to, for all the missed school events, all the trips that had never happened. She'd forgiven, because she'd known Betty wasn't like other people, that she was doing her best. But now, with the things that had come to light last summer ... there were limits to what she could understand and forgive.

'You were always much nicer to your mum than I was to my parents,' Susanne went on. 'You took care of her in a way that was ... it was heart-breaking, really. I remember thinking that back then even, that I didn't understand how you could be so understanding, I mean, Betty was so ... she was like my parents, but I was much less understanding than you.'

'Betty was worse.'

'What do you mean?'

'I mean that she ... she wasn't who I thought she was.'

Charlie instantly regretted saying anything, but it was too late now.

'Mum and Annabelle's mum were friends when they were younger,' she said.

'Nora Roos?' Susanne said. 'That's ... unexpected. But what's so horrible about that?'

'They killed a toddler.'

Susanne stared at her.

'I don't understand,' she said. 'I don't understand what you're saying, Charlie.'

'Mum and Nora killed a two-year-old boy when they were little.'

'What the fuck are you saying? How?'

'They smothered him, or Betty did, according to Nora.'

Susanne blanched. She glanced up at the photographs on the wall on her left where her boys were chubby babies on sheepskin rugs.

'Why?'

'According to the newspaper articles at the time, it may have been a game that went too far.'

'Oh my god, Charlie. What happened to them afterwards?'

'Institutional care, foster home and new identities. And then ... then Nora became a loner who wasn't able to protect her daughter, even though she dedicated her entire life to it. And Betty, well you know how she turned out.'

Silence fell again. They sipped their drinks.

'I don't know what to say,' Susanne said at length. 'I never thought ... so fucking cruel.'

She shook her head. Charlie studied her frowning face, knowing she was trying to process the fact that Betty was a cold-blooded child murderer.

'I don't understand it either,' she said.

'But why?' Susanne said again. 'Why did she do it?'

'Who can say? Genes, a terrible childhood?'

'Who the fuck didn't have a terrible childhood?' Susanne said. 'Since when is that an excuse?'

They both knocked back their drinks.

'I'm not making excuses,' Charlie said, 'I'm just trying to explain and understand, but that doesn't seem possible.'

'How do you deal with it?' Susanne said. 'How the fuck do you even process that your own mother ... I mean, Lola, she's not exactly a sunshiny person, but she would never hurt anyone like that. It's unthinkable.'

'I suppose you try to tackle it the same way people always have,' Charlie said.

'What way is that?'

'You endure. Take things one second at a time, then one minute, one hour, one day, just let time pass.'

'And that works for you?'

'Sometimes.'

'Painting is my only non-destructive method of combatting my anxiety,' Susanne said.

Charlie nodded towards Susanne's paintings on the walls.

'You have to start painting again,' she said.

'Who said I stopped?'

'I just assumed ...'

'Come with me,' Susanne said.

She got up and walked towards the hallway. Charlie followed. Susanne slipped into a pair of clogs and handed Charlie another pair.

'They're Isak's so they might be big for you, but we're not going far.'

'Where are you taking me?'

'You'll see.'

'But if the children wake up?'

'They'll know where to find me.'

They cut across the yard to the old barn.

Susanne flipped a switch. Nothing was the same in there. Gone were the stalls, the lambing pens and the hay feeders. The entire barn was one giant room and hung or leaning all along the white wooden walls: Susanne's paintings.

'Blimey,' Charlie said. 'Bloody hell, Susanne.'

She started walking around the room. Susanne sat down on a paint-flecked wooden chair in the middle of the room.

Charlie stopped in front of a painting of two little girls sitting on a stone wall, their backs to the viewer. They were holding hands. She could almost hear the music from Lyckebo. Betty's shrill voice singing 'It's my party' off key.

Charlie squinted and made her painted self turn round, look at the people dancing among the cherry trees: Betty in her red dress with a man who wasn't Mattias chasing after her. Betty breaking off a twig covered in half-wilted, browning blooms from one of the trees and sticking it in her hair.

'Recognise them?' Susanne said.

Charlie nodded. She took a step closer.

'Am I wearing Mum's nightgown?'

'Yes, it's the one you used to borrow from Betty.'

'It almost looks like a photograph,' Charlie said. 'I don't know how you do it.'

'I just painted what I remember,' Susanne said, as though she didn't understand that most people were unable to create such a detailed depiction, no matter how precise their memories. 'Remember that night?'

Charlie tried to remember sitting on a wall in her night-gown, but she couldn't.

'It doesn't look like night-time,' she said. 'It's light out, right?'

'Midsummer's Eve,' Susanne said. 'Night paling towards dawn. You can tell from the dew.'

She pointed to the painting. Charlie moved even closer and spotted the tiny droplets of water in the grass.

'It was the night Mattias disappeared. The last party in Lyckebo.'

Charlie studied the painting. Midsummer's Eve, the last party in Lyckebo.

'Mum and Mattias started fighting after the party ended,' she said.

'They were already fighting when we left, I think,' Susanne replied. 'Those drunken rows, it really is miserable to have parents who shout at and beat each other, who threaten divorce, suicide and god knows what. And then, the next day, everything's back to normal.'

'But there was no next day for Betty and Mattias,' Charlie said.

'I know. It must have been awful for Betty, for both of you.'

Charlie touched the girl in the painting. The girl that was her.

'Mum was never the same afterwards.'

'She wasn't exactly the most stable person before either,' Susanne said. 'It might not be much of a comfort, but ...'

It is, actually, Charlie thought to herself. It's a comfort to know it's not all on me. For a brief moment, she allowed herself to think about Mattias, his flailing hands in the water, her own paralysis as she just sat there at the water's edge, letting it happen.

'Are you working on anything right now?' Charlie said and walked over to the covered easel.

'Yes,' Susanne replied, 'but I'm not sure it's ready to be seen.'

'Oh, I'm sorry,' said Charlie, who had already removed the cloth hiding the painting. She gasped when she saw the motif.

'It's in bad taste,' Susanne said. 'I know, but the image just came to me. I never meant for anyone else to see it.'

She started to cover the painting back up.

'Hold on,' Charlie said. 'Can't you let me have a look since I've seen it now anyway?'

'Sure,' Susanne replied. 'But god help you if you tell anyone in town. They would think I'm a lunatic.'

Charlie nodded and continued to study the painting. There was the bridge by Vall's village shop, the sun-bleached green dam gates and the churning black water. But it wasn't the landscape that made it impossible for Charlie to tear her eyes from the canvas. It was the girl in the light blue dress on the wrong side of the bridge railing, her red hair caught in the wind, her face half turned away, her left hand raised as if she were waving.

Annabelle.

Francesca

I woke up at three in the morning and instantly knew I would struggle to go back to sleep. The wind was howling outside. The branches of the oak tree were scratching against my bedroom window. Mum was fast asleep on the sofa bed. Her breathing was laboured.

I crept out of bed and went down to the library. The massive oak doors were open and a fire was crackling on the hearth. Dad was sitting in his favourite armchair with a whisky in one hand and a lit cigar in the other.

'You're up?' he said when he noticed me.

'Evidently.'

'Aren't you cold?' he went on with a glance at Cécile's thin nightgown.

'I'm never cold.'

'Have a seat,' Dad said, pointing to the armchair next to his.

I sat down and put my feet on the footstool.

'What were you going to do down here?' Dad said and put his cigar out. 'I mean … how are you feeling?'

'It seems worse than it is,' I said.

Dad looked at my arms again and said he thought it seemed awful.

'This thing with Henrik Stiernberg and his gang,' I said to shift the focus of our conversation away from the *incident*. 'That night, behind the chapel, I was there. I found the yellow rose Paul had worn on his lapel and ...'

'You have to try and move past that now,' Dad broke in. 'It's not good for you to be so hung up on what you thought you saw that night.'

'What do you mean thought I saw? I did see.'

'You *thought* you saw,' Dad said. 'We spoke to the doctors and considering your level of intoxication and those other substances...'

'But I know I saw all those things.'

'I have two daughters telling me completely different stories and the only thing I can be sure of is that one of them is either lying or misremembering. And I absolutely don't want to doubt you, Francesca, but Cécile has never lied to me before.'

'What you mean to say is you've never caught her lying to you.'

'Yes, isn't that what I said?'

'You said she hasn't lied; there's a big difference.'

'Remember that business with Aron Vendt?' Dad asked.

'How could I forget?'

'All I'm saying is that our faith in you is slightly ...'

'Your faith in me? What do you think my faith in you is like after all of that?'

Dad got up and walked towards the door.

'You're just leaving now?'

'I need ice.'

I lay down in front of the fire and thought back to when Aron Vendt and his father came to visit us at Gudhammar. It was the summer after seventh grade. Dad and Aron's father had pulled off some business coup together and they were going to celebrate. Aron's brother, Erik, was away at sailing camp. Aron had finished school that year and was, according to the older girls in my dormitory, a guy to watch out for unless you wanted your heart broken.

Before dinner, Mum reminded me not to leave the table too soon, not to lick my knife, not to make sudden movements and not to spill. I was supposed to listen to whoever was speaking, answer seriously and ask relevant follow-up questions.

I did pretty well at first. Seated across from Aron at the large wooden table in the parlour, I pretended to be intensely interested in his studies and plans to make it into the upper-most echelons of society. Mum looked genuinely pleased but wrinkled her nose with annoyance when I excused myself and left the table on several occasions. I simply had to go to the kitchen and take surreptitious sips from the bottles of red wine set out to breathe on the counter.

Aron was going to spend a year studying abroad. If I had any interest in international studies, I should contact him.

I said that sounded amazing, that he would be my very first call. The evening was interminable; I was so relieved I wanted to run up the stairs to my room when dinner was finally over and the men started talking about retreating to the library to smoke and drink whisky. At first, Aron seemed to think he would be going with them, but when he got up, his dad gave him a long look, then told him he should take the young lady for a drive in his car. No, driving after a glass or two was fine. This was the country, no police here.

Just stick to the back roads and drive safely, he called after us as we walked towards the front door.

Minutes later, I was in the beige leather passenger seat of a Mercedes that smelled new.

We drove down the tree-lined road. Aron looked at me as he accelerated and told me about the car's copious horsepower.

'Eyes on the road,' I said, not bothering to stifle a yawn.

Playing the well-mannered, good girl was truly exhausting.

'So, what kind of music do you like?' Aron asked as he turned out onto the bigger, slightly winding road leading into town.

'Anything in a minor key,' I replied.

'I was actually thinking genre,' Aron said.

I pondered that for a while without coming up with a specific genre.

'I like Alice Cooper a lot,' I said.

Aron laughed. Alice Cooper, not what he had expected.

I asked what he had expected and Aron shrugged and said 'something else', then turned on the radio.

Alphaville's 'Forever Young' poured out of the speakers. I thought it was a pretty inane song, but on that small road with the dark woods on either side, the lyrics made me feel oddly wistful.

'Pretty lame lyrics,' I said.

Aron asked what I meant by that and I said you didn't really have much choice. Living forever was impossible so that only left dying young.

Aron laughed and said he'd never thought about it that way; he didn't usually analyse lyrics much.

I said it wasn't a matter of analysis, that it was literally what they were singing.

'It's just a song,' Aron said. Then he asked me to open the glove compartment and light us a cigarette each.

I thought to myself that I could never fall for a guy like Aron. There was something faintly ridiculous about his mouth, his deft handling of the gearstick, his self-satisfied, stupid smile. And yet, I couldn't help but wonder what a life with him would be like. A fancy flat in some metropolis or other. Dinners, dresses with spaghetti straps and trips to Paris. Aron, coming home from work and hoisting little boys in the air before setting off again on his next business trip. I envisioned myself, unhappy, drinking in secret, cheated on. No matter what I did, that seemed to be how it would end.

'What did you say?' Aron said suddenly.

'Nothing.'

'Sounded like you said "pointless".'

'I was just humming.'

We drove on, passing mist-covered fields, glittering predators' eyes and twinkling stars.

'Are we going into town?' I asked.

'Like there's a town around here,' Aron said.

'Fine, the village,' I said. 'You know what I mean.'

Aron didn't reply, but I assumed we weren't going into town, because he went straight past the sign for Gullspång town centre. I was starting to feel uneasy.

'Do you have a boyfriend?' Aron asked.

'Yes,' I said. It was a lie, of course, but something compelled me to make a split-second decision not to tell the truth. Maybe I hoped it would persuade Aron to leave me alone.

'So, what do you get up to with your boyfriend?' Aron wanted to know.

'Play chess,' I said. 'Play chess, analyse song lyrics and …'

'That's obviously not what I meant.' Aron laughing out loud.

I pretended not to understand, even though I knew perfectly

well what he'd meant. I wanted him to know I wasn't a sexual creature. I wanted to go home to my room at Gudhammar.

My tactic failed spectacularly because all of a sudden, Aron's hand landed on my thigh.

I stiffened, glanced at him to see if it was a bad joke. It wasn't. His hand just lay on my thigh like it had every right in the world to be there.

'What are you doing?' I said.

My voice was trembling with anger and fear.

'What?' Aron said, sliding his hand further up.

I removed it.

Aron smiled like I'd done something funny.

'Did I upset you?' he said.

'I just think it's strange,' I answered honestly, 'to do something like that without asking first.'

Aron laughed and shook his head.

'Let me tell you something, Fran,' he said.

'My name's Francesca.'

'Let me tell you something, *Francesca*, there's more than one way to ask permission and not to brag or anything but there are a lot of girls who don't mind my hands on them.'

'Could you turn round now?' I said. 'I'm starting to feel car sick.'

'You're drunk, too,' Aron said. 'I can tell. You must have been sneaking drinks from somewhere.'

'I want to go home,' I repeated.

'Soon,' Aron said.

He turned down a forest road and killed the engine.

'I just want to touch you,' he whispered, unbuckling his seatbelt. 'Why are you so angry?'

I wasn't angry any more; fear had taken over. I pulled on the door, but it was locked.

'I don't want to,' I breathed. 'Please stop.'

But Aron was already on top of me. His tongue pushed into my mouth, making it impossible to breathe. I felt paralysed. And then, his hands inside my top, squeezing my breast.

'It feels good, right?' he whispered between the forced kisses. 'This is what you want, isn't it, Fran?'

Breakfast with Aron and his family the day after the drive was horrible. I sat in complete silence, not answering when spoken to. It didn't matter that Mum almost kicked my shin off under the table. I just glared at everyone buttering their rolls, pouring juice and coffee. After a while, Mum got fed up and asked me to leave the table. I stayed in my seat. I wasn't trying to cause a scene, I just suddenly felt exhausted. It was only when Dad gave a stern look that I felt I'd had enough and declared I didn't feel like talking, that I was still in shock at what happened the night before. And then I told them about our drive, about Aron forcing himself on me. I told them like it was.

'What are you talking about?' Aron's father said.

It took me a second to realise he wasn't upset about what his son had done, he was upset about my accusation.

'I don't know what you're talking about,' Aron said and leaned back in his chair.

'I think you need more sleep, Fran,' Dad said.

'That might be true,' I said. 'I did have a hard time falling asleep after what he did to me last night.'

I nodded towards Aron.

'What the fuck's going on?' Aron burst out. 'I'm sorry, but I don't understand.'

'Calm down, Aron,' his father said, waving his napkin at his son. 'Let's get to the bottom of this.'

'There's nothing to get to the bottom of,' Aron said. His eyes were as black as they'd been in the car. 'You must have dreamt it; you must have dreamt the whole thing.'

'Then show them your arm,' I said, nodding at him across the table.

'What are you talking about?'

'If it didn't happen, if it was just a dream, then I must have dreamt that I bit your arm, too, right?'

'She's out of her mind,' Aron said, looking at his father.

'Show us your arm, Aron,' said his pale mother. 'Just let us see it so we can put an end to this.'

But instead of rolling up his sleeve, Aron got up so violently he knocked his chair over and left the table.

Later on, I was told he'd simply been offended by my accusation and both his parents confirmed there was no sign of a bite on him.

After Aron's family left, my parents had a serious talk with me. Was I sure about what had happened? What had he done? Had he touched me, done ... other things? It was important that I tell them what had happened.

I tried to tell them about our drive, give them the details the way I remembered them.

When I was done, Mum and Dad exchanged a long look, then Dad asked if that was all?

I didn't understand what he meant. That wasn't enough?

Not by a mile, Dad said. He shook his head and then, eagerly cheered on by Mum, launched into an explanation about how boys sometimes misinterpret signals and get pushy, especially with beautiful young girls like me. It wasn't okay, of course not, and of course he was going to have a serious conversation with Ola Vendt and his son about it.

A conversation? I said.

Dad nodded, he would have a very serious conversation with them.

And then what? I said. Everything just carries on like before? I mean, you're going to keep working with him?

Dad's eyes said it all.

I was quiet for a long time. Then, without even thinking it through, I looked Mum and Dad in the eyes and said the thing that would permanently end Dad's lucrative partnership with Ola Vendt. I said Aron Vendt had pinned me down and forcibly entered me. I said it had hurt and that I felt ... broken.

I must have dozed off because Dad prodded me awake, whispering it really was time for me to go to bed. I got up slowly. As I walked up the stairs, I felt wide awake again. I would have liked to take something to make me sleep deeply. I knew Mum kept Imovane somewhere, but given the situation they were probably locked in the safe with the family jewels.

There was a liquor cabinet in the shape of a globe in Dad's office. I pushed the small handle by the equator and was disappointed to find nothing but whisky. When it came to alcohol, I was far from picky, but whisky, I hated. I opened all the bottles and took a few sips from the one that smelled the least foul, then I went back to my room. I'd thought the booze would keep my thoughts from tormenting me, but instead, they returned to Paul. *Let it go, just stop thinking about it.* But my brain kept loading up picture after picture of Paul. Paul in the science classroom with a scalpel and a pig's heart. *See how it's practically the same as a human heart?* Paul on the jetty by the lake, the two swans with the downy cygnets. *It's not true that they mate for life.* And then, the images everyone claimed my sick brain had made up: Henrik and his friends, their wet clothes, the yellow rose on the ground.

II

The next morning, Charlie drove the twins to school, giving Susanne a chance to sleep in. Tim and Tom didn't want her to go in with them; they weren't babies. Once the boys had pulled open the heavy front door and disappeared into the building, Charlie got out of the car. She took a deep breath and smelled the familiar fragrance from the dog roses growing along the side of the elementary school. There were tunnels criss-crossing those bushes, tunnels where they'd played war and scratched themselves on the thorns. Charlie was reminded of her first teacher, the woman with the warm voice who had glued stars in her book and been upset Betty never came to any parent-teacher meetings. *Why do I have to go?* Betty said when Charlie reminded her. *I already know my kid's top of her class, what more is there to talk about?*

Charlie lit a cigarette and leaned back against the car. She was going to drive out to Gudhammar. She'd decided that last night, as she lay awake and thoughts of Annabelle had morphed into thoughts of Francesca.

The narrow road leading out to the manor curved unpredictably. As she got closer to Gudhammar, she passed fewer and fewer old wooden houses with gingerbread. Before long, the landscape began to change, too, turning into brown fields framed by forest. The shades of yellow, orange and green made the scene pretty like a painting. Charlie slowed down as she approached the oak-lined drive. She parked the car and continued up towards the yellow main house on foot. Squinting in the autumn sun, it was as though she could see the Mild family standing there on the stone steps, just like in the picture in Johan's article: Mum and Dad on the top step and in front of them their daughters, one fair with a forced smile and then the dark, serious one: Francesca.

When she spotted the big marble lions by the front door, the images from her dream returned with full force: Betty and her on the gravel road, the mist of the summer night, the oak branches above them.

Where are we going, Mummy?

To a friend's.

What friend?

No reply.

Mummy?

I've been here before, Charlie realised. This is where Betty took me. Why? What's going on?

She took a few deep breaths and walked up the wide steps. Her hand shook when she turned the large, round doorknob. Locked. What had she expected? She looked up at the knocker and saw Betty's pale hand tremblingly reach for it. Knocking tentatively at first, then increasingly insistently. Footsteps on other side. The door, opening a few inches and a deep voice telling them to go away. *I said go away!*

Betty, trying to force a foot in the door.

I just want to ... we have to ...

Leave before I call the police.

We need to talk. Betty whispering to the closed door. *Please.*

Charlie was suddenly overcome with nausea. She staggered down the steps, like she had in her dream, hurried back to the car and left Gudhammar without so much as a glance in the rear-view mirror.

12

Charlie's legs were still shaking when she drove into Gullspång town centre. She parked the car behind the supermarket and went over to the police station.

It was unchanged since the summer. The reception counter, the seventies wallpaper and the shelves full of binders. Charlie glanced into the messy kitchen and passed the room she and Anders had used last summer. It suddenly felt so long ago. If I hadn't come down here, I wouldn't know the truth about Betty, she thought. I wouldn't have been forced to go to therapy or take leave, I wouldn't have reconnected with Susanne. She passed Olof Jansson's office; the door was closed and she could see through the half-closed blinds he wasn't in there.

Micke Andersson was sitting at his desk and jumped when Charlie knocked on his half-open door.

'Lager?' he exclaimed. 'What are you doing here?'

'I need to talk to Olof,' Charlie said, 'but he seems to be out.'

'He's not in today,' Micke said. 'He's at the hospital with his wife. Can I help you with anything?'

No, Charlie wanted to say. She didn't trust Micke, not after last summer. But her impatience got the better of her.

'I'm looking for information on the Mild family, the ones who used to live at Gudhammar.'

'Why's that?' Micke said. His mocking smile made Charlie instantly regret saying anything.

'Never mind,' she replied. 'I'll give Olof a ring or come back tomorrow.'

'Did I do something wrong?' Micke asked. 'I really don't know what your problem is, Lager. Is it because I'm a man?'

Charlie laughed.

'What?' Micke demanded.

His cocky look had been replaced by an offended one she remembered all too well from the summer.

'Just your comment,' Charlie said. 'Why would being a man make me dislike you?'

'I don't know,' Micke replied. 'But you seem like the kind of woman who disapproves of men in general.'

'You're wrong about that,' Charlie said.

She felt like adding that his sex was the least of her problems, that what she took issue with was his patronising air, coupled with the fact that he was terrible at his job. But she wasn't there to pick a fight with a pathetic little man child. She turned to leave, still hoping he would give her more.

'What do you want to know?' Micke asked. 'They haven't been back here for years. Not since the daughter went missing, I think.'

'I'd like to have a look at the casefile.'

'The case was closed almost immediately. I think the verdict was that she'd left voluntarily.'

'Why do you know that?' Charlie said.

Micke shook his head.

'So now you're turning that against me too, that I'm answering your questions.'

'It just strikes me as odd that you would know,' Charlie said. 'I mean, it was a long time ago. You were barely born.'

'My family has lived here for generations; I know almost everything that's happened here since my great-grandmother was a child.'

'But it didn't come up last summer?'

'Sure it did,' Micke said. 'People around here remembered and talked about it.'

'Then why didn't I hear about it?'

'Maybe they didn't talk to you. And it was considered irrelevant in terms of the investigation. Correctly, as it turns out.'

'But it is another missing girl,' Charlie said.

'Annabelle's death was an accident as far as anyone could tell,' Micke said, 'and this missing girl ...'

'Francesca,' Charlie said. 'Francesca Mild.'

'Yes, that was her name. They say she was clinically depressed, which suggests she killed herself somewhere.'

'Then why wasn't she found?'

'I don't know all the details,' Micke said. 'But I think the family were convinced she wasn't dead, just off somewhere. They were very wealthy so maybe she had enough money to start over somewhere else?'

'You believe that?'

'Honestly, I've never given it much thought. Why don't you just read the casefile for yourself?'

'Because it's closed.' Charlie sighed.

'Ask for access to the archives then. I mean, if it's that important to you.'

'I'm on vacation,' Charlie said.

'Right now?'

'Yeah, so?'

'It's just that it's an unusual time to be on vacation; I figured maybe you'd gone rogue again.' Micke grinned.

'What are you talking about?' Charlie said, though she knew very well what he was alluding to. He'd obviously heard about her sleeping with Johan.

'Calm down,' Micke said, holding his hands up defensively. 'No judgement here. Though maybe you shouldn't have gone for a journalist. There were a lot of people in the pub that night who I'm sure wouldn't have minded a bit of ...'

'Shut up,' Charlie said. 'So long as it doesn't affect my work, I can sleep with whomever the fuck I please.'

'Clearly,' Micke retorted.

His eyes narrowed.

'What were you thinking?' he went on. 'How could you blab to a journalist?'

'He didn't get it from me,' Charlie said. 'Someone else did the blabbing.'

'How can you be so sure it was someone else?'

'Because I trust that particular journalist.'

Micke let out a laugh. Then he apologised and said it was just a bit funny to hear the word *trust* in the same sentence as the word *journalist*.

It was an effort for Charlie to keep calm.

'Why is that old case so important to you?' Micke asked. He leaned back in his chair and put his hands behind his head.

'I'm interested in cold cases,' Charlie said, 'but I understand if you can't help me. Sorry to disturb you.' She took a deep breath and forced herself to at least try to work on him. 'I know I was a bit brusque with you last summer, but ...'

'Brusque? You were condescending, unpleasant and ...'

'I'm sorry,' Charlie said. 'I guess that's just who I am. But I want you to know I really am impressed by the work you put into finding Annabelle.'

Micke smiled again, but without the insinuations this time. Was he really that gullible?

'It was easier for me,' Micke said. 'I know the area and the people.'

'Yes, you really do know the area,' Charlie said. 'Both the area and its history. That's why you're the one I'm talking to.'

Damn, she thought. I already told him I wanted to talk to Olof. But Micke seemed to have forgotten that, so she went on:

'I get if you can't help me, but I had to ask.'

'I'll see what I can do,' Micke replied. 'Let me think about it.'

Gaps in Time

Paul is sitting under the weeping willow. Knees pulled up, reading a book. I ask what he's reading and he says it's a French philosopher famous for his positive philosophy. I tell him I want to know more, because if there's one thing I love, it's positivity.

Paul laughs, marks his page with a dog ear, closes it and starts to talk. I listen distractedly while he describes the philosopher's take on free will, which argues that people create their own future. That doesn't sound very positive to me. I would feel less anxious about the future if it was predetermined and the onus wasn't entirely on me. But then Paul starts talking about the philosopher's take on time. Time, he claimed, is not a line or a series of points; time is more like a flow in which different parts bleed into each other.

Go on, I say when Paul breaks off. Tell me more.

You're interested?

I nod.

How do you see it? Paul asks. Time, I mean? Is your time linear or more like a circle?

It's many different circles, I tell him and close my eyes. Everything's always spinning.

Paul says it's the same for him.

It's almost like space, I say. Makes me dizzy.

Space scares me sometimes, Paul says.

How come?

Because it feels like I could lose my mind thinking about it, about how there's no beginning and no end. It's frightening.

Or it's reassuring, I say. Reassuring that we're just tiny dots in something infinitely big and that nothing really matters.

13

Charlie slumped into the driver's seat. She took a deep breath, then pulled out her phone and called Johan. He picked up almost before it started ringing.

After some awkward small talk, Johan apologised for leaving so abruptly the other night.

'No worries,' Charlie said. 'I'm calling because ...'

'Did something happen?'

'Not exactly, but I'm visiting a friend in Gullspång.'

'Susanne?'

'Yeah, she's having a hard time, so I've gone down to help her out. Isak, her husband, has abandoned her.'

'That sucks,' Johan said, 'but maybe it's for the best, being rid of him, I mean.'

'No doubt,' Charlie replied, 'but he ditched his four children, too.'

'Bloody hell. Are they alright?'

'I hope so.'

Johan cleared his throat.

'And otherwise?' he said as though he felt they'd strayed into sensitive territory. 'How are things down there, the same?'

'I suppose, for better or worse.' Charlie looked out the

windscreen, at the supermarket and the bench outside it, which was empty at the moment. 'I went out to Gudhammar today.'

'Why?'

'Because I was curious. I wanted to look around.'

'And how was it?'

'It's an imposing house, despite not being looked after. And ...'

Charlie closed her eyes and took a deep breath.

'What, Charlie?'

'I've been there before. With Betty. We walked to Gudhammar one night. Betty knocked on the door, but we weren't let in. I don't understand why we were there.'

There was a brief pause.

'Hey, Charlie,' Johan said, without commenting on her memory. 'I'm going to come down, too. I'd been toying with the idea anyway, before you ... I mean, there are things I want to check out. I don't feel done with Gullspång.'

That's what I thought, Charlie thought to herself, but now I'm not so sure. She also wasn't sure it was such a good idea for Johan to come. Her life was complicated enough already.

'Do you think there are rooms available at The Motel?' Johan asked.

'I'd be surprised if there weren't. It's not exactly peak season and I assume your colleagues are done writing about Annabelle. But it probably depends on how long you were planning on staying. This weekend's the Harvest Festival.'

'Harvest Festival, what's that?'

'As the name implies, it's a festival to celebrate the harvest.'

'So, is it worth celebrating? I mean, was it a good harvest?'

'I suppose you reap what you sow.'

Johan chuckled.

'I guess I should call ahead then,' he said.

'When were you thinking of coming down?'

'Now.'

'Now?'

'Yes.'

They hung up. Charlie was overcome with the restlessness she always felt when she was in the middle of an investigation. But it was more than that. She closed her eyes and summoned the images from her dream, Betty's hand on the knocker, being shooed away like animals. Why had she and Betty gone to Gudhammar? An unpleasant thought was taking root in her mind. Betty Lager. But no, she wasn't going to get ahead of herself. She simply had to find out what happened to Francesca Mild.

A large, colourful poster advertised *The Harvest Festival, Friday and Saturday* in the pub. Charlie had only attended one harvest festival before moving away from Gullspång. She'd been thirteen years old. She and Susanne had snuck in through the kitchen. Susanne had done their make-up and they wore short dresses and high-heeled shoes they could barely walk in. Betty had laughed when she spotted them in the pub and when the owner tried to throw them out, Betty had said he couldn't since both the girls' guardians were present. Surely the kids deserved a chance to celebrate the harvest, too.

Three men in overalls were sitting at one of the larger tables. Charlie felt their eyes on her when she walked up to the bar to order. Jonas Landell, one of Annabelle's friends, came out of the kitchen.

'So, you're back?' he said and Charlie thought she saw a shadow pass across his face.

'I'm just visiting a friend,' Charlie said.

'Susanne?'

Charlie nodded and checked her watch. It was quarter past eleven. No word from Susanne. Maybe she was enjoying a much-needed lie-in.

'I heard she threw him out,' Jonas said. 'About time, if you ask me.'

Charlie didn't bother responding. She just sat down at a window table and asked for coffee.

'It's self-serve,' Jonas said with a nod towards a small table with thermoses by the bar. 'But don't get up. I'll get it for you since I'm on my feet anyway.'

'Thanks.'

'You coming to the Harvest Festival?' Jonas said when he returned with her coffee.

'Not sure,' Charlie replied. 'Are you expecting a lot of people?'

'There's always a lot of people at the Harvest Festival.'

Jonas nodded to a group of men and women in overalls who had just entered.

'Of course you're coming to the Harvest Festival,' one of the men at the large table said. 'That and Waterfall Day are the only things that ever happen around here.'

Charlie turned to the man who had spoken. She wasn't used to being addressed so kindly by people she didn't know.

'Adam knows what he's talking about,' the other man said. 'He hasn't missed a Harvest Festival since the first one, back in the fifties.'

'Lay off, David,' said the one called Adam. 'I'm not that bloody old. But I happen to like music and it's the only time we can get a real band to play here. If you come, I promise you a dance.'

He smiled and winked at her.

'I'm afraid I'm not much of a dancer,' Charlie said.

'I know how to lead,' Adam said, 'all you have to do is follow.'

'That's the part I have trouble with,' Charlie said, thinking this was probably a man who was used to his come-ons paying dividends.

'What are you doing here, anyway?' David said. 'I mean, you're not from here, are you?'

'I'm visiting a friend,' Charlie said. 'And I'm writing about cold cases.'

She regretted her words the moment they left her lips.

'What do you mean, cold cases?' David wondered. 'Hey, why don't you join us and explain.' He patted the empty chair next to him. 'We want to know more.'

Charlie picked up her cup and went over to their table.

'Maybe you can help me,' she said. 'Do you know anything about Gudhammar Manor?'

Adam leaned forward, his elbows firmly on the table.

'Have you changed careers?' he asked.

'What do you mean?' Charlie could feel her cheeks flush.

'I mean that last time you were here, you worked for the police.'

I'm so fucking stupid, Charlie chided herself. She'd figured they didn't know who she was. Digging around the Francesca case as a private citizen wasn't going to be easy, she realised now.

'I'm off duty,' she said and fixed her eyes on Adam, 'and in my spare time, I like to write about cold cases.'

'When I'm off duty, I like to drink beer,' David said with a smile.

Adam laughed.

'But who knows,' David went on, clearly egged on by his colleague's appreciation, 'maybe next time I'm on holiday, I'll do some research?'

'So,' Charlie said when the two men had calmed down. 'Do you know anything about Gudhammar?'

'It's been a long time since anyone lived there,' David said. 'The place is completely abandoned. A well-to-do family used to own it, or I suppose they still do, even though they're never there.'

'Do you know anything about the family?' Charlie asked.

David shrugged.

'I don't think anyone knows all that much. They only ever used it as a summer house, posh people, but unhappy, or at least that's what people said about one of the daughters.'

'What else did people say?'

'That she was a nutcase – the girl, I mean. Tragic for that kind of posh family when one of the children turns out to be mentally ill.'

'What do you mean, mentally ill?' Charlie asked.

'I'm just saying that was the rumour. And no smoke without fire, put it that way. I actually saw her once, driving home from a nightshift. She was running down the road, pretty far from the house and wearing nothing but a flimsy nightgown, even though it was bloody cold. At first, I was convinced she was a ghost, but it was her, the Mild girl, wild-eyed she was and she didn't want a ride home, either. Maybe I wasn't posh enough.'

He smiled.

'When was that?' Charlie said. 'Do you know if it was the night she went missing?'

'No,' David replied. 'It was before, because I saw her again after.'

'Did you tell the police about it?'

'No, why would I have?'

Adam checked his watch and said they had to get going, that lunch was over a long time ago. They stood up and left the pub.

Charlie returned to her table but found that she was unable to relax with her coffee with everyone staring at her. Or was she imagining it? She had yet to get over the hyper-sensitivity she'd developed as a child, when Betty talked and laughed too loudly. During those periods, Betty was blind and deaf to other people's looks and whispers, but Charlie had seen and heard them all. Now she had the same unpleasant feeling as when she'd been with Betty: that people were looking at her, that there was nowhere to hide.

Francesca

'What are you doing?' Dad yelled the morning after our conversation.

He came out onto the patio in his dressing gown.

'What are you doing, Francesca?'

'I'm removing the rhododendron,' I shouted back.

Dad ran over to me.

'But Mum wanted it gone,' I said.

'And I wanted it kept,' Dad said. 'For god's sake, stop digging and come back inside.'

I put down my shovel and thought about how impossible Mum and Dad were to please. Try as I might, at least one of them was always angry or disappointed. Maybe it was no wonder I felt torn sometimes.

I didn't want to stop digging or go back inside. There was something about the crisp autumn air and the physical exertion that made me relax in a way I hadn't in a very long time. I told Dad I would carry on somewhere else and leave the bush alone.

'Why?' Dad demanded.

'Because I like digging, simple as that. Why do you have to question everything?'

'It's a very relevant question,' Dad said.

'Well, now you know,' I replied.

I picked up the shovel and went down to the pet cemetery, which was located off the path to the lake. A few of our sad little rodents were buried there under crooked homemade crosses. I walked round the tree and studied the small shrub I'd planted next to the grave that meant the most to me. There, under the heart-shaped little leaves, lay my beloved cat, Serafina. She'd been born on the farm next to ours, the same day as me. The mother cat had abandoned her litter and all but one kitten had died. The farmer's wife had stopped by and told my parents about the little miracle and when she heard that I'd been born, she felt it was a sign the tiny survivor belonged with us. Serafina was shy and unpredictable and liked only me. Whenever anyone else tried to pet her, she'd scratch them.

I was seven the summer she was hit by a car and dumped in a ditch a few hundred yards from Gudhammar. A few days after we said our farewells at the pet cemetery, I dug Serafina back up. I did it because I'd forgotten what her face looked like, I explained to Mum and Dad; I'd forgotten what she looked like. It turns out it was ill-advised, because if there was one thing I would now remember forever, it was what death had done to Serafina.

I read the text I'd carved into her cross ten years previously: *Serafina. Grief springs eternal!* I remember writing that because Mum told me I was overreacting, that the farms around Gudhammar were teeming with cats and I could have a new one whenever I wanted. We could probably even find one with the exact same markings. Mum had never been able to grasp that animals are unique, that they can't be replaced, that it's not about a particular colour combination. It made me think of something one of the older doctors had told me in the hospital. The grieving process, he said, follows a predictable trajectory, which is largely the same for everyone. Then he listed off a bunch of consecutive phases I could no longer remember the names of and said that most people went through roughly the same stages. It took a year, then the worst was behind you and you could go on with your life like before.

Grief was like a dog, he'd continued when I questioned the simplicity of his theory, a dog that stays very near its owner at first, but with time, if you just keep walking, gets tired and falls behind. It would be like that for me too. In time, I would no longer see my grief; I would barely be able to feel it.

That was obviously bullshit, but I was too tired to argue. And now, when I realised I was still sad about Serafina, that I still missed her warm body next to mine in bed, I knew Paul's death would be with me like a baying hound for the rest of my life. It would never go away.

I moved to a respectful distance from the tiny crosses, raised my shovel and started digging. The soil was softer than I'd thought it would be. My rapid progress was gratifying and it felt good to repeat the same monotonous motion over and over again.

'What are you doing?' said a voice behind me.

I turned around to see Ivan. He was looking at me with the expression that always made my stomach lurch, like I was an animal he'd crept up on in the woods.

'What are you doing?' I retorted. 'Don't you have anything better to do than to run around scaring people?'

'It's raining,' Ivan said, looking up at the sky.

I hadn't noticed, I'd been so absorbed by my labour.

'Great,' I said. 'Thanks for letting me know.'

I carried on digging without further comment. It was odd, I mused, that Vilhelm, who had been one of my favourite people, had created a person whose very existence aroused such uneasiness in me. Had Ivan ever even done anything to me? I pondered as I dumped soil inches from his black boots.

Ivan had helped his dad with his work on the farm when Vilhelm got too old to do it himself. Once, he and his dad had argued about the contract my grandfather had signed with Vilhelm, the agreement that said Vilhelm would be allowed to reside in the gatehouse in perpetuity, even after he stopped working. Because of that contract, Dad felt he could underpay Ivan, since his dad lived on our property for free. But eventually, Ivan had had enough and put his foot down and after that, he was no longer welcome. Even so, he showed up on the farm from time to time. There was always some tool to be retrieved, some saw that had belonged to his father. 'Like a restless spirit,' Dad would sigh occasionally, 'like a restless bloody spirit.'

'What's the hole for?' Ivan asked. 'There are no more animals to bury.'

'I just want to see how deep I can make it,' I said. 'The journey is the goal.'

'Your mother's not going to be happy with you.'

'My mother has never been happy with me.'

That night, after I'd gone to bed, the palms of my hands began to sting. I was an idiot for digging for so long without gloves. But it actually felt good, I thought to myself, I liked having physical pain to focus on, a pain that was more socially acceptable than the one emanating from the lacerations on my arms. I'd done physical labour, done a good day's work. A few hours ago, the ground down by the pet cemetery had been flat. Now it wasn't. I was a person who made a difference. But I was unable to sleep now. The palms of my hands were throbbing. For some reason, I started to think about Aron Vendt again. That was what this place had become to me, a place to remember horrible things. Aron Vendt, the name alone made me feel cold. Aron with his keys in his hand, that stupid grin, how proud he was about his car's horsepower, all the talk about bespoke rims and luxury trim. The feeling of being a passenger, of not being in control of where we went, whether we'd stop or ever go back home.

Aron's breath smelled of menthol when he reached across me and whisperingly told me to relax. He'd reclined my seat with practised, precise movements, nibbled on my ear and whispered that I should calm down, that it would hurt if I was tense.

I didn't want him on top of me, but I felt like my body had gone to sleep, like I wouldn't be able to make my limbs move, no matter how hard I tried. I was limp like a ragdoll.

It was only after he pulled down my knickers that I managed to bite his arm. I bit it so hard I tasted iron. He let out a yelp and recoiled into his own seat. Then he turned on the dome light and examined his injury.

'Do you have any idea what you've done?' he demanded, pointing at the wound. 'Look at this!'

He held his arm up in front of me and forced me to look.

'I'm sorry,' I said.

'Sorry? I might have to go get a rabies shot or something.'

'I don't have rabies,' I assured him.

'If you say so. Maybe I should even the score,' he said as

though he'd forgotten why I'd bitten him in the first place. 'I should really hurt you back, make you bleed.'

I gazed out into the night and realised I was about to burst into tears.

'You're lucky,' Aron went on and started the engine. 'You're bloody lucky I'm a gentleman.'

He reversed with a hand behind my headrest. Then he drove back to Gudhammar at top speed.

14

Susanne came out from the barn to greet her when Charlie turned into the driveway.

'Where have you been?' she said when Charlie climbed out of the car.

'I drove around for a while and then I had a coffee at the pub. Is everything okay?'

'I slept,' Susanne said. 'I slept like the dead.'

'That's great,' Charlie said and refrained from asking if the sleep had been natural or chemically induced. She hadn't come here to play morality police with a person who was just as broken as she was.

'Isak called,' Susanne said. 'He's going to pick the boys up tomorrow. Apparently, he's staying with an ex-colleague in town. He'll keep them for at least a week.'

'Is that good or bad?'

'I guess it's good for the boys. But the twisted thing is, I'll miss them. I've never been away from them for more than a night, if that.'

'You're going to be fine,' Charlie said. 'You really do need some time to yourself.'

'I was thinking about the Harvest Festival,' Susanne said.

'I usually love going, seeing people. This year it hasn't felt appealing at all, but if the children are gone and you're here, I'm bloody well going to go. I'm done feeling ashamed.'

'Why would you feel ashamed?'

'Because of what happened. I don't exactly relish leaving the house these days; when I go into town, people stare without saying anything. I really hate that. At the Harvest Festival, they're not going to pretend nothing happened; the alcohol is going to make them talk and I prefer dealing with honest drunks than silent judgement. Especially if I'm drunk too.'

'I get it,' Charlie said, 'but you shouldn't take it to heart. You haven't done anything wrong.'

'No one's ever completely blameless.'

Susanne looked up at the sky and said it was a bloody lovely autumn day, they should go for a walk.

'Where to?' Charlie asked.

'Does there have to be a destination? Can't we just walk?'

They walked down the gravel road behind the house. The wind was coming from the right direction today, no smell of the paper mill. It was odd, Charlie mused, that what looked like just a forest road like any other could be so full of memories. This was where they'd ridden Susanne's dad's old moped, this was where Charlie had given Susanne a croggy on her bike and they'd fallen off. When they got to the party in the village shop that time, they'd both had scraped up knees and gravel embedded in their palms.

Walking past the rock where they'd snuck their first cigarette, they laughed at how they'd kept at it until they could inhale without coughing even though it had made them sick.

'Do you know Gudhammar?' Charlie asked.

'Sure. Why do you ask?'

Charlie told her about the article she'd read about Francesca Mild, who had lived there and gone missing. Did Susanne know about that?

'I suppose I know it happened, that a girl disappeared. People who were the same age as her mentioned it occasionally. You never heard about it?'

'No,' Charlie said. 'Not as far as I recall anyway. But I think it's weird no one said anything about it last summer. I mean, given as how another local girl had gone missing.'

'Francesca wasn't local,' Susanne retorted.

'But she did go missing here. Francesca Mild disappeared from Gudhammar.'

'Yes.' Susanne stopped and looked at Charlie. 'What's this about?'

'I had a dream, about Betty, about me and her walking down a tree-lined gravel road; we were in a hurry. Betty knocked on a door and the man who opened it told us to clear off. This happened in real life, I'm sure it did. And the farm ... it was Gudhammar. I just don't understand why we were there.'

The images resurfaced. Betty's pleading voice rang in her ears. *We need to talk. Please.*

'Maybe it was about an outstanding booze payment,' Susanne suggested. 'You know how worked up Betty could get about that. Sometimes she forgot she'd been paid already and ... well, there were rows.'

Betty's wine business. She'd peddled the cherry wine that came with the house when she bought Lyckebo and later she'd started making her own wine, both to sell and for her own consumption. Sometimes, people were allowed to buy on credit and occasionally, when Betty was completely broke, she would walk around collecting her debts. She'd often taken Charlie along. Had their visit to Gudhammar been about something that trivial? But why had they gone at night? And why would a wealthy family ever do business with someone like Betty?

She thought that last thought out loud.

'No idea,' Susanne replied.

'They wouldn't.'

'No,' Susanne admitted. 'They probably wouldn't.'

'I don't understand why we were there,' Charlie said again.

'I can call Mum and see if she knows,' Susanne offered.

She pulled out her phone and dialled, but Lola didn't pick up. Susanne left a message asking her to call when she woke up.

'By the way, a friend of mine from Stockholm's coming down tonight,' Charlie said.

'Who?' Susanne asked. 'Why?'

'His name's Johan Ro and he's coming for work. He's going to stay at The Motel.'

'Wasn't he the guy who got you in trouble last summer?'

'I was the one who got me in trouble last summer.'

'But that is the guy, right, the journalist?'

'Yes.'

'So, a friend?' Susanne said with a grin.

It was her first real smile since Charlie came to Gullspång.

'Yes, it is possible to have male friends, you know.'

'It is?'

'Yes.'

'I just don't see the point of having male friends,' Susanne said with a shrug. 'Men are so ... they're spiritually deficient somehow, so alone in their little worlds. Even Isak, with his literature and big talk, once you scratched the surface, it became obvious there was very little depth there. You've never found that? That men usually only talk about concrete things?'

'I don't usually talk to men much,' Charlie said.

Susanne laughed.

'I thought you said the two of you were friends.'

'Johan might be the exception that proves the rule,' Charlie replied and recalled Betty's words about his father: *Mattias is the only person who knows everything about me and still likes me. Mattias is the exception that proves the rule.*

Susanne suddenly stopped dead.

'Goddamn piss knob,' she said. 'What week are we in?'

'No idea,' Charlie replied.

Susanne pulled out her phone.

'God-damn-it.'

'What?'

'School! The boys! They finished ten minutes ago.'

'But it's only ten past one.'

'They have half days every other week; uneven weeks they finish at one. Goddamn fucking shit!'

15

Tim and Tom were standing on the school steps with their backpacks when Susanne skidded into the car park and jumped out of the car.

Charlie heard her shout she was sorry and saw her hug the boys while gesticulating apologetically and saying something to the teacher who came outside.

Charlie remembered the rows Betty had got into with her teachers the few times she'd bothered to show up at school. *I'm not about to take any shit from those stuck-up windbags, Charline. Do you hear me? No more shit.*

'Oh my god,' Susanne exclaimed once they were all back in the car. 'I wouldn't be surprised if they reported this to children's services.'

'I'm sure children's services have their hands full,' Charlie said, 'and in my experience, they're not terribly efficient. Worse things than a late pickup have fallen through the cracks, put it that way.'

'It's okay, Mum,' Tim said. 'We were fine waiting, we even got sweets. Ow, stop hitting me, Tom.'

'From whom?' Susanne asked and shot him a look in the rear-view mirror. 'Who gave you sweets?'

'I found them in my backpack,' Tom said.

Susanne hit the brakes so hard Charlie almost smacked her head on the dashboard.

'What are you doing?' Tom shrieked.

'I'm going to stay here until you tell the truth.'

'But I ...'

'Be quiet, Tom. If you're not going to tell the truth, you're at least not going to interrupt your brother when he tries to.'

'A lady gave it to us,' Tim said.

'What lady?'

'I don't know. Just a lady.'

Susanne looked at Charlie, who turned round and asked in a warm voice if they could tell them what the lady looked like, but neither one of them had much to offer by way of description. Nor did they know if they'd seen her before. All she'd done was say hello and offer them sweets. And they'd both been hungry and unable to say no. And she was just an old lady.

'Have you ever heard me say you can't talk to strangers?' Susanne said. 'Even if they're just old ladies.'

'I'm sorry, Mum,' Tom said. 'We didn't mean to.'

'Did she poison us?' Tim shrieked.

When Susanne said there was no way of knowing, that time would tell, both twins started screaming hysterically.

They were still crying when they got home. Susanne sent them to their rooms.

'Maybe you should reassure them,' Charlie said. 'About the poisoning.'

'In a bit,' Susanne said. 'First I want to make sure they're so terrified they'll never do it again.'

'I think they're as terrified as they're going to get,' Charlie said. 'Who do you think it was?'

'No idea, an old person from the nursing home maybe.'

'Odd that they didn't recognise her.'

'All old ladies probably look alike to children,' Susanne said. 'But I'm going to let the school know.'

Charlie went upstairs to talk to the boys. As she walked up the stairs, she heard Susanne say something sharp about how it was the school's responsibility to make sure strangers didn't come into the schoolyard and offer students sweets, even if their parent happened to be late.

Tim and Tom were lying on Susanne's bed with their arms around each other. Charlie mused that they might have been like that in the womb, entwined, like one body.

She sat down on the bed.

'It's okay,' she said. 'You haven't been poisoned.'

'How do you know?'

Tim turned to her, wide-eyed.

'Because you would have felt it by now. Poisons act really quickly.'

'So we're not going to die?'

'No, you're not going to die.'

'Ever?'

Tim looked both frightened and hopeful.

Charlie opened her mouth to reply, but Tom beat her to it.

'Everyone dies,' he said, and when Tim clapped his hands to his ears, he repeated the sentence, louder and louder: 'Everyone dies, everyone dies, everyone dies.'

'Stop that,' Charlie said.

'But it's true!'

'Doesn't matter, keep it to yourself.'

*

Once Melker and Nils were back from school as well and they were all gathered in the kitchen, Susanne told them Isak had called. He wanted to come pick them up the next day. The twins cheered but Nils was quiet and Melker said he wasn't going.

'Not in front of your brothers, please,' Susanne told him in English.

'He can't just pick us up when it suits him,' Melker retorted.

'I think it would be good for you to have a talk about things,' Susanne said, 'and your brothers will be sad if you don't go with them.'

'I can stay here with him,' Nils said. 'Or actually, I don't know.'

Melker groaned and muttered something Charlie didn't catch.

'Why are any of us seeing him?' he said. 'Aren't you the one who always says actions have consequences, Mum?'

'He hasn't done anything to you,' Susanne replied.

'He left,' Melker retorted, 'and who knows what else.'

'What do you mean?'

'I'm not deaf, Mum. I can hear what people are saying at school and … everywhere.'

'We don't listen to stuff like that. Haven't I told you that in this family, we don't listen to gossip?'

'Yes, and you've also said people have to own up to what they've done.'

They were interrupted by Tim knocking over his chocolate milk, flooding the table.

'Damn it!' Susanne erupted, and in the next moment: 'I'm sorry.'

Melker got up quickly, fetched the dishrag and started mopping the milk up.

'When's Dad going to be here?' Tom asked.

'Tomorrow after school,' Susanne said.

'I miss Dad,' Tim said. 'I want to show him my spaceship and tell him I finished the alphabet book in school and ...'

'I finished the alphabet book, too!' Tom shouted. 'I finished it before you, before anyone else in class, before anyone else!'

'Stop goddamn shouting,' Susanne said.

She got up and asked if it was okay if she went out to the barn. She wanted to get a bit of painting in before starting dinner. Charlie said maybe they could all have dinner at The Motel later.

But Susanne didn't want to. She wasn't ready to answer questions about Isak or handle the angry or pitying looks, at least not without a beer in her. But Charlie could take the boys if she wanted.

Charlie checked her watch. Johan was probably already there. She wondered if the only reason she couldn't wait to see him was to talk about Francesca Mild.

'You drive as fast as Mum,' said Melker, who was in the passenger seat. 'Dad used to say she'll end up in a ditch one day if she doesn't slow down.'

Charlie noted his use of the past tense *used to*.

One of the twins shrieked in the back seat.

'What's going on?' Charlie demanded.

'Tom's pinching me to make me open my eyes.'

'I just think it's weird that his eyes are closed,' Tom said.

'He's obviously afraid, you git,' Nils commented.

Charlie slowed down and looked in the rear-view mirror.

'What are you afraid of, Tim?'

'He sees dead people,' Nils said.

'Tom,' Charlie said. 'Your brother's allowed to have his eyes closed as much as he likes, and the next time you pinch him or hurt him, I'm turning this car round and dropping you off at home. Have I made myself clear?'

'Watch out, or she'll throw you in prison,' Nils added.

'I don't think it was a dead person,' Tim said after a pause. 'It didn't look like a zombie. Zombie's move much weirder.'

'What are you talking about?' Melker sighed.

'I saw someone in the garden before,' Tim said. 'Over by the swings.'

Charlie met Tim's solemn eyes in the mirror.

'Why didn't you tell me or your mum?'

'I have a vivid imagination,' Tim said. 'I thought maybe it wasn't real.'

'If you ever think there's someone in the garden again, I want you to tell us.'

'I figured I should shut my eyes instead,' Tim said, 'so I don't have to see. I'm afraid of ...'

'What are you afraid of?'

'Being afraid. I'm afraid of being afraid.'

Nils sighed and said he shouldn't watch so many horror films then. If he's so afraid of being afraid.

Finally, Charlie's phone rang.

'Watch where you're going!' Nils bellowed as she started digging through her handbag for her phone. 'Chaaarlie!'

Charlie looked up. She just managed to avoid the ditch. A hot-cold feeling exploded in her head and rushed down her spine.

'Johan,' Charlie said once she had the car under control and was able to answer. 'How's tricks?'

'I'm fine, but there's something wrong with my phone. The battery is draining too fast and sometimes it refuses to charge. Where are you?'

'On my way to the pub with Susanne's boys. Where are you?'

'I just got here.'

'We were going to grab a bite to eat,' Charlie said. 'You're welcome to join us.'

'I'm going to have a shower,' Johan said. 'Then I'll be right down.'

Francesca

Dad was driving me to Doctor Molan's house. Doctor Molan was really from Stockholm, but conveniently enough, he had a summer residence just a few miles from Gudhammar on Lake Skagern. Since his retirement, the large house by the water had increasingly become his permanent home. Doctor Molan was a family friend; I'd been sent to him from time to time my whole life. He was an arrogant, caustic man I didn't trust. It was hard to confide in a person I knew could turn up in the parlour at Gudhammar for a whisky with my dad at any time. But neither Mum, Dad, nor Doctor Molan, seemed to understand that. I was seven the first time I was sent to talk to him. It was the day after I held Cécile's head under water. Doctor Molan talked to me as though I were a very small child. *Why did you hurt your sister? Do you understand what happens to a person if they can't breathe?*

The last time I'd seen Doctor Molan was a few weeks after that drive with Aron Vendt. Doctor Molan had given me a long lecture on the importance of telling the truth. Because the thing is, and I'd do well to remember it: a person who lies can't count on being believed in the future.

'It's a waste of money,' I said to Dad. 'Taking me to Doctor Molan.'

'It's not a matter of cost,' Dad replied. 'And besides, there's no such thing as waste if it makes you feel better.'

'It doesn't make me feel better.'

'It's either Doctor Molan or sectioning.'

'Why him?' I said. 'Why does it have to be someone I dislike?'

Dad pretended not to hear and just told me what a skilled professional Doctor Molan was.

'Have you forgotten?' I said.

'Forgotten what?'

'Forgotten that he didn't believe me last time.'

'If I were you, I'd tread carefully now,' Dad said.

'I haven't forgiven you, in case you were under the impression I had,' I said. 'I haven't forgiven you, Mum or Doctor Molan. I never will.'

'I'm aware of that, but as you know, we disagree with your version of events.'

'Is that why no one believes me this time? Because of what happened then?'

'Francesca,' Dad said, taking his eyes off the road. 'Your friend killed himself. It helps no one that you're trying to point fingers. Everyone knows he killed himself.'

'That's just because people didn't know him. No one knew him like me.'

'It looks the same,' I said when we turned into the driveway of Doctor Molan's moss green turn-of-the-century villa.

The house was beautifully situated on a hill with a view of the beach and the water. In Dad's motorboat, it took no more than ten minutes to get to it from Gudhammar. When the skies were clear like now and the leaves had fallen from the trees, you could actually see our house on the other side of the lake. Being back here caused a knot to form in my stomach. I remembered all the awkward hours I'd spent in his office while he tried to straighten out my little idiosyncrasies. Why did I lick my lips compulsively? Why did I break drinking glasses with my teeth when we had guests? Why did I refuse to answer when people asked friendly questions?

My first thought when Dad's car disappeared round a bend after he'd dropped me off, was to flee into the forest, but since that would only make things worse, I reluctantly shuffled up to the front door. I rang the bell and was struck by how inappropriate the jolly jingle was in a home frequented by mentally unstable patients.

Greta opened the door. She was Doctor Molan's ... cleaning lady? Maid?

'Francesca,' she said with a smile. She had kind brown eyes and hair that was turning white. 'It's so good to see you again. Please have a seat outside his office.'

After what felt like an eternity, Doctor Molan opened the door to his office on the first floor. He was dressed in a mustard-yellow cardigan and brown trousers that didn't look entirely clean. His hair was mussed as though he'd been napping.

'I'm glad you're here,' he said as he let me in. 'Your parents are very worried about you, Francesca.'

'Hello to you, too,' I replied.

His office was shrouded in pipe smoke. I made myself comfortable on the green velvet divan. Doctor Molan sat down behind his desk. I think he liked to sit there so he could take notes, but perhaps he also wanted to maintain a certain distance.

'I hear you're not feeling well,' Doctor Molan said, 'that it's very serious this time.'

'It was a cry for help,' I said with a nod to my arms.

'Yes, I suppose that's what we usually say.' Doctor Molan lit his pipe.

I wished he would open a window. What kind of person was he, anyway, smoking indoors, in front of his patients?

'Now, tell me, Francesca,' he said and crossed his legs. 'Tell me why you want to die?'

Why did I want to die?

I was grateful Doctor Molan was using the same approach as before, that he never gave me time to answer; I only managed a sigh and a shrug before he started posing his endless follow-up questions. Did I find life meaningless? Had I lost my faith in the future? Was I sleeping poorly?

'I think you're depressed,' Doctor Molan announced gravely after I managed to squeeze in brief answers to a few of his many questions.

'Is that right?' I said.

The sarcasm seemed to escape Doctor Molan, because he simply nodded and said everything I'd told him made him feel fairly certain of his diagnosis. That and my suicide attempt made it perfectly clear. I was deeply depressed.

'It was just a cry for help,' I said again.

'Fine, since you insist on calling it that,' Doctor Molan said. 'The point is, we heard you, Francesca. We heard your cry for help.'

'Great,' I said, 'good thing you're all so perceptive.'

'Have you ever considered ...' Doctor Molan sucked on his pipe again. 'Have you ever considered letting your intellect overrule your destructive impulses? Because you have a sharp intellect, Francesca, are you aware of that?'

'I don't know. I feel neither destructive nor intelligent.'

It was the truth. My whole life, people around me had gone on about this intelligence that lurked underneath all my little idiosyncrasies. It always made me feel uncomfortable, because deep down, I suspected I might be dumber than most. Maybe I was able to draw conclusions and read people's intentions and moods with relative ease (though Dad always said I shouldn't overestimate my talents in that area), but when it came to things like rivers, oceans and mountains, old philosophers, kings and theories, I was clueless. I could cram things like that for exams and get full marks (at least I used to be able to), but then it was like it all vanished in a haze. I wasn't even remotely able to point to countries on a map. I might get it in my head that Mexico was in Europe and Lisbon was the capital of Austria. But the worst part of all the talk about my intelligence was the stress I felt about it being wasted. Because intelligence was completely wasted in a person unable to do something sensible with it.

'Apparently I'm not intelligent enough to make the best of my situation,' I said, 'because then I would have a long time ago.'

'It's not too late,' Doctor Molan said, putting his fingertips together. 'It's a long life.'

It sounded like a threat.

'How do you see your future?'

'To be honest, I can't bear to think about that right now,' I said and realised that was completely true.

I was so incredibly sick of the future.

'But before you started feeling unwell, what were your hopes for the future?'

My life. No matter what happened, it was going to be a disaster. I thought of my favourite book, *The Bell Jar* by Sylvia Plath. Paul had given me it because he thought I'd love it and he'd been right. Now I recalled one of my favourite parts of that book, the part where Esther Greenwood says travelling is pointless since she can never get away from herself.

We talked about my parents, my anger, how I couldn't forgive them. Doctor Molan said I should try, for my own sake if nothing else.

I studied the wall behind Doctor Molan, all the diplomas he'd hung on it, and thought about how useless an education and awards were if you couldn't even comprehend that some things were unforgivable.

Doctor Molan asked me to tell him about the tragic death of my boyfriend. My parents had only given him a bare-bones account of the situation.

I said the information he'd been given was incorrect; I had never had a boyfriend.

'Your friend, then,' Doctor Molan said.

'I think he was murdered, that my sister's boyfriend and his mates killed him.'

'That's a very serious accusation, Francesca.'

'It's a very serious crime.'

'What do you base your suspicions on?' Doctor Molan asked.

I told him about my memories, about the yellow rose and the wet trouser legs. The eyes that avoided mine.

When I was done, Doctor Molan looked out the window, cleared his throat and launched into a speech about memories.

They were unreliable, he said, unreliable and mutable. They could be lost, manipulated and false, and if you added things like sedatives, alcohol and drugs, that obviously made a person's ability to remember even more unreliable.

I stopped listening and let my mind drift out of the room and take me elsewhere, somewhere where people believed me, where Paul and I would be vindicated, where the guilty would be punished.

'I would prefer to talk about what happened with Aron Vendt,' I said when Doctor Molan had finished his lecture on memory.

'Remind me,' Doctor Molan said, uncrossing and re-crossing his legs.

'Aron Vendt assaulted me. You don't remember?'

'I remember,' Doctor Molan said. 'But we were talking about your friend.'

'I would like to talk about Aron Vendt instead.'

'What is there to say about him?'

Doctor Molan sounded resigned and reached for his pipe again.

'Would you mind not smoking, please,' I said.

'Of course.'

He put his pipe down with a look of disappointment.

'It's not really about Aron Vendt, I said. 'It's about Mum and Dad, their betrayal.'

Doctor Molan cleared his throat and said his view of the event in question differed from mine. He didn't see it as a betrayal.

'Then how do you see it?' I asked.

'I see it as two parents doing what they could in that situation. I mean, they needed proof.'

I thought about the horrifying visit to the gynaecologist Mum and Dad had forced on me. The gynaecologist wasn't even a woman; it was a middle-aged man with hairy knuckles. I should just take deep, calm breaths and it would be over in the blink of an eye, he said before asking me to scooch further down, closer, closer.

After the examination, he spoke to Dad while I had to wait outside.

Dad gave me a stern talking to in the car on the way home. I had to stop lying, he told me, or things might end badly for me.

I screamed at him that I hadn't lied. Why didn't they believe me? Why didn't they believe their own daughter?

Dad said he wasn't about to go into details but that the gynaecologist had seemed fairly certain that what I'd told them about Aron never happened.

16

There was only one free table in the restaurant. Charlie told the boys to have a seat while she went to get one more chair. It was already slightly too loud. She looked out across the room and was struck by the strange notion that the people in it hadn't moved since she left last summer. The raucous group of older men that usually included Svenka was there, as was a number of middle-aged women she recognised. The regulars had reclaimed the place after last summer's invasion by the police, journalists and Missing People.

'Well, well, well.' A face appeared right next to Charlie's. 'Braved the pub, too, eh?'

'What do you want, Micke?' Charlie said, sounding considerably less enthusiastic than he.

She had no desire to talk to him again, not unless he was going to help her with the closed police investigation, and yet there he was, standing much too close, the way socially tone-deaf people tend to.

'I just wanted to say hi,' Micke said. There was alcohol on his breath.

'Hi.'

'Aren't those Susanne's boys?' He nodded towards their table.

'Yes.'

'And where's Susanne?'

'At home.'

Micke leaned in closer.

'Do you reckon Isak's coming back?'

'I don't know,' Charlie replied. 'And even if I did, I wouldn't discuss that with you.'

'I hope for his sake he stays away,' Micke said. 'I mean, I know he wouldn't be convicted, but people here don't care. What we know for sure he did is bad enough. We don't forgive things like that around here.'

'Was there anything else?' Charlie asked.

'Yes.' Micke lowered his voice. 'I had a look around the archive after you left and I think I might have something you'd like. I took it home, actually.'

Charlie was surprised. She'd figured she was out of luck.

'What's the catch?' she said.

'What do you mean?'

Charlie didn't want to explain what she meant since that might offend Micke and jeopardise her ability to get her hands on the case file.

'Never mind,' she said.

'I might let you have a look if you tell me what you're digging around for. I mean, I don't exactly feel like putting my job on the line ...'

'We can talk more tomorrow when you're sober,' Charlie said.

'I just had a couple of pints. I'm heading home now.'

'Tomorrow.'

'Why didn't you say something, by the way?' Micke went on.

'About what?'

'About being from here, about being Betty's daughter.'

'Because it was irrelevant.'

She turned round.

'My dad knew Betty,' Micke said. 'I'd go so far as to say he knew her pretty well. And if Betty's daughter needs my help, who am I to ...'

'Not here,' Charlie said. 'Are you trying to get sacked?'

'Are you going to rat me out?'

Micke smiled. He seemed unaware of how loudly he was talking.

Charlie went back to their table with Micke's words about Betty ringing in her ears. *My dad knew her pretty well.*

'What did he want?' Melker asked with a nod towards Micke.

'Nothing in particular.'

'He's a copper, too,' Nils said.

'Don't you think she knows that?' Melker rolled his eyes. 'She has worked with him before.'

'I didn't think of that,' Nils admitted.

And then Johan appeared in the door. When Charlie's eyes met his, she felt something in the pit of her stomach she hadn't felt since ... that she didn't know if she'd ever felt before. Stop being a ninny, she chided herself. He's just ... well, what was he?

Johan walked over to them. He gave Charlie a quick hug before shaking all four boys' hands and introducing himself. Jonas quickly brought them another chair.

'How are you?' Johan asked after taking his seat.

'Good,' she said. 'You?'

'Not bad, just struggling with the weather.' He nodded

towards the window where a light drizzle had started to fall. 'The lack of light is the worst part. I don't like it.'

'I do,' Charlie said. 'I find the lack of light liberating.'

'Liberating?'

Johan frowned.

'Why do you find the lack of light liberating, Charlie?'

Nils was looking at her solemnly.

Charlie hadn't realised the boys were listening; both Nils and Melker had seemed absorbed by their phones and the twins were folding their napkins into airplanes.

'I don't know,' Charlie said. 'Dark days make me feel calm for some reason.'

'You're not like other people,' Nils said.

Charlie met Johan's eyes across the table. He smiled at her and that feeling in her stomach came back.

Their food came; while they ate, Johan talked to the boys. Charlie watched him as he listened attentively to Tom's interminable ramblings about some new game he was amazing at, then just as patiently to Tim when he repeated almost the same thing.

Melker was the only one who asked him questions back.

'What's your job?' he wanted to know.

'Journalist,' Johan said and waved an invisible pen around as though the profession needed further explanation.

'You were a pain last summer,' Melker said candidly. 'Well, maybe not you, but the other journalists. They asked a lot of questions and followed Dad around.'

'I understand,' Johan said. 'That must have been hard for you.'

'Serves him right,' Melker retorted.

'What do you mean?' Tom demanded. 'What do you mean it serves Dad right?'

Charlie instantly regretted bringing the boys with her.

Just then, the music was turned up and Tim and Tom demonstratively covered their ears.

'Isn't there a pinball machine in the back?' Charlie said.

'Yes, there is,' Nils replied.

'Would you like to play?'

'We don't have any money.'

Charlie took out her wallet and pulled out a one-hundred-kronor note.

'Ask for change at the bar,' she said, handing it to Melker.

'Can we keep the whole thing?' Melker asked.

'If you want.'

The boys disappeared and Charlie met Johan's eyes across the table. He held her gaze a fraction too long.

'So, what's it like being back?' he said.

'It's alright.'

'Not much has changed.'

'We'll do small talk later,' Charlie said. 'The boys are going to use up that money in no time.'

She leaned forward and told him what Micke had said about the closed investigation.

'So it's at his house?' Johan said.

'Yes.'

'What's Micke's surname?'

'Andersson.'

'And you're going to go get it later?'

'That was my plan,' Charlie said.

She pulled her phone from her handbag and typed in 'Mikael Andersson Gullspång'. It turned out there was only one his age, so finding his address was easy.

'Do you want me to come with you?' Johan asked.

'No, I think I'd better go by myself. It's a matter of confidentiality and stuff like that.'

'I get it. Let me know if you actually manage to get it off him.'

When the twins returned, Tim and Tom were at loggerheads.

'He used up all the money,' Tim said, pointing at Tom. 'He's an idiot.'

Charlie stifled a smile, fixed Tim intently and told him he shouldn't use words like that about his brother, or anyone else.

'I think it's time for us to get going,' Charlie said. 'Boys, go tell your brothers we're leaving.'

The twins left. Charlie saw them elbowing each other as they walked.

'Well, I suppose we should ...'

Charlie nodded towards the exit.

'I'm off, too,' Johan said. 'Going back to my room, I mean.'

'So ... see you later.'

She realised she wanted to hug him, but she refrained.

Gaps in Time

Paul and I are sitting in our usual pew in the chapel, trying to sing along with a summer hymn that is far too high pitched for our voices. Paul turns to me with his eyes crossed and I have to fake a coughing fit to hide my laughing.

When the priest starts to speak again, Paul hands me a note.

The clergyman – that quintessence of nonsense done up in long clothes!

They're not his own words, he whispers when I say I like them. They're Kierkegaard's.

Paul! Francesca! The headmaster says behind us when the service is over. I would like to see both of you in my office. Yes, right now.

We follow the headmaster to his office, which is full of dark wooden furniture and dusty books. There, we're forced to endure a long lecture on the importance of obeying school rules. Because we both know what the consequences are of failing to do so: phone calls to our parents, warnings and ultimately ... we both knew very well what a third warning entailed. And if you are suspended, the headmaster went on, and now he was looking only at Paul, the tuition fee will not be returned. Are you aware of this?

We don't belong here, I say, when the headmaster finally releases us.

But we belong together, Paul replies. We're Paolo and Francesca. He bursts out laughing and says he's never thought about our names before.

Who are Paolo and Francesca?

You haven't read Dante?

Heard of him. He's the one who wrote about hell, right?

Paul nodded, that was right, and Paolo and Francesca were two characters trapped in the eternal winds of hell.

Why?

Lust. Adultery.

You go to hell for that? I have an instant mental image of Dad in a tornado.

There's no such thing as hell, Paul replies.

I still like it.

Hell?

That Paolo and Francesca exist in the eternal winds.

It's a nightmare, Paul says. I can't even ride a merry-go-round without feeling sick.

I want to tell him it's not the winds that appeal to me. That I, if I were flapping around in an eternal storm, can't imagine anyone I'd rather do it with than Paul Bergman.

17

They were back in the car. Melker and Nils were quietly discussing their winnings from a game you had to be eighteen to play.

'You said you didn't have a husband,' Tim piped up from the passenger seat.

'I don't,' Charlie replied.

'What about Johan?'

'He's just a friend. You can be friends, too, you know.'

'Dad always says that's impossible,' Melker piped in. 'He says there's always a certain attraction between the sexes.'

Charlie glanced up at the rear-view mirror and met Melker's grave eyes.

Your dad's wrong, she wanted to tell him. Your dad's judging others by his own standards. Your dad's a selfish fucking asshole.

'Why was that man so mean?' Tim asked.

'What man?' Charlie said.

'Just an old drunk who talked to us when we were playing,' Melker replied.

'But why did he say nasty things about Dad?' Tim pressed.

'Who was it? And what did he say?'

'I don't know his name,' Tim said. 'But he said ...'

Tim was cut off by Melker.

'You shouldn't pay any attention to old drunks, Tim. They're full of shit.'

'But ...'

'They're full of shit,' Melker repeated. 'It was a drunk,' he went on, turning to Charlie. 'I don't know his name, but I'm guessing you know what he was talking about.'

Charlie nodded and told them they should have come to her.

'That would only make it worse,' Melker said. 'It's better to pretend you can't hear them.'

'Sometimes it's better to put your foot down,' Charlie said.

Melker shrugged.

'You're going the wrong way,' Nils said.

'I just need to pick up something from a friend's house,' Charlie told him.

Micke lived in a light-blue terraced house in a part of town that must have been built after Charlie left Gullspång, because she had no recollection of it. Micke apparently saw her coming, because he opened the door before she could ring the bell.

'I knew it,' he said. 'I figured you wouldn't be able to stay away. Come in.' He threw the door open. 'Can I offer you a drink?'

'I have the boys in the car,' Charlie said, nodding in the direction of the driveway. 'Did you have something for me?'

'Sure.'

Micke disappeared into the house and Charlie thought to herself it was weird he was drinking alone on a Monday. She had no recollection of noticing signs of alcohol problems last summer. But maybe something had happened today to make him need it. She recognised the artificial sound of cards being shuffled and dealt on a computer. Micke returned with a green folder. When she reached for it and he pulled it away, she had to bite back a comment about how predictable he was.

'I don't even get to know why you want this?' Micke said. 'And what's in it for me; what do I get in return?'

That's as far as he got before Charlie snatched the folder out of his hands.

'Don't worry,' she said. 'I'm not going to tell anyone you've pocketed materials you need permission to access. My lips are sealed.'

'I haven't even bloody read it myself yet,' Micke said.

A string of curses followed her to the car.

'I'm going to choose not to hear any of that,' Charlie said loudly. 'Thank you so much for your help.'

It was odd, she mused as she climbed back into the car, odd and slightly stupid of Micke to bring that folder home. He really had everything to lose by doing it and no reason to want to help her out. It was no secret they'd disliked each other. But now Francesca Mild's case file was in her bag and she wanted nothing more than to dig into it. But she had to wait until she was alone.

18

Charlie was lying in the crack in Susanne's double bed, sand-wiched between two tousled-hair little boys. The heat from their pyjama-clad bodies made her feel calm and drowsy. They were reading *The Little Prince*. It was endlessly long, but the wide-eyed twins had told her their dad used to read it to them until they fell asleep and Charlie was determined to do the same. She realised it would take quite a long time, since they kept interrupting to ask questions and tell anecdotes. Before long, she reached the passage she had liked the most when she was a child, the one about the prince's love of sunsets, about how one day, he'd watched the sun set forty-three times.

'Impossible!' Tim objected.

'Totally possible,' Tom disagreed. 'It's a different planet, stupid, it's not like here.'

'Don't call me stupid, poophead,' Tim said and sat up.

'If you're going to fight, we're done reading,' Charlie declared.

They both fell silent and Charlie continued.

'I wish,' Tom said, 'Mum would be happy again soon.'

He rubbed his eyes.

'We're going to be good,' he continued and his brother

nodded solemnly. 'We're not going to make a mess or run around and chase each other in the house.'

Charlie's throat contracted. She was all too familiar with that kind of guilt. She remembered a social worker who had knelt down in front of her once and demanded eye contact. *Look at me, Charlie, look up. And listen to me. It's not your fault your mum's sad. Not. Your. Fault.*

Now she tried to convey the same message to Susanne's boys.

'Then whose fault is it?' Tom wanted to know.

'It's no one's fault,' Charlie replied.

'But if it's not our fault,' Tom said, 'then why are we the ones she's angry with?'

'Sometimes, sad people get angry, but she's not angry with you. She loves you.'

'How do you know?' Tim demanded.

Charlie said it was because she was Susanne's best friend and that meant she knew things like that.

'When's Dad coming tomorrow?' Tim asked.

'I don't know what time,' Charlie replied.

'But he is coming, right?'

'I think so.'

'Why did he move out?' Tom said. 'Was it just because Mum told him he was a fucking asshole?'

Charlie shook her head.

'Then why did he move out?'

Tom turned to Charlie and looked her in the eyes. She felt on the verge of tears.

'That's all very hard to understand.'

'When you're a child?'

'When you're a grown-up, too.'

'Keep reading,' Tim said.

Charlie continued to read about how the little prince journeyed to a planet on which there lived a man who drank too much.

'Why does he drink?' Tom asked.

'It says he drinks to forget,' Charlie replied.

'To forget what?'

'To forget that he's ashamed.'

'Ashamed about what?'

'Ashamed about drinking.'

'I need to pee,' Tim announced.

'Otherwise he wets the bed,' Tom whispered after Tim left.

'Tom,' Charlie said. 'Do you know what it means to be loyal?'

'No.'

They were interrupted by a loud shriek from Tim.

Charlie raced out into the hallway and saw Susanne coming up the stairs. Tim was sitting on the floor under the hallway window with his arms wrapped around his legs, screaming.

'Calm down, sweetheart,' soothed Susanne, who had reached the landing and gathered Tim up in her arms. 'There's nothing to be afraid of here.'

'I saw,' Tim sobbed. 'I saw someone outside again.'

'It might have been a deer,' Susanne said and looked up at Charlie. 'You don't have to be afraid. Do you want me to carry you back to bed?'

Tim nodded.

Charlie looked out the window. She could see nothing.

'Are you too tired to hear more?' Charlie said after they'd

made themselves comfortable in the bed and Tim had calmed down.

The boys snuggled in closer. The smell of their hair, grass, sand and something else she couldn't put her finger on made her feel wistful.

'Are you alright, Tim?' she said.

'Yes, but I don't want to go outside by myself any more.'

'You don't have to.'

Fifteen minutes later, both boys were asleep. Charlie closed the book and listened to their even breathing. She pondered what it would be like if they were hers. What it was like to be a mother in Susanne's situation, to live like this, with limited means, no work and a fragile safety net.

When she got out of bed, Tom woke up.

'Charlie,' he whispered. 'I don't think it was a deer in the garden. I saw something behind the swings, too. It looked more like a person.'

'Maybe it was just someone walking their dog,' Charlie said. 'Don't worry about it.'

In the doorway, she turned to look at the boys. What was it they had seen?

Francesca

When I got back from Doctor Molan, I pulled on a pair of gloves and went down to my hole. Then I dug until Mum called me in for lunch. With every plunge of the shovel, the image of Paul flashed before my eyes. I thought about his family, his dad, his brother and his grandmother, whom I'd never met. I thought about his funeral, which I'd missed because I'd been lying in a hospital bed with bandaged arms. And I thought about the night of the ball and the royals. Their wet trouser legs. The yellow rose.

'What are you up to, Francesca,' Mum exclaimed when I came back dripping sweat. 'Why are you digging like your life depended on it?'

I asked if it bothered her.

'I just don't understand the purpose,' Mum said. She looked at Dad. 'Do you?'

Dad didn't understand either.

'Does there always have to be a purpose?' I said. 'It just makes me feel calm.'

'At first, I thought you were digging that poor cat up again,' Dad said. 'I'll never forget when you did that.'

'Some things can't be forgotten,' I said.

'Either way, it doesn't look nice,' Mum said. 'It doesn't look nice at all.'

Later that day, Mum asked if I wanted to go into town and have a coffee with her. I thought she must have forgotten her many failed attempts to take me out. When I was younger, she'd brought me with her to have coffee with her girlfriends and their children sometimes, but since I didn't reliably answer when spoken to and licked my lips too much (why couldn't I just use lip balm like Cécile?) she'd eventually given up and started taking only my sister. Maybe it was no wonder Mum preferred Cécile's company to mine in situations like that. Cécile, who always asked relevant follow-up questions and laughed in the right places. Cécile, who let other people finish their sentences and never spilled on white tablecloths. But apparently Mum was ready to try again.

Mum parked outside the supermarket. When we crossed the square, the man with the lottery tickets called out after us. He was sitting in his usual spot outside the supermarket entrance, shouting at anyone who passed: 'Come buy looooot-tery tickets!'

I said we should buy some, but Mum just shook her head and whispered that he seemed unpredictable, that she didn't want to go near him.

An old bell tinkled above the door when we entered the café. Every time we came, Mum would make condescending comments about the furniture, about how it looked untouched since the fifties. That was probably true, but unlike my mother, I found the unmatched brown wooden furniture, the old jukebox and the floral curtains cosy. Besides, the pastries were delicious. It was because of all the butter, Mum said – they put more butter in everything out here, because in the country, people cared more about flavour than a few extra pounds.

Mum asked for a cup of black coffee. I ordered two pastries and a fizzy drink. One of the tables was occupied by men in blue coveralls. They looked like they were covered in red dust.

'Why are they red?' I said, nodding towards the men.

'Lower your voice, Fran,' Mum hissed between clenched teeth. 'Oxidised iron ore. It turns red, when it oxidises, and it clings to everything.'

I politely thanked her for the information.

Mum closed her eyes and said nothing for a while. Then she collected herself and asked if I was feeling any better.

I took a big bite of one of my pastries, not bothering to wipe the sugar from around my mouth, even though Mum was gesticulating furiously at me.

'I feel terrific.'

'There's no need to exaggerate,' Mum said, handing me a napkin. 'Just tell the truth, Francesca.'

'Alright. Paul's dead; no one believes me when I say something's not right; I've been expelled from school and you're watching over me like I'm a crazy person.'

Mum gave me a look I took to mean I just might be.

'I know it's hard,' she said, 'but it'll get better.'

'How do you know?'

'From experience. Everything gets better, everything passes.'

'Or maybe there's neither beginning nor end,' I said. 'Maybe everything just goes around and around, like in an eternal whirlwind.'

'Let's hope there's an end at some point,' Mum said.

'I think this grief is going to bark at my heels like a dog until I fall down dead. It will only pass when I die.'

'Please don't say things like that,' Mum said. 'How did it go with Doctor Molan?'

'There's only one way it can go with him and that's poorly. Surely you can understand that I can't trust him again after what happened with Aron Vendt.'

Mum passed a hand across her brow.

'I thought that was in the past,' she said.

'Maybe for you. But Doctor Molan and I have gone back to it.'

'Why? That's hardly the problem now, is it?'

'How is anyone to know where things start and end? That's what we're trying to figure out.'

'Great,' Mum said dully.

Was she ashamed? I hoped so. I certainly would have been if I'd let my own daughter down like she had.

Mum excused herself to go to the powder room.

Moments after she left, the bell above the front door tinkled again and a beautiful young woman holding a little girl by the hand entered. The woman looked dishevelled, with long, tousled hair and rumpled clothes.

'Hiya, Melinda,' she greeted the woman behind the counter. 'How are the chickens?'

'Fox has gone and bloody taken them,' the woman named Melinda replied. 'I don't understand how he got in.'

'Don't you have a roof?'

'He got in anyway.'

'I can help you build a new coop, if you want, a more secure one.'

I felt impressed by this woman who didn't bother brushing her hair and could build things.

'We'll have two juice boxes and two cinnamon buns,' the

woman continued. 'Or did you want something else?' She bent down to the little girl I assumed was her daughter. 'I can't hear you, sweetheart. You have to speak up.'

The little girl stared at the floor and said she just wanted a biscuit.

Melinda behind the counter swapped one of the buns for a biscuit and handed the tray over without charging.

I watched the woman move through the room. When she passed the table with the men, one of the younger ones patted his knee and told her to have a seat.

'Cut it the fuck out, Svenka,' the woman hissed. 'You're scaring my daughter.'

She put her tray down two tables behind ours. Then she led the girl over to the jukebox and picked her up so she could choose a song.

'I'm just going to nip to the loo, angel,' she said when the girl had pushed a button and the intro to Judy Garland's 'Over the Rainbow' filled the café. 'I'll be right back. You go sit down.'

The girl sat down at the table next to mine. Her hair was as tousled as her mother's and her face was dirty. Maybe it was the state of her, coupled with her resigned eyes and the melancholy music, that brought me to the verge of tears.

It was only when the song ended I started wondering where Mum had got to. She'd been in the bathroom forever. When she finally returned, her face was ashen. She almost looked like she was about to faint.

'Did you see a ghost?' I said.

'Something like that,' Mum replied. Then she told me we should go home. She was feeling dizzy.

19

Susanne had lit a fire in the living room. She was sitting on a sheepskin rug on the floor holding a big glass full of something pink, staring into the flames.

'Are they asleep?' she said without looking up.

'Yes.'

'Tim's really not himself,' Susanne said. 'He's always been anxious, but it's got a lot worse since Isak left.'

'Something happened in the car earlier as well,' Charlie said. 'He was scared and Nils said he sees dead people.'

'Nils and his film quotes,' Susanne sighed. 'But Tim, I'm genuinely worried. Remember Karla, my aunt, the one who saw butterflies on black walls and talked to people who didn't exist?'

'I remember you talking about it, but I don't think I ever met her.'

'You probably didn't because she was more or less locked up her entire life. Sometimes, my nana would tell me to be careful or I'd end up like her, she'd say that kind of nervous condition was genetic.'

'If that's true, then how would being careful help you?'

'I don't know. I suppose that's why I was scared. What if Tim has inherited Karla's mental illness?'

Charlie looked out the window; the autumn night had enveloped the yard; the only thing she could see was the faintly yellow glow from the lone light by the gate.

'Tom saw someone, too,' she said.

'What do you mean?' Susanne stared at her.

'Tom said he saw someone in the garden, too, down by the swings. Does he imagine things, too?'

A vague unease fluttered in Charlie's chest when Susanne shook her head. She'd hoped the boys' virtually identic genetic make-up would be able to reassure her, that Tom also had a habit of seeing things others didn't.

'Tom's nothing like Tim,' Susanne said gravely. 'Not when it comes to imagining things. I'm scared, Charlie. I'm really scared.'

'Is there anyone around here who doesn't like you?' Charlie asked.

'These days I feel like the whole town hates me.'

'I don't understand why,' Charlie said. 'If they want to be angry with anyone it should be Isak.'

'But Isak's not here,' Susanne replied. 'And the sins of the fathers, right?'

Charlie nodded. She was Betty Lager's daughter; she knew all about the sins of the fathers, or in her case, mothers.

'But you're not related to Isak.'

'I'm his wife. That's as close as it gets in most people's opinion.'

'But you didn't do anything wrong.'

'Tell that to the town gossips.'

'Who are?' Charlie said. 'Who are these people who judge you and spread rumours?'

'It's more sophisticated than that, Charlie. I can't believe you've actually forgotten what it can be like here.'

Charlie took a big gulp from her glass and closed her eyes. Betty and her at the supermarket. Betty throwing random things into their trolley, dog food instead of cat food, tinned goods, napkins and plastic cutlery. People turning to look at her, whispering, laughing. Betty is oblivious, but Charlie's not. She notices everything.

'I haven't forgotten,' Charlie said.

She thought about the looks she'd got in the pub earlier. She had forgotten nothing.

'It could be about you, too,' Susanne went on. 'Maybe some nutbag followed you down here from Stockholm.'

'Why would anyone do that?'

'Well, there must be nutbags in Stockholm, too.'

Charlie quickly ran down the list of men she'd met recently. Anders liked to joke that it was just a matter of time before she picked up a lunatic, that she should run her hook-ups through the system so she could at least weed out the worst of the creeps.

'Or it's someone from around here,' Susanne said. 'Someone wondering what the fuck you're doing here and why you're going around asking questions about Gudhammar and Francesca Mild.'

Charlie shook her head.

'Maybe we're blowing this out of proportion,' she said. 'It could just have been a neighbour walking their dog.'

'By our swings?' Susanne retorted. 'And besides, we don't have any neighbours.'

20

In the end, even Susanne felt it was time to go to bed. Charlie fired off a text to Johan about being in possession of the case file. And then, the question: *Do you want to read it together?*

His reply was instantaneous: *Absolutely. Come over.*

Hibben, who was asleep on the sofa, inevitably woke up when Charlie walked by. He started whining but quieted down when she stroked his back.

The darkness outside was compact. Charlie looked down towards the swings. Everything was quiet.

It was the same in Gullspång town centre; not a soul in sight. The dark, deserted town square made Charlie remember the fear that had overcome her on occasion when she was a child, the one about being the last person on Earth. How many times hadn't she slipped into Betty's bedroom in the middle of the night, just to make sure she was still in her bed, breathing? *Stop creeping around like a ghost, sweetheart. I'm here.*

The Motel's front door was locked; Charlie had to call Johan to ask him to come down.

'Isn't it funny,' he said, pointing towards the bar, 'that it's all in there, that we could just go in and pour ourselves a drink if we fancied.'

Charlie thought wonderful was a more appropriate word for what it was. She would have loved to mix herself something strong.

'Is everything okay?' Johan inquired. 'How's Susanne holding up?'

'She's having a rough go of it,' Charlie replied, 'but she'll be alright.'

Discovering that Johan was in the room she'd stayed in last summer made Charlie vaguely uneasy. It was the room she'd drunkenly dragged Johan back to, getting herself suspended from the investigation. She was having a hard time getting over how stupid she'd been.

For everything you do and don't do, forgive yourself.

Johan pulled out the desk chair for her and took a seat on the bed. Charlie opened the file to the first page.

'Why is the interviewer's name redacted?' Johan asked.

Charlie looked at the black blotch where the lead interviewer's name should be.

'Maybe because someone made a mistake.'

'Then why not get rid of the whole thing?'

'Good question; maybe because someone made two mistakes. We're going to have to look up who worked for the local police in the eighties.'

The first few pages contained a brief summary of events, most of which they knew about already.

Francesca Mild had disappeared sometime during the night of the 7th of October 1989. Her passport was missing as well as some cash. A few weeks before her disappearance, Francesca had discontinued her studies at the Adamsberg boarding school following a suicide attempt.

'Suicide attempt,' Johan said. 'Did you know about that?'

'No, but Micke said something about depression. And I talked to a man in the pub today who called her mentally ill.'

'That might point to suicide then, after all.'

'Sure, but they should have found her if that were the case, right?'

Francesca's parents had also mentioned their daughter's mental illness. Francesca had always tended towards destructiveness.

Were they suggesting Francesca might have taken her own life? the anonymous interviewer asked.

Neither parent thought so.

But hadn't she just been discharged from the hospital following a suicide attempt?

Fredrika Mild explained that it had been a misunderstanding, that it hadn't been a suicide attempt but rather a cry for help.

Johan's phone went off.

'I have to take this,' he said after a quick glance at the screen.

He picked up the phone and left the room while Charlie continued to read.

She'd reached a section of questions about whether the family had any enemies. According to Rikard Mild, they didn't, but his wife reported the occasional sinister visitor at the manor. Who they were, she couldn't say. She couldn't remember names or faces.

Charlie reread the passage. *Sinister visitors.* She closed her eyes. Betty's hand reaching for the knocker, the other one squeezing hers so hard it hurt. The cracked door, the pleading.

I just want ... we have to ...

Leave, before I call the police.

We need to talk. Please.

This was no time to think about Betty. But she couldn't hold it back any longer. Were there even more things Betty had kept from her? That incident when she and Nora were thirteen, the little boy they'd never meant to harm, but who had been found strangled ... had it in fact been premeditated? Was that boy the first victim of a murderer, a murderer who would continue to kill long after released into society? Charlie tried to tell herself what had happened had been the work of two vulnerable little girls, a joke that went too far and turned serious, a one-off event, an accident. Betty hadn't been evil. Betty had been impulsive, crazy and ... She closed her eyes. Betty's hands in her hair. Waltzing through the cherry orchard during warm summer nights: *Don't look down! Relax. It's just a game, sweetheart. It's not serious.* Betty Lager – dancer, party thrower, drinker: *Turn the music up and let your hair down, people! What's the point of going to a party if you won't dance?* And then, the other side of her. Betty Lager – mournful mother, hiding from light and sounds, blackout blankets, staring at the wall. And then, a third version: Betty the protector: *Don't catcall when I'm with my little girl!*

Anyone who touches a single hair on my daughter's head ...

She's too smart for you. She's smarter than all of you. I have the world's oldest daughter.

No one knew Betty Lager. Of all the friends that had come and gone in Lyckebo, there wasn't one who truly knew her. *Not even me,* Charlie mused. *I didn't know my own mother. The only thing I know for sure is that she kept secrets, that she wasn't who I thought she was.*

She walked over to the window. Somewhere out there was the river, the fields, the forest, but in the dark autumn night, she could only see as far as the closed old smelter. A handful of streetlights lit the entrance to the compound. How many times had Betty walked through those gates to the place that *could drive the most stable person insane*? Too many times, Charlie thought. Because Betty hadn't exactly become more stable after she started working among the *hell fires*.

Johan returned.

'You okay?' he said.

Charlie opened her mouth to say she was. But instead, she said no. No, she wasn't okay. She pointed to the documents and told him about the sinister visitors, how well that tallied with her own memories.

'I don't care how Betty was involved in this,' Charlie said. 'It's too much for me.'

'Just because she was there doesn't mean she ... I mean, it's like with the passport,' Johan said. 'Just because it was missing doesn't mean Francesca left of her own accord.'

'No, but it *could* mean that,' Charlie said. 'And that my mother with her violent background was one of the sinister visitors ... I'm having a hard time with it.'

Johan picked up the file from her lap and quickly read through the page he'd missed while on the phone.

'It doesn't necessarily mean ...' he tried again.

'We're going to have to find out,' Charlie said. 'We're going to have to find out what it means. Let's keep reading.'

Francesca

I lay awake, staring at the ceiling. It was two in the morning. Dawn was an eternity away and my thoughts were stuck in their usual loop. I remembered what Paul had said once, about the benefits of writing thoughts down, that it could help clarify things and illuminate patterns and contexts.

The only thing I could find to write on was a grid paper notepad, but it would have to do.

I wrote like a maniac for the rest of the night. I didn't bother with chronology or any other kind of system. I just wrote my memories down in the order they came to me; they ended up being short, dreamlike paragraphs.

Doctor Molan says memories are unreliable and mutable, I wrote, then I chewed the pencil for a while before continuing: *They can be lost, manipulated and false and if you add things like sedatives, alcohol and drugs, they obviously become even less reliable. Conclusion: My memories from the night of the ball need not be true. The yellow rose, the royals' wet clothes ... it could all be the result of intoxication, a dream, a hallucination. And no matter how much I want to, Doctor Molan says, I can't coax memories out of oblivion. I can't fill in the gaps. It's a complex process that can't be controlled by an effort of will. So instead of tormenting myself, trying to remember, I should focus on something else, according to Doctor Molan. I should simply forget about the whole thing.*

I would like to tell Doctor Molan that forgetting is a complex process that can't be controlled by an effort of will.

I read what I'd written and felt an unusual sense of pleasure course through me. I was going to turn over every rock, write down everything I remembered, dreamed, believed and suspected. Maybe that would kickstart my memory, and if not, at least it would impose some sort of structure on my thoughts.

The next day, Mum told me we were going to have dinner guests. When I asked why, Mum looked at me uncomprehendingly and said because it's nice to have company. It was a successful young couple who happened to be in the area. Perhaps a more festive atmosphere would do me good, she thought. Give me something else to think about.

Before the guests arrived, the house had to be cleaned and of course panic ensued when Mum realised the paper with the names and contact details of all the people who worked for us wasn't in its usual place on the noticeboard.

'Where's the note?' she asked me. 'Where's the note with all the numbers?'

I said I had no idea.

'What do we do now, Rikard?' Mum turned to Dad.

'Why don't you just use the phonebook,' I said. 'It has everyone's number, right?'

'Yes,' Mum said, 'we could do that. The problem is I can't remember her name, the woman who comes in. Do you recall, Rikard?'

Dad shook his head.

'Carola,' I said. 'Her name's Carola.'

They both stared at me. The two people who were incapable of doing their own cleaning had a daughter who at least knew the name of the woman who did it for them.

Carola came on a Friday, the day before the successful couple was joining us. She was a fairly recent hire; I'd only met her a few times the previous summer. All I knew about her was what I could see. Something told me she liked a tipple. I don't know what I based that on; it was just a hunch. A few times, she'd brought her daughter with her, a pig-nosed little girl who didn't answer when spoken to.

I sidled up to Carola while she was vacuuming the first-floor landing. She was working frantically; I clearly disturbed her rhythm when I unplugged the vacuum.

'What are you doing?' she demanded. Her face was red from the exertion.

I'd been planning to chat with her for a while, but now I couldn't think of a single thing to say, except my actual reason for addressing her.

'Would you mind buying me a bottle of wine?'

'Why would I …' Carola frowned. 'I mean … aren't you too young?'

'Yes,' I said. 'That's why I'm asking you.'

'How old are you?'

'Seventeen,' I said.

'You look younger. You're very … skinny.'

'That's just because I'm depressed.'

Carola reached for the vacuum plug.

'A Lambrusco Donelli,' I went on. 'It costs fifty kronor. I'll give you a hundred for it. Two hundred if you buy two.'

Carola's eyes flashed.

'But if something were to happen ...' she said.

'What could possibly happen?' I said. 'I'm not asking you to peddle drugs. A bit of wine's never killed anyone.'

Carola chuckled.

'You're funny.'

I thought to myself that if I was anything, it was thirsty.

'But you're wrong,' she went on.

'What?' I said, thinking she was referring to the thing about wine never killing anyone.

'About the price,' she replied. 'It's thirty-eight kronor a bottle, the Donelli, I mean.'

The next day, when she told me in a whisper that she'd hidden the bottles in the big hole down by the birch trees, like I'd asked her to, I gave her a hundred extra just for being honest about the price.

The successful young couple travelling through the area was due to arrive at five on Saturday. Mum asked me to help her with dinner prep at one. I said I was busy.

And what was I so busy with? Mum wanted to know. I said I was busy writing because I wanted to avoid a lot of follow-up questions. Writing took up more and more of my time; it had expanded to include other things than that particular night and Paul. I wrote about the future that might not be mine, about being a stranger in the world and in my own family. I wrote about what my day had been like, about simple things like what I'd had to eat and how the digging had progressed. I, who usually grew bored of things almost before I started, had never felt so motivated.

I pulled on my dressing gown and went out to the big barn that had once housed two hundred milk cows, sheep, pigs and horses. It was sad, I mused, that there were no animals left on the farm. Dad had sold the lot the moment he bought Gudhammar because animals required employees and were not profitable, plus, he and Mum spent most of the year in Switzerland.

The stable aisles were clean but there were still a number of hay bales in the loft. I started climbing the rickety ladder to the loft with my notebook under my arm. When I was halfway up, the barn door was thrown open behind me and Ivan entered.

'What are you doing?' he said when he spotted me on the ladder.

'I'm going up to the loft,' I said.

I felt uncomfortable accounting for my actions to Ivan. His frequent silent appearances at the farm were creepy.

'What are you going to do up there?'

'Be by myself.'

'That ladder's very old,' Ivan said.

'So?' I said.

'I'm just wondering if it might collapse. It's quite a fall.'

He nodded up at the hayloft.

'I think it'll hold,' I said. 'What are you doing here, anyway?'

I suddenly came to think of the time when Ivan killed a litter of kittens. He'd filled a sack with rocks, put the kittens in it, tied it up and thrown it off the bridge in town. He'd told me about it without a hint of emotion.

'I'm just picking up some things, my hacksaw, for one, and a hedge trimmer that belongs to me.

'Great,' I replied. 'I hope you find your things.'

Was I imagining, or was Ivan peeking in under my dressing gown? I was wearing nothing but pants and a tank top underneath. And why was he just standing there if he'd come to fetch his tools?

'Okay, see you, then,' I said, because I was done with Ivan.

'No,' Ivan said. 'You won't see me again; this is the last time I'm coming over.'

'Alright,' I said and pulled the dressing gown tighter around my body. 'Bye.'

I built myself a small hideout out of dusty hay bales. Then I picked up my notebook and began to write. I'd become increasingly poetic, I noticed. Even Miss Wilhelmsson would have approved of my similes.

I'm an odd bird. I'm the fifth wheel, the thirteenth fairy, the eternally unwelcome guest. I am a stranger in this world. I stopped writing and reread the last sentence: *I am a stranger in this world.* It felt familiar. I was sure I'd read it somewhere. But what difference did that make? My task was neither to write originally nor well. My task was to try to remember, to bring order to events and rehabilitate Paul.

When I heard Mum calling my name, it had been nearly an hour.

'You can't just wander off,' Mum told me when I returned to the house. She'd come out onto the front steps. 'You scared me half to death.'

'I was just in the barn so there's no need to get all tense.'

'How was I supposed to know that?' Mum retorted. 'You're supposed to let someone know if you leave. You seem to enjoy upsetting me.'

'I was just in the barn,' I repeated. 'I wanted to be alone for a while.'

Mum shook her head and went back into the house.

'What are we cooking,' I asked when I joined her in the kitchen.

'Just a roast,' Mum replied.

Only now did I notice that she looked sad.

'Is everything okay, Mum?'

Mum looked at me in surprise. I realised how unused she was to me sounding friendly.

'I'm fine,' she said. 'I'm just ... a bit tired.'

'Mum,' I said, 'are you happy?'

'Happy?' Mum said, as though she'd never heard the word before. 'Why do you ask?'

'I was just wondering. I didn't mean to upset you.'

'I'm not upset,' Mum said and cursed when she dropped a spoon into the pot.'

'Not upset and not happy?'

'I'm fine. I have everything I could ever want. If that's happiness, I guess I'm happy. What's happiness to you?'

'I know very little about happiness.'

'You can make the salad,' Mum said, handing me a very sharp knife.

'Isn't it a bit early?'

'No, we'll just cover it and stick it in the fridge.'

I started chopping tomatoes, cucumber and lettuce.

'Be careful not to cut yourself,' Mum admonished. 'It's a very sharp knife.'

She stopped what she was doing and looked at me.

'Are you in a hurry, Francesca?' she asked.

'No, I was just thinking ...'

'Don't tell me you're thinking of going back out to dig again.'

'What's wrong with digging?'

'It's very odd behaviour. Are you aware of that?'

'It's harmless,' I said, chopping even faster. 'It's harmless and I like it, so what's the problem?'

'The problem is we can't have giant holes in the ground in our garden. It's not a laughing matter, Fran, holes that deep can be a hazard.'

'*One* hole,' I said, holding up a finger. 'And it's several hundred yards from the house.'

'Either way, Adam's filling it up as we speak,' Mum said. 'Don't, Francesca,' she called after me when I dropped the knife and ran out, 'just let Adam sort it out.'

Adam had just started shovelling dirt back into the hole when I arrived. He paused and looked at me with something resembling fear.

'Stop,' I said. 'Stop it right now.'

'Are you alright, Francesca?' Adam stuck the shovel in the ground. 'Did something happen?'

'I just don't want you to fill the hole up.'

'But Fredrika said ...'

'I know what she said, but this is my hole.'

'I understand,' Adam said.

He looked lost, standing there next to the hole, holding his shovel; the poor sod probably didn't know what to do about the contradictory orders.

'You can stop now,' I said.

Adam put the shovel down and obeyed.

'Can I just ask you something?' he said.

'Sure.'

'Why is this hole so important to you. Why are you digging so much?'

'I just want to see how deep I can go,' I said.

21

Rikard Mild didn't take the sinister visitors as seriously as his wife. According to him, it was just random people from the town, people looking for work or to borrow money, or people who were simply intoxicated and looking for a chat. It had been like that since he was a boy. Maybe it was no wonder in a place like Gullspång. Lack of money really had a way of making people forget their pride. Charlie wished she could travel back in time and take the place of this anonymous interviewer. She wanted to bang her fist down in front of Rikard Mild and demand to know who these people were. He must have known.

In the next section, there was a statement from Francesca's psychiatrist, a Doctor Sixten Molan. According to him, Francesca was clinically depressed and suffered from delusions. Just a few weeks before she disappeared, he'd warned her parents that she was still an imminent suicide risk.

Charlie was surprised at how detached Molan seemed to be from his young patient; perhaps it was his frequent use of psychiatric terms that created that impression. He sounded so cold, as though this girl was just a collection of symptoms, a problem that existed inside her, which no one could solve.

'Did you talk to this psychiatrist when you worked on your article?' Charlie asked.

'No,' Johan replied, 'this is the first I've heard of him. But he certainly seems to have made his mind up about what happened to Francesca.'

But if she killed herself, Charlie mused, her body should have been found. Shouldn't it? The image of Mattias's body splitting the surface of Lake Skagern suddenly flashed before her, the ripples around him, and then, within a minute, the lake had been a mirror once more, completely still. Mattias had never been found, either. Lake Skagern was deep and dark. A body could get caught in the currents, get stuck somewhere and never resurface. But usually, as she was well aware, bodies floated back up.

They took a break and started googling Sixten Molan.

'If he's alive, we need to find him and talk to him,' Charlie said. 'If Francesca was his patient, he should have access to information no one else has.'

'If he's alive, we'll find him,' Johan replied.

'He's been very productive,' Charlie said, scrolling through Doctor Molan's many published works on mental illness.

She ended up on a site where someone had posted an article from Gullspång's local paper. It was from 1987, a man in his fifties was sitting on a white wooden bench suspended like a swing from the veranda roof of a green turn-of-the-century house. He had a lit cigar in his mouth and was smiling broadly at the camera. *Professor Molan relaxing at his summer residence*, was the headline; in the text that followed, Charlie read that Doctor Molan, after a long career in the capital, had now permanently relocated to Gullspång. The rest of the article was vapid drivel about green thumbs and the clinic in his home where he, when he wasn't gardening, would still see the occasional patient.

In the next section of the case file, there were interviews with students from Adamsberg. They were all very brief. Francesca was described as lonely, unmotivated and depressed. She'd had only one friend at the school, Paul Bergman, and after he died, it was as though she'd withdrawn into her own world.

'Paul Bergman,' Charlie said. 'I'll check him out.'

She pulled out her phone and did a google search.

'Too many hits,' she sighed.

She added Adamsberg to the search field and clicked the first link that came up. It was a webpage entitled 'The Autumn Ball', which turned out to contain photographs of dressed-up Adamsberg students since ... 1970. Johan leaned in over her shoulder and read. *On the first of September every year, the high school students at Adamsberg celebrate the start of a new term full of knowledge, development and friendship.* Then followed pictures of students from 1970 to the present.

Charlie scrolled down until she got to 1988. Both Paul and Francesca should be in those. But a quick glance at the names under the picture revealed that neither of them was. She had to scroll down to 1989 to find one of them. According to the caption, Paul Bergman was standing on the far left of the middle row. Charlie zoomed in. Dark, serious eyes under a long fringe, a tailcoat that looked several sizes too big and a yellow rose in his breast pocket. But it wasn't just the ill-fitting tailcoat that set Paul apart from his classmates, everyone else in the picture was coupled up, boy and girl; the boys' bowties matched the colours of their dates' dresses. Paul had no girl by his side. Was Francesca Mild supposed to have stood there? Why was he alone?

They returned to the case file. They'd reached the transcripts of the interviews with the servants at Gudhammar. Considering that Gudhammar had only been a summer residence, the Milds had had an impressively large staff. There were carpenters, cleaners, gardeners, nannies and handymen. The question of whether anyone wanted to harm the Milds had been posed to them, too, but there was unanimous agreement: the Mild family had no known enemies. And then there was a familiar name. Carola Johnsson, 'cleaning lady'. Charlie checked her personal identity number.

'I know her,' she said, pointing to Carola's name. 'It's Susanne's mother.'

'It is? Does she still live in town?'

'Yes, but I'm not sure talking to her would do much good.'

'Why not?'

'Booze. She was sober for a while, but she recently fell off the wagon again.'

'Tragic,' Johan said. 'Why are so many of the locals here having such a hard time?'

Charlie didn't respond. She could go into how unemployment and social vulnerability often led to meaninglessness, anxiety, illness. But right now, she wanted to focus on Francesca Mild.

'Did you know Susanne's mother used to work there?' Johan went on.

'No,' Charlie replied. 'I don't think Susanne knows. At least she didn't mention it when I talked to her about Gudhammar.'

Carola Johnsson had told the interviewer Francesca was depressed. The girl had told her herself when she'd asked Carola to buy her wine.

And then, when Carola was asked if she had bought

Francesca wine, the reply was firm. Of course not, the girl was underage.

The last person interviewed was a man by the name of Adam Rehn. He'd worked at the manor for a few years but had been let go right before Francesca disappeared. He was aware she wasn't well and had come home from school, but other than that, he had no information about the Milds. He just looked after the garden.

Why had Adam Rehn been fired? the interviewer had wanted to know.

He didn't know.

And he hadn't asked?

No.

Why was that?

He just hadn't asked.

Adam, Charlie mused. Was that a common name in Gullspång? She searched for his name. There was a forty-nine-year-old man in Gullspång by that name who owned a local business, Gullspång Landscaping. She did an image search and one look at the first photograph that came up confirmed he was the man she'd met in the pub.

'He still lives in Gullspång,' Charlie said. 'He runs Gullspång Landscaping. I talked to him and his co-workers earlier today.'

'Did he say anything useful?'

'It was before I'd seen the case file. But I did ask about Francesca. That's when I was told about her mental illness. But Adam didn't say anything about working for the family.'

'People here are like clams,' Johan observed, 'especially with outsiders.'

'I know,' Charlie replied.

'Isn't this just a few too many coincidences?' Johan said.

'I guess that should be expected in a small place,' Charlie replied, even though she felt he was right.

Her mother and Susanne's, a place she'd visited at night with Betty. There was some kind of connection and she knew she had to find out what it was. It was too late to back out.

'Did you talk to anyone when you were researching your article?' she asked.

'I just read clippings from back then,' Johan said. 'It was all there was. I tried to locate the Milds, but there was no trace of them anywhere. And I contacted a few of Francesca and her sister's old schoolmates, but no one wanted to talk to me. After that, I called Olof Jansson.'

'And what did he say?'

'That he didn't work in Gullspång at the time, but that he was familiar with the case. He said the girl had most likely left voluntarily or killed herself.'

'How hard would it have been to find a runaway teenage girl, especially given that the family had ample resources at their disposal?'

'Francesca had resources at her disposal, too,' Johan retorted.

'And if she killed herself,' Charlie pressed on without commenting on Francesca's resources, 'where's the body?'

'Some bodies are never found.'

'Is that what this is about?' Charlie exclaimed. 'Your dad? He drowned, Johan. I saw it with my own eyes. Lake Skagern's deep and ...'

'I know, but what are the chances of two people disappearing from here, never to be found? And most people who drown do resurface eventually. No matter how deep the water is.'

'You think Francesca Mild's disappearance is connected to your father's death?'

'Probably not. Do you?'

'What?'

'You seem pretty keen to dig into this, too. I'm guessing it's more than just a random cold case to you. I mean, what you said about your dreams, Gudhammar and Betty and ...'

'Maybe it's the other way round,' Charlie said. 'Maybe I'm hoping not to find out any more horrible things about Betty.'

'So it is about Betty.'

Charlie shrugged. She was sick of Betty. Sick of everything still revolving around her. She recalled her therapist's words: *if your aim is to avoid being your mother, you're still using her as your reference point. You may not be able to step out of her shadow until you start acting without reference to her.*

'Whatever it's about,' Charlie said, 'I want to know what happened.'

'I'm in,' Johan replied. 'But what do we do when people start asking why we're poking around?'

'We tell them you're writing a series of articles about missing people. What's the problem?'

'They know you work for the police.'

'So you do the talking. I'm just here on vacation and we know each other. Problem solved. But I think we've done what we can tonight.'

'Let's talk again tomorrow,' Johan said with a big yawn.

Charlie put a hand on his shoulder and was just about to say bye when he hugged her.

'What are you doing?' she said.

'Sorry,' Johan released her. 'I thought ...'

'Don't apologise.'

She leaned in closer.

'Are you sure you want to?' Johan asked as he pulled her top off.

She nodded.

It was only afterwards, as she staggered out of bed and started to pull her clothes back on, that she put her finger on why it had felt so odd. She'd just had sex without a drop of alcohol in her blood.

'See you tomorrow?' Johan said as she made towards the door.

'Of course. We have a case to crack.'

'Charlie?'

'Yes?'

'Drive safe.'

22

Summer, night. The tree-lined road to Gudhammar Manor.
Charlie and Betty. Charlie looks up at the sky and the trees,
but it's not trees flanking their path, it's shadowy people with
hands like claws, contours of faces she recognises but can't
place, girls in ballgowns and boys in tailcoats. And then, at
the end of the road, fluttering police tape. Betty's gone.

Charlie was woken up by something wet on her toes. She
pulled her legs up; for a second, she thought it was a badger
licking her toes. But it was the dog. Charlie pushed it away
and tried to gather her thoughts. Her brain felt tired and
sluggish. What time was it? She reached for her phone on the
nightstand. Quarter to nine.

There was no sign of Susanne downstairs, but the coffee was
fresh. Charlie poured herself a cup, sat down at the kitchen table
and stared out at the garden. She thought about the investigation into Francesca's disappearance. Why had it been wrapped
up so quickly and who was the interviewer whose name had
been redacted? She made a list of things to look into: find out
who worked at the police station in 1989. Find out if Doctor
Molan was still alive and if so, talk to him. Try to find anyone
who knew more about Paul Bergman and how his suicide had

affected Francesca. Ask Adam Rehn why he'd stopped working at Gudhammar. Locate the rest of the Mild family.

She fetched her laptop. It took her less than ten minutes to establish that she was unable to dig up contact details for anyone in the Mild family.

She slipped into Isak's clogs, pulled on a jacket and went outside to call Anders.

He answered straight away.

'Are you free to talk?' she said.

'And how do you do to you, too.'

Charlie sighed. Anders was always quick to point out her lack of social graces.

'How are you?' she said.

'I'm horrible, thanks for asking.'

Charlie realised she should have called him sooner. Considering what he'd told her about his marriage, she really should have, but she hadn't taken what he said all that seriously. But it was serious; she could tell from his voice.

'Maria and Sam have moved in with her parents. She needs time to think.'

'I'm so sorry, Anders.'

'Me too,' Anders replied. He coughed as if to hide a sob.

'Are you sure you should be at work?'

'Working's what's holding me together. I can't stand to be at home.'

Charlie didn't know what to say. In a way, it would be good for Anders to divorce Maria, but he was not receptive to that particular truth right now.

'I'm sure it'll work out,' she said.

'Anyway, what can I do for you?' Anders said.

Charlie told him what she needed help with.

'I'll look into it and get back to you,' Anders said.

'Hey, how's the investigation going? Made any progress?'

'Not even a little, I'm afraid. I'll keep you posted.'

'Thanks. I'll talk to you soon, okay?'

Susanne was walking towards her across the lawn. There was light-blue paint spatter on her clothes.

'Are you alright?' she asked. 'You look a bit low.'

'I slept poorly, is all.'

'Me too,' Susanne admitted. 'I lay there, listening for noises, imagining someone lurking in the yard.'

'I went to The Motel last night to talk to Johan, the journalist,' Charlie told her. 'I managed to get my hands on a case file yesterday, the Francesca Mild case, her disappearance.'

'Why did you want to talk to him about that?'

Charlie explained.

'And what did the case file say?'

'Some new things.'

'Any connection to Betty?'

'No, but did you know your mum used to clean at Gudhammar?'

'She did?'

'Yes, she was one of the people interviewed by the police.'

'What are you implying?' Susanne burst out. 'Are you telling me I might also have a mum who ...'

She trailed off as though she realised how inappropriate the rest of the sentence would be.

'I'm not implying anything,' Charlie said. 'I'm just telling you what I read in the case file.'

She briefly summarised what it had said about Carola.

'Buying booze for a minor seems to be all she's guilty of, then.' Susanne looked relieved.

'She didn't buy Francesca any booze,' Charlie said. 'At least not according to what she told the police.'

'Of course she did,' Susanne retorted. 'I know my mother. But admitting it to the police is a different matter.'

'Would she have lied about other things, too?' Charlie said. 'Or failed to mention them?'

'Don't know,' Susanne said. 'I guess we just have to ask her.'

She pulled her phone out of her trouser pocket. Charlie heard it ring and then go to voicemail.

Susanne checked the clock on the wall and said Lola was probably still asleep. She would try again later.

'I really hope she wasn't involved in anything bad,' Susanne said. 'I can't bear finding out about any more shit committed by my relatives. I feel like I've had more than my fair share of that.'

Me too, Charlie thought. We've both had more than our fair share.

Charlie sat alone in the kitchen. Susanne had returned to the barn. She took out her phone and called Johan.

'Did I wake you?' she asked when he answered, sounding drowsy.

'No, or actually, yes, you did.'

'Sorry.'

'No, I'm glad you did. I mean it's … fuck, it's almost ten.'

'Are you ready to start trying to talk to some people?'

Gaps in Time

Me and Paul under the Weeping Willow down by Adamsberg Lake.

Paul is reading to me from Sylvia Plath's *The Bell Jar*. He thinks I might like it and he's right. I'm destructive like Esther Greenwood, but sadly lack her passion. I giggle at her spot-on analyses of the meaninglessness of existence and her revulsion at being married to a stupid man.

Why would anyone ever want to marry a stupid man? I say, putting my head on Paul's shoulder.

You shouldn't, Paul tells me. If you do marry, it should be with someone on your level. Someone you can talk to.

I'm not the kind of girl who dreams of marriage, I tell him. I'm not normal. Besides, you're the only one I can talk to.

Paul looks up from the book, studies me and says he's not normal either, but that I'm the only one he could marry if he were.

23

There was no sign of Johan in the restaurant. Linda, the motel owner's frosty wife, was behind the bar; when Charlie asked if she could order breakfast, Linda replied it was too late, that the breakfast buffet had been cleared away an hour ago.

'Ask her what she wants,' her husband, Erik, called out from the kitchen regions. Moments later, he emerged through the swing door behind the bar.

'What would you like? We can rustle up pretty much all the usual things.'

'Just coffee and a sandwich. Or, actually, two coffees and two sandwiches,' she corrected herself. 'I'm waiting for someone.'

'Sure.' Erik threw his wife a sour look before going back into the kitchen.

'What's the point of having rules and structures if you're always breaking them?' Linda shouted after him.

Johan smelled of cologne, fabric softener and ... cleanness.

'I'm afraid the breakfast buffet's closed,' she said, 'so I hope you can make do with coffee and a sandwich.'

'Sounds perfect,' Johan replied. 'I'm not a breakfast person.'

He hid a yawn behind his hand.

'Oh my god, I'm tired,' he said. 'I couldn't fall asleep after you left. It was a lot to take in.'

They started talking softly about who should be at the top of their list of people to talk to. They were interrupted several times by Linda circling them, wiping down tables.

'I just tried Adam Rehn,' Charlie said, 'but he didn't pick up, on his mobile or at home.'

'Who even has a landline these days?' Johan said. 'But this Molan, is he alive?'

'I haven't been able to find anything on him,' Charlie said. 'But he's not registered as deceased in the databases either.'

Erik came out of the kitchen to ask if they needed anything else.

'Can I ask you something?' Charlie said.

'Ask away.'

'You've lived here a long time, right?'

'My whole life.'

'Do you know a Doctor Molan?'

Erik shook his head. He didn't know anyone by that name.

'But maybe you know who worked for the local police in the late eighties?'

'That I do, as it happens. I had some run-ins with the law back then, derestricting mopeds and making moonshine, you know.' He smiled as though those were things all teenagers did. 'It was Lars-Göran Edwardsson and one other bloke, Christer Mörk, but he killed himself, sadly.'

'How come?' Johan asked.

Erik shrugged.

'The usual; I guess he couldn't take it any more.'

'It was his nerves,' said a voice from behind the bar.

Everyone turned to Erik's mother, Margareta.

'Stop eavesdropping, Mum.' Erik rolled his eyes at Charlie

and Johan. 'She always does this, lurking about, eavesdropping and sticking her nose in.'

'I do not,' said Margareta. 'But that man had weak nerves, everyone knows that. I just wanted to let you know, since you asked. He hanged himself in the stable on his farm. His eldest girl found him. She was never the same after that, mark my words, because ...'

'I don't think they were looking for a local history lesson, Margareta,' Linda broke in. 'All they wanted to know was who worked at the police station back in the eighties.'

'How come?' Margareta asked.

'It's for me,' Johan said. 'I'm writing about people who have gone missing and ...'

'You're thinking of Francesca Mild,' Margareta said.

'Yes. Do you know about her?'

'Of course, she was that upper-class girl who ran away from her family.'

'Or something else might have happened to her.'

'Like what?'

Margareta looked troubled. Had she missed something?

'Well, she was never found.'

'So you think ...?'

'We don't know,' Johan told her. 'But I'm going to try to find out what I can.'

'Let me know if I can be of any help,' Margareta said. 'I don't mean to blow my own horn, but I know almost everything about the people in these parts.'

'Do you know a Doctor Sixten Molan?' Charlie asked.

'The man from Stockholm?' Margareta said in a tone that made it abundantly clear what she thought about people from Stockholm. 'I do, as a matter of fact. He's that stuck-up doctor.'

'Do you know where he lives?'

'The home,' Margareta replied without hesitation. 'The nursing home,' she clarified. 'Amnegården.'

'Do you know if he would be able to talk to us?' Johan asked.

'I couldn't tell you,' Margareta replied. 'Some of the people up there are completely batty and others are just there because they're ancient and can't look after themselves.'

24

The wind was picking up. Colourful autumn leaves swirled around their legs as they walked to the car. Charlie looked over at the laburnum outside the pub's dining room. The yellow racemes were wilted and brown now. Time was passing so quickly. She didn't know if that made her feel stressed or relieved.

'So, where do we start?' Johan asked. 'Want to head up to the nursing home?'

'Let's hold off on that for now. I'd like to go out to Gudhammar again,' Charlie said. 'Look around. Get a feel for the place.'

Charlie parked next to the small house at the end of the tree-lined road.

Johan looked up at the big yellow manor house looming up before them.

'Quite a place,' he said and then, when they got close enough to see the peeling paint, the missing roof tiles, the weeds carpeting the gravel driveway: 'Why would anyone let a house fall into this kind of disrepair? I don't understand why you don't just sell it if you're not bothered to maintain it.'

Charlie thought about Lyckebo. She understood all too well.

'Let's go inside.'

'Isn't it locked?' Johan said just as they reached the front doors. He tried the handle.

'Let's go inside anyway,' Charlie said.

'Are you saying we should break in?'

Charlie nodded and pointed to a ground-floor window with a missing pane.

'No,' Johan said, 'we can't do that.'

'Who would find out?' Charlie said. 'The place is abandoned. Come on, give me a hand.'

'I just don't get why?'

'Give me a boost,' Charlie said. 'I want to see what it looks like inside.'

Johan did as he was told. Charlie's fingers located the hook on the inside and the window swung open. She climbed in but misjudged the distance to the floor and fell when she jumped down. In front of her was an enormous table ringed with about twenty chairs. The walls were hung with paintings of grave-looking men. When she crossed the room to reach the hallway to open the door for Johan, she heard Challe's voice in her head: *This is breaking and entering, Charlie. What the fuck are you thinking?*

'Come on in,' she said once she'd managed to turn the bolt and open the door.

Johan looked over his shoulder and entered.

'This is bloody insane,' he whispered.

'I don't think there's any need to whisper,' Charlie said. 'I imagine you could shout at the top of your lungs without anyone hearing.'

*

Next to the parlour-like room Charlie had entered through was a library. The walls were covered by dark, built-in shelves.

'That's one high ceiling,' she said. 'It's enough to make you dizzy when you look up.'

'Could we please hurry up?' Johan said. 'Haven't we seen enough?'

'Let's just have a look upstairs first,' Charlie said.

'I'm staying down here,' Johan replied.

'Why?'

'In case someone comes.'

'I don't think you need to worry about that,' Charlie said.

Johan shook his head.

'I'll wait downstairs.'

Charlie climbed the long staircase to the first floor. It all reminded her of returning to Lyckebo last summer. There was a similar smell of wood, dust and abandonment in the air, the same feeling of abrupt departure: moth-eaten clothes hung over chair backs, wineglasses sitting out on the kitchen table, shoes ready to be put on in the hallway. The only thing missing was the people.

She entered a room that must have belonged to one of the sisters: a desk with several drawers, a long shelf with books on one wall and a large gold-framed mirror. She turned her flashlight on the bed and noticed a cushion with an embroidered, old-fashioned F. It was Francesca Mild's room. Charlie paused in the doorway, trying to imagine Francesca in the room. She conjured an image of her sitting cross-legged on the bed and behind her, her blonde sister, both wearing nightgowns. Her sister pulling a brush through Francesca's hair. But no, that wasn't right. Francesca hadn't been the type to spend evenings fussing with her hair and giggling. Charlie thought about the descriptions of her in the case file. Francesca was depressed, alone, grieving. She was a young girl drawn to darkness, a young woman who had tried to take her own life. Charlie entered the room and looked at the bed again. This time, Francesca was lying on it, alone, staring at the ceiling. Charlie placed the same weight on her chest that she herself had often wrestled with in the wee hours. Then she let Francesca get up, take out her passport and gather up some clothes before leaving the room. Was that what had happened? Had someone been waiting for her? And what had been so serious it had made a sixteen-year-old girl leave her home forever?

Charlie closed her eyes. When she opened them, Francesca was back. This time, she was sitting at her desk with her face in her hands. Was she crying? Was she scared? Charlie wanted to go up to her, put an arm around her shoulders and ask her what was wrong. What happened to you, Francesca? Where did you go?

Francesca

Our dinner guests arrived at quarter past five. They were both ridiculously beautiful and well-dressed, and effusively thrilled to see Mum and Dad's summer house.

'Such high ceilings,' the woman exclaimed, taking in the dining room.

'Don't be fooled,' I thought to myself.

'And this must be the daughter.' The woman smiled too broadly, shook my hand and told me her name was Mikaela.

I introduced myself.

'But you have a sister, too, right?' said the man, who was, comically, named Mikael.

His smile was as blindingly white as his wife's.

'She's at school this weekend,' I told him.

'What a shame,' Mikaela said. 'I've heard so much about both of you.'

I must have unconsciously pulled a face, because she hurried to add that it was all nice things, of course.

I couldn't bear joining them for their tour of the house, but I heard Mikaela's delighted exclamations as Mum guided them from room to room. It was going to be a long night; I spared a grateful thought for Carola, who had kept her promise and delivered my wine. I'd already downed two glasses in my room and given how thorough my Mum's tour of the house was turning out to be, I might have time for one more.

Mum had gone on and on about how she wanted to keep things simple, but the dinner was, predictably, extravagant. It became clear Mikael and Mikaela were unaware of my history, because they talked to me without restraint, asking questions as though I were just a regular teenager.

Then their focus moved on from me and Mikael started talking about his background. It felt like he was reading from a book. I did my best to look natural and interested. Whatever becomes of me, I thought, studying Mikael's exaggerated gestures as he described something I had long since stopped listening to, whatever becomes of me, I hope I never become the kind of person who smugly goes on and on about their own CV like this. Mikaela's account of herself was every bit as detailed as her husband's. She had studied law originally, but had found working as a lawyer too constricting. She had a need to think outside the box. She explained about the business idea she and Mikael had come up with. And then they'd met Dad, and he'd seen their potential and agreed to finance several of their recent ventures.

At that point, I had stopped listening entirely, because if there was one thing I was fed up hearing about, it was Dad's investments and partnerships; his success never failed to make me gloomy.

I thought about my future career. What was my CV going to look like? Who was I going to be?

No matter what life I imagined for myself, it always ended in darkness. I could picture myself with three well-behaved little children and a husband in a suit, family dinners, clinking crystal glasses, sparkling eyes in candlelight. Quick cut to: burnt-down candles, silence, the miserable mother of three rummaging through a cupboard for a bottle to drink straight out of.

Another scenario: Me in a run-down attic flat in a big city somewhere in the world, working as an artist, having dinner on the floor, friends with depth and soul. But then the perspective shifts to show the flipside: men who are nothing but husks, hangovers, exhaust fumes and loneliness.

I thought longingly of the wine in my room. When would I be able to leave the table without being rude?

Something was amiss with Mum; her hand was trembling visibly whenever she picked up her glass. She was never one to take up space around the dinner table, but this time she seemed even more self-effacing than usual. I couldn't help feeling sorry for her. Dad, who often claimed to be so proud of Mum, made no effort to include her in the conversation, as usual. He laughed and talked shop with the young couple as though they were the only three people in the room.

'Francesca?'

I looked up.

Mum shot me an embarrassed look.

'I'm sorry,' I said, not knowing what I'd done wrong.

'Well, go on, answer,' Mum said.

'Answer what?'

'I was just asking what your plans are after graduation?' Mikaela said, pushing her food around her plate like someone with an eating disorder.

I'd had enough classmates at Adamsberg with that problem to recognise the signs.

I said I hadn't decided, but that I was either going to study medicine or law. I added that I burned for so many different things I felt I might literally burn out. Mikaela laughed and said I had to make sure I didn't burn out, because if there was one thing the world needed more of, it was skilled doctors and lawyers.

Dad shot me a tense look. He was smart enough to know I was lampooning her and might drop the pretence at any moment.

'If you do choose law school,' Mikaela said, 'is the idea to work as a lawyer?'

I said that was the idea.

'And if you become a doctor,' Mikael said, 'are you thinking of any particular specialty?'

'I would love to be a cardiologist,' I said (where did I get these things from?). 'I've always been interested in the human heart. Did you know, by the way, that human hearts and pig's hearts are very similar?'

Dad laughed and said he thought he'd heard that somewhere.

Mikaela started talking about a failed heart transplant her friend had undergone. Everything had seemed fine at first, but then ... she paused for effect for far too long before telling us about the unhappy outcome.

When everyone was done eating, I was unable to keep pretending to be a normal young woman. I excused myself, saying I had some things to see to.

'Leave it,' Mum said when I picked up my plate.

I had planned to go up to my room, but instead I fetched the wine bottle and snuck out of the house. I wasn't tired enough to go to bed; I was just bored of the company.

When I reached the driveway in front of the house, I heard

something. I stopped and peered down the dark, treelined road.

'Hello!' I called out. 'Is anyone there?'

'It's me,' answered a voice I recognised as Adam's.

'What are you doing?' I said.

'I'm just taking a walk.'

Only then did I realise he was slurring his words. He approached me, swaying as he walked. A moment later, he had stepped into the light and became fully visible.

'Are you drunk?' I said, though it was obvious.

Adam nodded. He was very drunk.

'And you?'

'A bit tipsy,' I admitted.

'I've been down the pub,' Adam said, pointing in the wrong direction. 'I've been trying to drown my sorrows.'

'What sorrows?' I said, because I'd always thought of him as carefree.

'I don't work here any more. I'm out.'

'Why?'

'No idea. Rikard just told me I was fired.'

'I'm sorry,' I said. 'Want some?'

I held out the wine bottle. Adam nodded, took it and started drinking it down like it was water. I had to take the bottle from him to prevent him from emptying it completely.

'Thanks,' he said, wiping his mouth. 'So, what are they up to in there?'

He nodded towards the house. The light from the candelabras flickered in the living room window.

'Dinner,' I said.

'Isn't that nice.'

Adam fumblingly pulled a packet of cigarettes from his

jacket pocket, extracted two Prince and handed me one. I took it without comment and cupped my hands around it when he lit it. He was going home now, he said. He didn't know why he'd come out here at all.

'Take care,' he said as he staggered down the tree-lined road. 'I hope we meet again, Francesca. I hope we meet again once you're even more beautiful than your mother.'

'Thanks!' I called after him, though I didn't understand what he meant.

I finished the cigarette and took a few more big gulps of wine before I went back inside.

That night, Mum came up to my room and sat down on the edge of my bed. She asked if it was true I was considering studying law. Because if so ... well, then that was fantastic. I could already hear her twittering with her girlfriends: *Imagine, my youngest daughter, following in my footsteps. Maybe my interest in justice is genetic somehow?*

Mum prattled on about how perfect my choice of profession was. And so convenient too, because she still had all her coursebooks. Some of them might be outdated, but that was no problem; after all, they could just buy new ones.

25

What's that?' Johan said in the car on the way to the nursing home, pointing at the railroad.

'The draisines?' Charlie looked at Johan. 'Are you telling me you don't know what a draisine is?'

'I'm guessing it's a type of bike you ride on rails?'

'Not as dumb as you look, eh?'

'But why?' Johan said.

'Because it's fun, I guess.'

'Have you ever gone on one?'

'Everyone here has.'

But the truth was, Charlie had only ridden a draisine once. It had been one of those days when Betty was becoming manic and wanted to do things. She'd packed a lunch, scraping together whatever they had in the cupboards, and bathing suits for both of them. It had made no difference that it was raining out because it was bound to clear up, Betty felt. Charlie had been tasked with pedalling. They had been working their way up a mild incline and it had been heavy going. Betty had sat with her legs crossed next to her, singing one of the songs she always hummed when she was in a good mood. Charlie had felt relieved once they'd left the town behind and were surrounded by nothing but trees and water.

We could ride all the way to China this way, sweetheart.

Stop being weird, Mum.

I'm not being weird. This railroad goes all the way to China. We could go there. What's to stop us?

A couple of oceans.

You're a killjoy, Charline; how did I get such a serious child? I think you're the oldest person in the world. I have the world's oldest daughter.

The rain hadn't let up, but Betty thought they should stop and go for a quick swim anyway. *Don't be such a scaredy cat, sweetheart. Just get in. It feels cold at first, but you get used to it, you get used to the cold quickly.*

On the way home, Betty had wanted to pedal. They'd flown through the forest. Charlie had sat curled up for warmth and not seen the boom barrier, the one you were supposed to stop at and open. It had struck Betty in the chest and Charlie in the head. She'd been unconscious for a while and came to with Betty crying next to her. *I thought you were dead, sweetheart. I thought it was all over.*

Charlie had been to the nursing home once before, with school. She remembered thinking all the shrivelled faces had been sad. When she'd told Betty about it afterward, Betty had said she never, ever, ever wanted to end up in a place like that. She never wanted to be abandoned, confused and ill, to the care of strangers. *If I get confused and ill, sweetheart, you have to promise to help me.* And Charlie had nodded and pretended she knew what Betty meant by help.

The place was the same, Charlie noted. Long hallways with striped yellow and brown linoleum floors and sofas, tables and spinning wheels that looked like they were from the turn of the century in the bay windows. The antique furniture looked strangely misplaced in the seventies building. The walls were hung with black-and-white photographs, all from Gullspäng. Charlie stopped in front of a picture of children staring intently at men digging holes in the ground. *A fifth-grade class from Gullsten School at an archaeological dig at the ancient monument, 1975*, said a note under the photograph.

'Recognise anyone?' Johan said.

'No, that's before my time.'

The hallways were strangely deserted, but they soon came across a man mopping the floor.

Charlie apologised and asked if he knew where Doctor Molan's room was.

'Straight ahead and then the first door on your right,' the man said, pointing. 'And don't ring the bell,' he warned them. 'The gentleman doesn't like loud noises.'

Charlie gently tapped a door with a sign on it that said Sixten Molan. A wheezy voice on the other side called out: 'Come in.'

They entered straight into a room that served as both hallway and living room. A white-haired man was sitting by the window with his back to them.

'Doctor Sixten Molan?' Charlie said.

The man slowly turned to them.

'I didn't know I was expecting visitors,' he said.

Johan briefly explained why they'd come, that they were writing about missing people; Charlie noted a faint hint of something akin to apprehension in the old man's face when Johan mentioned Francesca Mild.

'I'm a psychiatrist,' said Doctor Molan. 'I'm not at liberty to discuss my patients.'

He's not confused, Charlie thought, and he doesn't seem to have forgotten the rules of his profession.

'Maybe you could at least listen to our questions,' Johan said. 'And then you can see if you want to answer them.'

'Unfortunately, I'm not going to be of any help to you. I have my physician-patient privilege to consider.' Doctor Molan had put a finger across his lips as though his words needed underscoring.

His way of talking reinforced Charlie's impression of him from the case file. He spoke with the kind of upper-class accent that always rankled her.

'Surely you are allowed to breach that privilege if murder is suspected?' Charlie said.

'Murder?' Doctor Molan raised his bushy white eyebrows. 'I thought the girl ran away? Or did something to herself. I didn't realise there was ever any proof of a crime having been committed?'

'New information has come to light,' Charlie said, not caring that she was treading on very thin ice.

'What new information?'

'I'm not at liberty to discuss that,' Charlie said, resisting the impulse to put a finger across her lips. 'Are you in touch with the Mild family?'

'They live abroad,' Doctor Molan replied. 'In Switzerland.'

'I see,' Charlie said. So that's why they hadn't been able to find any Swedish contact information. 'But you are in touch with them?'

'No, I'm not.'

'Any particular reason why not?'

'As I said, they don't live in Sweden,' said Doctor Molan, as though that were reason enough. 'I haven't heard from them in decades.'

'So there's no unfinished business between you?' Johan said.

'Such as?'

'I'm just asking.'

There was a brief pause.

'Coffee?' Doctor Molan said. 'Can I offer you some coffee?'

He pushed a red button dangling from a strap around his left wrist; moments later, a nurse dressed in blue entered.

'What is it this time, Sixten?' she said.

'I was wondering if you wouldn't mind fetching us some coffee; I've run out and I believe there must be some left over from this morning?'

'Sixten,' the nurse said sternly, 'your alarm button is for emergencies, if you fall down or can't breathe. You can't use it for things like this; how many times do I have to tell you that? What if someone else had needed me right now? What if I run over here unnecessarily and someone dies because of it? Can't you understand how serious this is?'

'I'm terribly sorry, Annelie,' Doctor Molan said in a tone that revealed he wasn't particularly sorry at all. 'It won't happen again. But since you're here anyway, would you mind bringing the coffee?'

Annelie sighed and said she didn't have time to run to the kitchen and back.

'If you show me the way, I can do it,' Charlie offered.

She followed Annelie into the hallway. The nurse's rubber-soled shoes clacked a rapid staccato against the floor.

'Are you family?' she asked.

'No, we're here to talk to him about an old patient of his.

My friend Johan is writing an article series about cold cases, missing people who were never found.'

'Is it a case I might have …'

Annelie broke off.

'Take those cards from him,' she told a young nurse's assistant sitting next to an old man in one of the windows. And then, to Charlie: 'He just rips them up. I don't know how many decks of cards he's turned into confetti, and we have no money to buy new ones.'

'Is that The Motel?' Charlie said, without commenting on the home's lack of funds.

Annelie glanced at the picture and confirmed that it was.

'All the pictures are from around here. The old people like it; they find relatives, friends and remember buildings that have been torn down. The idea was to hang them in chronological order, so they would show how the town has developed, new buildings, events and everyday scenes through the decades, but they ended up jumbled. A good thing too, I reckon, because they barely build anything new; it would be depressing to look at.'

They'd reached the kitchen. An old woman in a wheelchair with her foot in a cast and rollers in her hair was sitting alone at the table. She was mumbling something.

'Did you say something, Asta?' Annelie asked.

'I was asking if this is it?' said the woman named Asta. 'If there's nothing more?'

'We're out of pastries,' Annelie said.

Asta sighed; Charlie sensed her question hadn't been about baked goods.

'Here,' Annelie said, handing Charlie a thermos she'd filled. 'It's still warm. He has cups in his room. Make sure he washes them, even if he tells you he can't.'

Charlie took the thermos, thanked the nurse and started back towards Doctor Molan's room. She walked slowly, studying the pictures on the walls. She stopped in front of the picture of The Motel again. Stepped in closer and read the caption underneath. *Preparations for the Harvest Festival, 1986.* A man (Erik's dad?) was hanging a banner above the entrance; at the edge of the photograph, a small group of men and women could be seen carrying amplifiers and microphone stands.

'Did you have to make the coffee?' Doctor Molan asked when she returned.

'No,' Charlie replied. 'I just took the opportunity to look around, all the pictures on the walls. It's fun to see what the area used to look like.'

'You think? I'm not from here so it's lost on me. I used to come down for the summers, but then I stayed and ... well, that's how things turned out. I should really find a nicer assisted living facility in Stockholm, but the truth is I'm too tired.'

He sighed.

'Let's sit in the parlour,' he went on. 'The colour palette of this room makes me miserable.'

As they drank their coffee, Doctor Molan boasted about himself, his years in Stockholm, his education and research. He could have gone on forever if Johan hadn't eventually cut him off and reminded him why they were there.

'This doesn't feel like an interview,' Doctor Molan said. 'More like an interrogation.'

'We just want to talk to you and see if you remember anything you didn't tell the police at the time,' Charlie said.

'I barely remember what I said. It's almost thirty years ago.

And unless this is a formal police interview, I'm not going to discuss my patients.'

'That might make you guilty of obstruction of justice,' Charlie said.

'You can't be serious, girl.' Doctor Molan put his cup down with a bang.

'I'm a woman,' Charlie said, 'not a girl.'

Doctor Molan shrugged as though it was all the same to him.

'My name is Charlie and I'm a detective inspector,' she continued. 'And as I said before, there's no physician-patient privilege in murder cases.'

'Why didn't you say so straight away?' Doctor Molan asked. 'That you're with the police, I mean? And how do we know it's a murder case? That girl was her own worst enemy, that much I know. And after what happened to her best friend, well ... maybe it's no wonder she chose to end it all.'

'You're referring to Paul Bergman?'

'Yes, that was his name. He killed himself but Francesca refused to accept it.'

'That he was dead?' Johan asked.

'That he killed himself. She'd got it into her head he was murdered. In fact, she was obsessed with it.'

'Maybe he was,' Charlie said.

'No.'

Doctor Molan shook his head.

'How can you be so sure?'

'Because Miss Mild was unable to tell fantasy from reality. Perhaps she didn't mean to lie; sometimes I think she believed her own stories, but that didn't mean they were true.'

'Surely it doesn't follow that you can't believe anything she says?' Charlie said.

'No, just that you can't believe everything she says.'

'Do you know if anyone looked into whether Paul Bergman's death might have been suspicious?'

'I don't know. I'm not a detective inspector.' Doctor Molan smiled condescendingly.

'Did she tell you who she thought had killed him?' Charlie asked.

'I don't remember a name. But, as I said, it wasn't something anyone around her took seriously.'

Charlie stood up.

'If you think of anything else, please don't hesitate to call.' She handed him a card with her number. 'And I would appreciate if you didn't tell anyone we were here.'

'Who would I tell?' Doctor Moran said. 'I have no friends here.'

Big shock, Charlie wanted to say.

'If you see Annelie or anyone else in the hallway, please tell them I need help with the washing up,' Doctor Molan said when they were putting their shoes on.

'Annelie told me you're supposed to do it yourself,' Charlie replied.

'What happened to you lying low and letting me do the talking?' Johan asked as they walked to the car.

'The only thing that man cares about is status and authority; I felt I had no choice.'

'What do you think about Paul's suicide?' Johan said. 'Could Francesca have been on to something?'

'I think we should look into it. I don't trust Doctor Molan's judgement, and if he was in fact murdered, we might have a motive for Francesca's disappearance. Maybe someone had a reason to want to get rid of her.'

Francesca

'Fran?' Mum said on the other side of my door. 'Can I come in?'

I put my notes away. 'Is it important?'

'I have something for you.'

'Fine, come in.'

Mum came in and handed me a black box with gold lettering.

'What is it?' I asked.

'Open it and see.'

I opened the box and held up the necklace it contained. The pendant was a pair of golden scales.

'My dad gave it to me when I started studying law,' Mum said. 'My old initials are etched on the back. It's the first two letters of your name, so that's nice.'

I turned the scales over and saw a tiny F on one of them and an R on the other.

'Let's see if it looks good on,' Mum said. 'Hold your hair up.'

I felt the weight of it around my neck when Mum closed the clasp. I liked it.

'It looks lovely on you,' Mum said.

'What about Cécile?' I asked.

'She wants to study finance,' Mum replied, 'so I figured it would suit you better.'

I walked over to my large full-length mirror. Mum came up behind me.

'It's beautiful,' I said. 'Why don't you ever wear it?'

'I don't know,' Mum said. 'Actually, I think it's because it makes me sad.'

'Why?'

'Because I dropped out of my studies and the necklace reminds me of that.'

Mum's voice cracked a little and I felt like something broke inside me. I looked at her face; maybe I'd misjudged her. She had wanted something else once, something more. I had reduced her to a puppet, a person without dreams and goals, a shallow soul. But she was more than that. She'd been more than that. She's not happy, I thought to myself. She's as unhappy as I am.

'With an education, you can have a different life from me,' Mum went on. 'It will make you more ... free.'

'Thank you,' I said.

After Mum left, I took off the necklace and turned it over in my hand, studying the F and the R. I pulled out one of my desk drawers and found the small pocket knife I used to whittle with when I was little. In the space after the two letters, I carved in two Es. FREE. Then I put the necklace back on.

26

They climbed in the car and drove away from the nursing home.

'I think I should contact more of Francesca's classmates from Adamsberg,' Johan said. 'I still have the lists of former students.'

'Good,' Charlie replied. 'How about we talk to Adam Rehn next, since we're out and about anyway? His company's in Nunnestad.'

'And where's Nunnestad?'

'A few miles outside town.'

Gullspång Landscaping was based in a shed-like building next to a residential house not far from the church.

'Hard to imagine he's a gardener,' Johan commented, nodding towards the garden, which was neglected, to say the least.

They walked up to the residential house and knocked on the door. After a while, shuffling steps could be heard from inside. An older woman in a dressing gown with old-fashioned curlers in her hair opened the door a crack and peered out at them suspiciously.

Charlie introduced herself and asked if Adam was home.

'Is this about Alexander?' the woman asked. 'Has he been causing trouble again? I've told him to stay in his room when he's not in school, but what can I do when he keeps sneaking out?'

'Adam doesn't live here?' Johan asked.

'He does, but he's at school, isn't he?' The woman looked at them worriedly. 'Is he causing trouble now, too?'

Charlie exchanged a quick look with Johan.

The woman began to fumble through the pockets of her dressing gown and at length pulled out a packet of cigarettes. She put one in her mouth and sighed when she couldn't find a lighter.

'Here,' Charlie offered.

She dug a box of matches out of her bag and held them out to the woman.

'Thanks.'

A car turned into the driveway. It was Adam.

'Mum,' he said as soon as he got out of the car. 'Is everything okay?'

'Oh yes,' his mum said. 'I'm just talking to these nice people. They're from the school; they've come to sort your brother out.'

'Go inside, Mum,' Adam said. 'And please don't smoke.'

The woman sighed and dropped her half-smoked cigarette on the porch without stubbing it out, before turning and going back into the house.

Adam studied them with eyes that held none of the warmth that had been there when he talked to Charlie in the pub the day before.

'What do you want?'

'We just wanted a word with you,' Johan said. 'I'm writing an article about ...'

'I don't give a toss about your articles,' Adam said. 'You can't just go to a confused old person's home and bother her.'

'We thought you lived here,' Charlie said.

'I do live here, with my mum. And as you might have noticed, she's not well and strangers make her nervous.'

'We're very sorry,' Charlie said. 'I tried to call before coming out, but you didn't pick up.'

'I've been busy with work and Mum never picks up unless she knows the number.'

Charlie looked towards the closed door. Tried to imagine the isolated life the woman inside must lead. She couldn't.

'Do you have a minute to talk to us?'

'I'm working,' Adam replied. 'I don't have time for idle chitchat. I only came back to check on Mum.'

'When are you done for the day?' Johan asked.

'I don't know. But it doesn't matter. I have nothing to say.'

'I understand,' Johan said. 'But it would be really helpful. You worked for the Mild family, right?'

'As I said,' Adam said. 'I don't want to talk to you; that's a closed chapter as far as I'm concerned. Now you'll have to excuse me.'

He walked past them into the house.

'We just wanted to know why you quit,' Charlie called after him.

Adam slammed the door shut behind him without replying.

'We're off to a great start,' Johan commented as they climbed back into the car.

'That he doesn't want to talk to us suggests he has something to hide.'

'But where do we go from here?'

'You have to be patient,' Charlie told him.

'Patience isn't my forte.'

'Mine neither.'

The restaurant part of the pub was almost full. Most of the guests were dressed in work clothes, hi-vis jackets and trousers with reflectors or more traditional blue overalls. A lot of them probably worked in the plywood factory.

Margareta was clearing a table. Charlie studied her sweaty forehead. She looked tired. How old was she anyway? Sixty-five? Older?

'You pay at the bar,' she said when she noticed them, 'then you can grab salad and bread from over there. We'll bring the food out to you.'

Was Charlie imagining it, or were people staring at her and Johan as they went to pay?

When they got back, Margareta was already bringing their food out.

'Are you coming to the Harvest Festival tomorrow?' she asked. 'It's going to be a night to remember.'

She was interrupted by a snort of laughter from one of the men at the table behind her.

'What's so funny, Ralf?' she said.

'Nothing,' he replied.

'Then why are you laughing?'

'It was just your choice of words.'

'Which words?'

'That it was going to be a night to remember. It just struck me as funny given as how a lot of people tend to have trouble remembering the Harvest Festivals. Surely that's no secret?' he went on when Margareta glared at him.

'I think a lot of people do remember,' Margareta said.

'Susanne and I will be here,' said Charlie, who wanted to end the conversation so she and Johan could talk in peace.

'Susanne Johnsson?' Margareta asked.

'Yes.'

'I haven't seen her in here since I don't know when.'

'Well, she's coming tomorrow,' Charlie said.

Fifteen minutes later, the dining hall was empty.

'What happened?' Johan asked. 'How quickly do these people eat?'

'Probably as quickly as they have to,' Charlie replied. 'It's a workday.'

'Surely they get lunchbreaks like everyone else?'

Charlie shrugged and recalled Betty's complaints about vile shift leaders who timed every break. It sucked, she'd griped, that people had to choose between going to the toilet and eating. If she was ever made a manager, she'd let her employees do both.

Margareta had started to clear the table next to theirs.

'Can I ask you something?' Charlie said.

'Of course,' Margareta replied, 'ask away.'

'Do you know Adam Rehn?'

'Of course I do. He's one of our regulars.'

'What's he like?'

'What he's like?' Margareta seemed thrown by the question.

'Yeah, what's he like as a person?'

'I don't know him that way.'

Charlie waited. She could tell from the look on Margareta's face there would be more.

'But I suppose he's what people call a womaniser,' Margareta said at length.

'Oh yes?' Johan urged her on.

'I'm not sure there's much more to say than that he likes women, simply put.'

'And the women?' Charlie said. 'Do they like him?'

'They do,' Margareta said with a grin. 'At least they seem to.' She looked around. 'He's broken up quite a few marriages in these parts, let me tell you. One time, he even tried it on with my daughter-in-law, but that made Erik put his foot down. I reckon it was six months if it was a day before we saw him in here again.'

'But he's not married himself?' Charlie said, even though she knew the answer.

'No, he lives with his sick mother.'

'We just met her.'

'Poor woman.' Margareta shook her head. 'It's a wonder Adam manages, with her being so senile. She lives in a different time, thinks her boys are still children and ... well, maybe it's for the best, that way she doesn't have to remember what happened to the older of them.'

Johan put his cutlery down.

'What happened to her oldest?'

'That boy, Adam's brother, oh, what was his name ... Alexander. He caused trouble, set things on fire, stole things, was violent. When he was fourteen, he got drunk, took his mother's car and drove straight into a lorry. Dearie me.'

Margareta was interrupted by the sharp ringing of a phone behind the bar and rushed off.

'So many people are dead here,' Johan commented.

'No more than in other places, I reckon,' Charlie retorted.

'Maybe not, but I feel like there are more. Too many people who died young, a lot of accidents and tragedy. It's just so sad.'

Charlie agreed; it was sad.

She brought the conversation back to Adam Rehn, a womaniser and homewrecker, a man who had worked as a gardener for a family whose youngest daughter had disappeared. How come he'd been fired from Gudhammar?

Margareta returned to their table.

'Why are you so interested in Adam Rehn?' she asked. 'He's not suspected of anything, is he? I mean, considering what you're writing about? Well, that poor rich girl didn't seem very happy, despite being so … rich.'

Charlie fixed Margareta with a stare.

'What do you think happened to her?'

'She disappeared.'

Yeah, we got that, Charlie thought to herself.

'We're thinking that's not what happened,' Johan put in, 'that she didn't disappear of her own accord, I mean.'

'You think she was murdered?' Margareta asked.

Her eyes widened; Charlie could almost hear her relaying this information to other patrons: *someone killed that poor girl.*

'We don't know,' Charlie replied. 'The case was never solved.'

'It's like with Annabelle,' Margareta said. 'I know, there was no evidence of foul play or however the papers put it. But that doesn't necessarily mean there wasn't foul play.'

'True,' Charlie agreed.

She couldn't quite decide if Margareta was stupid or shrewd; her analyses were so … uneven.

'We have no reason to believe the cases are connected,' Johan said. 'We don't know if either girl was the victim of a crime.'

He sounded like a police press officer to Charlie's ears.

'As I mentioned, I'm writing an article series about unsolved cases,' he went on.

Charlie didn't know if she found it impressive or frightening that he sounded so believable.

'You're counting the Annabelle case as solved then,' Margareta said. 'People around here aren't as sure about that, I'll have you know.'

'Who?' Charlie said.

Margareta turned to her and said it was a widespread opinion and she wasn't about to name names. But surely they could agree it was strange that a girl would 'fall' into the river from a high bridge in the middle of the night.

'If you know anything that could warrant the police reopening the case, it's important you tell me,' Charlie replied.

'I'm just saying it's strange,' Margareta said, spreading her hands. 'That's all I know, that it's strange.'

Charlie thought to herself that it was, but that it was also perfectly possible, that unfortunately, accidents involving drunk young people were fairly common.

'Do you know anything else about the Gudhammar family?' Johan said. 'Anything at all.'

'I don't think anyone around here knows much about them,' Margareta replied. 'Well, I suppose maybe the gatekeeper.'

'Who's the gatekeeper?' Charlie asked.

'The man who lived in the gatehouse at Gudhammar.'

'And where is he now?' Johan said.

'I'm afraid he's dead.'

Johan sighed.

'But he has a son,' Margareta went on. 'Ivan. Ivan Hedlund.'

'Is he alive?'

'He definitely was last week when he came in for lunch.'

'Where does he live?' Charlie asked.

'Eel Island.'

'And the address?' Johan asked.

Margareta said she had no idea, that it was a big red house at the end of the road.

'Just head towards the water.'

Gaps in Time

I'm in my bed in the dormitory. My housemistress is standing next to me in her yellowing nightgown and a nightcap that looks like it's from the nineteenth century.

What have you been up to, Francesca? she whispers. What on Earth were you doing outside in the middle of the night, and in your nightgown?

I tell her I was just out for a walk, that I was unable to lie still. Because of the air in here. It's so heavy to breathe.

My housemistress says that's nonsense, that no girl has ever complained about the air at Högsäter before.

It's inside me, I say softly. It doesn't really have anything to do with the air.

Then why are you going outside? My housemistress asks. If the problem is inside you, it doesn't matter where you are.

I open my mouth to tell her I feel better outdoors where I can move about freely, but there's no point. My housemistress and I belong to different species. We don't understand each other.

So, where did you go? my housemistress demands. You're not getting yourself into trouble, are you?

I shake my head and tell her I was just wandering about

randomly, that all I wanted was to take deep breaths. That's not true. I went over to Paul's dormitory to see if he had anything to calm me down. But when I peeked into the room he shares with a weird, quiet boy, his bed was empty. Where had Paul gone in the middle of the night? Where had Paul gone without me?

27

The farms were becoming increasingly few and far between. Charlie had visited the area a few times as a child; there had been a school field trip and Betty had taken her to visit an old man who had lambs. But she hadn't paid any attention to the beautiful old houses and farms. They passed an old schoolhouse that looked like it had first been converted into a residence and then an elaborate mansion that had probably been something to see once. The drainpipes had detached from the walls and withering climbers covered the walls. There was something both beautiful and melancholic about the dilapidation.

'He's in the barn!' a man in a green Helly Hansen jumper shouted to them as Charlie and Johan walked towards the entrance of the house at the end of the road. Charlie jumped; she hadn't seen him coming.

'Thanks,' she said.

'I'll go with you,' the man said. 'I have to help him with the piglets anyway.'

Charlie breathed in the familiar smell of hay, manure and animals as they stepped through the barn door.

'I found these in your garden, Ivan,' said the man, who still hadn't introduced himself. 'Figured I'd bring them over.'

'What do you want?' Ivan said.

'He was leaning over a blue plastic bin on wheels. His hands were covered in blood, Charlie realised.

'Stay!' he said to a large, wolf-like dog who was about to approach them. The dog stopped dead.

They introduced themselves and Johan gave his usual spiel about how he was writing about missing people.

'Is it urgent?' Ivan asked. 'I have some piglets here who need castrating.'

He nodded to the plastic bin.

Charlie took a step closer and realised the bin was full of sleeping piglets.

'I need to get it done before the anaesthesia wears off,' Ivan said, 'so if you want to talk to me, you'll have to do it while I take care of their balls. Or you can wait.'

'Maybe we should ...' Johan shifted uneasily.

'We want to talk to you about your father,' Charlie said.

'He's not missing,' Ivan replied, frowning. 'My dad's in the cemetery. Hand me one, Helmer.'

Helmer picked up a piglet by the legs and handed it to Ivan. Careless, Charlie thought as they strapped the small animal into a kind of steel device. Ivan cursed when he realised one of the parts was loose.

'Your dad's not the missing person,' Johan said. 'A young girl in the family he worked for is.'

'The Milds?'

'Yes.'

'I don't know much about it. I only went out there for the weekend sometimes. I'm a bastard,' Ivan said and spat in the manure gutter.

Who isn't? Charlie thought to herself.

'Can I ask why you ...' Johan nodded towards the piglets. 'Why you're removing their testicles?'

'The boar flavour,' Ivan said. 'Makes the meat taste bad.'

'Have they been properly anaesthetised?'

'Of course they have, why would I want to hurt them?'

Helmer handed Ivan a knife; he grabbed the tiny scrotum, made two quick cuts and pushed out two testicles the size of cherry pits. Then he picked them up and tossed them on the barn floor. Moments later, the dog had gobbled them up.

'Where are you going?' Charlie asked Johan who was heading for the exit.

'For a smoke.'

The two men worked in silence for a while. It was as though they'd forgotten Charlie was there. She could tell they were used to working together because they communicated without words. They handled the piglets together; Helmer handed Ivan the tools and the dog took care of the waste.

Charlie went outside to check on Johan. He was standing by the gable, smoking.

'Can I bum one?'

Johan nodded and handed her a cigarette and a lighter.

Charlie gazed out across the field and meadows. Far in the distance, between trees that had lost their leaves, she glimpsed the lake.

'Are you okay?'

'Yes, but it's unpleasant. They're so careless, treating them like ...'

'Animals?'

Johan smiled.

'I think those animals will have a better life than most,' Charlie said. 'Just look where they're kept.'

She pointed to a fenced-in pen behind the dunghill.

'But still,' Johan said. 'It bothers me.'

'That's a double standard.'

'That it bothers me to see them lift piglets by their hindlegs, cut out their testicles and throw them to the dog?'

'But you eat meat?'

Johan sighed. 'So do you, right?'

'Yes, but I'm not a hypocrite.'

'So you didn't feel anything in there?'

'I did.'

'So, what did you feel?'

'That maybe I should stop eating meat.'

The dog came outside. There were blood smears in the light fur around its mouth.

'I don't want it near me,' Johan said.

'I thought you were a friend of the animals,' Charlie said. 'You don't like dogs?'

'Not when their mouths are full of piglet balls.'

'You're from town, right?' Ivan said when they went back inside.

'Stockholm,' Johan said.

'No kidding,' Helmer commented drily.

'Like we said, we'd like to talk to you about the Milds,' Johan said, looking at Ivan.

'I don't think I'll be much help. I grew up with my mother. I spent some weekends at Gudhammar, but that was back when Mild Senior was running the farm, Rikard's father.'

'And you haven't been out there since? You never met Rikard or his family?'

'Obviously I was there, but that was much later, when I

was a grown-up. Dad had aches and pains and couldn't keep up with the work, so I helped him out. He felt like a burden sometimes and wanted to do right by Rikard.'

'Burden?' Johan said. 'I thought he worked for them?'

'Rikard's father, Ingemar Mild, hired him. In his will, he gave Dad the right to stay on the farm as long as he wished, rent-free, even if he was no longer able to work. But after Dad's back packed in, he felt redundant so sometimes I would pitch in and do some chores.'

'Did you ever meet Francesca?'

Charlie looked at him. Why was he taking so long to answer?

'I don't know about met,' Ivan said. 'I guess I would run into her from time to time, but we weren't friends or anything.'

'Were you enemies?'

'We were nothing. It was her father I couldn't stand.'

'Why's that?'

'Because he was a fucking prick.'

'Could you expand on that?' Charlie said.

'He was an evil bastard with a habit of exploiting people. Like what I told you about my dad, for instance. Rikard's father had promised him a pension and security and all that, but Rikard didn't give a shit. Dad lived off virtually nothing in his last years.'

'And Francesca Mild?' Charlie said in an attempt to bring the conversation back to why they were there. 'Any idea what happened to her?'

Ivan turned round and spat on the floor, next to the blood smear.

'No, but I shouldn't wonder if she did do herself in. She didn't seem well.'

'In what way?' Johan said.

'Well, it wasn't hard to put two and two together when she came back in the middle of term with sliced up wrists, acting weird.'

'Do you know if anyone disliked the family?'

Ivan let out a chuckle.

'Well, they weren't exactly popular, put it that way,' he said. 'Because they thought themselves above the rest of us. People who waitered parties they threw have told me they weren't allowed to use the fancy people's bathrooms. The Milds made no distinction between regular people and animals.'

Ivan pulled yet another sleeping piglet out of the bin.

'I suppose the short version is that they weren't much liked around here.'

'But do you know anyone who harboured a proper grudge? Someone who might have ...?'

'Killed?' Ivan asked.

Charlie nodded.

'No, I don't.'

'Thank you for taking the time to talk to us,' Charlie said. 'If you think of anything else, anything at all, call me, okay?'

She handed him her business card, the one that didn't have her professional title on it, just her name and contact details.

'This sounds like a police matter,' Helmer commented.

Charlie had almost forgotten he was there. He'd lit an old pipe and was eyeing her suspiciously.

'It's not,' Johan said. 'I just like to have all the facts when I write.'

'Well, now you know everything I know, anyway,' Ivan said. 'And you can have this back.'

He was about to hand the business card back to Charlie

when he dropped it in the yellow and red slurry in the gutter.

'Sorry,' he said.

As they were walking back to the car, Susanne called to ask if Charlie wanted dinner. Charlie glanced at the time. It was already half past four.

'I'm on my way,' she said.

She turned to Johan.

'Susanne's made dinner. Do you want me to call her back and ask if there's enough for you?'

'Thanks, but I think I'll eat down the pub tonight,' Johan said. 'Maybe you could drop me off there?'

'You look a bit pale. Was it the blood?'

'More like the whole situation, I think.'

'You really are from Stockholm.'

Charlie shot him a smile.

'Because I have feelings?'

'Because you don't understand how food gets on your plate.'

'I imagine it would have been different if I'd grown up out here.'

Johan looked out the window at a field where a flock of blackbirds was taking flight.

'If you'd grown up here, *you* would be different,' Charlie retorted.

Francesca

I'd been thinking more and more about visiting Paul's family. What prevented me was that I had such a hard time talking to people I didn't know, even more so if they were grieving. But I wanted to go. I wanted to meet his family, tell them about my suspicions and see what they thought about the whole thing. If Paul's father or brother told me to drop it, maybe I would.

I asked Mum to give me a ride to Paul's house after calling to ask if I could come by.

'Bergman's Funeral Home,' Mum read on the sign by the driveway. 'Paul's parents run it?'

'His dad and uncle,' I said, 'and his brother Jacob works extra there, too.'

'How old is his brother?'

'Nineteen or twenty, I think.'

'That's hardly an appropriate job for a young man,' Mum said.

'A job's a job. Paul used to help out as well sometimes.'

'Doing what?'

'Preparing the dead.'

Mum shook her head.

'Maybe it's no wonder he wasn't doing well.'

'It had nothing to do with the dead,' I said. 'The living were the problem.'

Mum dropped me off and told me to call if I wanted to be picked up.

I started up the gravel path to the house where Paul grew up. Even from the outside, I could sense this was a place of sadness, as if the trees and plants were drooping dejectedly. A rusty burgundy Citroën was parked in the driveway and under a big tarpaulin I glimpsed the boat Paul had told me about, the one they couldn't launch because there were so many cracks in its hull. I could picture Paul in the garden. This was where he'd been a little boy who made fires in the woods and followed his dad around while he worked with the dead. This was where he'd learnt to walk, ride a bike and drive a tractor. This was where he'd been stung by hornets and almost died of anaphylactic shock. That was one of the most dangerous things about living in the middle of nowhere, he'd told me, that it was so bloody far to the hospital.

The front door opened before I had time to knock.

'Did I scare you?' Jacob said when I took a step back. 'The doorbell's broken. Come in. Don't bother taking your shoes off; we haven't cleaned in a while.'

I followed Jacob inside. He was taller than Paul, I realised now, and more muscular, but his colouring, his dark hair and eyes, were exactly like Paul's.

We stepped into a dark, outdated kitchen. The lighting was so dim I didn't notice a man and an older, white-haired woman sitting at the kitchen table at first. They slowly got up when they saw me.

'This is Paul's best friend,' Jacob said. 'Please sit, Nana,' he went on when Paul's grandmother swayed and grabbed hold of the edge of the table.

I went over and shook their hands.

'Christer,' Paul's dad said.

'I'm his grandmother,' said the white-haired woman, who introduced herself as Annie.

She had the same warm brown eyes as her son and grand-sons.

'You're sweet to come by,' Christer said.

He was dressed in work trousers and a washed-out vest top. His clothes somehow clashed with the tears that suddenly started to stream down his cheeks and disappear into his beard.

'Would you like some coffee?' he said.

'Thank you. If it's not a bother.'

'There's a fresh pot,' Christer said and went over to a coffee maker on the kitchen counter.

He was stooped like a very old person even though he can't have been much older than forty. I mused that it was the kind of posture you might expect from a parent who had lost a child.

The absence of Paul seemed to fill every inch of the kitchen.

'Have a seat,' Annie said, nodding towards a chair. 'Sit, sit.'

I did as I was told and took a dry biscuit from the plate Christer brought.

'We haven't exactly been spoiled with visits from the posh people at Adamsberg,' Annie said. 'Not a peep from anyone since the funeral.'

'Not that we heard much from them before the funeral either,' Christer said. 'They just sent flowers, a bouquet that must have cost a fortune. Isn't it a waste, though, all those flowers?'

He turned and pointed into the house, to where I assumed the flowers were.

'They're keen on tradition,' I said, 'and given the tuition fees they charge, they can afford it.'

'Certainly can,' Christer agreed.

'We should never have sent him there,' Annie said. 'We shouldn't have sent him there to begin with.'

'We did what we thought was best.'

'You shouldn't have spent every last penny you had on sending him to a school like that. You shouldn't have.'

'Maybe you've forgotten what it was like for him here, Mum. Maybe you've forgotten what they did to him at the local school.'

Annie shook her head. She hadn't forgot anything. But the boy could have gone to some other state school, for god's sake. They could have moved somewhere else even. Anywhere.

'Nana,' Jacob put in, dunking his biscuit in his coffee, 'if we don't stop dwelling, we're going to lose our minds.'

'What's so bad about losing your mind?' Annie said. She reached for a biscuit. 'With the world the way it is, it makes more sense to lose your mind than to keep it. What do you think, Francesca?'

'I don't think either is easy,' I said. 'But the worst thing might be to be somewhere in between, I mean, to be aware of your madness.'

Annie smiled at me.

'You're wise,' she said. 'I can see why Paul liked you so much. You must have had a lot to talk about.'

'We did.' I coughed a few times to force back the tears threatening to well up at any moment. 'I want you to know that Paul was the smartest and funniest person I ever met.'

*

'Do you want to see his room?' Jacob asked after I'd eaten two biscuits and finished my coffee.

I nodded and followed Jacob into a parlour with the kind of old-fashioned, mismatched furniture that gave my mother a headache. The walls were hung with framed photographs of the family, two almost identical pictures of gap-toothed little boys.

'We both had very large heads,' Jacob said, nodding towards the pictures.

'Don't all children? I mean, relative to their bodies?'

'Sure, but ours were extreme.'

'Is that your mother?' I said, pointing to another photograph.

It was an unnecessary question because it was obvious the woman holding one boy by the hand and another on her lap and with the protective hand of a younger Christer on her shoulder was the mother Paul had been so reluctant to talk about.

'Yes,' Jacob replied. 'That's Mum.'

We walked through the rest of the house. It was large and in terrible need of cleaning: a house in which grief had settled like a layer of dust and dirt.

'Can I see Paul's room now?' I said at length, because I wanted to smell his pillow, see the things he'd touched, the clothes he'd worn. I wanted to be as close to him as possible.

We were interrupted by the phone ringing.

'Jacob!' Christer called. 'Would you mind?'

'Sure,' Jacob said and nodded to me. 'It's up the stairs on the left. Take all the time you need.'

I climbed the stairs, turned into the first room on the left and shut the door behind me. The room was, unlike the rest of the house, clean and tidy. The bed was made the same way they made us do it at Adamsberg, with everything stretched flat and tucked in under the mattress. I went over to the window. It overlooked a dense evergreen forest. I pictured Paul sitting there, gazing out at the woods, dreaming of a better future. I opened the drawers of his massive desk, one after the other. They contained nothing unusual: pencils, erasers and notepads. I got up and walked over to the dresser squeezed in under the slanted ceiling and started going through it. Since I didn't know what I was looking for, I made sure to be systematic and thorough. I moved on to the wardrobe and paused briefly, taken aback, when I saw Paul's familiar clothes. There was the shirt he'd worn on his first day at Adamsberg and the brown knit jumper that had lost its shape after he washed it on hot. I lifted piles of clothing, ran my hand under socks and T-shirts, but found nothing. I closed the wardrobe doors, sighed and scanned the room again. Then I got down on my knees and looked under the bed. Nothing. What am I doing? I asked myself. This isn't a story where I stumble across straightforward clues and explanations. I sat down on the bed and studied the books on the shelf on the other side of the room: *The Trial, War and Peace* and *In Search of Lost Time* next to philosophical works by Sartre, Camus and Rousseau. Typical Paul books, I mused, until my eyes found a title I would never have expected to find on Paul's shelf: The Holy Scriptures. The Bible.

28

The table was set and Susanne had lit candles.

'The idea was for me to help you, not the other way around,' Charlie said as she sat down.

'You have helped me, can't you tell?'

Susanne smiled and Charlie thought how different she was from the woman she'd found when she arrived a mere three days ago.

'How are you getting on?' Susanne continued. 'Have you found out anything else?'

'Not much. Do you know Adam Rehn?'

'I know of him, but no more than that.'

'Do you know anything about him?'

'Not personally, he's much older than me. But I've heard he's pretty flirtatious. You think he might know things?'

'Don't know,' Charlie said. 'But he used to work at Gudhammar.'

'So ask him.'

'He's not keen to chat.'

Isak wasn't scheduled to pick the children up until six, but by twenty past five, the twins were asking if they could go wait by the gate.

Charlie watched them go through the kitchen window. They were wearing identical football jerseys over their fleeces and pulling red suitcases. They went down to the bottom of the garden, clambered onto the gateposts and settled in to stare down the road. Time passed and dusk fell. Six o'clock came and went, then five past, ten past.

'What if he doesn't show up?' Charlie said. 'He will, right?'

'I certainly hope so.'

'Call him.'

Susanne picked up her phone.

'Turned off,' she said after a minute.

'Why isn't he here yet?' asked Melker, who had come downstairs. 'What's the holdup?'

'I thought you didn't want to go anyway?' Susanne retorted.

'I was going to, for their sakes,' Melker said. He'd gone over to the window and was nodding towards the two little people on the gateposts who were now barely visible in the gloom. 'I'll never forgive him if he stands us up.'

Yes, you will, Charlie thought to herself.

Ten minutes later, Susanne opened the kitchen window and called Tim and Tom back in. Ten minutes after that, she had to go out and get them. Their hands and feet were freezing, but they had no interest in hot chocolate or warmth. All they wanted to know was why their father hadn't shown up.

Tim started to cry when Susanne explained that something must have come up.

What did she mean by that? Didn't he want to see them?

'Of course he does,' Susanne assured him. She hugged both boys tight and kissed their heads. 'Of course he wants to see you, but right now, everything's very ...'

Charlie could tell Susanne was on the verge of tears.

Nils had come downstairs, too. He opened the packed suit-case he'd left in the hallway and started dumping the contents out on the floor.

'I'm going to go paint for a while,' Susanne announced.

She slipped on her clogs and disappeared.

Charlie didn't know what to do with the boys. This must be the worst part of being a parent, she thought, that you can't protect your children from life's many betrayals and dis-appointments.

'Stop it, Hibben,' Nils told the dog, who had appeared, curi-ous about the commotion. 'Fuck off, will you?' he continued when Hibben anxiously started to lick his face. He lashed out with one arm, sending the dog skittering across the floor.

'What the fuck are you doing?' Melker bellowed.

He dashed over to his brother with his hand raised as if to strike him.

'Cut it out,' Charlie said.

She grabbed Melker, who wrenched free. She took a new, firmer hold and forced Melker to back down. Both Tim and Tom were wailing.

'It's gone!' Susanne was suddenly shouting from the hallway.

She came into the kitchen, eyes wide.

'The painting's gone,' she said. 'The one of her. Of Annabelle.'

29

Charlie was having trouble falling asleep. She tried to close her eyes, but the slightest creak in the house made her open them again and listen into the dark. She thought about the painting of Annabelle, her dress, the wind in her hair, the bridge, the dam gates. Then Annabelle's face morphed into Francesca's. Francesca's hand raised in a wave, a smile.

She eventually drifted off but woke up before six. Restlessness drove her out of bed immediately. She walked over to the window, pulled the curtain aside and looked out at the mist-shrouded garden: no sign of an intruder. She crept down the stairs not to disturb Susanne, but when she reached the ground floor, she realised Susanne was already on the sofa.

'I couldn't sleep,' she said. 'I like to come down here when that happens. I've been told a change of locale can help.'

'Doesn't seem to have,' Charlie replied.

'I feel unsafe. I feel unsafe in my own home.'

'I'm not surprised. But I don't think you need to worry.'

Charlie thought about the stolen painting, the old woman who had given the twins sweets, the mystery person in the garden, the gossip about Isak in town. She could see why Susanne would feel unsafe.

*

'Have you heard from Isak?' Charlie said when Susanne returned from dropping the boys off at school.

'Yes, he called and said I must have misunderstood, that we had agreed today.'

'Do you believe him?'

'I don't know that I have much choice. And he really did sound like he missed the children.'

'Want to pop over to Lola's later?' Charlie said. 'I really need to talk to her.'

'About what?'

'I want to see if she remembers anything about Gudhammar and Francesca.'

'It's half past eight,' Susanne said. 'She'll be sleeping like the dead at this hour.'

'In a bit then?' Charlie said.

'Sure. I reckon it's time to check in on her anyway. I can't believe I have to mother my own mother. It fucking sucks.'

Charlie nodded. It definitely did fucking suck.

Lola lived in a rented flat above the little take-away on Gullspång's high street. The C on the sign had fallen off so now it just said 'arola Johnsson'. The door was unlocked. Susanne opened it without knocking.

'Mum?' Susanne called out as they entered. 'Are you here?'

No answer.

The flat smelled of ethanol and filth, but when they passed the kitchen, Charlie noted fading traces of Lola's sober period. The curtains matched the tablecloth and the geraniums on the windowsill had once been alive. But there was no sign of Lola.

'Mum!' Susanne called again.

Charlie met her eyes. Were they thinking the same thing? A wave of nausea broke over her.

Don't let her be dead, Charlie thought. Dear bloody lord, spare us that.

Lola was in her bed.

'What are you doing here?' she said drowsily when she noticed them. 'What's wrong with you, just walking into other people's homes without notice?'

'I'm your daughter,' Susanne replied dourly. 'And maybe you should be thanking us.'

She pointed at the floor.

Only now did Charlie spot the smouldering cigarette butt that had burnt a hole through the linoleum. Next to it were other black marks that revealed it wasn't the first time Lola had fallen asleep holding a lit cigarette.

'Stop treating me like a child, Susanne,' Lola said, sitting up.

'Then stop fucking acting like one.'

'Mind your tone,' Lola said, raising a finger to her daughter. 'Don't take that tone with me in my own home.'

She turned to Charlie and her face softened.

'Charline?' she said, rubbing her eyes theatrically. 'Is it really you?'

'Put some clothes on, Mum,' Susanne said before Charlie could answer. 'We'll wait in the kitchen.'

After they sat down at the kitchen table, Susanne spread her arms in dismay.

'Completely fucking unbelievable. One of these days, she's going to burn down the whole building.'

'I heard that,' Lola shouted from the bedroom. 'I heard everything.'

'Good!' Susanne shouted back. 'I meant you to.'

'I'm doing the best I can,' Lola said as she entered the kitchen.

She was wearing a floral dressing gown and a strange, wide headband.

'Charline Lager,' she said, shaking her head. 'You really are the spitting image of your mother.'

She walked over to the hob, turned on the fan and lit a cigarette.

'I can't believe you girls have reconnected,' she went on. 'You were like sisters when you were kids, slept in the same bed, combed each other's hair, took baths together.'

'Yes,' Susanne said. 'We relied on each other when life felt unsafe.'

Lola pretended not to hear the criticism in her voice. She took a tube of aspirin from the shelf above the hob. The fizzling sound of the effervescent tablet sinking into the water made Charlie think of Betty. How many mornings had Betty started with a glass of fizzing aspirin? Lola downed her drink in a few deep gulps, then started rummaging through the cupboards for something to offer them.

'Coffee's fine, Mum,' Susanne said.

'Why are you here?' Lola said after turning on the coffee machine. 'I thought you'd washed your hands of me, Susanne.'

She shot her daughter an injured look.

'We want to ask you about the Mild family,' Charlie said. 'The people who own Gudhammar. You used to clean there, right?'

'Yes, I did,' Lola replied. 'I cleaned for that stuck-up couple and their weird daughters.'

'Why have you never told me that?' Susanne asked.

'Why would I have?' Lola retorted. 'It was a lifetime ago. Besides, I think I took you with me a few times. But you were very young, four or five maybe. Can I ask why you're so interested in that old place?'

'Betty took me there a few times when I was little,' Charlie said. 'And I remember there being a fight.'

'Betty had a way of bringing that out in people,' Lola said with a smile. 'I really loved that woman, but when she was down, she was ...'

'I think Charlie knows what she was like,' Susanne broke in.

'Did my mum clean for them, too?' Charlie asked, though she was fairly certain what the answer would be.

Lola let out a surprised laugh and said no. Betty was far too useless at cleaning and at Gudhammar, they wanted things done just so, mark her words. There were no shortcuts there. And now, it was abandoned. It's insane, Lola said, to just leave a place like that and not even sell it, just let a posh old house like that fall into ruin. But after what happened to the girl ... maybe they didn't want to be reminded, Lola reasoned.

'What do you think happened to her?' Charlie said. 'What do you think happened to Francesca Mild?'

'No idea,' Lola replied. 'I guess no one knows. She either ran away or killed herself; at least that's what people said. I haven't seen any of them back here since.'

A phone rang. Lola stood up and left the room. They heard her pick up and say of course she was, sure but she would have said if she was going to.

'A friend,' she said when she returned. 'She was asking me about the Harvest Festival tonight. Are you going?'

'Yes,' Susanne said. 'I think we'll stop by.'

'Great,' Lola said. Then she frowned as if suddenly struck by an important insight. 'Where are the boys?'

'At school,' Susanne said. 'Yes, they go to school, you know,' she added when Lola looked surprised.

'I thought it was Saturday,' Lola said. 'But I'll be damned if it's not still Friday. And the Harvest Festival,' she went on. 'The Harvest Festival's today, too.'

Susanne sighed at Lola's repetition.

'I know,' Susanne said. 'Like I said, we're probably going to stop by.'

'What about the boys?'

'They're going to be with their dad,' Susanne replied. And when Lola just stared at her, befuddled, she added: 'They have a dad, too, you know. His name is Isak.'

'I know his name,' Lola said. 'It's just that I thought he'd left.'

'He has. But apparently, he's recently remembered that he has four children. They're going to spend a week with him. And since I don't exactly have a wealth of appropriate relatives to help out with them, I'm bloody happy about it.'

Charlie felt awkward. She didn't like it when people argued as though they'd forgotten they weren't alone.

'Tell me about Francesca Mild,' she cut in.

'I thought I had,' Lola retorted. 'Everything I know, at least. I just cleaned their house. If I remember correctly, her room was messy. She didn't really want me in there. She said it made her uncomfortable to have other people pick up after her.'

Lola smiled.

'She was depressed. I remember thinking: how is it even possible to be depressed with a silver spoon in your mouth? But she was.'

Charlie had to stop herself from saying: Have you forgotten that she asked you to buy her booze? She must have had some contact with you if she felt comfortable enough to ask. But instead, she said something Anders had told her once, a maxim that had made her laugh at the time.

'There's no correlation between money and happiness.'

Lola looked at her and shook her head.

'I assume that means money and happiness don't go together? But you have a fancier way of putting it? I'm no scholar, but if there's one thing I know for sure, it's that a lack of money can make you bloody miserable.'

'Couldn't agree more,' Charlie said.

Lola stood up and poured herself more coffee without asking if either of them wanted a top-up. She sat back down, shaking her head.

'What?' Susanne asked.

'I'm just thinking about all these bloody men.'

'Mum.'

Susanne walked over to the coffee machine and divided what was left between her cup and Charlie's.

'They're all the bloody same,' Lola went on. 'Your father, Isak, the lot of them.'

'I don't want to hear this, Mum.'

'I'm just telling you the truth. I'm just letting you know that all men are pigs, deep down, they all are. You might think you've found an exception, but sooner or later you'll realise there are no exceptions.'

Charlie thought that was almost verbatim what Betty had used to say before Mattias entered the picture.

'Not Mattias,' she said without thinking. 'Mattias was the exception that proved the rule.'

Lola smiled sadly.

'Yes, your mum used to say that. But if that was the case, I don't understand why she didn't do anything to save her exception.'

'What do you mean?' Charlie said, putting her cup down.

'I mean, she shouldn't just have watched him drown, she should have tried to save him if that was the case.'

'What the fuck are you on about, Mum?' Susanne said.

'She told me,' Lola said. 'She told me she and Charline just sat there on the beach, letting him sink.'

'Wait!' Susanne called after Charlie as she stormed out.

'Why is she so upset?' Charlie heard Lola say. 'She was there, for god's sake. She knows as well as anyone what happened.'

Gaps in Time

Where did you find these? I ask Paul. I hold up the brown glass jar with the orange pills. We're in his dorm room. Everyone else is down by the lake, cheering on the school team in the annual rowing race.

A secret contact, Paul says.

I'm reminded of what Dad likes to tell me about Adamsberg: that it's a school that opens the door to closed worlds, important contacts that'll be useful for the rest of my life. This is the first time I've appreciated it.

But what is it? I say.

Psych drugs. I can't remember what for.

You have to get more, I say and settle into his window nook. Whatever it is, you need to get more.

Paul says the best effect is still to come. He sits down across from me in the window, the soles of his feet against mine. Then the world changes shape and colour. It grows brighter, softer, and a bubbling feeling fills me and turns into laughter. Paul is laughing, too. We laugh at the yellow leaves on the birch trees outside the window, at the janitor digging in the flowerbeds by the Major. We laugh at the man who peed in the human soup.

I laugh as though it's the funniest thing I've ever heard.

We pop more pills. It's not because we want to die or anything like that. We just want to keep laughing. But it doesn't get funnier. I make a mental note to remember that next time. More pills don't equal more fun.

30

Charlie only realised she'd left her jacket when she stepped out onto the street. Susanne was carrying it when she came running after her.

'Never mind that old drunk,' she said and handed Charlie her jacket.

'I need to go for a walk,' Charlie said.

'I'll stop by the shops then,' Susanne said. 'Meet you back at the car in a bit? Don't take what Mum says to heart, okay? She doesn't know what she's talking about.'

Charlie had already started walking. Her heart was pounding as though she'd been running. She returned to her memory of the beach behind Lyckebo, placed Betty next to herself where she was sitting with her knees pulled up, staring at Mattias's unsteady progress across the lake. Why hadn't Betty bloody done something?

Watch out for men of big words

Mattias is the exception that proves the rule.

It's too bright. Why can't we just get rid of all this light?

Charlie stopped. She'd reached a building that had housed an old-fashioned café once upon a time. On the old notice-board next to the entrance, among hundreds of rusty staples and torn scraps of white paper, was a handwritten note about puppies for sale and next to that, another poster advertising the weekend's festivities. *Let's celebrate the harvest!*

Charlie sat down on the steps. The same question that had haunted her since the summer hit her again with renewed force: *Who were you, Betty Lager? Who were you and what were you capable of?*

It had been horrifying to discover that she couldn't even trust her own mother, but now she was realising she couldn't trust herself either. How was she supposed to when her memory seemed to expunge the most pivotal details?

Who am I? Who is Charlie Lager?

The answer had never been further from her grasp. It was as though she had one foot in each world, in two different times. She was all her ages at once: the little girl trying to keep up with Betty, the grown woman trying to trace Betty's footsteps. Wasn't it enough now? She felt strangely light, as though a wind could snatch her up and blow her away. What was keeping her here?

Her phone rang. It was Susanne, telling her she was waiting in the car in the car park behind the supermarket.

'On my way,' Charlie said.

She stood up too quickly and had to hold on to the railing to keep from falling. It was loose; she staggered slightly before regaining her equilibrium.

As she passed the supermarket, she heard someone shouting. It took her a while to realise it was at her.

'Too posh to talk, eh?'

She was overcome with a feeling of unreality again. She was little, holding Betty's hand. *You look radiant today, Betty. And your little girl. More and more like her mother every day.*

I am like her, Charlie thought. It doesn't matter what I do. I'm always going to be Betty's daughter.

She looked at the men. There were three of them, all dressed too lightly and sporting unkempt, bushy beards. Were they the same men who had used to sit on that bench back then? They did look old, but that's what alcohol did to people, it made them age prematurely.

'Too posh to talk, eh?' the same voice shouted again.

'I'm just not in the mood,' Charlie hollered back.

She kept walking.

'Thirsty, though, maybe?' another voice suggested. 'Want a drink?'

She shook her head, though she had never felt thirstier in her life.

'You sure? You look cold. I have something that'll warm your cockles. It's a completely unopened mini bottle,' he went on. 'But fine, suit yourself; I'm not about to waste a good thing on people who don't want it.'

She turned round, walked up to the bench and accepted the tiny bottle without comment. She unscrewed the top that had quite obviously been unscrewed before and took a big, burning swig. Warmth spread through her chest and slid down into her stomach like a ball of fire. She quickly took another swig, then handed the bottle back to the man, thanked him and started to jog towards the car park and Susanne.

'I'm so sorry about Mum,' Susanne said when Charlie climbed into the passenger seat. 'I hope you realise she doesn't always know what she's saying.'

'I'm sure she does,' Charlie replied. 'How else would she know?'

'It really happened?' Susanne exclaimed. 'You watched him drown?'

'I did,' Charlie said, 'but I have no recollection of Mum being there. As far as I remember, it was just me. I just sat there and did nothing.'

'You were a child,' Susanne said. 'You were a child and Betty was a grown-up. It's all Betty's fault.'

Charlie opened her mouth to say more, maybe something extenuating about Betty, but she didn't have it in her. It was all Betty's fault; everything began and ended with Betty.

31

Johan called. Charlie didn't pick up. She just wanted to be alone.

'I'm going for a drive,' she said when they reached the house.

'I was going to make lunch,' Susanne said.

'I'll eat later,' Charlie said. 'Do you have any cigarettes I can bum?'

'Sure.'

Susanne patted her jacket and pulled out a packet of Marlboro with a lighter in it.

Charlie drove down to the church. She parked next to the high, mossy wall, went through the gates and followed the dimly lit gravel path to Betty's grave. There, under the chestnut tree, was her simple headstone. It looked as abandoned as it had done the first (and only) time she'd visited. Maybe she should plant something that could survive the winter? Then she thought about Betty's loathing of traditional graveyards. She didn't want to be stuck in one place, not even after she was dead, so she'd made Charlie promise to scatter her ashes in Lake Skagern. But that hadn't happened. Charlie couldn't recall if anyone had even asked her about the funeral. The period following Betty's death was one big blank. She reached out to touch the pecking dove on the headstone. It was dirty. Charlie used her sleeve to clean it as best she could.

Fuck you, Betty. Why didn't you do something? If he really was the one man who knew everything about you and still liked you, how could you just let him sink?

I couldn't move, sweetheart, Betty's voice replied in her head. *I don't know why.*

Charlie squatted down behind the headstone to get out of the wind while she lit a cigarette.

Betty's voice inside her again: *Maybe it's because he knew everything about me that he had to die? I couldn't bear who I was in his eyes.* The statements sounded so real Charlie wondered if she had in fact heard them. Or am I losing it, she thought. Maybe I'll be seeing butterflies on empty walls soon.

'I don't understand you, Betty,' she whispered and stubbed her cigarette out on the ground.

When she stood back up, dark clouds covered the sky. It was like night in the middle of the day. She started walking down the neatly raked path. There were other graves she wanted to visit.

She heard something. Footsteps? She froze and scanned the cemetery. There were no shadows. Her serenity had morphed into watchfulness. It didn't take her long to locate an area that seemed newer. The headstones were less mossy and the soil in front of them raised. When she saw the flickering light of burning candles, she knew she'd found it. Annabelle's final resting place was covered in teddy bears, framed messages and candles. How long did grave candles burn for? Had someone just been there? She read the inscription on the dark, polished stone. *Annabelle Roos, loved, missed,* followed by the years of her birth and death. And under that, her parents' names and birth years, followed by a smooth area for the years of their deaths. Charlie had seen that before and it had always seemed creepy to her, as though the grave was just waiting to be filled. She sat down and started reading the framed messages. It was everything from the usual clichés about sweet dreams to more personal sentiments like: *Nothing will ever be the same without you, Anna-beautiful.* And then, a big, black semicolon, just like the ones Annabelle and her best friend Rebecca had tattooed on their wrists. *There's more to come.* And then, a Latin quote. *Alis volat propriis.* Charlie pulled out her phone and googled it. *She flies with her own wings.* Charlie thought about all the things this girl had lost, all the things that had lain before her that she would never experience, all her thoughts, dreams, goals: one moment and they were gone. Now her name would be spoken in hushed tones, as a cautionary example: *Don't forget what happened to that girl. Don't forget what happened to Annabelle.*

'Aren't you cold, sitting on the ground?' someone said behind her.

Charlie jumped. She turned and the familiar voice was given a face. It was Fredrik Roos, Annabelle's father.

'Fredrik?' she said. 'I ...'

'There's no need to apologise, Charlie.'

'It's lovely,' Charlie said, pointing at the flowers.

'Rebecca and William come here a lot,' Fredrik said. 'I'm glad she's not alone. It's silly, but I often worry she might feel abandoned, or cold or that the darkness out here scares her. That's why the candles never burn down. I keep bringing new ones to keep things bright and warm for her.'

'I understand,' Charlie said.

'What are you doing here anyway?' Fredrik asked. 'I mean, in Gullspång?'

'I'm visiting … visiting some friends,' she said, realising mentioning Susanne might make things uncomfortable.

'Did you read about your mother afterwards?' Fredrik asked. 'Did you read the things I gave you?'

Charlie nodded. She really didn't want to discuss that now.

'No wonder Betty and Nora felt bad,' Fredrik went on.

'I heard she's been sectioned,' Charlie said.

'You did, did you? Well, news travels fast around here. But it's true. She's at Solhem.'

'I'm so sorry.'

'Me too.' Fredrik cleared his throat. 'Sometimes I just miss …'

He nodded towards the headstone; there was no need for him to finish his sentence.

Francesca

I was taking the Bible off the shelf when Jacob entered the room.

'Not exactly his style,' I said, holding the book up for him to see.

'Definitely not.' Jacob smiled. 'I think he read it mainly to be able to critique it. He would make little notes in the margin.'

'Would you mind if I borrowed it?' I asked. 'I'd love to read his notes.'

'Keep it,' Jacob said.

He offered to give me a ride home. I said there was no need, that I could just call my mum. But he was heading into town anyway; he had some errands to run.

As we backed out of the driveway, it began to rain. A few tentative drops soon turned into a deluge.

'It's been a dry autumn,' I said.

'Is that right?' Jacob replied. 'I haven't been paying much attention to the weather.'

'It's been the warmest autumn in decades,' I told him, just to have something to say.

I felt I'd heard that somewhere, but it might have been the year before.

'Is that right,' Jacob said.

He popped a tape into the cassette player and Janis Joplin's wheezing voice poured out of the speakers.

We talked about normal things. Jacob told me he was studying economics in Uppsala. He'd taken some time off but was going back soon.

'I can't imagine Paul having a brother who likes economics,' I said.

'I don't, but it might come in handy when I take over the family business one day.'

'Is that what you're doing? Taking over the family business?'

'Yes. You think that's weird?'

'Not at all.'

I studied Jacob's big hands on the steering wheel and tried to imagine them preparing my ashen corpse for its eternal rest.

'Paul was in love with someone,' I said.

'With whom?'

Jacob turned to me.

'He didn't tell me. He was going to the night of the ball, but it never happened. That's why I wanted to ask you if maybe you knew who it was, if he'd mentioned anyone to you?'

'No, he never said anything about being in love.'

Jacob fell silent.

'Is it … I mean, does it matter now?'

'Maybe not, but I have a feeling it's important.'

'The only girl he ever talked about was you. He liked you a lot, Francesca.'

I swallowed hard and tried to think of other things to keep the tears from coming: cross stitch embroidery, flowering meadows, jokes. *I peed in the soup.* It didn't work.

'Do you think he killed himself?' I said, staring out the window to hide my tears.

'No,' Jacob said. 'He didn't kill himself.'

'Are you sure?'

'Yes. Paul would never willingly go into a lake. He hated water.'

'I know, but if it wasn't suicide,' I said, 'then what was it?'

'A drowning,' Jacob replied. 'That's all they know. An accident.'

I quickly dried my eyes.

'But what was he doing down by the lake that night?' I said. 'What was he doing down there all by himself on the night of the ball?'

'I don't know,' Jacob said. 'I have no idea. Do you know something I don't?'

That's when I started telling him about the night of the ball, the pills we'd taken, that Paul was going to tell me whom he was in love with. I told him about the first dance, that Paul had seemed happy. We had been happy. But then ... he was just gone, I couldn't find him anywhere.

Jacob wanted to know at what time he disappeared, but I couldn't tell him. I was bad with time under the best of circumstances and that night was fuzzy, but I felt like I'd searched for him for an eternity, checking any place he could be. And then, about how I'd gone over to the chapel, the last place I would ever expect to find him.

'But he wasn't there?'

'No, Paul wasn't, but this group of guys was.' I listed the names of everyone in the royals, and gave brief descriptions of them. 'Paul's rose was on the ground and their trouser legs were dripping. They were soaked.'

'What are you saying?' Jacob said.

He shifted down, pulled over by the side of the road and stared at me.

'I don't know. I'm just telling you what I saw.'

'But could they have done something to him?'

'I guess that's the feeling I've had,' I said. 'But no one around me wants to hear it. Everyone just keeps telling me I was drunk and I can't deny that; I was both drunk and high and my parents don't think I'm trustworthy even when I'm sober, so ... And anyway, it might be impossible to prove regardless.'

'Tell me more about that clique,' Jacob said.

So I did. I told him about the shoving, the bullying, the laughing.

Jacob listened and his eyes grew darker.

I didn't know if I should feel relieved to finally be talking to someone who took me seriously. Maybe part of me wanted to drop the whole thing, accept the easiest truth and move on. But I wasn't the kind of person who let things go and moved on. I was the kind of person who didn't mind hitting rock bottom, no matter how badly it hurt.

'I'm going to contact the police,' Jacob said. 'I'm going to tell them what you've told me and leave it to them to decide what to do.'

'What I really want to do is kill them,' I said. 'What I know for sure they've done is easily enough to make me want to beat them all to death.'

'Yes,' Jacob said. 'It's what they deserve.'

Then he burst into tears.

Without thinking, I turned to him and put my arms around his neck.

'I'm sorry,' I said. 'I don't know what I'm doing.'

But before I had time to pull back, Jacob had leaned in closer.

'Drive somewhere,' I whispered in a voice that didn't sound like my own. 'Take me somewhere where no one can see us.'

Jacob turned down a grass road. It ended at an old red house.

'It looks abandoned,' he said.

I nodded without looking. Then we fumblingly removed our clothes. I'd never been naked with a man before; maybe it should have made me feel shy and insecure, but it was as though someone had taken over my body. I wanted him in a way I'd never wanted anyone before. What was happening was worlds away from the suffocating French kissing and groping I'd subjected myself to with the boys at Adamsberg.

'What happened to your arms?' Jacob whispered.

'Just a cry for help,' I replied.

'It looks like more than that.' Jacob propped himself up on his elbow and looked at me gravely. 'The next time you want help, just cry, don't ...'

'No one heard me,' I whispered.

Then I regretted saying anything, because I didn't want to talk about it just then.

'Maybe you need to cry out to someone else,' Jacob said, 'someone who'll listen, so you don't have to ...'

I nodded. Kept my eyes closed for a minute.

'You look like a lot of the people around here.' Jacob caressed my lacerations. 'Almost everyone who works at the plywood factory looks just like this. Does it hurt?'

'No,' I said. 'I can barely feel it.'

'Don't do it again, Francesca. Don't ever do it again.'

'Okay.'

'Promise me.'

'I promise,' I said.

Then I kissed him. I didn't want to talk about scars, cries for help or factory workers. I didn't want to talk at all.

His breathing grew heavy again.

'Are you sure you want to do this?' Jacob whispered when he was as close as he could get without passing the point of no return.

'Yes,' I said. 'Please, don't stop.'

'But we have no ... protection.'

'Don't worry about it,' I whispered.

He thrust a few times before he managed to enter, and for a few seconds pleasure turned into a searing pain I could feel all the way up my back. But then, as he slowly started to move again, the pain dissipated, replaced by a pleasure I'd never experienced before. Maybe I'd had it wrong all this time, I thought to myself; maybe there are things that make life worth living?

The windows of the car had fogged up. Jacob suddenly froze.

'What?' I asked.

'There was a tap on the window,' he said. 'Someone's out there.'

He slid out of me. We lay dead still as though we were praying the tap hadn't happened. But there it was again. Jacob leaned over me and rubbed at the foggy glass. I slipped further down the seat and shut my eyes as if that could make everything go away.

'It's a little girl,' Jacob said.

'No,' I said when he rolled down the window.

'Hi,' he said.

'What are you doing?' said a high-pitched child's voice.

'We didn't know anyone lived here,' Jacob said.

'I live here with my mum.'

I shut my eyes tighter, hoping her mother was far away.

'So where's your mum?' Jacob asked.

'She's asleep,' the girl replied, 'and you're not allowed to wake her. She told me she doesn't want to be disturbed. You can't come in.'

'I understand,' Jacob said. 'We're going to go now.'

He rolled up the window.

'Oh my god,' he whispered. 'She appeared out of nowhere.'

'Are you sure she even exists?' I asked.

We put our clothes back on. They were scattered all over the car. I felt strangely dizzy, as though I'd just had an out-of-body experience.

Jacob turned on the fan and the windows cleared. I looked up at the house. It looked as uninhabited now as it had done through the haze I'd been in before. The windows on the ground floor were covered with fabric or blankets and there were no lights on. When Jacob backed out towards the main road, I saw a small sign pushed into the ground; I leaned forward and just managed to read it before the car's headlights swept past it: Lyckebo.

32

Charlie sat in her car, thinking about Nora Roos. She was the only person Charlie knew who had known Betty as a child. Was there more darkness in Betty's past than what she'd learnt from the letters she'd read? Did Nora know something? She pulled out her phone and googled Solhem Hospital. It was less than twenty miles from Gullspång. They might not accept spontaneous visitors, but it was worth a try. She put the address into the GPS and was told it was a twenty-five-minute drive.

Solhem Hospital was a brown brick building surrounded by a large garden with benches under tall birch trees. The paths winding between well-trimmed shrubberies reminded Charlie of the pictures of old-timey mental institutions she'd seen in her psychology coursebooks.

A text made her phone ding as she was parking. It was from Johan. *Call me*, it said. *I think I have something*.

She called, but he didn't pick up.

She left a message saying where she was and that he could call anytime.

Getting to talk to Nora Roos was not easy. Charlie had to pull out her police ID before the young woman at reception would agree to let her in.

'But don't upset her,' she admonished.

'I just need a quick word,' Charlie replied, hoping no one would think to ask her what for.

Nora was sitting on a bed in a white room with her back to the half-open door. Charlie knocked but Nora didn't react.

'Nora?' Charlie said.

Nora slowly turned round. She was pale and emaciated and her hair was so thin Charlie could see her pale scalp.

'You?' she said, staring blankly at Charlie. 'What are you doing here?'

'I'd like to have a word with you.'

'Annabelle's dead,' Nora said slowly.

'I know. Can I come in?'

Nora nodded and shrugged simultaneously.

'What do you want?' Nora said when Charlie had sat down on a chair next to her bed.

'I want to talk about my mother, about Betty.'

Nora seemed to shudder.

'She'll always be Rosa to me,' she said. 'But we can call her Betty if you prefer.'

'I would like to talk to you about her,' Charlie repeated.

'I've said what I have to say about Betty.'

'I know what happened. I know what you did to that little boy.'

'Not *we*,' Nora said. She sounded more alert now. '*We* didn't do anything. It was Betty. It was all Betty's fault.'

'Okay,' Charlie said. 'I understand. I'm not really sure why I'm here. It's just that my mum has no past, I don't know anyone else who knew her as a child and my memories of her feel ... unreliable.'

'Betty was unreliable.'

'You didn't see her at all after she moved to Gullspång?'

'Never.'

'So you didn't know her boyfriend? Mattias Andersson?'

'No, but I spoke with him once.'

'When?'

'What does it matter?'

'I'm just curious.'

Nora closed her eyes for a long while. She must have been given a fair amount of sedatives.

'It was in the summer,' she said at length, 'right before he disappeared. I ran into him in the woods. He was gathering birch branches for a maypole and I ... I guess I was just out for a walk. We started talking and when he said he was living with Betty, that his son was coming to stay with them, I told him everything. I told him what Betty had done to that little boy. I guess I just figured he should know who he was with, that maybe he should keep his son away from her. I wanted to warn him.'

Betty's words about Mattias echoed in Charlie's mind when she left Nora and Solhem.

Mattias is the exception that proves the rule. He's the only person who knows everything about me and still likes me.

Who had Betty been trying to fool? Mattias was a man who had liked her until he found out who she was. When he did, he couldn't love her any more, couldn't let her take care of his little boy. And Betty had let him die. She and Betty had sat there together, watching Johan's dad sink into the lake.

Gaps in Time

'Did you know a pig's heart is very similar to a human heart?'
Paul says.

It's late August and we're walking past the pig farm a mile
or so from the school.

I tell him I know almost nothing about hearts.

Then Paul tells me that in the future, they might be able to
put pigs' hearts in people, maybe even in our lifetime.

'Can you imagine that,' he says, 'having a pig's heart inside
you?'

'Why not? Better that than a stone heart.'

'You don't have a stone heart, Fran. Quite the opposite.'

Paul stops and looks at me.

I want to keep walking. Because of the reek of pig piss and
pig shit and because I feel embarrassed. I always think I want
to hear people say good things about me, but once they do, I
want to run away, oddly enough.

'What do you know about my heart?' I say.

'I know it's big.'

'I guess it's about the size of my fist, neither bigger nor
smaller.'

'It could be I didn't mean it literally.'

'I know, but you're wrong. My heart is tiny and dark.'

As we walk back towards the school, I think about Cécile's head under the water, my hands holding it down. I just wanted to help her beat the record. I wanted …

I don't know what I wanted any more.

33

Susanne was in the living room when Charlie got back.

'Hear that?' she said.

'What?'

'The silence. Isak picked up the boys. We're alone.'

'How was it?'

Charlie sat down in the armchair next to the sofa.

'The little ones were ecstatic, Nils sceptical and Melker was on the fence about going right up until the moment they left. If not for Tim and Tom, I don't think he would have gone.'

'That's understandable, right?' Charlie said.

'It's absolutely understandable.' Susanne heaved a sigh. 'What a vile fucking day it's been. What do you say to forgetting all about missing girls, peeping toms and drunken mothers?'

'Sounds good to me,' Charlie replied, wishing those were things you could just forget about.

'We need something to drink,' Susanne said. 'How else are we supposed to stop thinking about it?'

'It would be impossible,' Charlie said. 'Even booze might not do it.'

'True, but it can't hurt.'

Susanne went out to the kitchen.

Charlie called Johan again, but he still wasn't answering.

Susanne came back with two glasses filled to the brim. She handed one to Charlie.

When they'd finished the first round, Susanne made more, then she turned on music.

'You remember this one, don't you, Lager?'

Susanne danced towards her and held out her hand. Charlie took it, got up and sang along to the chorus of 'Life is a Party'.

The alcohol had numbed her thoughts; Francesca's face faded away and Betty seemed increasingly peripheral.

'Fuck me, Svenka really nailed the alcohol content this time!' Susanne laughed as they danced into the coffee table.

Charlie could only nod.

'Don't you think we should pop over to the Harvest Festival after all?' Susanne said when they sat down next to the fire-place for a smoke. 'I mean, sitting at home isn't going to help anything.'

'Of course we should go,' Charlie replied.

As they were putting on make-up with their drinks balanced on the sink, Charlie felt thirteen again. She and Susanne were thirteen and dressing up for a party in the village shop.

'Might as well go all out,' Susanne said as she smeared on a thick layer of eyeshadow. 'No point in half-measures. Do you need help?'

Charlie nodded, sat down on the edge of the bathtub and closed her eyes. The few times she'd worn make-up as a teen-ager, Susanne had always been the one to put it on. She felt Susanne's warm breath on her face and obediently followed her instructions about opening her eyes, closing them and opening them again.

'So fucking good-looking,' Susanne said as she backed up to inspect her work.

Charlie looked in the mirror and had to agree.

'Ready for me to call a ride?'

'I didn't know you had taxis out here?'

'You have to know the right people. There's a guy on a farm a few miles down the road; we help each other out. If he's unavailable, I'll just call my gypsy cab.'

'Here,' Susanne said, handing Charlie the flask.

They were both in the back seat. The car was an ancient Volvo Amazon and the driver looked far too young to have his own farm.

'Odd,' Susanne said. 'Would you mind turning the music up?'

Odd did as he was told.

Charlie read the text on the window. Looking at it from the inside it was mirrored; it took her addled brain a minute to decipher the sentence. *Don't laugh, Svensson, your daughter might be in the back seat.*

She checked her phone. Nothing from Johan. She fired off a text asking if he was alright, saying she was on her way to the pub, that maybe they'd see each other there. A second later, she pondered writing that she missed him, but quickly decided not to.

'I need to pee,' Susanne giggled when they reached the pub.

She jumped out of the car and ran off without thanking Odd for the ride.

'How much?' Charlie asked and met Odd's eyes in the rear-view mirror.

'Nothing,' he replied. 'Out here we help each other out.'

He looked at Charlie as though she didn't understand what it meant to help one another.

'Okay, thanks,' Charlie said. 'I hope I can help you back sometime.'

'I try to steer clear of coppers,' Odd said. 'But thanks anyway.'

How do you know I'm a copper? Charlie wanted to ask, but she refrained because she already knew the answer: Out here we tell each other things and we keep an eye on outsiders.

A girl was standing on the pub's front steps. She was leaning over the railing, vomiting onto the asphalt.

'You alright?' Charlie said. She put a hand on the girl's back.

'Fantastic, thanks.'

'Sara?'

'You again?' Sara exclaimed.

She tried to add something else, but was cut off by more vomit.

'I'm going to get someone to drive you home,' Charlie said.

'I'm fine,' Sara replied. 'I'll be heading back in there in a minute.'

'You're not supposed to be here. You're only thirteen.'

'Fourteen,' Sara said, holding up four fingers. 'I turned fourteen in September, actually.'

'But you're not eighteen,' Charlie said.

'Dad's here.' Sara nodded towards the bar. 'I'm allowed to be here with a guardian.'

'But you're not allowed to drink alcohol.'

'I'm not even drunk,' Sara said. She wiped her mouth on her shirt sleeve. 'Liquorice just makes me sick. I'm fine now.'

'Be careful,' Charlie said.

'Of course I'm careful,' Sara replied and held the door for her.

The pub was loud and warm and packed with everything from pensioners to teenagers who looked no older than Sara. Most people were wearing short-sleeved T-shirts. Charlie noted the familiar lacerations from the plywood factory on a number of arms. Betty's arms had looked like that. Worse, even, because she liked picking at her scabs. *First they took my body, then my soul.*

A band was playing on the stage; the singer was a girl who looked no older than fifteen. Charlie stopped.

'She has an incredible voice,' she said, turning to Susanne. 'Who is she?'

'That's Janis Rainen. And yes, she sings like an angel. She gets it from her mother. But let's hope she doesn't end up like her.'

Charlie didn't want to know what had happened to the girl's mother or the many ways in which the odds were stacked against Janis. She didn't want to think about the generations of grief and disappointments. She just wanted to close her eyes and listen to that magical voice.

'Charlie?' Susanne nudged her. 'Are you okay? Would you like a glass of water?'

Charlie shook her head. Up on stage, Janis grabbed the microphone in both hands and closed her eyes.

When the song was over, the audience clapped and cheered. One of the band members thanked their young guest singer and said it was time to get dancing.

'Because you want to dance, right?'

He looked out at the room.

'Yeeees!'

'Alright then, here's a golden oldie.'

The man in the leather jacket struck a chord on his guitar that everyone seemed to recognise.

Charlie watched the young girl step off the stage and walk up to the bar where Jonas was waiting with a pint.

But where was Johan? She couldn't see him anywhere. She wrote him another text, letting him know she was at the pub now. Was he coming down?

No answer.

Should she go upstairs and knock on his door? No, it could wait.

More and more people were dancing on the small dance-floor in front of the stage. Charlie spotted Adam Rehn and a blonde woman in a black dress. When they turned, Adam's hand slid down to her behind. The woman pulled it back up, but as soon as they turned again, his hand moved back down and she seemed to have given up on doing anything about it.

Charlie went to the toilet. As she was washing her hands, she spotted a familiar face behind her in the mirror: high cheekbones, big eyes, dark curls.

'Helena?' she said, turning round.

The girl laughed and said her name was Alva, that Helena was her mother.

'You look a lot alike,' Charlie said.

'Not any more,' Alva replied, 'but I suppose Mum did look a bit like this when she was younger. Do you know her?'

'She was a few years ahead of me in school.'

Charlie thought about Helena, who used to hitchhike into town and had seemed to have unfettered access to cigarettes and booze. And now here she was, still the same age, but in the form of a daughter.

'Your mother must have been very young when she had you,' Charlie said.

'She was seventeen,' Alva replied. 'Bloody poor decision if you ask me.'

'What do you mean?' Charlie said, even though she knew full well.

'She wanted to be something, but once she had me, she had to put food on the table and she got stuck at the sawmill and then her back gave out and she ended up on long-term disability.'

Alva turned round when someone in one of the stalls shouted that there was no loo roll. Alva sighed and pulled a wad of grey hand towels from the holder above the sink.

'I'll tell Mum I bumped into you,' she said, pushing the towels through the gap under the stall door. 'What's your name?'

'Charlie. Charlie Lager.'

When Charlie came back out, Susanne pulled her aside.

'Check him out,' she said, nodding towards a table by the window occupied by a group of men. 'The one by the wall.'

'Should I know who he is?'

'His name's Christoffer,' Susanne said. 'He used to spend summers here when we were younger and sometimes he comes back for special occasions. We were ridiculously in love once upon a time, or, to be honest, it was probably mostly me who was in love. He seemed to forget me the moment autumn came and he went back to town. I was his summer cat.'

'Doesn't sound great.'

'Oh, it was fun,' Susanne said. 'At least in the summers.'

Francesca

'What's wrong?' Dad said when I returned from my visit to Paul's house. He and Mum were sipping wine on the sofa in the parlour, looking like a couple in a film.

'Why do you ask?' I said.

I'd never believed what they say about it showing when a girl has lost her virginity, but with the way Mum was looking at me, I suddenly thought I might have been wrong about that.

'You look like you've been crying.'

'Wouldn't it be weird if I hadn't?' I retorted.

'Maybe we should set up another session with Doctor Molan,' Mum suggested.

'No, I'm fine.'

'You don't look fine,' Dad said.

'I feel better than I have in a long time.'

'I thought you said you've been crying.'

'Sure,' I said. 'But I also think I might have discovered the meaning of life.'

I grabbed Paul's Bible, headed up to my room and lay down on my bed. Flipping through the pages, I was overcome with disappointment. I'd hoped to find jotted down musings, highlighting, critical remarks, but unfortunately, Paul's Bible seemed to contain nothing of the kind. I flipped faster and faster and finally came across a blotted-out paragraph. I tried to read through the black ink, but it was impossible. When I carried on, I noticed some pages were missing. Why?

I brought the Bible down to the library, placed it on the table in front of the fireplace and started to look for an intact copy on the shelves.

It must have been fifteen minutes before I found one and could flip to Leviticus 18:22 and the lines that were unreadable in Paul's Bible:

Thou shalt not lie with mankind, as with womankind: it is an abomination.

I soon found another crossed-out section; when I located the corresponding lines in the unharmed Bible, they were on the same theme: *Know ye not that the unrighteous shall not inherit the kingdom of God? Be not deceived: neither fornicators, nor idolaters, nor adulterers, nor effeminate, nor abusers of themselves with mankind, nor thieves, nor covetous, nor drunkards, nor revilers, nor extortioners, shall inherit the kingdom of God.*

I sat down in front of the fire and rebuked myself for having been a blind idiot. No wonder I couldn't figure out which of the Adamsberg girls Paul had been in love with; it hadn't been a girl at all. I thought about how sad it was Paul hadn't told me the truth. It made me absolutely heartbroken that he hadn't felt able to confide in me.

'Where are you going now?' Dad asked as I walked towards the door.

'Just down to the lake.'

Dad felt I should stay in since there was a chill in the air and it would be dark soon.

'I want to be alone,' I said. And then, when I saw Dad was about to object: 'Surely I have to be allowed to move about freely on our own property at least?'

'Fine. But don't forget the jetty's slippery and not in great shape. We're tearing it down in the spring. I'm tearing the whole thing down and having a new one built.'

The path down to the water was almost completely overgrown. The ground was covered in brown leaves from the oak and elm trees. My body felt tender in a nice way. It had only been a few hours since I slept with Jacob in his car, but it already felt like a lifetime ago. Was it going to happen again? Then I felt ashamed about even thinking about something so banal when my friend was rotting in the ground. Doctor Molan had told me there was a thin line between sorrow and joy, that they could exist side by side. It might have been the wisest thing he ever said.

You're the only one I could marry if I were normal.

How could I have failed to understand, I thought to myself, how could I have missed what he was trying to tell me? Did anyone else know? Jacob? If not, it must have been terribly lonely.

But he had found someone.

Dad was not mistaken about the jetty not being in great shape. I carefully walked to the end and lay down on my stomach on the damp, cold wood. I dipped my hands into the water and studied my pale face in the ripples. It looked old. I turned over and looked up at the sky instead, but the serene feeling of being insignificant in the vastness that it usually induced in me failed to appear. I lay there contracting a urinary tract infection, thinking about what Paul had said about space, that it made him dizzy. I felt the same thing now. The fact that it had neither beginning nor end made me dizzy.

'What did you do to your hands?' was the first thing Dad said when I returned to the house.

'I was enjoying the water.'

'You're bright red. I'm going to light a fire in the library.'

'I'm not even cold,' I said.

It was true. I should feel cold because I could see the goose bumps on my arms, but I felt nothing.

It was only after I took a seat in the armchair in front of the fire that I realised I was freezing. Dad had wrapped a blanket around me and, to my relief, left me alone in the room.

When I woke up, I was in my bed with no recollection of how I'd got there or of falling asleep. There was a thudding sound. The front door knocker. I turned on my bedside light and checked the time: three in the morning. It had to be bad news.

I heard Mum's light tread outside my door.

'Rikard,' she said shrilly. 'You're going to have to come with me. I'm not going down by myself.'

I got up and padded out onto the landing where I waited to see who was coming in. But no one did. Instead I heard Dad talk in the voice he reserved for when he was furious.

'Go away,' he said. 'No, I never want to see you again.'

And then, a woman crying and pleading for something I couldn't catch.

'No,' Dad said and slammed the door shut.

The determined knocking resumed. I crept into the guest-room and looked out the window to see who had made Dad so livid. All I could see was the back of a woman holding a child by the hand. The little one had to run to keep up. Who were they? What had they done to make my dad so angry?

34

Susanne had sat down next to her old summer love. They seemed deep in conversation. Charlie felt oddly out of place. And then, there he was again, Micke. He was talking to Adam. So they knew each other? Micke looked up and straight at her. He leaned closer to Adam and said something before leaving him and walking up to Charlie.

'Can I buy you a pint?'

'I already have one,' Charlie replied, nodding at her glass. 'But thanks anyway. By the way, have you been talking to people?'

'About what?'

'The case.'

'That's what I wanted to talk to you about. I want the file back,' he said, moving in much too close. 'I want you to forget all about it.'

'Why?'

'It's for the best. I was an idiot to let you have it in the first place.'

'Who told you that?' Charlie asked.

'What do you mean?'

Micke's face revealed that he knew very well what she meant.

'I'm just wondering why it's so important that I forget it.'

'Because I'm dead certain they were right to close the case. Dead certain.'

'People who are dead certain always fill me with doubt,' Charlie commented.

Micke let out a chuckle.

'What do you mean?'

'I just find it unsettling, people who think they have all the answers, who aren't willing to reassess what they know.'

She was interrupted by a voice behind Micke.

'There you are!' exclaimed a tall, powerfully built man in his fifties.

He came up to them.

'I was just about to call you,' Micke said.

Charlie noticed that his eyes were suddenly nervously darting back and forth.

'Were you now? Then how come you don't pick up when I call?'

'Would you mind talking about this tomorrow? Let me buy you a pint and we'll talk tomorrow.'

'No, thanks, I reckon it would be better to stick to settling our business.' The man prodded Micke in the chest. 'When I call tomorrow, you are going to pick up.'

'What was that about?' Charlie said when the man left.

'Nothing.'

'Nothing?'

'Just a small debt, since you have to know.'

'Sounds risky.'

'I've just been unlucky,' Micke said. 'It'll be fine.'

'Gambling?' Charlie said, remembering the sound of cards being dealt on his computer when she picked up the case file.

'I don't want to talk about it.'

Dead on, Charlie thought.

'Can I buy you a drink?' she said when Micke knocked back what was left in his glass. He was really putting them away.

Micke shrugged. Charlie leaned over the bar and ordered two beers from Jonas.

'A modern woman,' Micke said when their drinks arrived.

'Do you find that intimidating?' Charlie couldn't resist asking.

'The woman hasn't been born yet who intimidates me,' Micke replied with a smile.

'Good for you,' Charlie said. 'What did you mean about leaving the case alone?'

'I think it's for the best.'

'But I can't just forget about it now I've read the file.'

Micke took a big gulp of beer.

'How are things with that journalist, by the way?' he asked. 'I heard he's been sniffing around, too.'

'Smooth segue,' Charlie said. 'Yes, he's here.'

'Mattias Andersson's son, right?'

Charlie put her glass down.

'What are you talking about?'

'I know who you are, Charline. I know who you are and where you're from.'

Charlie felt her brain summon all available resources to shake off the alcohol-induced haze shrouding it. Alarm bells had gone off the moment Micke said her birth name.

'What do you want from me?' she said.

'I want the case file back. I was a bloody idiot for letting you take it. I want you to forget about it and go back to Stockholm.

It's for everyone's sake. And this journalist you seem so fond of, how well do you really know him?'

'What do you care?' Charlie asked.

'I don't, but if I were you, I'd stay away from him, as well. Just a piece of friendly advice.'

'What are you talking about?' Charlie said. 'What the fuck are you talking about?'

'Cheers,' Micke said, raising his glass.

Then, before Charlie could say anything else, he stalked off and disappeared into the crowd.

Charlie turned to Jonas behind the bar.

'Could I have a glass of water, please?'

'Sparkling or still?'

'Just give me a glass of water.'

Charlie downed the water and looked out at the room. There was no sign of Micke anywhere. Or Johan. She checked her phone. No new messages.

How well do you really know him? Charlie pictured Johan's face. The night before. That feeling that was new to her. *Proceed with caution, Charlie.*

People were dancing off-beat in front of the small stage. Their faces looked strangely familiar. They slowly morphed into the faces of people she'd known once. In the middle of the crowd, she thought she saw Betty twirling in her red dress.

35

'Charlie?'

Susanne was tapping her arm. Her cheeks were glowing and her eyes were sparkling with intoxication and happiness.

'He wants me to go home with him.' She nodded towards the summer guy. 'Would that be okay by you? I mean ...'

'Of course it's okay,' Charlie replied.

'Great.' Susanne rummaged through her handbag and pulled out a small card. 'Just call this number when you're ready to go home.'

Charlie studied the rumpled business card. It had a picture of a road on it and the text: *Jesus is the way, the truth and the life.*

'Jesus is driving me home?' she said.

'No, but a fairly devout man is,' Susanne retorted. 'A Jehovah's Witness who earns some extra cash driving a gypsy cab on the weekend. His name's Josef.'

Susanne and the summer guy left. Charlie walked towards the staircase leading to the motel rooms. She had to talk to Johan right now.

A minute later, she was knocking on his door.

'Johan,' she called out when no one answered. 'Are you there?'

No answer. She walked back down the stairs and pushed her way to the bar.

'Jonas!' she said. 'I need ...'

'Wait your turn, lass!' exclaimed Svenka, who was standing next to her. 'We're all equals here, you know. You can't cut in line because you feel like it.'

'You mind your daughter instead of me,' Charlie retorted.

'My daughter ...' Svenka said as though he'd forgotten that he had one. 'My daughter can look after herself, I'll have you know.'

He pointed to the dancefloor where Charlie spotted Sara with a guy in a denim jacket. She was waving her hands about and looked like she'd recovered from her bout of nausea.

'Everything alright, Charlie?' Jonas said from behind the bar.

'Yeah, I just need to know if Johan Ro has checked out.'

'Why?'

'I just want to know.'

'Hold on, I'll check.'

Jonas disappeared through the swing doors and came back seconds later.

'No, he's still here. Is there a problem?'

'He's not in his room. Have you seen him here tonight?'

Jonas shook his head.

'Are you going to let me order or what?' Svenka put in.

He put a hand on Charlie's arm.

'Don't touch me,' Charlie said.

'What the fuck's wrong with you? This is a bar where you order booze. If you're looking for conversation you should go somewhere else.'

He burst out laughing, a laugh that quickly turned into a coughing fit.

'Two tequilas,' he said once he'd recovered. He held up to fingers. 'Two tequilas, please.'

'Maybe you should slow down,' Jonas said.

'Slow down?' Svenka shook his head. He hadn't slowed down in the last two decades and wasn't about to start now.

Jonas shrugged and started preparing his order.

'Never mind the lemon and all that,' Svenka told him. 'Just give me the booze.'

'When did you last see Johan?' Charlie tried again after Svenka had paid.

'He had coffee here this afternoon,' Jonas said. 'Then he left.'

'Did he come back?'

'No idea,' Jonas replied.

He raised a hand to a woman who had started waving her card about at the other end of the bar.

'I don't keep track of when guests come and go. Are you worried about something?'

'No,' Charlie said. 'I just want to know where he is.'

'If he shows up, I'll tell him you're looking for him.'

'Thanks.'

Charlie turned away from the bar. She didn't feel all that drunk any more, mostly nauseous and something else. She was … afraid.

Gaps in Time

I think I'm in love, Fran. I'd like to talk to you about it later.

I stop and say: with whom?

I need a few more drinks in me before I tell you. Come back in an hour.

Don't be ridiculous! Tell me.

I'll give you a rebus.

That's the same as saying nothing at all. You know I've never solved even one rebus.

True, but this is a fairly easy one.

Fine, go.

The first name of the author of *Time and Free Will* plus K.

Huh?

Time and Free Will plus K.

36

Charlie spotted Micke walking towards the exit with a young girl. She quickly dashed after them.

'Did you want something?' he said when he noticed her.

'I need to talk to you.'

'We were just heading outside for a smoke.'

Micke nodded at the girl who laughed as though he'd said something funny.

'Alone,' Charlie said.

'Milla,' Micke said. 'I just need a minute with my colleague.'

'What about the cigarettes?' Milla said. She tilted her head to the side.

'Here,' Micke said. He handed her one of the two cigarettes he was holding. 'We'll be right back.'

'I don't have a lighter,' Milla called after them, but that problem was quickly solved by a young man who rushed to the rescue.

'Let's walk down towards the river,' Micke suggested.

Charlie felt vaguely uneasy about being alone on a dark footpath with Micke. It made no difference that he was a police officer; he was creepy and what he'd said earlier had set her on edge. And yet, she followed him.

'Cigarette?'

Micke handed her a packet. They'd reached the outdoor dancefloor next to the river's edge.

She nodded, pulled out a cigarette and let Micke light it.

'So, Charline, what do you want?' Micke said.

He pulled hard on his cigarette. In the moonlight, he looked old, even though he had to be younger than her.

'My name is Charlie.'

'You're *called* Charlie,' Micke said. 'But your name is Charline, right?'

'I didn't ask to talk to you so we could bicker about my name,' Charlie said.

'Then why did you want to talk?' Micke smiled.

'I want to know who threatened you. Why you need the case file back and ...'

'And?'

'And why you're so eager to remind me about my background?'

'It's for your own good,' Micke replied. 'It's all for your own good. That's all I can tell you.'

'It's not enough,' Charlie said. 'If you want the file back, I'm going to need more.'

'And what's in it for me?' Micke's eyes flashed.

'The case file,' Charlie said.

My god, he was stupid.

'Where are you going?' Micke exclaimed when Charlie started back towards The Motel. 'We're not done yet. I just meant that I want you to promise me you'll stop digging around that old case, as well.'

'Why?' Charlie stopped and turned round. 'You're the one

who gave me the case file. Why are you so against me digging around now?'

'Fine, it's Olof. He discovered the file had been removed from the archive; don't ask me how. I need it back.'

'What does Olof care?' Charlie asked.

'I don't know. Ask him.'

Charlie didn't trust Micke, but something inside her said he was telling the truth. Either way, she was unlikely to get any further, so she changed tack.

'Why did you tell me to be careful around Johan?' she asked.

'Forget it, we should get back.' Micke started walking.

'Why do I need to be careful around Johan?' Charlie caught up to him. 'I promise I'll drop the case if you tell me,' she lied.

'Because,' Micke replied. 'Because I found out some things about him.'

'What things? What things do you know about him?'

'His dad and your mum lived together.'

'Yeah, I know,' Charlie replied. 'I lived there too.'

'I've been told they'd met before that, though,' Micke went on. 'By certain sources.'

'What fucking sources?' Charlie said.

Her body grew warm when she realised what Micke meant.

'I can't tell you, but I wouldn't shag him if I were you. Unless you enjoy shagging your own brother.'

Charlie stared at Micke, trying to take in what he'd just said. She couldn't. It wasn't true.

'He's not my brother,' Charlie said. Her voice cracked.

'According to my sources, that's exactly what he is. But you can always hope they're wrong; I mean, your mum, not exactly known for being monogamous, was she?'

Don't listen to him, Charlie told herself. He's just an idiot.

Not a person to take seriously. She tripped on a rock and fell. Her head smacked into the ground. The impact made her ears ring.

Micke was beside her in an instant.

'I'm fine,' she snapped when he tried to help her up.

'Suit yourself.'

He started to walk away.

'I'm not going to stop,' she said. 'I'm going to find out what this is all about.'

'No,' Micke said without turning round. 'You won't.'

She slowly got to her feet and called Johan.

'Where are you?' she barked when she was put through to voicemail. 'Where the bloody hell are you?'

When Charlie reached The Motel's car park, she pulled out the card with the number for the gypsy cab. Ten minutes later, an old, white Mercedes pulled up next to her and a man leaned across the passenger seat to open the door.

'My name is Josef,' he said once she had climbed in.

'Is that right,' Charlie replied.

'What happened to you?'

'Nothing,' Charlie said. 'Why do you ask?'

'Your face.'

Charlie pulled out her phone, started the camera app and understood his question. She had dark mud smears on her cheeks.

'Wet wipe?' Josef offered, handing her a strongly scented moist towelette.

She wiped her face.

'And where do we want to go?' Josef asked.

Charlie gave him the address.

'So, Susanne's house,' Josef said as he turned out onto the road.

'Exactly.'

'Are you a friend of hers?'

'I'm her sister,' Charlie said without thinking.

'Is that so? I didn't realise she had a sister, but I guess that's good, that she has someone staying with her now that she's alone. I've tried to persuade her to come to one of our services, but to no avail. Susanne is simply ... she walks her own path, put it that way.'

Josef's words turned into a strange kind of background noise as thoughts screamed ever louder in Charlie's head. *He might be your brother! You might be fucking your own brother!* She pulled out her phone and dialled Johan's number again. No answer.

'You came quickly,' she said, flailing to find a neutral topic of conversation, something to stave off her panic.

'I was out driving anyway,' Josef replied. 'On nights like tonight, I'm always needed. I pull people out of ditches and drive wobbly teenagers home. And not just when there's a party at the pub. The other day, I spotted poor Nora out on Smedstorpsvägen.'

'Nora Roos?'

'Yes. You know her? Oh, silly me, of course you know of her if you're Susanne's sister.'

'All I know is that she's Annabelle's mother,' Charlie said. 'But I thought she was at Solhem.'

'I guess she gets some kind of home leave,' Josef replied. 'She was in the middle of the road several miles from her house, with no coat on. Fredrik was very grateful when I brought her home.'

'What day was that?' Charlie asked.

'I believe it was last Thursday, because I always do a big shop on Thursdays and ...'

'Would you mind taking me there instead?' Charlie said.

'The Roos' house? Now?'

'Yes.'

'I don't think ... I mean, is that such a good idea?'

'I really need to go there.'

Francesca

I woke up in the middle of the night because I felt like someone had wrapped their fingers around my throat and was trying to strangle me. Someone was sitting on my chest, killing me. I flailed about. There was nothing there.

I need to get outside, I thought. I need to get out of this house, out of this body. A minute later, I was on the tree-lined road. I had only my nightgown on, but I didn't feel the cold. I ran like someone was chasing me. I ran as though I thought it was possible to outrun myself.

And then blinding headlights. I put an arm across my eyes. The car stopped; a man climbed out.

'Are you okay?' he said.

'Please turn off the lights,' I said.

He switched to low beams.

'Where are you going?'

'I don't know,' I said. 'I'm just ... running.'

'It looks cold.'

'It's okay.'

'Where do you live?'

'Gudhammar,' I said and waved my hand in the direction of the farm.

'That's kind of far. Are you sure you don't want me to give you a ride?'

'My mum told me not to accept rides from strangers.'

'But she's fine with you running around in freezing weather wearing nothing but a nightgown?'

I laughed. What were the odds of bumping into a man with a sense of humour in the middle of nowhere?

'She doesn't know,' I said and turned round. 'I'd better run back now.'

'Yes, I think that would be best.'

'But thanks anyway. Thank you so much for asking.'

It was only on the way back I started to feel cold.

When morning arrived, my feet were still cold. They were red and white. It would be typical, I mused, if I had got frostbite now, too.

'You're going to have to pull yourself together,' Mum said later that day; I'd lain in bed for hours, staring at the ceiling.

I asked if she was referring to anything in particular and she said it was several things. This hole I'd dug, for example, it couldn't stay like that. She and Dad had been letting me carry on in the hopes that it might have some kind of therapeutic effect, but enough was enough. It was going to be filled in before someone fell into it and got hurt.

'And what else?' I said.

'Well, for example, you've just shoved your suitcase in the closet without unpacking. How long were you planning on leaving it like that?'

I watched Mum's back and thought to myself that, for better or worse, I was never going to become the kind of person who had opinions about how other people kept their closets.

After Mum left, I pulled out my suitcase. At the bottom of it was a book that wasn't mine. I assumed Paul had put it somewhere in my room like he usually did when he thought he'd come across something I should read. I read the title. *Time and Free Will* by Henri Bergson. I flipped through the pages and found a dog-eared one. I realised this was the philosopher Paul had been talking about last spring. The one who had a positive philosophy and his own ideas about time. *Time, I read, is not linear, but amorphous and in flux.*

I lay down on the floor with the book on my stomach and tried to find the gap in time that would take me back to the autumn ball. The same memory as before: Paul and me by the lake. The drinking, the pills, the laughter and then the sudden seriousness: *I think I'm in love, Fran. I'd like to talk to you about it later.*

Time and Free Will. I sat up and started breathing faster.

I think I'm in love, Fran. I'd like to talk to you about it later.

I felt like I was going to pass out so I lay back down and closed my eyes.

The first name of the author of Time and Free Will *plus K.*

The first name of the author of this book, *Time and Free Will*, was Henri. Henri plus K.

Love isn't always rational. Henrik.

Paul had been in love with Henrik Stiernberg.

37

'Please wait here,' Charlie told Josef when they reached the Roos' house.

She walked up to the front door and knocked.

'It's the middle of the night,' Josef said behind her. He'd climbed out of the car and followed her anyway. She was just about to tell him there didn't seem to be anyone home when a rumple-haired Fredrik opened the door.

'What's this about?' he said.

'I'm sorry,' Charlie said. 'I didn't mean to disturb you in the middle of the night, but ...'

'Did something happen?'

Fredrik pulled his dressing gown tighter around himself.

'I just wanted to talk to you about Nora.'

'Is she ...?'

'No, nothing like that,' Charlie said when she saw the panic in his eyes. 'I think she's been going to Susanne Johnsson's house. The children have seen someone lurking in the garden and a woman gave the youngest ones sweets outside the school and now a painting Susanne made has disappeared.'

'What makes you think Nora would do things like that?' Fredrik said. 'Just because she's mentally unstable doesn't mean she'd ...'

'The painting was of your daughter,' Charlie said.

'What are you talking about?' Fredrik exclaimed. 'Honestly, I'm starting to think you're mentally unstable?'

'I'm sorry,' Charlie said. 'I'm not sure what I'm doing. It was an impulse. I should have called first.'

'You certainly shouldn't be banging on people's doors in the middle of the night, accusing them of theft, anyway, that much I can tell you. Don't you think we've been through enough?'

'I'm sorry,' Charlie said again. 'I'm terribly sorry.'

She turned round to leave. Josef had already got back into the car.

'She was doing something in the garage,' Fredrik said. 'We can go out and have a look. But I don't want any charges pressed against Nora if we find the painting.'

'No one's pressing charges,' Charlie said.

They saw it the moment the garage door opened. The painting was only half-covered with a sheet. Fredrik went over and pulled the sheet off completely. He let out a gasp when he saw the motif. Then he reached out and gently stroked the painted cheek.

38

Josef dropped Charlie off at the gate, having reluctantly accepted three hundred kronor for his trouble. It was really too much, he felt.

Susanne wasn't home. Charlie sat down on the living room sofa and resisted the temptation to down what was left in the glasses still sitting on the coffee table.

Her temples had begun to throb. With pressure mounting in her skull and her mind racing, sleep would be impossible. She went into the kitchen and filled a big glass with water from the tap. Then she went upstairs to Nils' room, picked up her laptop and sat down on the bed. She quickly typed in Johan's full name and clicked on images. The first hit was a black-and-white photograph of him smiling. It had to be a few years old because his face was smooth and unlined. She clicked through the images, studying them carefully, his colouring, the shape of his eyes, his smile. Was Mattias her father, too? No, he couldn't be. He just couldn't be.

When she called Johan again and still had no answer, she was overcome with a fear more immediate than the one about their possible blood ties. Had something happened to him? She found the number to The Motel and dialled. It was close to two in the morning. She didn't expect anyone to pick up, so she was surprised to hear Erik's voice. After explaining why she was calling, Erik said he would check his room. Charlie heard him tell someone the bar was closed, and no, there was no more beer to be had. And then, more firmly: It's time for you and your friends to leave now, Svenka.

Erik's breathing became laboured, so Charlie assumed he was about to reach Johan's room. Seconds later, she heard him knocking on the door.

'He's not here,' Erik said after a while. 'Or he's fast asleep.'

'Are you able to open the door?' Charlie asked.

'I'm not in the habit of doing that in the middle of the night,' Erik said. 'Is this urgent?'

'I'm worried something's happened to him,' Charlie said. 'I haven't been able to reach him all night and he hasn't checked out. I know he was planning to go to the Harvest Festival and ...'

'So you want me to go in?'

'Yes,' Charlie said. 'That would be great.'

'I just have to go grab the key.'

Charlie's heart started pounding hard. It felt like an eternity before she heard Erik open the door.

'Is he there?' she asked when Erik didn't say anything.

'No, there's no one here.'

'But his things?' Charlie said. 'Are his things still there?'

Please say no; tell me the room is empty so I can hope he just went back to Stockholm.

'Yes,' Erik replied. 'Everything's still here.'

Charlie didn't know what to do. She couldn't report a grown man missing after only twelve hours. And who would she report it to? She could get in the car and go looking herself, but she'd been drinking. She tried to calm herself down by listing every possible natural explanation she could think of, but she found none of them believable. Had he gone back to Stockholm after all? But if so, why were his things still in his room? Maybe he'd been in a hurry. But how rushed could he have been? She reread Johan's text. *Call me. I think I've found something.*

What had he found?

I'm never going to fall asleep, she thought and looked up at the ceiling. But a while later, she did sink into a fitful, sweaty slumber.

39

Susanne came home at dawn. Her hair was mussed and her make-up smeared. 'You're awake?' she exclaimed.

She stared at Charlie who was sitting at the kitchen table with her laptop open.

'I can't get hold of Johan.'

'Since when?'

'Yesterday. He's not answering his phone, he hasn't checked out and he's not in his room. Or at least he wasn't last night.'

'Maybe he's there now?'

'Maybe,' Charlie said. 'I'm just waiting to sober up so I can go down there and check. No one's answering the phone over there now.'

'I'm sure he's fine,' Susanne said. 'It doesn't necessarily mean ...'

Susanne didn't finish her sentence. Charlie could tell from the look in her eyes that she knew it could mean anything.

'Oh, I know where your painting is, by the way,' Charlie remembered.

'What?'

'Nora Roos took it and I'm guessing she's the one who has been lurking around the garden. At least the time of the lurking tallied with when she was on leave from the hospital.'

'But how?' Susanne stared at her.

'The taxi bloke told me he'd given her a ride home the same day the painting disappeared, so I went over there.'

'You went over to Fredrik and Nora's last night? Are you out of your mind, Charlie?'

'I just wanted to see if the painting was there. And it was, so at least that mystery's solved.'

'It's not bloody solved,' Susanne said. 'You think they're going to like me any better now that I've painted a picture of their daughter in the place where she was found dead?'

Charlie walked out to her car. The wind had shifted, she noted, because today she could smell the paper mill clearly. The olfactory sense was the one most closely linked to memory; Charlie had read that somewhere. Had it been in a psychology textbook or a tabloid? Either way, it appeared to be true, because the unique smell of . . . shit immediately made her think of her bed out in Lyckebo. Betty never figured out the trick of not hanging laundry out to dry in a northerly wind.

She cursed the fact that she hadn't brought her breathalyser. She could have used it now. But she was fairly certain she wasn't over the limit. Her body had an amazing ability to burn alcohol. That had been proven to her several times over.

The morning was fragile and clear. Sunshine set the forest and muddy fields alight. Charlie tuned in to the local radio station where a reporter was interviewing a farmer about the Harvest Festival. There was nothing to celebrate, he griped. Because it didn't have anything to do with the harvest these days, it wasn't what it used to be. Besides, it had been a bone-dry summer and what little rain they'd had had fallen right after they cut the hay. There was nothing to celebrate.

Charlie had no sooner turned out onto the slightly bigger road than a car came up behind her and flashed its high beams.

'Goddamn it,' she said out loud when she checked the rear-view mirror and realised it was a police car. She pulled over and stopped.

Micke and Olof appeared outside her window moments later.

'Hi there, Lager,' Olof said. 'I heard you were back. Came for the Harvest Festival, did you?'

Charlie couldn't tell if it was an attempt at a joke.

'Going a bit fast, aren't we?' Micke said.

'Come off it,' Charlie said.

'Maybe you should come off it,' Micke retorted. 'You were doing ninety on a seventy road and I think you know what that means.'

'I wasn't doing ninety,' Charlie said. 'No way.'

'You were doing ninety-one kilometres an hour,' Micke said.

'What the fuck.' Charlie banged the steering wheel. 'What do you want?'

'We just want you to obey the laws of the land,' Micke said. 'Police officers aren't exempt from the law, not even the high and mighty ones from Stockholm. Now, now, you don't have to look so upset, we're just doing our job. If you don't like it, you can go back to Stockholm.'

'Are you always this meticulous about the rules and regulations?' Charlie asked when Micke pulled out his pocket notebook.

'Hold your horses, Micke,' Olof intervened. 'Let's look the other way just this once.'

*

The police radio crackled. Charlie heard something about a man being found at the smelter.

'We have to go,' Micke said.

'What's going on?' Charlie felt her pulse rising.

Neither Olof nor Micke replied. They just turned on both lights and sirens and drove off. Charlie quickly started the engine and followed. A tractor turned out in front of her. She had to slam on the brakes to avoid rear-ending it. She leaned on her horn, but the man driving the tractor refused to move onto the verge to allow her to overtake. It felt like hours before she could get past him.

A crowd of curious onlookers had gathered at the smelter gates. Charlie stopped, jumped out of the car and ran into the smelter yard. Red dust swirled around her feet. She couldn't see the police car anywhere. Everything was strangely quiet. A flock of blackbirds flew past above the rusty old façades and rooftops. The smelter was enormous, like a small city made of iron, steel and furnaces. *Hell*, Betty had called it. *A hell with room for countless lost souls.*

Charlie spun round; she could hear sirens again. An ambulance entered the yard. And then Micke was there. He came out of one of the big sheds and waved the ambulance over. Charlie ran to him.

'Who?' she said. 'Who is it?'

'We don't have time now,' Micke said. 'Let us do our jobs.'

Charlie looked over his shoulder and saw a man being carried out on a stretcher.

'Is it Johan?' she asked, but she already knew the answer. She had caught a glimpse of the blue shirt he'd worn the last time she saw him. 'What happened?'

'He's hurt,' Micke said.

'Where? In what way?'
'The back of his head. Looks like a crush injury.'
'Who? Who did it?'
'How should I know?' Micke replied.

Charlie followed the ambulance in her car. Her mind was racing. A head injury. How bad could it be? It could be really bad. She went over the functions located in that area of the brain: the occipital lobe which handled visual stimuli or, if the blow had landed further down, the cerebellum which did balance and gross motor skills and ... that was as far as she got, the hemispheres were muddled in her mind.

Skaraborg Hospital said a sign in front of the main entrance to the large blue and grey concrete building. Charlie ran into the revolving door. She stepped too close to the glass. Everything stopped. The pressure across her chest intensified and her heart raced faster. Not now. But the panic attack was already in full swing. Then the doors slowly began to rotate again. Charlie hurried inside and collapsed on a bench. She put her head in her hands and breathed as calmly as she was able. A few minutes later, she was ready to stand back up and walk over to the information counter. The man behind it was aggravatingly calm when she asked for directions to the A&E. There were red and yellow hallways and ...

'Just point,' Charlie said. Then she took off running in the direction of the man's wave.

'There are signs,' he called after her.

Francesca

I had lain awake half the night, pondering Paul's infatuation with Henrik Stiernberg. He was the very last person I would ever have guessed. Had it been requited? I wondered now. Was that why Henrik had always behaved like a fucking prick towards Paul in front of others, because he was ashamed of his feelings? And the night of the ball? Had something maybe happened between them that ... I had to talk to Henrik, I thought, sitting in bed in Céline's nightgown, writing down everything I'd discovered. Then I added a title to my text: *Gaps in Time*. I read the words and felt a bit proud that I'd managed to work Henri Bergson's ideas in; maybe the circle was complete now.

My whole body itched. I felt awake in that way that had made me sneak out at Adamsberg. I twisted and turned in bed for a long time before giving up. I had to go outside.

The moment I stepped out the front door, I could tell something wasn't right. A light was burning where it shouldn't; a flame was flickering in the window of the gatehouse. My first thought was that Vilhelm was back, that he was sitting on his creaky kitchen chair with his deck of cards at the ready, waiting to play one last game of poker. But I didn't believe in ghosts. There was someone else in there, someone who had lit a candle. *Turn back*, my mind told me as I started walking down the driveway barefoot. The stones were sharp and cold under my feet, but I could barely feel it; my attention was fixed on the gatehouse. Maybe it was Ivan? Who had thought of something else he needed to reclaim.

I'd reached the tiny porch now. I hesitated for a second on the last step before taking a big step forward and carefully peering in through the window. It wasn't a candle burning inside; it was a fire in the fireplace. But it wasn't the fire that made me back away from the window and stagger backwards down the steps. It was the scene it illuminated. Because there, on a blanket in front of the fireplace, lay my mother. Stark naked. Her hands entwined in the dark hair of the undressed man kissing her breasts. I didn't have to see his face to know who he was. It was Adam. Mum and Adam Rehn.

When I woke up the next day, I tried to convince myself what I'd seen had been a dream, but of course, I failed. What was I going to do? Tell Dad? Never. Besides, he probably already knew since Adam had been fired. And why would I tell Dad anyway? I'd never ratted him out when I'd accidentally caught him being 'friendly' with women at parties, so it was only fair to keep Mum's secret, too. Somewhere inside, I felt a new respect for her, but mostly I was surprised. I'd always thought of her as the victim, the one who knew and suffered in silence, but apparently she was more than just a pawn in Dad's game. The scales were more closely balanced than I'd imagined.

I thought about Paul again. *Love isn't rational.* Had he been thinking of Henrik when he said that? Either way, I couldn't think of anything more irrational than falling in love with

Henrik Stiernberg. I was overcome with a strong urge to talk to Paul, ask him how he could be in love with such a jerk. *You deserve so much better, Paul Bergman.*

When I got up, I'd come to a decision. I was going to go over to the cemetery, to Paul's grave. I knew Mum and Dad wouldn't let me go alone and I didn't want them waiting in the car for me, so when they sat down on the veranda after lunch to enjoy the autumn sun, I took Nana's old bicycle and set off for town. The small town square was virtually deserted. The only people I saw were a few old men sitting on a bench outside the supermarket. They were a sorry sight with their cans of lager, talking too loudly. I was thirsty after my bike ride and decided to buy a drink.

'Why hello there, Miss,' said one of the men on the bench when I parked the bike in the rack. 'Whose lass are you, then?'

Mum had told me never to speak to the drunks on the bench. I was supposed to pretend they didn't exist. The rules of looking people in the eye, answering politely and not forgetting to ask questions back didn't apply to everyone.

But I was on my own now, so I did as I pleased.

'I'm Rikard and Fredrika Mild's daughter,' I said.

'Gudhammar?' said the man next to the one who had addressed me first. He was wearing only a T-shirt but didn't seem cold. 'You're the daughter of the fancy folk up at Gudhammar?'

I nodded.

'I used to stack hay for your grandfather when I was young,' said the third man, who hadn't spoken yet, a toothless, bony, drawn little man. 'Your grandfather was a good man. He treated us like ...'

'Humans,' laughed the man in the T-shirt and held out a flask to me.

I opened it and took a big swig, relishing the burning sensation in my throat. The three men were suddenly eyeing me with a lot more appreciation.

'Are you coming to the party?' the man who had given me the booze asked when I handed back the flat, leather-covered bottle.

'What party?'

'The Harvest Festival,' he replied, as though it was something everyone ought to know about.

'When is it?'

'This Friday and Saturday.'

'What lies are you people telling her?' a voice suddenly said behind me.

I turned round and saw a woman in a floral dress under a knit jumper. I recognised her from the café. She was the one with the young daughter.

'I never tell lies,' the man retorted. 'I was just telling young Miss Mild here that there's going to be one hell of a party here this weekend.'

The woman looked me up and down with an expression I couldn't read. Curious? Disapproving? Then she smiled and said she was going to have a pre-party at her house before the Harvest Festival.

'You're welcome to come.' She looked at the men and then me. 'You too. There's going to be singing and dancing and ...'

'A lot of bloody drinking,' the scrawny man added. 'Betty always shares her goodies.'

'You're being rude,' the woman snapped.

Her voice was suddenly harsh.

'I wasn't being rude,' the man called after her. 'It's the truth. It's the truth, Betty!'

Betty didn't reply; the scrawny man shook his head and said something about that lady being far too hot-tempered.

I had been to Gullspång Church for Christmas a few times as a child and had just thought of it as a regular church. But now, compared to the chapel at Adamsberg, it looked splendid and warm. I found Paul's grave almost immediately. It was located off one of the aisles shaded by big horse chestnut trees. His headstone was made of a material that stood out in the otherwise grey row. It looked like green marble. I slowly traced the inscription with my finger.

Our beloved Paul Bergman. 29.1.1972 – 1.9.1989

I sat down in the damp grass. Then I lay back in the same position I imagined Paul was in inside his coffin with my hands crossed on my chest. Or had Paul been cremated? And if he hadn't been, were maggots writhing around his eye sockets now?

I blinked hard to get rid of that image. He can't feel anything anyway. He's in a no-man's-land, I told myself. He's where he was before he was born, where he can't feel or see anything, not even darkness.

I closed my eyes and felt damp seep through my clothes. The cold should have made me shiver, but strangely enough, I felt warm. I imagined Paul underneath me and I no longer saw maggots in his eyes, instead he was alive, tanned and excited.

Did you know that if you cover a kitten's eyes during a certain period of its development, it can never learn to see? It's like a window closes and can never be opened again.

*

I was prodded awake. The cemetery was dark and I screamed when I saw a man with a rake standing over me. I tried to get up quickly, but I was stiff and slow with cold.

'Calm down,' said a voice I recognised. 'Calm down.'

I'd managed to get up on my hands and knees and now I was able to see his face.

'Adam?'

'Yes. What are you doing here, Francesca? And barely dressed. Are you trying to kill yourself?'

'I just dozed off.'

'You gave me a fright.'

'Likewise,' I said, feeling my pulse slow.

I figured Adam wasn't the type to beat me to death with a rake and dump me into an open grave. After what I'd seen him do with my mum the night before, he seemed, more than anything, like ... a passionate person.

'You were friends, weren't you?' Adam said, nodding towards the grave.

'Yes.'

'It's just too sad.' Adam put a hand on the headstone. 'Just too sad, the whole thing.'

'Did you know him?' I said.

'No, but his father. I've been working extra here for a few years.' He nodded at the graves all around us. 'And I guess I'll be here for a few more, now.'

'What time is it?' I asked.

'Quarter past seven,' Adam replied without checking his watch.

'Fuck.'

'Want a ride home?'

'I rode my bike here.'

'I've got a fairly big car.'

Adam pointed towards the car park.

As I sat in the car with Adam, it occurred to me that I'd just broken two of Mum's strictest rules: never to allow my nether regions to get cold and never to accept a ride from a stranger. But Adam didn't count as a stranger, I corrected myself; he worked for us, for god's sake. Used to work for us. And apparently provided other services, too.

'Why did you stop working for us?' I asked, because I was curious to hear his answer.

'Your father wanted it that way.'

'Did you accidentally trim the wrong bush?' I said. 'My parents take things like that very seriously.'

'No,' Adam said, his face expressionless.

I'd thought he would attempt to provide at least a half-wise plausible explanation, but he didn't say anything else. We were halfway up the tree-lined drive when he pulled over. I was just about to close the door behind me when he leaned over and told me to say hi to my mum from him.

Mum and Dad were livid when I got back. It didn't matter that I owned up to what I'd done, to betraying their confidence. How could I leave without telling them? After everything that had happened. How could I?

I said sorry and sorry again. I promised to be a better person from now on; I was going to make things right; fill in the hole, tidy my room, stop sneaking off.

'Adam says hi,' I told Mum on my way up to my room.

40

Charlie walked up to the nurse manning the reception desk in the A&E and said she wanted to know how Johan Ro was doing; he had just been brought in.

'Who are you?' said the nurse.

'I'm ...'

She didn't know what to tell her. Who was she? She was ... a police officer. She quickly pulled her wallet out of her bag and showed the nurse her ID.

'We have no information yet,' the nurse said. 'He was just admitted, but you're welcome to have a seat and wait.'

Charlie took a seat. Across from her in the waiting room sat an old man whose eyes were red from crying and next to him a middle-aged woman who looked to be his daughter. Further down the room, a man and a woman were having an agitated discussion in a foreign language.

A young doctor entered the room and walked over to the counter. Charlie saw the man behind the glass nod in her direction.

'How is he?' Charlie burst out before the doctor had a chance to speak.

'Do you know if Johan has any relatives we could contact?' the doctor said, ignoring her question.

'Is he alive?'

Charlie waited for his reply. It was a long time coming. *Fucking just tell me he's alive.*

'Yes,' the doctor said, 'but he's in critical condition. Do you know if there are any ...?'

'His parents are dead,' Charlie said. 'And he's single and has no children. I suppose you might say I'm his closest relative.'

'I thought you were from the police.' The doctor looked confused. 'I thought you were a police officer from Gullspång.'

'I am,' Charlie replied. 'I'm a police officer from Gullspång *and* Johan's friend.'

'I understand,' the doctor replied in a tone that Charlie interpreted to mean that friendship was irrelevant.

'I'm his girlfriend,' she said to elevate her status.

'Aha, I see,' said the doctor, looking bewildered.

'What do you know?'

'Not much. But you will be kept informed. He's in surgery now. He has been hit in the back of the head with a blunt object. I'll be back when I have more information.'

Time stood still. Charlie stared at the magazines in the rack next to her. She picked one up and flipped through it distractedly. They must have been old because one of them had an article with tips on how to decorate a patio. Happy-looking women in sweeping skirts planting seeds and hanging up wild strawberry plants.

He had to survive.

Because if he didn't?

He just had to survive.

A nurse appeared and showed her to another waiting room. 'It's a bit quieter in here,' she said.

Charlie took in the empty room. Had she been brought here to be told Johan was dead?

'What's happening to him?'

'He's still in surgery. You can talk to the doctors when they're done.'

The nurse left. Charlie walked over to the coffee machine. She picked up a brown paper cup, placed it in the right spot and inserted a ten-kronor coin into the coin slot. Nothing happened. She went back to her seat only to get up again moments later. She walked over to the window and looked out across the dreary hospital car park. Then she pulled out her phone and started surfing the internet at random.

Please let him be okay. She sat back down. Stared into space, focusing on her breathing. After a while – an hour? Two hours? – she put her head down on the armrest and dozed off.

A party in Lyckebo, big bonfire on the lawn. Dangerously close to the house.

What if our house burns down? Charlie says to Betty.

Betty just laughs and says there's no need to fret. It's autumn, everything's wet, so if a stray spark were to reach the façade, it would go out straight away. It wouldn't stand a chance against the damp wood.

The guests arrive. *What's with the Walpurgis bonfire, Betty? It's October, not April!*

It's an October bonfire, Betty laughs. She's dressed too lightly. A thin, white dress, or is it a nightgown?

Aren't you cold, Mummy?

Why would I be?

More people arrive. A man is trying to barbecue something over the flames. A pig? A boar?

Welcome! Betty exclaims when a new face joins them in the

garden. It's a girl. She's too young to be at a Lyckebo party, even Charlie can see that.

Come say hello, sweetheart, Betty shouts. *Come over here, Charline, and say hello to Francesca. Come and say hello to Francesca Mild.*

41

'Charline?' A hand on her shoulder.

Charlie sat up.

'How is he?'

'We've operated to alleviate the pressure in his skull and he is about to be taken to Karolinska in Stockholm.'

'Is he going to live?'

'We've done everything we can; the doctors at Karolinska are neurosurgical specialists. They will take over from here.'

'So you don't know.'

'His condition is critical; that's all I can tell you. We'll be keeping you informed.'

'Can I go with him to Karolinska?'

'Not in the ambulance.'

'Can I see him? I mean before he goes?'

Charlie had prepared herself for worst, but it was still a shock to see Johan in the hospital bed. His face was swollen beyond recognition; there were tubes everywhere and part of his head had been shaved.

'How are you feeling?' she whispered, not caring how stupid the question was and then: 'Who did this to you? Who did you go to meet?'

She reached out and stroked his cheek, bent down and whispered in his ear that he was going to live, that he just had to live.

She stayed behind when they took him away. They'd taken down her contact details; they were going to keep her appraised of any changes.

Should she head up to Karolinska straight away? Where would she be most useful? Were Olof and Micke going to catch whoever had done this to Johan? She thought about Susanne and the children. About Francesca. She had to stay in Gullspång. At least for now.

Images of Johan followed her back to Gullspång. It was only when she began to cast about for anything else to focus on that she remembered her dream, the party in Lyckebo, the big bonfire right in front of the house. The party had happened in real life, she knew that now. And the visit? *Come over here, Charline, and say hello to Francesca. Come and say hello to Francesca Mild.*

Yes, it had happened.

What was Francesca doing at our house, Betty? What was a teenage girl doing at your party?

Charlie went straight to the police station and knocked on Olof's door.

'Charlie!' he said when he saw it was her. 'I was just about to ...'

'We need to talk,' Charlie said.

'It'll have to wait. As I'm sure you understand, I have my hands full at the moment.'

'It's important.'

Olof sighed.

'Fine, come in.'

She entered; Olof shut the door behind her.

'I want to talk about Francesca Mild,' she said. 'About why the case was dropped.'

'We don't really have time for that right now, Charlie.'

'Yes, you do, because I'm pretty sure it has something to do with what happened to Johan. I want to know why the investigation into Francesca's disappearance was dropped so quickly. What really happened?'

'I didn't work here back then. Lars-Göran handled the case. Lars-Göran Edwardsson. He was the senior officer here for a long time. A bloody good one, too, let me tell you. He and I were friends.'

'Where is he now?'

'He died a few years ago, sadly. He was the best copper I've ever worked with.'

He pointed to a photograph of two uniformed police officers with their arms around each other's shoulders. One was a younger Olof, the other Lars-Göran Edwardsson.

'If he was so bloody good, how come he closed the investigation into Francesca's disappearance so quickly? There were lots of loose ends to tie up, I've read the case file.'

Olof shrugged.

'Bloody hell, Olof,' Charlie went on. 'Johan's in the hospital, fighting for his life; he was attacked after we started sniffing around that case. Maybe Francesca Mild was murdered and the murderer was trying to silence Johan. This is serious, can't you see that?'

'Lars-Göran was coerced,' Olof said. 'He was asked to drop the case. Maybe he was paid to do it; I don't know.'

'And his name has been blacked out because he was forced to drop the case.'

'I don't know why his name was blacked out; it was before my time. But the person who asked him to drop the case didn't kill Francesca, that much I can guarantee.'

'How can you be so sure?' Charlie asked.

'It was her father,' Olof said. 'Rikard Mild. It was Francesca's dad who made Lars-Göran drop the whole thing.'

'Why?'

'Lars-Göran said it was because Rikard Mild preferred to think of her as missing, not dead. He was absolutely certain she was dead and wanted to spare his family.'

'And Lars-Göran never asked how he could be so sure she was dead? It never occurred to him that her father might have had something to do with it?'

Olof frowned.

'I suppose he didn't think he would have killed his own daughter.'

'Why not?' Charlie said. 'Was he unaware that it happens? That fathers kill their children.'

'If that were the case, Lars-Göran would never have closed the investigation. I'm sure of that.'

'We need to get hold of Rikard Mild right now,' Charlie said.

Olof put his hand up to stop her.

'Easy now,' he said. 'Rikard Mild must be over seventy years old and given the overwhelming force used against Johan Ro ...'

'We have to talk to him anyway,' Charlie cut him off, 'as soon as possible. Do you have any suspects?'

'Not at present.'

'Check out Adam Rehn,' Charlie said. 'As you might recall, he was fired from Gudhammar for unknown reasons just before Francesca disappeared. Ask him why.'

'Like I said, we're not investigating the Francesca case,' Olof said. 'This is an assault.'

'It's both,' Charlie countered. 'Who found Johan?'

'A man walking his dog. It ran off and got into the smelter yard and started to bark. It was a pointer,' Olof went on, as though the breed was somehow significant. 'A hunting dog.'

'Do you have pen and paper?'

Olof handed her a sheet of paper and a pen.

Adam Rehn, Charlie wrote at the top. *Worked at Gudhammar but was fired for unknown reasons just before Francesca disappeared. Didn't want to talk to us. Is known as a 'womaniser'.*

Sixten Molan, family friend and Francesca's therapist, has informed us that Francesca told him her friend at Adamsberg, Paul Bergman, was murdered. According to Doctor Molan, Francesca was confused and delusional, but it might be useful to look into this.

Ivan Hedlund; his dad worked at Gudhammar almost his entire life. Johan and I met him and asked questions about this.

Charlie paused and then, after a moment's hesitation, added Carola Johnsson. If she wanted to make a list of everyone they had spoken to, she had to mention Lola, even though she was a highly unlikely perpetrator. That being said, she could know more than she'd let on, or maybe she'd been blabbing to the wrong people.

As part of his research, Johan has also contacted Adamsberg Boarding School and students who attended it together with Francesca. What really happened at the school?

When she was done, Charlie handed the list to Olof. He looked at it and repeated that they were focusing on the assault.

'An assault that is most likely connected to this,' Charlie said insistently, pointing to the paper.

'We'll do everything we can,' Olof said. 'I really will do it right this time.'

He paused, as though he were expecting a gold star.

'Make sure you get hold of Francesca's family,' Charlie said. 'Where are they? Why would her father pay to have the case dropped?'

'I already told you why!'

'The problem is, Olof, that it doesn't make sense. It just doesn't make sense.'

42

Charlie didn't take her eyes off her phone. The hospital had promised to call if there was any change, positive or negative. She was wrestling with the idea of going to Stockholm, but Johan was sedated. She could be more useful here. She left the police station, got into her car and called Anders.

'How are you?' she said.

'Crap. You?'

'Bad.'

She quickly filled him in about Johan.

'Hold on a minute,' Anders said. 'What's going on?'

'I don't know.'

'But you think it has something to do with that old case?'

'A lot of things seem to suggest it.'

'I'll find the family,' Anders said. 'I'm sorry I haven't yet, but I ... A lot of things have come up. We've identified an ex-boyfriend of one of the women. A man with a less than immaculate past, to say the least.'

'Estonian?'

'Yes, but he was in Sweden at the time the women disappeared. We're just waiting for the DNA analysis.'

'Good. I hope he's the guy.'

'Me too. I'll be in touch about the Milds asap.'

'Thanks.'

Anders called back minutes later to tell her he'd found them.

'Rikard Mild is registered in Switzerland; there's an address but no phone number.'

'And his wife?'

'Ex-wife, they're divorced. Her name's Fredrika Reimer and she's registered in Switzerland, too. Same thing there, an address, but no phone number.'

Charlie sighed.

'Surely you can go through a police liaison in Switzerland?'

'I'm on it,' Anders said. 'But there's a sister, too, Cécile Stiernberg. She's registered at an address in Stockholm. Are you writing this down?'

'Yes,' Charlie said, even though she wasn't. 'And the phone number?' she said after Anders told her the address.

Anders gave her the number.

Charlie hung up and immediately called Cécile Stiernberg.

Her call went to voicemail after just one ring: *You've reached Cécile Stiernberg. Please leave a message.*

Charlie hung up without saying anything. She wrote down the address in the notes app on her phone, started the car and set off for Gullspång Landscaping.

Adam's car wasn't in the driveway. Charlie saw a curtain twitch in a window as she approached the door and knocked. Adam's mum opened. She looked terrified.

'Is Adam home?' Charlie asked.

The old woman shook her head.

'Do you know where he is?'

'No. I don't know.'

'What do you want?' said someone from inside the house.

As he got closer, Charlie saw it was one of the men who had been sitting with Adam in the pub. David?

'I want to talk to Adam.'

'He's out. What do you need him for?'

'I need to talk to him,' Charlie said.

'You too? Micke from the police was just here. Has something happened?'

'My boy!' the old woman suddenly screamed. 'My darling boy! He promised not to take the car. He promised.' She grabbed Charlie's arm. 'Take me to him. Let me see the body. Let me hold him one last time.'

She broke down, sobbing. David put his arm around her shoulders and told her to calm down, that Adam was just running an errand, that he would be back soon.

David didn't seem to realise Adam's mum was stuck in a time warp, that she wasn't talking about Adam.

'I think you'd better leave,' David said, shooting Charlie an accusatory look.

'Do you know where I can find Adam?' Charlie asked.

'I think he went to the cemetery.'

There was only one car parked in the street outside the cemetery; it had *Gullspång Landscaping* written on the sides. A black cat with flashing yellow eyes was slinking along the top of the stone wall. Charlie walked past the large, fenced-in family tombs towards the more modest resting places where she imagined Adam's brother might be interred. But she found neither his grave nor Adam. Maybe he'd just parked by the cemetery and then gone elsewhere? She was just about to turn back when she spotted him. He was standing by the water tap under the big chestnut tree and he started when he heard her approaching.

'You scared me!' he said. 'What do you want?'

'I want to talk to you.'

Adam turned off the tap.

'I was going to water the plants on my brother's grave.' And then, looking up at the darkening sky: 'But it looks like I won't have to.'

What was there even there to water? Charlie wondered to herself.

'Where were you last night?' she said.

'I was at the pub; you bloody saw me there.'

'But before that?'

'At home. Why do you want to know?'

'My friend was assaulted yesterday. He might not make it.'

'Really?' Adam raised his eyebrows theatrically. 'But what does that have to do with me?'

'What happened to your hand?' Charlie said, pointing to a wound between the thumb and forefinger of Adam's right hand.

'What do you mean?' Adam took a step towards Charlie. 'What are you trying to say? Do you think I ...?'

He raised his hand and for a moment Charlie thought he was going to strike her.

'It's Mum,' he said, holding his hand up inches from her face. 'She gets ideas and when she does, she bites and scratches.'

Someone called out behind them. Charlie turned round and saw Micke and Olof walking towards them from the car park.

'What are you doing here, Charlie?' Olof said when they got nearer.

'She's stalking me,' Adam said. 'I'm just trying to visit my brother's grave and she's accusing me of all kinds of things.'

'I just wanted to ask a couple of questions,' Charlie said.

'I think you should go home now, Charlie,' Olof said. He turned to Adam. 'Would you mind coming with us? We need to talk to you.'

'Why?' Adam let out a laugh. 'Is this some sort of joke, Olof? Micke?'

'You'd better come with us so we can talk without being disturbed.'

Charlie watched the trio walk off towards the car park. She thought about Adam's intimate dancing the night before. Was it possible to be so carefree right after beating another human being to a pulp?

Yes, was the answer to that. For some people, it was possible.

Please, let it be him, Charlie thought. Let it be Adam who's behind this whole thing, the assault and Francesca's disappearance, so this can be over. She tried to shake off the images from her dream, the one she knew came from a real memory: *Come over here, Charline, and say hello to Francesca. Come and say hello to Francesca Mild.*

Francesca

I was restless in a way I'd never been before. I wanted to get really drunk, to talk to people, to be … normal? I wanted to go to the party that woman I'd met in town and seen in the café, the one with the tangled hair and the wild eyes, was throwing. Something told me it might be exactly what I needed.

But she hadn't told me where she lived.

I called Jacob and asked. We hadn't talked since my visit and I suppose I should have felt awkward, but one good thing about my mental state was that I didn't care about things like I normally would have. I'd come back from the dead. I had neither the energy nor the ability to feel much.

I said I had been invited to a party by a woman named Betty, but that I didn't know where she lived.

'Betty Lager?' Jacob said.

'You know her?'

'Everyone knows Betty.'

A slight hesitation in his voice.

'Is something wrong?'

'I don't know about wrong. Her parties are pretty wild, that's all. At least from what I hear.'

I almost told him I liked when things got wild, but then I realised that might have a sexual undertone to it.

'Where does she live?' I asked instead.

'I don't know exactly, but it's on the other side of town. It's definitely pretty far from Gudhammar. I could give you a ride, if you want.'

'I think they were going to some kind of harvest festival afterwards. Why don't you come?'

Jacob said he didn't want to. He wasn't a party person.

Was that disappointment in his voice at me apparently being one?

'That's a shame,' I said.

'But I'd be happy to give you a ride,' Jacob said again. 'I just have to find out exactly where it is.'

'Thanks,' I said. 'Maybe you can pick me up at the end of our road? Is seven okay?'

'Are you running away?'

'I'm just going to a party.'

When I reached the end of our tree-lined drive at five to seven, Jacob was already waiting for me. I had snuck down the fire escape outside my window and taken a circuitous route across the field behind the gatehouse. I'd told Mum and Dad I was going to bed, that I had a terrible headache and didn't want to be disturbed. With luck, I'd be able to climb back up the way I'd come when I got home and they would never even know I'd been gone.

Jacob smelled fresh out of the shower. When I climbed in, he started to lean over as though he wanted to hug me, but then stopped himself mid-motion.

'You look pretty,' he said.

I looked down at my clothes. I'd borrowed one of Cécile's expensive shiny dresses. This particular one was green and showed just the right amount of cleavage. Since I was taller than Cécile, it was, admittedly, possibly slightly on the short side – at least that would have been Mum's comment if she'd seen me. I'd brought one of Cécile's lamb's wool jumpers, as well, but I was probably going to be cold anyway, especially if I had to walk back to Gudhammar; was there even a taxi service in Gullspång?

'We've been here before,' I said when Jacob turned onto the grass road.

I pointed to the sign that said Lyckebo.

'Right,' Jacob replied.

I noticed that his ears were bright red.

'What's going on?' he went on, pointing up at the house where a large bonfire was burning. 'What the hell is going on?'

'It's a bonfire,' I said, like that wasn't obvious.

Jacob parked the car.

'Are you sure you want to be here?' he said.

I looked at the bonfire, at the people around it, and then I spotted her. Betty. She was dressed too lightly, but maybe it was warmer by the fire. She was standing really close to it.

'Francesca,' Jacob said when I climbed out of the car. 'Be careful.'

A song our French nanny used to sing sometimes was playing at a loud volume. The theme was the same as in the English version: It's my party and I'll cry if I want to. *C'est ma fête, je fais ce qui me plaît.*

Around twenty people were out in the garden and I could see more inside the house through the lit windows. Something was being barbecued; I could smell it but not see what it was. For a minute, I just stood there staring at the drunken mayhem, thinking there was still time to turn round. But I barely had time to finish that thought before Betty looked up and spotted me.

She walked over to me with her arms outstretched as though we were old friends reuniting.

Come over and say hello, sweetheart, she called to someone behind her and then her little girl came running over. She was barefoot and when she stopped a few feet away, I noticed her feet were red from cold. *Come over here, Charline, and say hello to Francesca. Come and say hello to Francesca Mild.*

'Hi,' said the girl, whose name was Charline. She took a step closer.

'Properly,' Betty laughed. 'Shake her hand.'

The girl shot her mother a confused look. Then she held out her hand. It was as cold as ice.

'And introduce yourself.'

Betty nudged her daughter in the back.

'But you already told her my name, Mum,' the girl said.

Betty burst out laughing.

'That's right. That's absolutely right, sweetheart.' She ruffled the girl's tangled hair. 'Alright, well, come with me, Francesca; I'll get you something to drink. We have a bonfire going and we're roasting a whole fucking pig, so I hope you're hungry and thirsty. I have my own wine, you see, a whole root cellar full of it.'

We'd reached the fire; the little girl was worriedly eyeing the flames, which came dangerously close to the house. Betty ushered me around so I could say hello to everyone. Most were very drunk yet shy, as though unused to strangers.

'This is Svenka,' Betty said, grabbing and shaking the

shoulder of a man dozing on a bench by the porch. 'Svenka. You're missing the party.'

'I'm just having a little rest,' slurred the man called Svenka. I recognised him from the café.

Then someone called out for Betty and she left without apologising.

I pondered whether to go into the house or stay outside. Just when I had decided to go in, the man on the bench coughed and opened his eyes wide.

'Who are you?' he said.

I told him I was Francesca Mild.

The man whistled and his bleary eyes looked me up and down. I felt naked in my short dress.

'Svenka,' said the man, offering his hand.

He had cuts on his forearm, probably from the factory.

'So what is a beautiful girl like you doing in a place like this?' Svenka said. And before I had a chance to respond: 'Why haven't you got a bloody drink yet?'

He stood up, swayed and grabbed my shoulder for balance.

'I just got here,' I told him, 'but I'd love a glass of whatever.'

I knew I wouldn't be able to stand this place for another second unless I could get intoxicated right quick.

'Follow me.'

Svenka staggered off; it was as though an invisible force was pulling him left.

'Where are we going?' I said.

'To fetch more wine. Oh, come on. I don't bite.'

I followed Svenka to a mound of dirt with a brown door in it. He turned a rusty key and motioned for me to go inside ahead of him. I thought to myself that I was an idiot for going into a dark cellar with a stranger, and yet, that was exactly what I did. The room was damp and dimly lit.

'Don't be scared,' Svenka said behind me.

'I'm not scared,' I lied.

'I'm not going to do anything to you,' Svenka went on. 'Unless you want me to, of course.'

He was standing very close to me; I could smell the tobacco and alcohol on his breath.

'All I want is a glass of wine,' I said, as firmly as I could.

To my relief, Svenka backed away and flipped a switch. A light turned on overhead. I forgot my fear when I saw all the shelves full of wine bottles around me.

'It's cherry wine,' Svenka said, as though showing off his own life's work. 'Want some?'

I nodded. He took a glass down from a shelf and pulled out one of the green screw-cap bottles. The glugging sound of the wine filling my glass to the brim was heavenly.

'Try it,' he said; I raised the glass to my lips.

I took a big gulp and closed my eyes.

'Amazing,' I said.

I really knew nothing about wine, but this one tasted wonderful. I brought my glass back outside to where the others were.

'Is everyone going on to the Harvest Festival later?' I asked.

Svenka chuckled and told me most were unlikely to make it there.

43

Charlie paced around Susanne's kitchen. She'd heard nothing from the hospital and as far as Adam was concerned, all she could do was wait. But she still had one lead to chase down: Betty. She had to talk to someone who had been at Betty's party. She had to try to find out why Francesca Mild had been to one of the Lyckebo bashes. Of the many people who had come and gone at Betty's parties, most were dead now. She'd gone through the list last summer with Susanne; they'd concluded Lola was one of the few who were both alive and living in the area. Might Lola have some information? But if Francesca had attended a Lyckebo party, shouldn't Lola have mentioned that when they'd talked about the Mild family? It was worth another shot. Charlie googled Lola's phone number; it rang four times and she was just about to hang up when a slurred voice said: 'Hello.'

'Hi Lola. It's me, Charlie.'

'Hiya, Charlie.'

'I need to talk to you. Do you have a minute?'

'I'm at the pub. But why don't you join me?'

*

Lola was sitting at the bar, noticeably inebriated, letting Jonas top up her glass. She seemed to have forgotten their phone conversation, because her face lit up when she spotted Charlie.

'Lovely,' she said, patting the stool next to her. 'What can I get you?'

'I just want to talk to you.'

'No reason we can't drink while we talk.'

Lola burst out laughing. Her teeth were full of fillers.

'It's about Betty.'

'Betty, Betty, Betty.' Lola sighed. 'So many things are still about Betty.'

'It's about someone else, too,' Charlie said. 'Francesca Mild. I remembered that she came to Lyckebo once. To one of the parties.'

'Is that right? Tell me more.'

'I was hoping you could tell me. What was Francesca Mild doing at a party in Lyckebo? She was so much younger.'

'That's right.' Lola lit up. 'It's true she was there once.'

'Do you remember anything from that night?'

Lola was silent for a while, then she shook her head. Nothing.

'Do you know if it was the night of the party Francesca Mild disappeared?' Charlie asked. 'It was in October, and ...'

'I have no idea what date or even what year it was. All I remember is that Francesca Mild was there once, the time Betty had a bonfire. She was feeding it like crazy, squirting lighter fluid everywhere. It was pure luck it didn't spread to the house. I think the Mild girl got pretty drunk. Then she left. I don't think she was there for long.'

'Do you remember whether Betty was still at the party after Francesca left?'

'Lord, how am I supposed to remember something like that?'

'I understand if you don't,' Charlie replied. 'I just thought I'd ask.'

'Charline!' Lola called after her as she walked towards the door. 'I thought of something.'

Charlie turned round.

'Francesca left in a car. She was picked up by one of the Burial Brothers.'

'The Burial Brothers?'

'Yes, the undertaker's lads.'

'What lads?'

'Christer Bergman's boys,' Lola said, as though Charlie should know who Christer Bergman was. 'The man who ran the funeral home. He had two sons, you know, Paul and … I don't remember the other one's name. But I think Paul was dead by then.'

'Paul Bergman?' Charlie said. Her heart was starting to beat faster. 'Do you know if he attended a boarding school?' she asked.

'Sure,' Lola said. 'He was at Adamsberg. So what?'

'He was Francesca's best friend.'

'All I know is he was bullied so bloody badly in school his dad took all the money he had to pay the tuition fees at Adamsberg. And it all went to hell anyway.'

Charlie thought about the pictures from the autumn ball: Paul in his ill-fitting tailcoat. The feeling she and Johan had had, that he was different from the other boys in the picture: this was why. Paul Bergman was a local boy. He was the son of an undertaker. He wasn't one of them.

'And his brother?'

'He took over the funeral home, I think,' Lola said. 'He might be called Jens or Johannes or something like that. Bloody hell, why can't I remember his name! Maggan!'

Lola reached out and rang the old call bell on the counter. Margareta immediately emerged from the kitchen.

'Where's the fire, Lola?' she asked.

'What's the name of Christer Bergman's oldest lad? The one who runs the funeral home now?'

'Jacob,' Margareta replied.

'That's it,' Lola turned to Charlie. 'Jacob,' she said, as though Charlie hadn't been able to hear Margareta. 'His name's Jacob Bergman.'

'Thanks, Lola,' Charlie said.

She was already on her way out.

'What's the rush?' Lola called after her as she left.

Charlie rested her head against the steering wheel. Paul Bergman had been from Gullspång. His brother, Jacob, had driven Francesca home from a party in Lyckebo. She tried to remember more from the night Francesca came to Lyckebo, but all she could summon was the images from her dream: the bonfire, the pig roasting over the flames, Betty calling her over to say hi to Francesca.

She pulled out her phone, searched for the only funeral home in Gullspång and dialled the number.

'Jacob Bergman,' said a voice on the other end.

Charlie said hi and introduced herself.

'Lager?' Jacob Bergman said. 'Are you Betty Lager's daughter?'

'Yes,' Charlie replied.

She found it unsettling that this stranger seemed to know who she and Betty were.

'So, what can I do for you?' Jacob asked.

Charlie explained. She could tell she was speaking too fast and slightly incoherently, but Jacob didn't hang up on her, at least. When she was done, he suggested it might be a good idea for them to meet.

44

Ten minutes later, Charlie rang a doorbell on the other side of town.

The man who opened it was very attractive, she noted as he held out his hand. Dark eyes, deep voice. He invited her into the house, which turned out to be a mess.

'Pardon the chaos,' Jacob said. 'I was halfway through a big renovation when my wife told me she wanted a divorce.'

Charlie contemplated the half-torn-up floor in the hallway. Plywood boards stamped with the local factory logo had been laid down to allow entry.

'What happened?' she had to ask.

'She met someone else,' Jacob said. 'It was all very difficult.'

'I understand,' Charlie said. 'Long time ago?'

'A second and an eternity.' Jacob smiled. 'We were supposed to run the business together after my dad passed away, but it didn't turn out that way. Now I have only the dead to keep me company. Can I get you anything? Tea? Coffee? I only have instant, but ...'

'Instant's fine.'

Jacob turned on a kettle and set out two cups and two teaspoons.

They sat down at the large kitchen table. Charlie put her phone down with the screen facing up. She looked out at the garden through the window behind Jacob. It was neglected and overgrown, but underneath the dead leaves, the tired trees and the uneven hedge, there was something that gave Charlie the feeling it had once been loved and cared for.

Jacob looked at her like he was waiting for her to start talking, so Charlie told him why she'd called, that she wanted to know more about Francesca.

'We've met before,' Jacob said. 'You and me, I mean.'

'We have?'

'Yes, in connection with her funeral. Betty's.'

Something stabbed at Charlie's chest.

When I die, scatter me over Lake Skagern. Yes, I know it's not allowed, but who's going to stop you? Just bring the urn one night and row out there.

'I don't remember much from that time,' she said. 'But I remember that Mum didn't want a traditional burial.'

'I remember,' Jacob said. 'She wanted her ashes scattered at the sea. You told my dad. I honestly don't know why that didn't happen, but we're too far from the sea here.'

Charlie mused that she must have misspoken, because she'd meant Lake Skagern, though Betty had often referred to it as the sea. She'd often had to point out to her mother that Lake Skagern wasn't the sea, that it ended at the dam gates, but Betty had refused to listen.

Sooner or later, we all return to the sea.

'I think I meant Lake Skagern,' she said. 'I was probably just in shock. Maybe that's why I've forgotten almost everything about the funeral.'

'I understand,' Jacob said. 'My mum died when I was little,

too. Maybe people forget what they need to in order to survive.'

Charlie nodded, thinking he was probably right.

'Did you have any contact with Francesca Mild?'

'We met up a few times after Paul's death. She was pretty upset about how it was handled.'

'What do you mean?'

'She was convinced he was murdered, but no one listened to her. Well, except me.'

'And?'

'And no one listened to me, either. Everyone kept pointing out that he was prone to depression, that he'd been bullied, that there had been alcohol and even drugs in his system and ... well, you get it. The police didn't care that many things in fact pointed to something other than suicide.'

'Such as?'

'Such as the fact that he was found in the lake, for instance. Paul hated water. And the things Francesca told me, about a gang that terrorised him, that she'd seen them that night, that she was certain they had something to do with his death.'

'But no one took you seriously?'

'No. Francesca was delusional, they said. Apparently she'd been known to make baseless accusations before and in the end, I just dropped the whole thing. I felt I had to if I wanted to move on.'

'But you believed her?'

'Yes.'

'Do you have the names of the people who terrorised your brother?'

Jacob shook his head. He had put all of it behind him.

'But do you have any idea what happened to Francesca afterwards?'

'Unless I'm mistaken, no one does. But she called a few days before she disappeared and asked for my address. I wasn't home so Dad gave her it. She wanted to send me something she'd written, but I never had a letter and then it was too late. I'm pretty sure it had something to do with Paul.'

Charlie nodded and cursed the fact that Francesca's letter had never reached its recipient. It had, in all likeliness, never been posted.

'I've been told you picked her up from a party once,' Charlie said. 'A party out in Lyckebo. At my mum's house.'

Jacob gave her a surprised look.

'That's true,' he said. 'I gave her a ride there and a few hours later I went back to ... to check on her. Those parties were rumoured to be pretty wild, so ...'

Driving out to check on a girl at a party, Charlie mused. That suggested more than a fleeting acquaintance.

'I suppose there was something between us,' Jacob said as though he'd read her mind. 'But I think it was mostly about comfort; we comforted each other.'

'You don't have to justify it to me,' Charlie said. 'I just want to know what happened to Francesca and rule out that my mother was somehow involved in her disappearance.'

'Why would she be?' Jacob asked.

'It's a long story. Do you remember when this was? I mean the exact date you picked her up from the party?'

'I don't remember the exact date, but it was a week or so before she disappeared.'

'And where did you take her?'

'I guess we drove around for a bit and then ... well, you know.'

Charlie nodded. She did know.

'Do you think it's possible they were both murdered?' she said. 'Your brother and Francesca.'

'I've often wondered,' Jacob said. 'But I don't think about it as much any more. After a while, I decided to let it go and try to accept that I will never get any answers. It might not have been the right thing to do, but ...'

'If you're convinced you're not going to find the answers, I imagine it's what you have to do to stay afloat.'

'The problem is I never quite believed it,' Jacob said. 'I reckon I've always felt there must be a way of finding out, but I guess I've been too ... I don't know, but in the first few years after Paul's death, I barely felt alive myself and then ... I buried myself in work, simply put.'

He chuckled, maybe at his choice of words.

'I understand,' Charlie said, really meaning it.

They were interrupted by Jacob's phone vibrating between them on the table.

'I'm sorry,' he said, 'I have to take that. Why don't you have a look around the mess while you wait.'

He disappeared into the hallway. It was probably work-related because Charlie heard him offer his condolences and say that of course he was happy to help.

She got up and walked into the living room. The renovation didn't seem to have started in there; everything – furniture, wallpaper and décor – looked like it was from the eighties. She studied the dusty pictures on the walls, the family photographs, the two boys who looked so alike and yet ... Charlie moved closer to a picture in which they were standing next to each other, Jacob's arm protectively around his younger brother's shoulders. Both were looking straight into the camera with big, brown eyes. In a large photograph on the other side of the room, the whole family was gathered. A young mother with her youngest sitting on her lap and her oldest standing next to her and behind them, a father whose eyes were as beautiful as his sons'.

Charlie went into the hallway next to the living room. There was a flight of stairs leading down to what had to be the basement. Jacob was still on the phone in the kitchen. She hesitated briefly before starting down the steps. It felt like the temperature dropped with each one. Then she reached a door. She slowly pushed the handle down. Unlocked. It was an office, a desk, a computer, a filing cabinet and on the other side of the room, another door. Charlie was just about to close the door again when her eyes caught on something on the desk. A handful of pictures were spread out there. She quickly slipped into the room. At first, she couldn't believe her eyes. It was four almost identical photographs, of a girl in a white dress on a gurney, pale hands crossed on her chest, her dark hair loose and that determined and familiar mouth. Francesca. The girl in the pictures was Francesca Mild.

Francesca

The next day, I woke up to the 'good' news that my sister was coming home. And wouldn't it be lovely, Mum said, if the two of us could agree to bury the hatchet for just a little while and have a nice time.

I said I had no idea what she was talking about. Cécile and I always had a nice time together, didn't we?

Cécile looked almost translucent in the sunlight on the front steps. I had, at my mother's urging, gone out to greet her when she and Dad pulled up in front of the house.

'Those lions are beautiful,' Cécile said flatly.

'They weigh over two hundred pounds,' I offered. 'Each.'

Cécile made no reply, but came over and air kissed me like I was a fleeting acquaintance.

'We have to take a picture,' Dad said. 'All of us here at the farm for the first time in so long.'

He called for Mum to join us. She didn't want to be in any picture at first, but she soon relented and Dad fetched his camera with the tripod and self-timer. Then he lined us up between the lions and told us to smile.

'I had my eyes closed,' I said.

'Oh, I'm sure you were fine,' Dad replied. 'It's not unusual to blink after the flash goes off. It's going to be a lovely picture.'

At dinner, everything was so correct and stage-managed, I had an overwhelming urge to spill something or break my glass with my teeth like I used to when I was younger. Talking about inane things was exhausting. It was all loose barn roof shingles and the state of the grounds, the mushrooms. Never before had Dad experienced such a mushroom-rich autumn. I started talking about the rhododendron, saying it really ought to be cut back, that trimming it would help give the front of the house a cleaner look. When Mum and Dad started in on possibly planting an arborvitae hedge by the gatehouse, I suddenly felt deflated. I leaned back in my chair and stared at the ceiling. That's when I noticed the stain. The greyish-yellow stain on the ceiling.

'Damp,' I said, pointing. 'We have damp.'

And that brought the discussion around to how serious the damp might be, if it was just a roof issue or if the water was coming from inside somewhere, if it was rainwater or a broken pipe. Mum thought it might just be a one-off leak that had dried, that maybe it could be painted over.

I said we were probably going to have to tear up the entire roof to get to the bottom of what had caused it. Yes, because otherwise it would spread and one day, the roof would cave in on us.

'There's no need to be so dramatic,' Mum sighed. 'It could be champagne from a New Year's party, anything.'

Cécile didn't say much. She gave the water stain one weary look and then went back to pushing her food around her plate.

'What's the matter, Cécile?' Mum said finally. 'You look a bit pale.'

'I'm guessing she just has a lot on right now, what with the national exams,' I said. 'They're enough to make anyone exhausted.'

Cécile ignored my comment, just sighed and said she was tired.

'Maybe you and your sister should go for a walk before it gets dark,' Dad suggested.

'I'm very tired,' Cécile said.

'Some fresh air might wake you up,' I said, because I really wanted to talk to Cécile alone.

We made it out onto the front steps before coming to an undecided halt between the gaping lions. Neither one of us seemed to know where to go.

'Want to walk down to the lake?' I said.

Cécile shrugged.

We started down the path.

'What the fuck is that?' Cécile said, pointing at the hole.

'It's a hole,' I said. 'I've been doing some digging.'

'Have Mum and Dad seen it?'

'Yes, and I'm going to fill it in.'

'Why did you dig it in the first place?'

'I wanted to see how deep I could get.'

Cécile studied me searchingly. It was as though she was trying to figure out how on Earth the two of us were related.

'What's that?' she said, pointing at my necklace.

I put my hand over it and said it was just a regular necklace.

'Can I see?'

Cécile took a step towards me. I backed away.

'What, is it a secret or something? Stop being weird.'

She reached out and snatched up the pendant. I wanted to back away again but was afraid the chain would break.

'Who gave it to you?'

'Mum. Mum gave it to me.'

'Why?'

Cécile stared at me as though I'd said something highly improbable.

'Because I'm going to study law,' I said. 'It's the scales of justice. Justitia and whatnot.'

'I know what it symbolises,' Cécile said. 'I just don't understand ...'

'Why she didn't give it to you?'

'I didn't say that.'

Cécile turned her eyes from the necklace to me.

'So you're going to study law? Maybe you should consider coming back to school soon if that's the case.'

'I'm a year ahead,' I reminded her.

The fact that I had skipped a year was always the ace up my sleeve.

'You have to have top grades to get into law school,' Cécile said.

'I know,' I said. 'I know what's required.'

'Can I try it on?'

Cécile pointed at the necklace.

'Why?'

'I just want to try it on.'

I sighed, undid the clasp and handed it to Cécile.

'It's scratched,' she exclaimed after turning the scales over.

'It's two Es,' I said. 'It says FREE.'

'Does Mum know you ruined her necklace?'

'It's not hers, it's mine,' I countered. 'I can do whatever I want with it. Can I have it back now?'

'Sure,' Cécile said. 'In a minute. Help me put it on.'

She held her hair up. I sighed but did what she asked. We started walking towards the lake again.

'Remember?' I said, pointing to a bare, drooping tree. 'Wasn't it from that one you got the leaf buds you shoved into your ears?'

'You really never forget anything,' Cécile said with a sigh.

That wasn't true; I forgot lots of things, just not outright injustices or comical interludes and the thing with the buds still brought a smile to my lips sometimes. We must have been four or five that spring when Cécile suddenly stopped answering when spoken to. Mum and Dad thought she had a hearing problem, but when they took her to the doctor, it turned out her ear canals were full of green little buds.

'Why did you do it?' I asked.

'Because I didn't want to hear you,' Cécile said. 'Your voice hurt. Don't you remember how much you screamed?'

'Couldn't you have used something other than leaves?'

'I was five,' Cécile said. 'I assume I panicked and used whatever I could find. Your screaming almost drove our whole family over the edge.'

'You're exaggerating.'

Cécile stared at me like she couldn't believe her ears.

'I'm really not. You screamed so much I couldn't have friends over; Mum cried and Dad locked himself in the library. That's why we had to have nannies. If not for you, we wouldn't have had nannies or gone to nursery school. We might not even have been sent to Adamsberg. Mum and Dad just couldn't handle you.'

'I don't understand why people choose to have children if that's the case,' I said. 'If they can't handle it.'

'How were they supposed to know what you'd be like.'

'You get the children you get,' I said. 'You have to take care of them no matter how they turn out.'

'Sometimes, right before I fall asleep, I can still hear you screaming,' Cécile said.

We had almost reached the lake now and Cécile was walking slowly, talking in a dreamy voice that sounded different from her normal one.

'It's like it's stuck in my brain,' she went on. 'Your voice, I mean. The screaming.'

'Fine, I'm sorry,' I said. 'I'm sorry I've ruined everyone's lives.'

45

Charlie was so intent on the pictures, she didn't hear Jacob approaching.

'What are you doing?' he exclaimed, suddenly standing behind her in the doorway. 'When I said you could have a look around, I didn't mean for you to come in here.'

'I . . .'

She didn't know what to say.

'It's not what you think,' Jacob said, nodding at the photographs on the table.

'Okay,' Charlie replied.

She had an urge to run, but Jacob was blocking the only exit.

'Don't be scared,' Jacob said. 'I can explain.'

'Fine, but upstairs.'

Charlie followed Jacob up the flight of steps. The relief of no longer being underground made her tremble.

'I realise it must seem odd,' Jacob said once they were back in the kitchen.

'You have pictures of a dead girl,' Charlie said. 'A girl who went missing almost thirty years ago.'

'She's not dead,' Jacob said. 'At least not in those pictures.'

'You lost me,' Charlie said.

'It was a game. I know it sounds twisted, but Francesca wanted, she wanted me to prepare her like I would a corpse.'

'Why?'

'Don't know,' Jacob replied. 'I suppose she had a pretty unique sense of humour and was drawn to things like that. That was the night I picked her up from that party. She was hammered. I didn't want to at first, but she talked me into it. Hold on, I'll show you.'

He stepped out of the room and returned moments later with the pictures of Francesca.

'The date,' he said, pointing to the numbers stamped along the edge of one of the photographs.

It had been taken on the first of October 1989, a week before Francesca disappeared.

'But why did you have those pictures out?' Charlie wanted to know.

'A man came here yesterday, asking questions about Francesca,' Jacob said. 'I got them out after he left to ... I don't know ... reminisce.'

'Johan Ro?' Charlie asked. 'Was that his name, the man who was here?'

Jacob nodded.

'Why didn't you tell me that?'

'He asked me not to tell anyone. What is this about?'

'Johan Ro was assaulted yesterday,' Charlie told him. 'He may not survive.'

'Why?' Jacob exclaimed. 'Who?'

'I don't know. When was he here?'

'After lunch sometime, around two, I think.'

Jacob's phone went off again. He apologised, stood up

and left the room. Charlie heard him offer condolences in a professional tone.

'I'm sorry,' Jacob said. 'There's been a death.'

'Who?' Charlie had to ask. 'Actually, no, I'm sorry, that's none of my business.'

Jacob smiled and said he wasn't really at liberty to say, but since she was bound to find out anyway, in the supermarket or down the pub ...

'Sven-Erik Larsson,' he said.

'Svenka?'

'Yes, that's what they call him. You know him?'

'No, well, I know of him. I talked to him last night at the pub. What happened?'

'It was unclear. That was his sister calling. She was still in shock.'

Charlie pictured Sara, the heavy eyeliner around her eyes, her vulnerability, her dejection, as though she were already an old person. But she was only fourteen. How was she going to get by now? How much was she going to have to forget to survive?

'I need to know what you told Johan,' Charlie said when they were done lamenting the sad life that had reached its end.

'I guess he asked much the same questions you did.'

'Did he say where he was going afterwards?'

'No, he didn't. I really hope he pulls through and that they catch the lunatic who did it.'

'Have you told anyone else he was here?'

'No,' Jacob replied. 'No one.'

'I have to go,' Charlie said.

She thanked him for the coffee and started towards the door. Jacob went with her.

'If you discover anything about my brother or Francesca, please call me,' he said when they reached the hallway.

'Sure,' Charlie replied. 'And you call me if you think of anything else. You have my number in your call list.'

46

Charlie called Olof the moment she had reversed out of Bergman's Funeral Home's driveway. His voice sounded strained.

'Has Adam confessed?'

'No. He has an alibi. He was at home and then down the pub.'

'He could have nipped out,' Charlie retorted. 'The smelter's only a few hundred yards from the pub. You have to put the screws to him.'

'We're doing everything we can,' Olof said. 'Are you still there, Charlie?'

Charlie hung up to answer an incoming call from a local number.

The person on the other end was in the middle of a coughing fit.

'Who is this?' Charlie said at length.

'Annelie Karlsson. I'm a nurse at the nursing home; we met the other day when you and your friend visited Sixten Molan.'

Charlie remembered the no-nonsense nurse well.

'Well, I heard about what happened to your ... friend. It was your friend who was assaulted at the smelter, right?'

'Yes.'

'And then I was told you work for the police. And so I thought you might want to know that he was here yesterday, your friend, talking to Sixten. The doctor was peevish afterwards, saying he was tired of people poking their noses in where they don't belong and ... I'm not sure it's important, really.'

'It is,' Charlie told her. 'Thank you so much for calling.'

Sixten Molan was not in his room. A man with a rollator shuffled past as Charlie tried the locked door.

'He's gone to play the piano,' the man said, nodding down a hallway.

Charlie followed his directions. Molan was, indeed, sitting at a piano. His old hands were placed on the keyboard as though he were just about to start playing, but he was staring vacantly at the music rack and didn't notice her until she was right next to him. He didn't seem surprised to see her.

'Doctor Molan,' Charlie said. 'I need to talk to you.'

'Again?'

'Yes, if you have a minute.'

'Would you mind if we do it outside?' He nodded towards a door opening out onto a patio. 'I need a smoke.'

Charlie didn't realise the patio was occupied until they stepped out and she saw a woman sitting there in a white plastic chair.

'Mr Molan!' she said with a hint of irony in her voice. 'What a pleasure.'

'Greta!'

Doctor Molan doffed an invisible hat and bowed. He walked over to the table and picked up a pipe and a box of matches. Then he lit the pipe and sat down next to Greta.

'And who is your lucky guest?'

Greta studied Charlie with brown eyes sparkling with curiosity.

'Charlie,' Charlie said.

'Is that right,' Greta said. She squinted as though trying to remember something. 'Sounds like a man's name.'

'It works on women, too,' Charlie replied.

'Yes, it seems to be working just fine.'

Greta stubbed out her cigarette in an upside-down flower-pot and immediately pulled another from her packet.

'Greta,' Doctor Molan said. 'Charlie and I would like to speak privately.'

Greta let out a chuckle, spread her hands and said God's nature belonged to everyone and she wasn't about to be run off by him.

Charlie smiled at her. Doctor Molan rolled his eyes and took a few more puffs on his pipe before turning to Charlie to suggest they go to his room instead.

'She's tricky,' Molan muttered as they walked towards his room.

'I thought she seemed nice,' Charlie replied.

'She used to work for me,' Doctor Molan said. 'Cleaned and cooked. She wasn't as impertinent back then.'

'I suppose people don't tend to bite the hand that feeds them.'

'She bites all the more now.'

They had reached the door to his room; his hand shook when he put the key in the lock.

'Have a seat,' he said, pointing at the sofa.

He himself sat down in an armchair on the other side of the table and crossed his legs. It was as though he had slipped into his professional role, as though he were waiting for her to lie down, close her eyes and open up to him.

'I heard your friend is hurt,' he said. 'I do hope he recovers.'

'And I heard he came back here,' Charlie said. 'Johan, that is. My friend.'

'Yes, he came back. I don't really understand why. He asked a lot of questions.'

'What did he ask you?'

'About people I had met at Gudhammar, whether I had forgotten to mention anything before. Things like that.'

'And?'

'I told him everything that came to mind, all sorts of trivial episodes.'

'Do you remember exactly what you told him?'

'Why wouldn't I?' Doctor Molan retorted, looking offended. 'I told him about a man Francesca claimed had forced himself on her. It was later shown to be a lie, but ...'

'Who?' Charlie said. 'And how can you be so sure it was a lie?'

'It's a long story, but the point is that Rikard and Fredrika had Francesca examined and it turned out she was untouched.'

'Untouched.'

'Yes, I'm sure you understand what I mean.'

Charlie nodded. She knew what he meant by untouched. What she didn't understand was how parents could fail to believe their daughter and compound the violation by forcing her to undergo that kind of examination.

'Sexual assault doesn't require vaginal penetration,' she informed Doctor Molan.

'Is that right?' Doctor Molan said, as though this was news to him.

'What was his name?' Charlie said. 'What was the name of the man who forced himself on Francesca?'

'I don't recall,' Molan replied. 'I honestly don't remember.'

'Adam? Adam Rehn?'

'Like I said, it was many years ago. I don't recall the names.'

Charlie sighed. Was this visit nothing but a waste of time?

'I think that's enough for today,' Doctor Molan said, leaning back in his chair. 'I hope things work out for your friend. Sometimes it's better not to stick one's nose in,' he said when Charlie reached the door.

'What do you mean?'

'I mean some things are best left alone. That might be a strange thing for a psychiatrist to say, but if there's one thing I've learnt in my profession, it's that some stones are best left unturned.'

'And if there's one thing I've learnt in my profession,' Charlie replied, 'it's the importance of sticking one's nose in when it comes to assault and suspected murder.'

On her way from Doctor Molan's room, Charlie studied the black-and-white photographs on the hallway walls. She stopped in front of the Harvest Festival again, then moved in closer for a better look at the young men carrying amplifiers and microphone stands. And there, at the very edge of the picture, she noticed a woman she'd missed before. A tall, long-legged woman in a dress. She was watching the other people as though she were looking at a painting or a life she wasn't entirely a part of.

'Nice, huh?'

Charlie turned round. Greta was standing behind her, smiling broadly.

'I like to call these hallways the Corridors of Reminiscence,' she went on. 'I suppose putting up pictures of times gone by is supposed to make us feel safe. But they make me wistful, too.'

Charlie nodded.

'The Harvest Festival.' Greta nodded to the picture.

'Do you know who that is?'

Charlie pointed to the woman in the beautiful dress.

'That's Mrs Mild, that is,' Greta said with a smile.

'Did you know her?'

Greta shook her head.

'The Doctor would have Mr and Mrs Mild over for dinner from time to time, but I was staff and therefore probably invisible to them. They didn't mix with ordinary folk. That was why it was surprising to see Mrs Mild that time at the Harvest Festival. And alone, too. It turned out to be a memorable night.'

'How so?'

'Her husband,' Greta replied. 'Her husband turned up and there were fisticuffs.'

'Between whom?'

'Between Rikard Mild and Ivan Hedlund,' Greta said. 'But Ivan did most of the punching. It was a proper spectacle. That's odd. I just told that story to a young man who was here. We started talking about the Harvest Festival and ...'

'Johan?' Charlie broke in.

'I don't remember his name, but he was a handsome lad. Curly hair.'

Greta raised a hand to her head.

'And you told him the same thing you just told me?'

'I think so,' Greta said. 'Did I do something wrong?'

374

47

Charlie drove out to Eel Island, parked and caught the smell of manure as she walked up towards Ivan Hedlund's house.

'You again?' Ivan said when he opened the door.

He was dressed in a washed-out T-shirt and a pair of old jeans. Charlie couldn't stop herself from ogling his muscular arms. He didn't seem happy to see her.

'I'm here for a different reason this time,' Charlie said. 'May I come in?'

'Sure.'

Ivan backed up.

The house smelled ... unclean. A mix of wet dog, barn and something Charlie had woken up to out in Lyckebo more times than she could count: hangover.

'Stay,' Ivan told the dog, which padded over and sniffed Charlie's crotch. 'Oh, lay off, Nima.'

Ivan raised his hand and smacked the dog. It whimpered, crouched low and quickly slinked off.

'Eight years old and impossible to train,' Ivan sighed.

Charlie said nothing. The blow had been too sudden and much too hard.

'So, why are you here this time?' Ivan demanded.

He crossed his arms, apparently not planning to invite her in any further than the hallway.

'It's about an assault,' Charlie said, showing him her ID.

'Police?' Ivan raised an eyebrow. 'How come you didn't tell me that last time?'

'Because last time, I was here in a private capacity.'

'Should I be worried?' Ivan said.

'I don't know,' Charlie replied. 'My friend Johan, who was here with me last Thursday, has been assaulted.'

'I'm sorry to hear that,' Ivan said. 'But what does that have to do with me?'

'We have reason to believe there's a connection between the assault and the case we were asking you about. The Francesca Mild case. Did Johan contact you again? I mean, after we were here?'

'No. Am I under suspicion?'

'We're contacting everyone we talked to regarding Francesca Mild. You're no more a suspect than anyone else.'

She knew it was wrong to pretend she was working on the case, but she didn't care. Doing nothing when Johan was fighting for his life was unacceptable. Charlie glanced around. Behind a half-drawn curtain, she could see the heavy black wellies Ivan had been wearing in the barn and his blue overalls, the legs of which were covered in ... blood? From the pigs?

Something hissed in the kitchen.

'Fuck, it's boiling over,' Ivan said. 'Hold on.'

He disappeared into the house.

When Charlie took a step closer to the curtain and the work clothes behind it, she realised it wasn't blood on the trouser legs but something else entirely. Red dust. She knew where she'd seen it before. It had been clinging to her shoes just the day before. It was the dust from the oxidised iron ore that covered every inch of the smelter floor, the dust that according to Betty destroyed both lungs and souls.

48

On her way back from Ivan Hedlund's house, Charlie called Olof. When he didn't answer, she tried Micke.

'I hope this is important,' he said by way of greeting.

'Ivan has been to Gea,' she said. 'The smelter,' she clarified when there was no reaction.

'Don't you think I bloody know what Gea is?' Micke said. 'How do you know?'

Charlie told him about Ivan's trousers.

'And I think Johan went to see him the day he was assaulted.'

'Based on what?'

Charlie told him about her conversation with Greta at the nursing home, about the fight between Ivan Hedlund and Rikard Mild, that she was sure Johan had gone looking for Ivan.

'So what was the fight about?' Micke asked.

'No idea, but I'm sure Johan asked Ivan some uncomfortable questions. And now Johan has been assaulted and there's dust from the smelter on Ivan's clothes. What more do you need to bring him in?'

'I'll let Olof know,' Micke said.

Then he hung up.

*

Charlie drove straight out to Gudhammar. She wanted to search Francesca's room, on the off chance the piece of text she'd intended to send to Jacob was still there.

Dusk had fallen over the farm. Charlie parked halfway down the tree-lined drive. As she started walking up towards the house, she had a strange feeling she wasn't alone, that someone was walking next to her, holding her hand, telling her to hurry.

The lions with their gaping maws shone white in the gloom. The front door was unlocked since Johan and Charlie's last visit. It creaked open when Charlie pushed the handle down. Outside, dusk was darkening into night; she turned on her flashlight.

She went straight to Francesca's room and once more felt she could almost see her, lying on her bed, battling her demons. She quickly walked over to the desk and started opening drawers. They were all empty. Had someone emptied them? She moved on to the dresser and then the closet. Nothing. What had she expected? The police must have searched it after Francesca went missing. Or someone else had, she mused. Someone else could have gone through Francesca's things before the police. Nothing in the room stood out. The bed was the only place left to check. Charlie aimed her flashlight at the crocheted bedspread. She pulled it off and let out a curse. Something had been born there, or possibly died. Even so, she forced herself to lift up the mattress. Her pulse began to race when she spotted something underneath it. It looked like a school notebook.

She picked it up, opened it to the first page, turned her flashlight on it and read: *Gaps in Time.*

There was a light thud from the ground floor.

Charlie froze. Her heart skipped a beat. She tried to tell herself it was probably just a draught, a rat, a bird colliding with a window, but then she heard footsteps. Her hand instinctively moved to her side, where her gun would have been if she'd been on duty. There was, of course, nothing there. She quickly slipped under the bed and turned her phone off. She fought to get her breathing under control. The sound of approaching footsteps made her think of playing hide-and-seek as a child. Lying curled up somewhere with Betty slowly moving through the rooms, calling in an affected voice: *Where is that little girl? Is she gone? No, she must be here somewhere ... she wouldn't have snuck out, now, would she? Charli-ine?*

But this wasn't a game. The footsteps had been moving around the first floor for a while and now they were right outside the door. She lay stock-still. Who could it be? Had the person followed her out here? Whoever it was, he was in the room with her now. He walked back and forth across the floor, only feet away from her. She held her breath, thought about Johan's crushed skull. Was it her turn now?

Francesca

I didn't understand why Dad had suggested we take a walk. What was the point of spending time with one's sister if all she did was throw insults? We had reached the water now.

'Be careful,' I said when Cécile stepped onto the jetty. 'Some of the boards are rotting away.'

'I don't care,' Cécile replied.

'Fine, but it's not my fault if you put your foot through one of them.'

We sat down on the cold, damp wood. Mum wouldn't have approved. She was always worried we'd catch a urinary tract infection and become sterile, as though not being able to have children was the worst thing that could ever befall a woman.

'Oh my god,' Cécile said when I pulled out the bottle of wine I'd hidden inside Mum's big fur coat. 'Maybe you shouldn't be drinking.'

'Why not?'

'On account of how you seem to be feeling.'

'That's exactly why I need to drink,' I said, handing Cécile the bottle.

She accepted it and took several long swigs.

'Drink it with reverence,' I told her. 'It cost a hundred kronor.'

'Right,' Cécile said indifferently.

Without so much as a glance up at the house, she pulled out a small silver cigarette case, which she opened and held out to me.

'They'll kill us,' I said.

'Not if we don't make it a habit.'

'I wasn't referring to the cigarettes,' I said, nodding in the direction of the house.

'What could they possibly do?' Cécile countered.

We lit our cigarettes.

'I brought mints,' I said. 'You know how sensitive Mum's nose is.'

'She seems less alert than usual,' Cécile said. 'I reckon all this stuff has been pretty hard on her.'

'It's not just about me,' I said.

'What do you mean?' Cécile asked. 'What else is it about?'

'This might come as a complete surprise to you,' I said, 'but I'm not the only person in this family capable of making mistakes.'

'Dad?'

'Sure, but what else is new, right?'

'Mum?'

Cécile looked at me uncomprehendingly.

I nodded.

'I suppose you might say Mum is walking in Dad's footsteps, at least when it comes to adultery.'

'Stop it, Fran,' Cécile said. 'Stop throwing accusations around.'

'But it's true, I saw them with my own eyes, I ...'

'I can't trust what you feel you've seen,' Cécile cut me off. Her voice was frosty. 'It's not the first time you've seen and experienced things that only existed in your own little world. Mum and Dad love each other. They would never . . .'

'Blind,' I said.

'Excuse me?'

'It's what your name means: blind. I looked it up.'

'I don't care.'

'Did you know kittens become permanently blind if you cover their eyes during a certain period of development?' I said. 'They never learn to see if . . .'

'Stop talking,' Cécile said. 'You sound deranged.'

'I'm not.'

'You talk too fast. Everyone agrees. No one else can keep up. It's too fast.'

'Maybe it's just that everyone else thinks too slowly.'

Cécile sighed.

'And what about your name?' she said after a while. 'What does your name mean?'

'Free,' I said. 'Francesca means free.'

'How lovely.'

'Never mind,' I said. 'Are you okay?'

'I'm not falling for that,' Cécile replied. 'I'm not falling for your fake concern, so just cut to the chase, will you? What do you want to know?'

'I want to know if you broke up with Henrik.'

Cécile pulled on her cigarette and looked out across the lake.

'Let me tell you something about Henrik. He's not always like you think he is. He has a different side to him, a funny side, clever, creative, deep even.'

'So you didn't break up with him?' I said, ignoring her boyfriend's many positive qualities.

'No. Why would I have?'

'Paul was in love with him,' I said.

Cécile burst out laughing.

'I'm serious,' I said. 'It wouldn't surprise me if they had some kind of relationship.'

'Have you actually lost your mind, Fran?'

Cécile suddenly looked worried.

I briefly told her about the rebus, Paul's words, the memories that had come back to me.

'You have to let that go,' Cécile said. 'Whatever Paul might have felt for Henrik is moot. I can assure you Henrik is not gay.'

'But he might be a murderer,' I said, with my face right next to hers.

'Stop it,' Cécile said. 'I mean it. Stop acting like a fucking nut case.'

I punched her lightly.

'Ow!' she shrieked, rubbing her arm. She never wasted an opportunity to exaggerate.

'When are you going to stop hitting me?' Cécile said. 'How old are you? You're like a stupid child.'

I hit her again.

'What the fuck?' Cécile screamed.

'What's going on,' Mum called from the veranda.

'She's hitting me!' Cécile shouted back. 'Francesca's hitting me!'

Always running to Mummy. Cécile never seemed to grow out of it. Now who was the stupid child?

'Stop it, Francesca!' Mum shrieked from the veranda. 'Stop it right now!'

'I was just joshing!' I called back.

'Stop it anyway!'

'If you don't cut it out, she's going to come down here and she won't be happy,' Cécile said.

She continued to rub her arm and nodded at the wine and the cigarette case.

'Seriously, you're acting like a lunatic, Francesca.'

'You might not have been the epitome of perfection either, if you'd lost your best friend.'

'I've lost a sister,' Cécile retorted and flicked her smouldering cigarette butt into the lake.

My nose was suddenly stinging.

'That's your own choice,' I said, 'since you don't believe me. Isn't that what sisters do, believe each other?'

'I believed you last time,' Cécile said. 'We all believed you.'

'Clearly, you didn't.'

'I'm not getting sucked into that again,' Cécile said. 'Really, Fran, I'm done.'

We looked out across the water.

'Remember when we used to compete?' I said at length.

'Compete about what?'

'About who could stay under water longer.'

'How could I forget?'

'I was trying to help you. I just wanted to help you stay under.'

'That's not what it felt like.'

'You really think I was trying to drown you?'

Cécile was quiet for a long time before answering: 'I don't remember what I thought. I guess my memory's not as good as yours.'

'It seems a bit selective,' I agreed.

'Why are you even bringing that up now? It must be at least ten years ago.'

'Nine. It's just over nine years ago.'

'Fine, what's your point?'

'My point is that sometimes you withhold truths, too; you never told Mum and Dad you knew I wasn't going to drown you. You never told them it was just a game.'

'Was it just a game?' Cécile said.

It was getting dark. Cécile and I walked back up towards the house.

'Remember the bird's eggs?' she said.

'I'm done reminiscing,' I told her.

'So you're the only one who gets to remember things?'

It was typical, I thought to myself, that Cécile had to come home and remind me of even more horrible things. Had she forgotten that I was depressed? We'd found the little gull eggs by the water's edge one summer, thought they were abandoned and brought them up to my room to keep them warm so they could hatch. The only problem was that I was impatient. I felt I'd held the eggs under the lamp for an eternity without anything happening and I just wanted to have a look inside the shells to see if anything was happening and then ... I could still remember the bloody mess in front of me. It had got on my bedspread and the stains never fully came out.

'You know what they say about children who harm animals, don't you?' Cécile said.

'No.'

'That they're not right in the head, that they're psychopaths.'

'I didn't kill them,' I said. 'Or at least I didn't mean to. I just wanted them to hatch.'

'You should have known they would die,' Cécile retorted. 'That bird foetuses die if you crack their shells.'

'Then shouldn't you have known that, too? Have you forgotten that you're a year older and that you were there as well?'

'But I didn't crack the eggs,' Cécile replied. 'I never even touched them.'

49

Charlie closed her eyes and waited to be pulled out of her hiding place. But then, a phone rang. The man left the room. She heard him run down the stairs and then ... silence. How long did she stay under the bed after that? Thirty minutes? An hour? It felt like an eternity.

After tremblingly creeping back outside and locking herself in her car, Charlie called Olof again.

'Did you bring him in?' she said. 'Did you bring Ivan Hedlund in?'

'No, we ...'

'What the fuck!'

'Don't swear at me!' Olof snapped. 'And don't interrupt.'

'Don't you fucking tell me what I can and can't do.'

'We went to his house a while ago, but he wasn't home.'

'Maybe because you took too long and he went chasing after me.'

'What are you talking about?'

'I'm telling you he came after me,' Charlie said and before Olof had a chance to ask her for more information, she bellowed into the phone that they had to find him, find him before someone else got hurt.

She tossed her phone onto the passenger seat. Her eyes fell on the notebook she'd found under Francesca's mattress. Charlie wanted to feel safe when she read it. She started the car and drove away from Gudhammar, glancing up at the rear-view mirror every few seconds. No one seemed to be following her.

Fifteen minutes later, she turned down the narrow road to Lyckebo. She climbed out of the car and listened for the sound of another vehicle, but all she could hear was birdsong and the wind soughing through the trees.

The Lyckebo sign had sunk almost completely into the ground. When Charlie grabbed it to pull it up, a chunk of rotting wood came off. She gave up and continued towards the house. When she'd been there the previous summer, for the first time since she was fourteen, she'd been on edge. The images from that night ... Betty collapsed on her make-up table, the flies buzzing around her body, Charlie's unsuccessful attempts to resuscitate her.

She received a text. It was from Micke, who wrote that Ivan had been brought in for questioning. Charlie dialled his number and while waiting for him to pick up, she walked to the wooden pallets that constituted the front steps, bent down and pulled a key out of a terracotta pot and unlocked the door. Micke didn't answer his phone.

The hallway was dark; she turned on her phone flashlight once more. She knew something was wrong the moment she entered the kitchen. There were several empty wine bottles on the kitchen table. They hadn't been there when she left the house last summer. She clearly remembered putting all the empty bottles out on the porch. Someone had been in the house. Someone might be in it right now. She stood still for a long time, listening, but the only sounds she could hear were the familiar creaks from her childhood. Maybe she hadn't taken all the bottles out after all? Maybe she'd just intended to.

Charlie found some tealights and lit them. Then she opened the notebook entitled *Gaps in Time* and started to read. Each page transported her further into Francesca Mild's world.

Doctor Molan says memories are unreliable and mutable, I wrote, then I chewed the pencil for a while before continuing: *They can be lost, manipulated and false and if you add things like sedatives, alcohol and drugs, they obviously become even less reliable. Conclusion: my memories from the night of the ball need not be true. The yellow rose, the royals' wet clothes ... it could all be the result of intoxication, a dream, a hallucination. And no matter how much I want to, Doctor Molan says, I can't coax memories out of oblivion. I can't fill in the gaps. It's a complex process that can't be controlled by an effort of will. So instead of tormenting myself, trying to remember, I should focus on something else, according to Doctor Molan. I should simply forget about the whole thing.*

I would like to tell Doctor Molan that forgetting is a complex process that can't be controlled by an effort of will.

And then, the paragraphs that made Charlie certain, once and for all, that her dreams about visiting Gudhammar with Betty were in fact real memories: *Last night someone banged on our door. I heard Mum wake up Dad. Heard him run downstairs, a woman crying, Dad's voice so full of rage. 'Go away.' And when I looked out the window, I saw a woman and a small child walk down the drive.*

The letters were small and the hand hard to decipher. Francesca seemed not to have cared about coherence. In the middle of an account of a nocturnal walk at her school, she'd suddenly insert a poem Paul had read to her.

This life is a breeze, a fable, a dream
A droplet falling into Time's endless stream
Shimmering briefly like a rainbow in the sun
Bursting and falling and the dream is done

There was a click. Charlie knew the house; there was no mistaking that sound. The front door. Someone was inside the house. Charlie got up and took two quick steps over to the cutlery drawer next to the sink, snatching up the first knife she could find. She wasn't going to hide this time.

'Freeze!' Charlie shouted at the shape in the hallway. 'Don't move. Step into the light so I can see you.'

'I can't step into the light if you don't want me to move,' said a girl's voice.

Charlie lowered the knife.

'Sara?' she said. 'What are you doing here?'

50

'I'm sorry about the wine.' Sara nodded towards the empty bottles on the table. 'But there were so many left in the basement and even more out in the root cellar and ...'

'Don't worry about the wine,' Charlie said.

They were sitting across from each other at the kitchen table. Sara's face was white in the candlelight.

'And for breaking into your house.'

'It's okay,' Charlie said. 'I'm glad it can be of use to someone.'

'I liked having a place where I could be alone.'

'I get that.'

Charlie put a hand on Sara's hand on the table.

'Dad's dead,' Sara said.

'I heard. I'm so sorry.'

'I think I must be a psychopath, because I feel ... I feel nothing.'

'You're in shock. Have you talked to anyone?'

Sara shook her head.

'My aunt's here, but I don't want to talk to her, or anyone. Do you have cigarettes?'

Charlie nodded, took out her pack and gave her one. Sara

leaned forward and lit it on the flame of one of the tealights. Charlie did the same.

They smoked in silence for a while.

'We went to Stockholm once,' Sara said, 'Dad and me. Mum drove me to the station where we were supposed to meet. This was back when I still lived with her every other week, before she left. Dad came staggering towards us on the platform, wearing big glasses, I mean, those giant gag glasses, you know, and he'd bought me a pair, too.'

Sara smiled as though it were a treasured memory.

'Mum told him to get it together, that maybe I shouldn't be going anywhere with him if he was going to be like this. She asked me if I really wanted to go to Stockholm with Daddy and of course I didn't, because he was shitfaced, but I didn't want to make him sad so I said I did. It was one fucked up trip, let me tell you.'

Sara shook her head.

'Dad was a fucking drunk, but I loved him. I haven't told him that since … I don't remember when I last said it, and now it's too late.'

'He knows,' Charlie said.

She felt her throat constricting; she saw herself kneeling next to Betty's lifeless body, saw herself trying to blow life into what was already dead. *I love you, Mummy. I love you. Mummy!*

'I don't know how much more I can take,' Sara said. 'I feel like this is the end, that my life's over, too.'

Charlie wanted to tell her it was far from over, that she was only fourteen, but it wasn't a matter of years, she knew that all too well. And it wasn't a young girl's eyes that met hers across the table. It was the eyes of a person who has seen too much darkness.

*

A text came through from Micke. *Was there something in particular you wanted?*

'I need to make a phone call,' Charlie told Sara. 'I'll only be a minute.'

She got up and walked into the living room.

'Has Ivan confessed to anything?' she said when Micke picked up.

'Yes, he admits to the assault.'

'Why?' Charlie said. 'The motive?'

'Johan called him up and wanted to talk. Ivan was at Gea to pick up some old welding tool and Johan came over and . . .'

'But why? The motive?'

'He says he snaps when people get up in his face. He was abused as a child and . . . Johan pressed him and so Ivan shoved him and then Johan punched him and . . . he says there was no weapon, that Johan must have fallen and hit his head on something. He didn't realise how serious it was until much later and then he was scared. That's why he didn't say anything straight away.'

'Quite the storyteller, this Ivan,' Charlie said.

'Don't jump down my throat for telling you what he said. I'm under no obligation to talk to you at all.'

'You have an obligation to solve this,' Charlie said. 'You have to get it into your heads that there's a connection, that we have to keep looking into Francesca's disappearance. Putting the lid on won't work.'

'You're not my boss,' Micke said. 'It's not up to you what I look into.'

'He's been in fights before,' Charlie said. 'Ivan Hedlund. It's not the first time he's beaten someone up.'

'I know.'

'Do you know what it was about?'

'A misunderstanding, if I've understood things right. Rikard Mild, Francesca's father, thought they were in a relationship, but they weren't, so she must have been going around with someone else.'

'Who?'

'How should I know?'

Francesca

The next day, Mum and Dad told us they were going to a dinner party at Doctor Molan's. I pictured them sipping expensive champagne out of crystal flutes while making light conversation about their youngest daughter's adjustment disorder.

'I thought we were supposed to spend time together as a family,' I said. 'Now that Cécile's finally home.'

Mum said they were only going to be gone for a few hours and that I could call Doctor Molan if there was a problem. I had his number, after all.

'And while we're gone, why don't you start filling in that hole,' Mum said. 'You surely can't get much deeper, now can you? It's already as deep as a grave.'

'I don't think so.'

'Great. Then we're in agreement. When we get back, that hole is gone.'

'I thought that was Adam's job.'

'Adam doesn't work for us any more, as you are well aware. You're going to have to take care of it yourself.'

'Okay, I will,' I promised, thinking: *But I'm not going to. I have better things to do than to fill in graves.*

*

'There's a storm coming,' I told Cécile after Mum and Dad left.

I was standing at the kitchen window, looking out at the swaying trees down by the lake.

'It's just a bit of wind,' Cécile replied. 'Don't overstate it.'

'When am I getting my necklace back?' I said, turning round.

Cécile had slipped the scales into her blouse. Maybe she'd figured I would forget.

'Can't we share it?' Cécile said. 'I like it, too.'

'It's mine,' I said. 'You're not taking it back to Adamsberg.'

Cécile sighed and said she wouldn't.

Cécile went to bed early that night. As soon as she disappeared into her room, I fetched my notebook, sat down at the kitchen table and began to write. I wrote about how angry I was with my sister. How petty it was for her, who had always been our parents' favourite, not to let me have our mother's old necklace to myself. Writing it made me so upset I had to take a number of deep swigs from the wine bottle I'd found the previous day. No wonder so many writers had a drinking problem, I thought half a bottle later; it really did quicken the mind and lighten the hand. Maybe one day I could turn my musings into a novel? Or? Alcohol affected people's judgement, too. That much was obvious. After a few more swigs, my mood took a turn for the worse; I felt both angry and vengeful. I thought about Henrik Stiernberg's callous eyes and spiteful smile, about how fake he and his friends had been during Paul's memorial service. How could they sit there, pretending to grieve, when they were the ones who killed him? I pictured their pathetic little lives, saw their successful future careers and businesses, cigars, back-slapping, cheek kisses. One thing's for sure, I thought, even if the truth never comes out, they will not be allowed to forget. As long as I live, I will be there like a constant reminder of what they've done. I brought my glass over to the phone and called a certain dormitory at Adamsberg. I'd expected some poor first-year to pick up and was surprised to hear Henrik's voice on the other end.

'It's Francesca,' I said.

'So I hear,' Henrik said. 'What do you want?'

'I just want you to confess.'

'Confess what?'

'Don't play stupid.'

'You're imagining things, Francesca,' Henrik said.

He sounded pleading, as though he were genuinely tired of my baseless accusations.

'I know things,' I said. 'About you and Paul.'

He breathed into the receiver. It took a while before he replied.

'Maybe we should meet and talk about this. Are you at Gudhammar?'

When I said I was, he said: 'I'm coming over.'

'Now?'

'Yes, I think it would be best to have it out, once and for all. I mean, if I'm going to be with your sister ...'

I stopped myself from saying he wasn't going to be.

'Do you need directions?' I said instead.

Henrik said he didn't, that he and Cécile had driven by before. He would be there in a couple of hours.

'Cécile's asleep,' I said. 'Just so you know.'

'Then I'll pick you up and we'll go for a drive.'

'I don't like drives,' I said. 'I'll meet you on the jetty behind the house in an hour and a half. Don't drive all the way up to the front door; you might wake Cécile.'

My heart was pounding when I hung up. I felt dizzy, happy, angry and ... relieved. I lay down on the floor and thought about Paul, pictured his dark eyes, heard his voice. *If you cover a kitten's eyes during a certain period of its development, it'll be permanently blind.*

The final scene draws near, I wrote in my notebook. There were just a few pages left and my writing was getting smaller and smaller. What had started as an attempt to fill in the holes in my memory had turned into a brooding, diary-like text littered with digressions that would have made Miss Wilhelmsson question both the dramaturgy and the underlying purpose. *Where's the narrative? What do you want to convey, Francesca?*

The truth, I thought to myself. I just want to tell the truth.

Henrik Stiernberg, I wrote. *Soon, he won't have my sister or his freedom. Maybe there is some form of divine justice after all?*

51

Susanne was watching a film in the living room when Charlie came back.

'Charlie,' she said when she spotted her, 'you look exhausted.'

'I am exhausted.'

'Any news about Johan?'

'He's still unconscious.'

'It's going to be okay,' Susanne said. 'Everything's going to be okay.'

Charlie could tell from her tone she didn't quite believe it herself. They both knew things didn't always get better, that they could go from bad to much, much worse.

'Do they have a suspect?' Susanne continued.

'Ivan Hedlund.'

'Ivan? Why?'

'Don't know.'

'Bloody lunatic. You think you know everything about everyone and then it turns out you don't even know everything about your own family.'

'I know the feeling,' Charlie said.

'Did you hear about Svenka?'

Charlie nodded.

'I saw Sara at Lyckebo.'

'What was she doing there?'

'She's been using my house as a sanctuary.'

'How is she holding up?'

'She's in shock. I have this impulse to take her back to Stockholm with me, so she can put all of this behind her.'

'Does that actually work?' Susanne asked. 'Moving away to Stockholm and putting everything behind you, I mean. You could give her a good home, though.'

Charlie thought about Lillith. The poor cat hadn't survived a month in her care. Was she capable of looking after any living creature besides herself?

'I think I'm going to turn in,' she said. 'I've had an awful day.'

After closing the door to Nils' room, she pulled out Francesca's notes. She had a lot left to get through.

I saw them last night, in the gatehouse. Mum and Adam. They were making the beast with two backs.

Charlie stared vacantly into space for a minute, trying to process what she'd read. Adam was the one who had had an affair with Francesca's mother, Fredrika. That's why he'd been fired from Gudhammar. Why hadn't he just said so?

Francesca wrote about her school, the dormitories, the rowing races and all the rules she had to follow. Charlie thought about centuries-old traditions of peer discipline, elitism and networking. Francesca hadn't fit into that cookie-cutter world. *I'm an odd bird. I'm the fifth wheel, the thirteenth fairy, the eternally unwelcome guest.*

And then, about Paul:

Two wrongs don't make a right, but now we have each other.

The only thing I'm sure of is that he didn't kill himself. He wouldn't, not like that, not without me.

Charlie thought about the picture painted of Francesca in the police investigation, how her family and friends had described her as an inherently untrustworthy girl widely known to have a tenuous relationship with reality, a suicidal young woman who had been born destructive. It was odd, Charlie mused, that no one had mentioned that Francesca was clearly gifted. It had been clear to Charlie from the very first paragraphs that Francesca was an intelligent and analytical person. She seemed a lot older than sixteen.

She turned to the last page of the notebook. Her stomach flipped when she saw the date at the top: *Gudhammar, 7 October 1989.*

She swallowed a few times before starting to read. The first paragraph was about the weather. It had been so windy Francesca had thought the house might collapse.

I just told Cécile we're both going to die in this house. When Mum and Dad come back from their little dinner party, they're going to have to dig their daughters out of the ruins. It would be interesting to see how they would react to that.

Cécile told me to stop being so melodramatic and morbid.

I said I couldn't help it, it's just my nature.

Cécile said she didn't have it in her to talk about my nature, but that I shouldn't worry; Gudhammar had withstood the weather for hundreds of years; it was unlikely to fall down tonight.

I didn't have it in me to tell her that everything falls down sooner or later, that nothing lasts forever.

And then, the section about Paul's secret love, those final lines, which for a moment took Charlie's breath away.

Henrik Stiernberg. Soon, he won't have my sister or his freedom.

Maybe there is some form of divine justice after all?

Charlie let the notebook fall and stared straight ahead. On the last night before she disappeared, Francesca had met up with Henrik Stiernberg, the person she had accused of murdering Paul Bergman, the man who now shared a surname with her sister, Cécile.

The next morning, Charlie called the hospital. Johan's condition was still critical, she was told, they were not going to risk trying to wake him.

So when would that happen?

The doctor couldn't say.

Charlie wanted to ask: But you are going to try eventually, right? He's going to wake up, isn't he? But she already knew the answer. Doctors weren't gods, they couldn't work miracles with broken skulls, no matter how badly they might want to.

When Charlie went downstairs, Susanne was sitting on the sofa, wearing the same clothes as the day before.

'Good morning?' she said. 'Any news from the hospital?'

'He's not ready to be woken up,' Charlie said. 'I guess that's all they can tell me. I have to go to him, Susanne. I think I have to go home now.'

'I understand.' Susanne patted the sofa. 'Come have a seat.'

Charlie sat down. Susanne put her arm around her.

'You're going to get through this.'

Charlie hid her face in Susanne's hair. It smelled of nectar and hairspray. For a long time, they just sat there, holding each other.

52

This time, Charlie left Gullspång knowing she would be back. Back to see Susanne and the boys, Sara Larsson, the fields, the woods, the river, Lyckebo.

An hour and a half later, she stopped at a roadside restaurant, pulled out her phone and dialled Henrik Stiernberg's number. The result was the same as the other times she'd called: *The number you have called is unavailable.* She tried his wife instead, expecting to be put through to voicemail; to her surprise, after three rings, she answered.

'Cécile Stiernberg.'

'My name is Charlie Lager. I'm calling because I need to get hold of your husband.'

A long silence followed. Charlie checked the display to see if the call had cut out.

'Then why aren't you calling my husband?' Cécile said at length.

'I have, but he's not answering.'

'He's away. He's a busy man. But perhaps I can help?'

'I would like to meet,' Charlie said. 'As soon as possible.'

'That's fine,' Cécile said. 'I assume you have my address since you've found my phone number.'

'Can I come by today? Later this afternoon?'
'That's fine. I'll be home.'

53

Charlie was back in Stockholm, the city that had never really felt like home. Now, it was more alien than ever. In Stockholm, a person could die alone in their flat and not be missed by anyone. There were people in the city no one ever gossiped about, whose existence was inconsequential to the rest of the world. Here, where there were people everywhere, Charlie was fundamentally alone in a way she could never be in Gullspång.

But you like being alone, Charlie.

She went straight to Karolinska. The big car park by the entrance was full. She turned up towards the Astrid Lindgren Children's Hospital and found an empty space. Then she walked down the hill towards the main entrance. She looked over at the statue of Astrid Lindgren and thought about how she'd longed to join the Brothers Lionheart in Nangijala and Nangilima as a child, until Betty had ruined it by telling her that outside of children's books, death was a big nothingness. That had frightened Charlie, the thought that there would be no flowering cherry trees in the next life, just an endless darkness.

Who said anything about an endless darkness? Betty had said. *Put a hand over your eye. What do you see?* And when Charlie

had started to describe what she could see with her open eye:
With your covered eye, silly.

Nothing.

Not even darkness?

No, nothing.

Exactly. That's what it's going to be like, like before you were born: nothing.

An emaciated man with an IV pole was standing by the entrance, pulling hard on a thin cigarette. A passing nurse chided him and pointed over towards an area where smoking was allowed. The man slowly tottered off across the asphalt, his IV pole rattling along next to him.

Johan had his own room on the eighth floor. A nurse showed Charlie the way.

'All the machines can look a bit scary,' she said. 'But they're just there to help us monitor him. Go on.'

Charlie walked up to the bed. Johan's eyes were closed. She'd been hoping he'd look better than the last time she saw him, but if anything, he looked worse. His pale skin was covered with contusions and his bloodless lips looked like the lips of a dead person.

'It looks worse than it is,' the nurse told her.

She walked over to a dispenser on the wall and tore off a piece of tissue that she handed to Charlie as though she were crying. Maybe that's what was expected of the partner of a patient who was hovering between life and death.

'It's pretty bad, though, isn't it?' Charlie said. 'I mean, it looks like what it is, right?'

'At least he's stable,' the nurse said.

Charlie looked at Johan's chest, which rose and fell evenly

with the aid of the respirator. What is the point of being stable, she thought, if you may never wake up and breathe on your own again?

The nurse leaned in over Johan, felt his forehead and adjusted his pillow. Charlie noticed a small gold cross around her neck. More than ever before, she wished she had a faith, hope, a God to pray to. But she was alone.

An alarm sounded in the hallway. The nurse excused herself and quickly left the room.

Charlie gently put a hand on Johan's ribcage. She wanted to say something, whisper calm, encouraging words, but none came.

54

The mansion on Strandvägen in Djursholm made even Gudhammar look small. With its towers and turrets, it rose majestically above the rest of the neighbourhood. The CCTV-monitored electric gates stood open. There were contractors at work in the garden. So, this was where they lived, Cécile and Henrik Stiernberg.

Charlie rang the doorbell but couldn't tell if it was working.

A young woman opened the door and asked her to come in in broken Swedish.

Charlie entered an enormous hallway, complete with a glittering crystal chandelier. There was no sign of coats or shoes. *Soulless*, would have been Betty's assessment. *A house without a soul.*

'They're waiting for you in the parlour,' the woman said, signalling with a nod that Charlie should follow her.

Cécile Stiernberg and a woman who judging by her age and appearance might be her mother were occupying opposite ends of a dark-green velvet sofa. They had blonde hair and identical haircuts and were both dressed in elegant trousers, blouses and low-heeled pumps.

'Welcome,' Cécile said. She stood up and shook Charlie's hand. 'This is my mother.'

The woman on the sofa rose and extended her hand to Charlie.

'Fredrika,' she said. 'Pleased to meet you.'

'Do have a seat,' Cécile said, nodding to an armchair.

She looked grave.

Charlie sat down. It was odd to be face to face with the sister Francesca had written so much about. Charlie remembered the paragraph about the lake, Francesca's hands on her sister's head. *I no longer know what I wanted.*

A girl of about ten entered the room. She was wearing a skirt and blouse, like a pint-sized woman.

'When is Daddy coming home?' she said.

'Tomorrow,' Cécile replied. 'I just told you that.'

'Mum, I want to show you ...'

'Not now, Beatrice,' Cécile said. 'This is a private conversation.'

When her daughter didn't immediately leave, she called out something in French and the woman who had opened the door came running, ushered the child out of the room and closed the big double doors behind her.

Charlie was just about to speak when Fredrika beat her to it.

'I expected you sooner, Charline,' she said.

Charlie froze. Why was this woman calling her Charline and what did she mean by *sooner?*

'Regarding the inheritance,' Fredrika went on. 'I mean, if you are your mother's daughter ...'

'What are you talking about?' Charlie said.

She felt hot and cold at the same time and the parquet floor in front of her suddenly seemed to roll and pitch.

'I'm talking about the fact that Rikard is dead. He's been

dead for a month now; I thought it was odd that we hadn't heard from you or your mother yet.'

'What do you mean?' Charlie said. 'I don't know what you're talking about.'

But she did know. It was slowly dawning on her who she was.

That night. The gravel road. Betty's fists banging on the double doors.

Get out of here. Leave us alone.

'Are you alright?' Cécile said. She got up and walked over to Charlie. 'You really don't look so good. We're not going to fight you, Charline. Mum forced the truth out of Dad during the divorce; I assume Betty still has the paternity test and ... You don't have to worry.'

She turned round.

'Mum, would you mind fetching a glass of water from the kitchen?'

Fredrika disappeared.

'How are you feeling?' Cécile asked.

Charlie didn't know what to say. Betty's words were ringing in her ears.

Don't trust men who talk big. Don't trust any men, for that matter. Never forget that all men are swine.

Even my dad?

Especially him, sweetheart.

Who is he?

He was just passing through.

But who was he?

He was nobody, sweetheart. He was nothing.

'Charlie?' Cécile said again. 'You didn't know?'

Charlie shook her head. Her knees had started bouncing

up and down. She put her hands on them to keep them still. Betty's face behind hers in the mirror. *'Do we look fancy now?'*

'Then why did you want to see me?' Cécile said. 'Why are you here?'

Fredrika returned with a glass of ice water. She put it on the marble table in front of Charlie and left the room again.

Cécile handed her the glass. Charlie took it but didn't drink. She studied Cécile's pale face, trying to make out shared features. But nothing. Cécile was her mother's daughter.

But she's your sister. And then, as if it were too immense to take in at first. *And Francesca. Francesca is your sister, too.* Charlie's mind raced. How long had this family known? Why hadn't they contacted her?

All they care about is appearances. Mum wanted us to paint over the water stain on the ceiling. She doesn't understand that the damp would still be there, invisible, that it would continue to spread beneath the surface.

'I have something for you,' Charlie said.

She spilled a little when she put her glass down on the table. She pulled copies of Francesca's notes out of her bag and handed them to Cécile.

'What is this?'

'It's the reason I'm here.'

'Where are you going?' Cécile said when Charlie stood up and made for the door.

'Call me when you've read it,' Charlie said. 'I need ... some fresh air.'

Back in the hallway, Charlie felt as though the house were shrinking around her. The walls and ceiling were closing in on her. The nanny or maid or whatever she was appeared behind her, holding her jacket. Charlie thanked her and put it on. When she got outside, she took a deep breath and started digging through her bag for diazepam. She found a single pill rattling around the inside pocket and swallowed it.

'Where are you going?'

Charlie turned round. Cécile's daughter was eyeing her curiously. The girl was wearing a hat with a fur bauble that looked real, and a thin, dark-blue quilted jacket.

'I'm just going for a walk,' Charlie said. 'I'll be right back.'

'I saw a wolf yesterday,' the girl said.

'Oh really?' Charlie said. 'There are wolves here?'

'Everyone says there aren't. But I saw one. I saw it with my own eyes. It crossed the path down there.'

She pointed down the gravel path.

'Well, then maybe there are wolves here,' Charlie said. 'Since you saw one.'

'Exactly. That's exactly what I told Mum.'

55

Charlie walked along the water towards Djursholm town centre. Work had brought her to the area a few times before and each time, she'd been stunned by the grandness of the houses and gardens. Now, in the autumn sunshine, the stately turn-of-the-century villas seemed even bigger than she remembered. She studied the beautiful exteriors, the meticulously cared-for grounds and wondered what it would have been like to grow up in one of those mansions, with their pools, dinner parties and staff. She could have been one of those children. She could have been a bilingual little girl dressed like an adult, with a nanny and upper-class mannerisms. She could have been, if the man who was her father hadn't rejected her. What would have happened if he'd taken his responsibility? What would her life have been like? Who would she have grown up to be if she had gone to boarding school and been the daughter of someone important, if she had been something more than just Betty Lager's kid?

Happier?

She thought about Francesca's notes. *I'm an odd bird. I'm the fifth wheel, the thirteenth fairy, the eternally unwelcome guest. I am a stranger in this world.*

No, that wasn't a given. But some things might have been ... easier? All the days Betty had spent cooped up in the dark, the light that had to be blocked out, all the nights she'd paced about, the wild parties. And the whole time, he had been there, Rikard Mild, every summer, just a mile or two away. Now she understood why it had been important that she look pretty. Betty had been trying to make Rikard Mild recognise her. How many times had she been to Gudhammar as a child? How many times had Betty pleaded, begged and humiliated herself before she gave up?

Why didn't you tell me, Betty? Why didn't you just tell me the truth?

Because it wouldn't have made you any happier. I tried, sweetheart. But he was ... unfortunately, he was just an ordinary man.

The diazepam was unable to numb her feelings; confusion, grief and something else she couldn't quite put her finger on were churning inside her.

She had reached the town centre, a high street with quaint little shops. It was about the same size as Gullpsäng's town square, but there the similarity ended. In Djursholm, nothing was shuttered, shattered or demolished. She walked past a florist displaying tidy autumnal flower arrangements, a charity shop full of luxury handbags and a bookshop with hardback classics in the window. It would take Cécile at least an hour to read Francesca's notes. How well did she really know her husband? Maybe none of it was news to her?

Charlie crossed a small square and entered a café that according to its menu catered to people who didn't eat sugar, gluten or lactose. She ordered a large latte and sat down at the only free table. The walls were green with rows of little ... beetroots. There was not a man to be seen in the whole café and almost everyone seemed to be speaking English. Charlie let the din of conversation fade into the background while she tried to process what she'd been told. She hadn't been the kind of fatherless child who fantasized about reuniting with her dad. She'd had her hands full with Betty. And now, he was dead.

Fifty minutes later, Charlie got up and started walking back.

Cécile was sitting on the sofa with her sister's photocopied notebook on her lap. There was no sign of her mother or her daughter. A glass half full of what looked like whisky was sitting on the table in front of her.

'I don't quite know what to say,' Cécile said. 'I don't know, I'm ... in shock, I think.'

'I can understand that,' Charlie said.

She tried to read Cécile's facial expression. Was she acting? Had she never suspected her husband?

'She was going to hold Henrik to account,' Charlie said. 'Well, you read it for yourself. If that's true, your husband was the last person to see your sister alive.'

'I don't understand,' Cécile said. 'I don't understand what you're implying. My husband would never, I mean, he's ... he's not the one, he would never ...'

'He seems to have been the last person to see her alive,' Charlie repeated.

'Where did you find this?'

Cécile held up the notebook.

'I work for the police,' Charlie said, as though that explained it.

'And you've reopened the case without telling us?'

Cécile studied her sceptically.

She was no idiot. That much was clear.

'It's a long story,' Charlie said.

'I can imagine,' Cécile replied. 'I can certainly imagine.'

She looked angry, as though everything in the notebook was Charlie's fault. She glanced at the door.

'I think you had better leave now. If it's money you want, we can come to an arrangement. We have been expecting you.'

'What do you mean?' Charlie said. 'I didn't even know he was my dad.'

'Are you sure you didn't know?' Cécile said, an edge to her voice.

'I don't understand what you're getting at.'

'Maybe you're thinking you can get more money than you have a right to by bringing all of this up.'

'Keep your money.'

Charlie stood up.

'What is it you want, Charline?' said Fredrika, who had silently appeared in the doorway.

'Answers,' Charlie said. 'I want to know what happened to Francesca and Paul Bergman.'

'I have no idea what you're talking about,' Fredrika said.

'Leave us alone, Mother,' Cécile said. 'Get out!'

Fredrika backed out of the room and shut the double doors behind her with a bang.

Cécile turned back to Charlie.

'I think you should drop whatever it is you think you've discovered. Our family has suffered enough. Digging around helps no one.'

'It helps *me*,' Charlie retorted. She looked straight into Cécile's pale eyes. 'I'm not the kind of person who paints over water stains and leaves the ceiling to rot underneath.'

'I honestly don't care what kind of person you are. Just

send me your bank details and we'll transfer your share of the inheritance.'

'Like I said,' Charlie said. 'That's not why I'm here. I want to speak to your husband when he gets home.'

'I don't think he'll be interested in talking to you,' Cécile replied.

Charlie was treading on thin ice now and she knew it. It would be easy for Cécile to check if the case had in fact been reopened. She could make Charlie's life hell, but just then, in that moment, she didn't care.

Cécile followed her into the hallway.

'She was my sister,' she said when Charlie was halfway out the door. 'I loved her. We were very different and butted heads constantly, but she was my sister.'

And mine, too, Charlie thought to herself. She was my sister, too.

'Ask your husband to call me when he gets home,' she said. 'You have my number.'

56

She felt like she'd been away from her flat for months. Charlie often had that feeling when she'd been gone for a while, but this time, it was stronger than ever. The smell, she didn't recognise it, her furniture and things felt alien, like they belonged to someone else. Maybe because she was no longer the person she'd thought she was. She had assumed her dad was a wastrel just passing through town, but he was ... well, what had he been?

Heartless, she heard Betty say. *And what good was a heartless man to us, Charline? We got by fine without him.*

Henrik Stiernberg called the next day. He pronounced his surname in a way that made it impossible to doubt his pedigree.

'My wife tells me you came by,' he said, 'and that it wasn't a particularly pleasant visit, so I think we should finish this business as quickly as possible.'

'Business?'

'Yes, no one's going to fight you, Charline. You will get your share of the inheritance; there's no need to stir up family tragedies.'

'I think you've misunderstood,' Charlie told him. 'Maybe we should meet.'

'I have meetings in town all day.'

'Great, then I'll see you between two of them. Just give me a call; I'll be there.'

She hung up.

Charlie didn't think Henrik would contact her, but he called again around six and said he had thirty minutes free. Could she be at The Frog in twenty minutes?

'On my way,' Charlie said.

Henrik wasn't there yet when she arrived. Ten minutes later, a well-dressed man entered the restaurant and looked around.

'Henrik Stiernberg?' Charlie said.

He nodded and shook her hand. They were shown to a table.

'Do you want anything?' Henrik asked.

'Just a glass of water, please.'

Henrik ordered two waters and a whisky.

Charlie couldn't bear the thought of making polite small talk, so she got straight to the point.

'Have you read what Francesca wrote?' she asked. 'The copy I left with your wife.'

Henrik nodded. He had clearly been good-looking once, probably still was, but there was something unsympathetic about him that made him unattractive. Maybe she was biased by what Francesca had written about him: his condescending tone, the way he pushed Paul around, his arrogance.

'If you've read it, I assume you realise things are looking less than great for you,' Charlie said.

'What do you mean?' Henrik said.

'You and Paul, what Francesca saw that night, the suicide that seems not to have been a suicide and a missing person who didn't . . .'

'Paul Bergman was depressed,' Henrik said, cutting her off. 'You can ask anyone.'

'Were you in a relationship?'

'A relationship?' Henrik chuckled. 'Absolutely not! But at that age ... well, I suppose people experiment.'

He leaned across the table.

'I don't think you can imagine how hard it can be to be accused of something like that in a place like Adamsberg, and back then ... and I, I'm not a homosexual, I ...'

'I couldn't care less about your sexual orientation,' Charlie said. 'I just want to know what happened to Paul and Francesca.'

'I don't like your tone,' Henrik said.

And I don't like you, Charlie countered inwardly.

Henrik was quiet for a moment before reluctantly returning to the subject.

'Paul and I ... we hung out sometimes. I liked him and he liked me, but I ... I was very unsure and had my reputation to consider. Paul was angry with me for not standing up for who I was, but come on, I didn't bloody know who I was yet.'

'And then?' Charlie said.

'He got very drunk at the Autumn Ball and wanted to have it out with me. I was with my friends and he wouldn't shut up. I really tried, but he just carried on, so ...'

'So what?'

'It was an accident.'

'What was?'

'We started arguing. I told him we should talk, just him and me, down by the lake. I didn't want one of the housemasters or housemistresses to see us, so we went down to the lake and ...'

'And what?'

'He said horrible things to me.' Henrik raised his empty glass to a waiter. 'I don't remember all of it, but he was going to destroy my entire life, he was going to tell everyone about us, he was going to ...'

'So, what happened?'

'I just wanted to scare him. I'd just turned eighteen, I had my whole life in front of me and this person was going to destroy everything.'

'His name was Paul,' Charlie said.

'Pardon?'

'That person who loved you. His name was Paul Bergman.'

'I know what his name was.'

The waiter brought another glass of whisky. Henrik's hand shook slightly when he raised it to his lips.

'So, what did you do?' Charlie demanded.

'I just wanted to scare him,' Henrik said again. 'I pushed him under. He was flailing and squirming, but he didn't have a chance, I was so much stronger. I was furious with him and when I pulled him back up again, he ... he wasn't breathing.'

'That's the kind of thing that happens when you hold someone's head under water,' Charlie said.

'I didn't mean to kill him!'

'But that's what you did.'

She clenched her fists. Her mind was roaring.

'Did your friends know?' she said.

Henrik nodded. They'd helped him out of the water. He'd been in shock.

'And no one did anything to save Paul?'

'He was dead,' Henrik said.

'You could have told the truth,' Charlie said.

'It wouldn't have changed anything. All it would have done is ruin my life.'

It was strange, Charlie mused, that it never seemed to have occurred to this man that it might have been meaningful to Paul's family.

'What's going to happen to me now?' Henrik said.

'There's no statute of limitations for murder,' Charlie replied, 'so I guess that's up to a prosecutor.'

'I was young, I ...' Henrik scratched his head and for the first time looked properly miserable. How typical of someone completely devoid of empathy, Charlie mused; people like him only get worried once they realised their actions are going to have consequences for themselves.

'And Francesca?' she said.

'What about Francesca?' Henrik knocked back what was left in his glass. 'She was crazy and she went missing.'

'I know she went missing,' Charlie said. 'The question is where to and how.'

'Are you saying I ...?'

Henrik slammed his glass down so hard whisky sloshed out onto the tablecloth.

'Are you surprised?' Charlie said. 'Francesca knew about you and Paul and you were the last person to see her alive.'

'That's not true,' Henrik countered.

'You didn't read her notes?'

'Yes.'

'Are you saying you didn't go out to Gudhammar?'

'I did,' Henrik said. 'I did go, but ...'

'But what?'

'Francesca wasn't there. I never saw her.'

423

Gaps in Time

'Sometimes life just seems so unfathomable, so unjust and so incredibly painful.'

The priest pauses for effect in the speech he's written to honour Paul's memory. Some of the royals are sitting a few pews in front of me, their heads lowered.

'Paul was such a good friend and a diligent student,' the priest droned on. 'He was … curious, questioning and analytical. He was … unique. And now, let us sing together.'

'Fuck,' I whisper into the hymnal on my lap.

My tears blur the lyrics of hymn 256, 'Be not Afraid', the one we're supposed to sing now.

I belt the text out as loudly as I can. My housemistress, sitting one pew ahead of me, turns round and glares reprovingly.

I glower back. She's always so determined to have everybody sing along, shouldn't she be pleased? I stand up; my hymnal falls to the floor.

The organ stops playing, but I keep singing. I don't know the words, and yet I'm singing about the Lord and love and loneliness. All eyes are on me, all the phony students, all the pompous teachers, all the venal housemasters and housemistresses, the sermonising priest, our pig of a headmaster.

I move towards the aisle, still singing. The row of knees folds aside like the sea before Moses.

57

Charlie called Anders on her way back from seeing Henrik Stiernberg,

He immediately asked about Johan.

'No change,' Charlie replied.

'Have they caught the person who did it?'

'I think so.'

She told him about Ivan Hedlund.

'Good,' Anders said. 'I'm glad it's over.'

'It's not,' Charlie said. 'Can we meet up?'

'Now?'

'Yes.'

'I'm off in half an hour. Where do you want to go?'

'I'm leaving The Frog as we speak.'

'The Frog? What are you doing there? I thought you made a point of avoiding the posh part of town.'

'I don't avoid anything; I just prefer certain places over others. How are you holding up, by the way?'

'Still crap, but it turns out you can get used to that, too.'

'You're never given more than you can handle,' Charlie said.

Where had she got that from? Some church person or other had told her that when Betty died. Either way, it hadn't comforted her back then and she was sure it didn't comfort Anders now. Most people who had been around for a while knew it wasn't true: a person could easily be given far more than they could handle.

'The DNA on the women's bodies did end up matching the ex-boyfriend's, by the way,' Anders said. 'He's going down.'

'Nice work,' Charlie replied.

I should have stayed and worked on that case, she chided herself. If I had, Johan wouldn't be unconscious in the hospital and I could have lived my life like before, but now ... everything had changed.

'So, where do you want to meet up?' Anders asked.

Charlie had started to walk down the street. A man with despondent eyes was curled up in a sleeping bag outside Seven Eleven. He had definitively been given more than he could handle.

'Charlie?' Anders said again. 'Where do you want to meet up?'

Forty-five minutes later, Anders entered the Scottish pub across the street from The Frog. Charlie noted him eyeing the staff, who were all traditionally attired in kilts, knee socks and patent leather shoes, with amusement.

She waved him over to her table.

'I ordered,' she said, pointing to the pints in front of her. 'I didn't know if you were driving, but ...'

'I've just moved into my dad's flat two blocks away,' Anders replied. 'So, no, no car.'

'Is it that serious?'

'I don't want to talk about it right now. How have you been getting on? Did you manage to get hold of the family?'

Charlie filled him in on the contents of the notebook, her visit to the Stiernberg residence and her meeting with Henrik Stiernberg. But she didn't mention that she was related to the Milds. She didn't want the conversation to be about that.

'So you think Henrik killed both of them?' Anders said. 'Both Paul and Francesca?'

'Definitely Paul, though he claims it was an accident.'

'Was it?'

'If you consider drowning someone an accident. He also claims he didn't see Francesca the night she disappeared.'

'But that could be a lie, right?'

'Sure, but then why did he confess about Paul?'

'But didn't you say you read about it in Francesca's notes?'

'Yes, but no one believed her before, so ... I don't get it.'

Charlie emptied her glass.

'I have to go home,' she said.

'Didn't I just get here?' Anders said.

'I'm sorry, I just realised something. Talk to you later.'

When Charlie got back to her flat, she took out Francesca's notes again. She quickly skimmed the pages until she found what she was looking for.

A paragraph in which Francesca wrote about her digging, the calming effect the physical labour had on her. *It's as deep as a grave.* She turned to the last few pages where Francesca had written about how insane her parents were to go to a dinner party when they had two half-dead daughters at home.

And when we get back, that hole is gone, Mum said.

I said I thought that was Adam's job.

Adam doesn't work for us any more, as you are well aware, Mum replied. You're going to have to take care of it yourself.

I promised I would. But it was obviously a lie. I have better things to do than to fill in graves.

Charlie called Olof.

'I heard you're back in Stockholm,' he said. 'Have you been to see Johan? How is he doing?'

'Stable,' Charlie told him. 'I'm calling to ask if you know whether your old boss and his colleagues searched the farm properly after Francesca disappeared?'

'I assume they did.'

'There's a pet cemetery. The daughters had a burial site for their pets.'

'That's news to me, but I'm not sure what you're getting at.'

Charlie explained what she'd read in Francesca's notebook.

'How did you get hold of her notebook?' Olof asked.

'It doesn't matter,' Charlie said.

Then she ended the call.

She had to go back to Gullspång.

58

After three hours behind the wheel, Charlie parked her car next to the gatehouse, climbed out and stretched before proceeding up the tree-lined road towards Gudhammar on foot. The autumn sun beamed down on the dilapidated roof and walls of the main house and glittered in the water of Lake Skagern on the other side of the fields. She followed the path down towards the lake, stopping when she reached the grove of birch trees. There could be no doubt this was a cemetery. The small homemade crosses that had sunk into the ground reminded Charlie of Stephen King's *Pet Sematary*. At first glance, there was no sign of a larger grave. She bent down for a closer look, pushed the tall grass aside and ran her hands over the soil. There, wasn't the ground raised just there? Charlie sat down. What was she going to do now? Calling Micke or Olof would be pointless. After a moment's hesitation, she pulled out her phone and found a number she'd called just a few days earlier.

'Adam,' she said when he answered. 'This is Charlie Lager. I need your help.'

She had expected him to be annoyed and maybe even hang up, so she was surprised when he calmly replied: 'What's the problem?'

*

Half an hour later, Adam arrived armed with sharp-edged spades and a small digger. Charlie met him in front of the house.

'It's down by the pet cemetery,' she said, pointing.

'I remember where the hole was,' Adam said. 'We can start with the digger, but then I think we'll have to switch to spades, or we might ... if there's something there, we might want to be careful.'

Charlie nodded.

'Thank you for coming so quickly,' she said. 'Thank you for coming at all.'

'There's no need to thank me,' Adam said. 'It really is time to get to the bottom of this once and for all. I'm tired of people looking at me sideways.'

'Is that how you've felt?'

'Yes, a certain level of suspicion seems to have lingered ever since that first police interview. My brother was a delinquent and I've done some things I'm not proud of, but I would never hurt a woman, or any human for that matter. And I liked them, both Francesca and Fredrika. I want to put an end to this whole affair.'

Me too, Charlie thought.

'We're lucky it's been a warm autumn; the ground's not frozen yet' Adam said.

He started up the digger and Charlie noted the precision with which he steered the machine. Once he had removed the topsoil, it was time to start digging by hand. Adam handed Charlie a spade and a pair of gloves.

'Otherwise you'll get blisters.'

They started digging at opposite ends of the rectangle. It

suddenly occurred to Charlie that she was doing exactly the same thing Francesca had been doing three decades previously. She could almost see her. Francesca with a spade, hacking at the ground. For her, the digging had been aimless; for Charlie, it was anything but. *I'm digging for her. I'm digging for my sister.*

'There doesn't seem to be anything here,' Adam said when they had been at it for thirty minutes.

'We need to get deeper,' Charlie replied.

She thought to herself she might be wrong about this; she fervently hoped she was. If there's nothing here, she told herself, I will drop the whole thing and assume Francesca is alive and well somewhere else in the world, alive, happy and far from all the things she clearly didn't want to be a part of.

'There's something here,' Adam said.

He held up a bone fragment.

Charlie stared at it. It might be part of a femur.

'It could be from an animal,' Adam said.

'We have to keep digging.'

Charlie's heart beat faster and her hands shook as she resumed her work.

Just a few minutes later, she caught something glinting in the sunlight. She bent down, picked up a necklace and rubbed the dirt off it. It was a set of golden scales: the pendant Francesca's mother had given her.

'What is it?' Adam said. 'What have you found?'

'A necklace,' Charlie said. 'It's hers.'

'You're white as a ghost,' Adam said. 'It's just a necklace. It doesn't mean ...'

Charlie didn't reply. She knew what it meant.

The world around her disappeared. She was in Francesca's notes, the part where Cécile takes her necklace and refuses to give it back. The planned meeting with Henrik Stiernberg. *Francesca wasn't there. I never saw her.*

The notes again. That last night: *I have better things to do than to fill in graves.*

'Charlie?'

Adam put a hand on her shoulder.

'Hold on,' Charlie said. 'I just need to think.'

'I'm going to go get my cigarettes.'

Charlie sat down on the ground, oblivious to the damp seeping through her clothes. She closed her eyes. The images came to her like scenes from a film: Francesca runs down the front steps, rounds the house and continues down the path to the lake. A light is turned on in a room on the first floor. It's the room with the view of the water. Then the front door opens and closes again. *Where are you going, Francesca? What are you doing?* Cécile runs after her sister. She catches up by the pet cemetery, grabs Francesca's arm and tells her to go back inside, that she's lost her mind. Francesca tears free and says she knows everything. She knows and she's not going to stay quiet. Screaming and fighting and then ... Francesca loses her footing. She fumbles for something to stop her from falling, something to hold on to. The necklace. The chain snaps. Francesca falls. The scales of justice follow her into the grave, the deep, stony grave. Her head meets the ground and ... it's over.

Cécile leaps down after her sister, presses her face against hers: Francesca's not breathing. Two fingers against her throat: no pulse. Panic. Screams, echoing across the lake. It's over, all over. And then, Cécile heaves herself out of the hole, grabs the shovel and starts covering her sister with dirt, crying all the while.

Charlie opened her eyes and tried to shake off the images. She couldn't. Everything was crystal clear, as though she'd been there to witness it. She remembered Cécile's pale, nervous face. *I loved her. We were very different and butted heads constantly, but she was my sister.*

What now? Who was going to deal with all of this?

Not me, she thought. I'm done.

She should have felt relieved, but there was no room for anything but grief. She had wanted this story to have a happy ending.

> This life is a breeze, a fable, a dream
> A droplet falling into Time's endless stream
> Shimmering briefly like a rainbow in the sun
> Bursting and falling and the dream is done

Charlie looked at the golden scales in her hand. She turned them over, rubbed away the dirt and read the letters engraved there. FREE.

Credits

Orion Fiction would like to thank everyone at Orion who worked on the publication of *For The Dead* in the UK.

Editorial
Ben Willis
Lucy Frederick

Copy Editor
Francine Brody

Proof Reader
Linda Joyce

Audio
Paul Stark
Amber Bates

Design
Debbie Holmes
Joanna Ridley
Nick May

Editorial Management
Charlie Panayiotou
Jane Hughes
Alice Davis

Production
Ruth Sharvell

Marketing
Lucy Cameron

Publicity
Alex Layt

Finance
Jasdip Nandra
Afeera Ahmed
Elizabeth Beaumont
Sue Baker

Rights
Susan Howe
Krystyna Kujawinska
Jessica Purdue
Richard King
Louise Henderson

Contracts
Anne Goddard

Paul Bulos
Jake Alderson

Sales
Jen Wilson
Esther Waters
Victoria Laws
Rachael Hum
Ellie Kyrke-Smith

Frances Doyle
Georgina Cutler

Operations
Jo Jacobs
Sharon Willis
Lisa Pryde
Lucy Brem

If you loved *For The Dead*, don't miss Lina's first novel featuring DI Charlie Lager: *For The Missing*

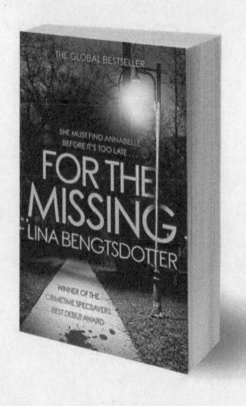